ONE QUARTER VILLAIN

CORI COOPER

To Hepzibah:
Whose excitement was so contagious I submitted the manuscript
waaaaaaaaaay earlier than I planned to! Thanks for being there, friend.

ONE

Every good fairy tale needs a villain.

Of all the gifts Maddy thought she might receive for her seventeenth birthday, a DNA kit from Heritage Hunt was not on the list.

Not even in the top ten.

Or the top one thousand.

"Wow, Grams. This is..." She stretched a smile that she hoped looked more convincing than it felt. "...um, great. Thank you so much."

It was a good thing Grams wasn't there in person. Maddy would have a much harder time faking enthusiasm if Grams were sitting across the kitchen table instead of watching her open presents through the computer screen.

"Do you like it, dearie?" Grams moved forward so quickly that her image buffered. For a couple of seconds, Maddy watched tiny pixels of Grams rearrange to form her face again.

Maddy examined the writing on the back of the box. "I've never done one of these before. How does it work?"

"Oh, it's easy as pie, dearie. You just swipe your cheek with a cotton swab—I do believe there is one included—pop it in the envelope, and send it back to the company."

Her smile was so bright that Maddy felt like a despicable human being. What was she expecting from Grams, anyway? Two years ago, she sent Maddy a dusty mirror that looked like it came from a yard sale, and last year Grams had sent a six-foot staff she had whittled out of wood. When the mail guy delivered it, he was so curious that he stuck around to see what was inside.

Remembering *that* birthday made Maddy grateful that at least this year she didn't have Herman the postman watching her pretend to smile while she opened Gram's gift.

Maddy set the genealogy kit next to the computer and dug deep for some real sincerity this time.

"Thanks for always remembering my birthday, Grams. You're the best."

"Oh!" Grams placed a hand over her heart. "You sweet, sweet thing. Please make sure you call me as soon as you get those results back. I want to see what you are made of." Her laugh sounded like fairy bells.

"I will..." Maddy's voice trailed off as footsteps pounded up the driveway. "Hey, Grams, don't go yet, okay? It sounds like Leo's here. He'll want to say hi."

Grams pulled her small, square glasses to her nose, making the chain swing gently in front of her neck. "I just love that Leo. Is he still handsome as paint?"

Maddy hid a laugh behind her hand. Who came up with these sayings? Like, who was the person who first thought paint was so handsome that they decided to compare it to someone they liked?

The doorknob rattled a few times, then the hinges screeched as Leo pushed the door open.

"Leo!" Maddy turned all the way around in her chair so he could get the full range of her exasperated look. "We talked about this a zillion times! You don't actually live here, you know? It's common courtesy to knock before you barge into someone's house."

"Maddy!" Her mom glanced over from the kitchen sink where she was washing dishes. And eavesdropping. "Leo is part of this family. He's welcome to walk in without knocking."

"Okay, sorry." Maddy sighed back into her chair and let the subject drop. That was easier than trying to explain that while the common courtesy thing was important, she was really thinking of Leo here. Sometimes her dad walked around the house in just Darth Vader boxers and mismatched knee socks.

No one should have to experience that.

"Who are you talking to?" Leo rested his chin on Maddy's head so he could see the computer screen. "Oh, hey, Grams. How's France?"

"Her name is Agathe," Maddy reminded him.

"Oh, dear," Grams shuddered. "Please do let him call me Grams. Agathe is such a dreadful name."

"I think it's lovely," called Maddy's mom.

"Thank you, love." Grams blew a kiss, probably aiming for Maddy's mom, but it went toward the bay window instead. "What do you kids have planned for Maddy's special day?"

"I'm glad you asked." Leo's chin created a tender spot on the top of Maddy's skull as his jaw went up and down. She didn't want to interrupt what he was saying to ask him to move, so she slouched in the chair to take the pressure off.

Leo lifted one hand to tick things off his fingers. "First, we're going to meet the gang to try out the new escape room by Target. Then we're going to play laser tag for at least three hours. After that, I thought a couple of games of paintball would totally rock. Then we're taking Maddy to a sports bar downtown where she can get her fill of greasy burgers, fried cheese curds, and boneless wings in sauce guaranteed to bring on epic heartburn." His voice raised into a rousing sportscaster impersonation, almost making "epic heartburn" sound like a good thing.

"Well." Grams's smile was more than a little forced. "Doesn't that sound lovely?"

"He's joking, Grams." Maddy rolled her eyes. "We aren't doing any of those things."

Grams let out a long breath of air. "I was quite surprised, I own. You are a tease, Leo." She shook her finger at him.

Leo ducked his head in false remorse. Maddy knew it was false because the real thing *never* showed up for Leo.

Maddy pressed her lips together to hold back a smile. "What Leo just described would be his dream birthday, not mine."

"Come on, Maddy, that isn't true." Leo looked serious—too serious, which meant he wasn't serious at all. "You know I hate fried cheese curds."

Grams chuckled, encouraging Leo even more. Before he could ham it up to the next level, Maddy hooked her foot around the leg of the nearest kitchen chair and pulled it closer.

"You know, we have chairs. You can sit like a normal person." The seat hit him behind the knees, so he wobbled a bit until he caught his balance.

"And how does a normal person sit?" Leo grinned but plopped into the chair. He scooted until his knees bumped into Maddy's legs, then he leaned forward so his face showed up on the camera. Something about the lighting made his features point upward more than usual. He was like an Italian version of Peter Pan, about to lead the Lost Boys on an expedition against Captain Hook. Leo, the olive-skinned elf with dark hair that curled around his ears.

No, not an elf. Elves weren't always mischievous, but Leo sure was. He was more like Puck from the Shakespeare play.

Puck, for sure.

A sharp elbow jabbed into Maddy's side. She blinked and looked around. The room was strangely quiet, and Grams watched her with raised eyebrows.

Apparently, Maddy had missed something. "What?"

"Space cadet," Leo nudged her with his shoulder. "Grams asked what you really want to do on your birthday date."

"It's not a date!" Warmth crept up the back of Maddy's neck like someone had just flipped on a space heater right behind her.

Leo gave her a strange look. "I know. I meant, like, outing."

"Oh, right." Maddy concentrated all her energy on Grams's image on the screen so she wouldn't have to look at Leo until her cheeks turned back to their normal color. "You want to know what we're doing today?"

Or was it *Leo* who wanted to know what they were doing?

Out of the corner of her eye, Maddy noticed Leo start to squirm. He was probably questioning his life decisions right about now. Instead of a gift, Leo always gave Maddy a *day* to do whatever she wanted. This was bold because the things Maddy liked and the things that Leo liked rarely ever matched up.

"Yes, dearie," Grams smiled. "That's exactly what I asked."

Maddy smiled sweetly. "We're going to go see *Beauty and the Beast* at Gammage." She paused there to let Leo get his squirming under control, but it increased as soon as she said the word *Beauty*, and now he looked like he was sitting on a chair made of beetles.

"Then I want to eat at Cupbop." Maddy knew this would be sticky because Leo was a guy, and food was super important. It would have been easier all around if she decided to go out for pizza or something, but Maddy really loved Asian food and it was *her* birthday, after all. She hurried to the next thing before he had a chance to decide he wasn't going to like it, even though he couldn't possibly know what kind of food it was based on the name.

"*Then* I want to go get ice cream from Handel's."

Leo relaxed at last, just like she knew he would. Maddy chose Handel's on purpose because of how much he loved it. He was her best friend, and she didn't want him to be totally miserable the whole time. He needed something to look forward to.

Something safe and ice creamy.

"That sounds like a wonderful day." Grams clasped her hands under her chin. "I have a soft spot for the story of *Beauty and the Beast*, I must say, and the musical is just lovely."

"Wait a sec." Leo sat up straight. "Going to a play isn't the same as a movie theater, right? Don't those shows sell out? You have to buy tickets way far in advance, I'm pretty sure."

Maddy tried not to laugh at how hopeful he looked. "Mom and Dad bought me tickets months ago. I was going to take Izzy or Savannah, but then I decided to use them for your present."

"Oh," Leo's shoulders drooped. "That's lucky, then."

It was Maddy's turn to nudge Leo. "Come on, you can use a little culture. It will be fun!"

"Right," Leo recovered quickly; he always did. "Yeah, of course. Sure it will. What time is this show...play...thing?"

Maddy checked the time. "Oh! Oops, we better go, Grams, just in case there's traffic. Thanks again for the present. Love you!"

"Love you, too, my Madelena. Have a wonderful birthday. And please do call me when you get your test results back."

"I will! Talk to you next week. Same time?"

Grams nodded and blew a kiss aimed right at the center of Maddy's forehead. This time she was spot on. Maddy waved until Grams's screen went black, then she shut the lid of her laptop. Leo reached for the Heritage Hunt box.

"What test? She gave you a test? Is this it? What kind of test is this?"

Maddy didn't bother answering as she stood up and stretched her arms above her head. Leo was doing the thing where he rapid-fired questions while he was figuring out the answers for himself. He didn't really need her to respond.

"Oh, this is one of those genealogy things. Why did she give you that? David did one of these when he found out he was adopted, but I don't know why other people do them." Leo tossed the box back onto the table.

Time screeched to a halt. Maddy's heartbeat slammed against her ribs so hard it was painful to breathe. "Mom?"

"Yes?" Her mom was focused on wiping counters, so she didn't look at Maddy.

Pounding filled Maddy's ears as her knees began knocking together. "Mom?"

"Yes, Maddy? I answered you the first time."

"Yeah, but you won't look at me." Her voice sounded shrill. "Mom!"

Maddy's mom finally stopped what she was doing and placed one fist on her hip. "You have my full, undivided attention. What is it?"

Words rushed up Maddy's throat and got stuck there. She swallowed and tried again. "Am I adopted? Is that why Grams gave me this DNA test?" Now that the words were out, irritation followed close behind. "Grams said she couldn't wait to find out what I'm made of. Is that because she doesn't *know* what I'm made of? Who am I, really? Where did I come from? And why didn't you and Dad tell me yourselves instead of making Grams do it? This is a horrible way to break that kind of news!"

Leo snickered, but Maddy ignored him. She couldn't put up with his nonsense in the middle of an identity crisis.

"Adopted?" Her mom dropped the grody rag and stepped closer. "Whatever gave you such an idea?"

Maddy jabbed a thumb at Leo. "His step-dad was adopted and took this test to find out his family history."

Her mom stopped in front of Maddy and rested both hands on her shoulders. "Look into my eyes."

Maddy did.

They were vivid green—like, unnaturally green—with a ring of blue right around the pupil.

Just like Grams's eyes.

And just like Maddy's.

"Of course you aren't adopted." Maddy's mom wrapped her arms around her daughter. "You are one hundred percent ours."

Maddy took a couple of deep breaths, letting her mom's words calm her down. She had to be telling the truth; both of Maddy's parents were horrific liars. Plus, since Maddy was an only child, they usually told her everything about everything. She actually quit asking them questions and started using Google because they didn't know when to stop telling her things. They for sure would have told her if she was adopted.

She should have remembered that before she ran away with herself.

"I wish I was adopted," Leo said.

"Leo!" Maddy's mom swatted his shoulder with the back of her hand. "What a thing to say!"

He ran his fingers through his hair. "Seriously, have you been to my house? My family put the 'crazy' in 'crazy town.'"

"Leo Romano, you be grateful for your family. You would miss them if they were gone." Maddy's mom had to cover her smile with an exaggerated frown.

"Yes, ma'am." Leo stood up, his posture stiff as a soldier.

She shook her head. "Are you two headed out?"

Maddy checked her watch, grateful for something to do other than feel stupid about overreacting. "Yeah. Are you ready, Leo?"

"Born ready." Leo rubbed his hands together like a supervillain. "Let's go watch a chick show, eat food I don't know anything about, and have some great ice cream!"

"That's the spirit." Maddy shot him a look on her way down the hall to fix her hair. She was pretty sure there was a chin-shaped dip she needed to brush out before she went out in public.

The first bite of ice cream was always Maddy's favorite, before the ice numbed her taste buds and she couldn't taste anything anymore. She closed her eyes to shut out the noise around her and let her tongue tingle with chocolate and honeycomb in silky smooth vanilla ice cream.

When she opened her eyes, Leo stared at her like she was all kinds of nuts.

"What?" She sat up straighter, trying not to feel like an idiot. "I believe ice cream should be savored."

"Oh, I know." Leo took a huge bite of his cone, spraying bits on the table while he chewed. "I just think you're weird, is all."

"It goes both ways." Maddy tucked a lock of hair behind her ear. "Thanks for the play and dinner and this ice cream. It really was the best birthday outing ever."

"Yeah?" Leo grinned. "I'm glad you made me go to Cupbop. I never would've done that on my own."

"You liked it?"

"Crazy liked it." He shoved the rest of his cone in his mouth. There was so much left that he couldn't close his lips all the way around it.

"You are a heathen!" Maddy threw a handful of napkins at him. "Take smaller bites!"

Leo opened his mouth wider and chewed as obnoxiously as he possibly could.

"Ew!" She looked away until he swallowed loudly. "Leo!"

"What? It's good." His eyes flicked to her ice cream bowl, still mostly full.

Maddy sighed. She thought she had more time. Leo always ate fast, but football season made him even worse. She handed him the extra spoon she'd snagged before they sat down and pushed her bowl closer to the middle of the table. Leo didn't waste any time. He scooped up a big spoonful of ice cream and stuck it into his mouth.

His eyes lit up. "Okay, I get you now. This is awesome."

"Right?" She carved out a boundary to show Leo how much more she wanted, then pointed her spoon at it to make sure he saw.

Leo saluted.

His mouth was too full to answer.

Maddy couldn't resist a smile. He was just so...Leo. "What did you think about the play?"

Leo paused with his spoon hovering in the air. "Honestly?"

Maddy nodded.

His eyes darted to the sides as he leaned forward. Leo spoke so quietly that Maddy had to focus on his lips to hear his words. "I actually really liked it. But if you tell anyone that, I will destroy you."

Maddy pressed her tongue to the roof of her mouth to stop all the *I told you so*'s from sliding out. It was tempting to dance around Handel's singing about how right she was, with a couple neener-neeners thrown in for fun. But Maddy was better than that.

And she really didn't need to say anything. It was satisfying in her soul that they both knew she was right.

"Tell me what you liked best." She leaned back in the chair and watched his face.

"The Beast." Leo dipped his spoon back into the bowl. "He was sic! Like, that part where he flips out and then saves her from the wolves? Epic."

"Actually, she saved him from the wolves."

Leo paused to give Maddy an incredulous look. "Whatever, that's not even possible. She's half his size."

"That's what makes it such a powerful moment."

"Uh, no."

Maddy glanced down, gearing up to argue her point until he conceded or ran away screaming, whichever came first. Except there was a streak of melted chocolate across her fingers. It totally distracted her from what they were talking about. She reached for a napkin to wipe it away and remembered she just touched her face when her hair was tickling her nose.

Great.

That meant she probably had chocolate all over her face now too. Should she pull out her phone and do the selfie mode to check? No, she hated it when people did that. She should just go to the bathroom and use the mirrors. Except that earlier Leo had to wait forever for her to get through the enormous line at the restrooms after *Beauty and the Beast*. She could only imagine what he would say if she told him she needed to go *again*.

Maddy put the napkin down and sighed. "Do I have anything on my face?"

Leo nodded solemnly.

"I mean, besides my nose, eyes, freckles, mouth..."

Leo continued to nod, the corner of his mouth twitching in and out of a smile.

Maddy let out a huff of air. "I mean, anything that isn't supposed to be there, like chocolate. Is there chocolate or ice cream or bits of food on my face?"

Leo shook his head with a grin.

"Why are you such a booger?" Maddy stole his clean napkin to wipe her face, just to be sure. "I can't trust you at all."

His spoon dropped with a clatter as Leo placed a hand over his heart. "Savage."

Maddy tossed the napkin at his head, but it just fluttered to the table harmlessly.

"I was saying"—Leo raised his voice and sniffed like he was mortally offended—"before I was so rudely interrupted, that the Beast was seriously lit. Way better than that Gaston guy. He was a hun. I'm glad Belle didn't fall for his garbage."

Maddy shook her head. She actually agreed with what Leo was saying about Gaston; it was all the nonsense he said before that she took issue with.

Leo kept talking. "So, I was thinking about that Enchantress chick—"

"The *evil* Enchantress," Maddy corrected him.

"Naw, that's what I mean. I don't think she was evil."

"What?"

"Is that a 'what' because you didn't hear me or a 'what' because you heard me and think I'm an idiot?" Leo smirked.

Maddy shook her head, refusing to get distracted by his question. "The Enchantress used her magic to curse the Beast. That makes her the villain."

"Does it, though?" Leo pulled the ice cream bowl closer, not even pretending anymore that it was Maddy's.

"Does what though?"

"Does cursing the Beast make her evil? He sort of deserved it. The dude was a jerk."

Maddy squinted her eyes. "I thought you just said he was *sic*." She deepened her voice to sound as much like Leo as possible.

"Pathetic. I do not sound like that," Leo said. "And I do think he's sic."

"So...jerkiness is awesome?"

"No, Maddy." Leo scraped his spoon around the edges of his side of the bowl, trying to catch every last drop of ice cream. "Jerkiness is not awesome. All I mean is it's interesting, right? The Enchantress is supposed to be bad, but if she hadn't cursed the Beast, he wouldn't have changed who he was. Right?"

"No." Maddy was not about to get swept up in one of Leo's philosophical debates. Not on her birthday. "It's this simple: Gaston, the Enchantress, and the asylum guy are all bad. The Beast, Belle, and her father are all good. It's black and white, Leo."

"What about the townspeople?" Leo raised an eyebrow.

"Bad, obviously. They wouldn't help Belle and tried to kill the Beast."

"What about Belle?"

"Good, Leo. She's the protagonist."

"Just because she's the protagonist doesn't mean she's good. I actually think she's kind of stuck up. Why did everyone want her? I don't get the hype."

Maddy was struck dumb for several seconds in the face of such blasphemy. After working her mouth a few times, she finally got words out. "I can't believe you just said that. Everyone loves Belle."

"Just because people like her doesn't mean she's all good."

"That's not what I said. Obviously, people liking Belle doesn't make her good. People like her because she's already all good."

"But no one is *all* good." Leo pointed his spoon at Maddy before he dropped it into the empty bowl with a dull *thunk*.

Maddy gave herself a little shake to get her thoughts in order. "Remember when we were in second grade and Ms. Hinkle taught us about elections by having a class poll on our favorite Disney princesses?"

"No," Leo said.

"Yes, you do," Maddy exclaimed. "Belle won, and guess who voted for her the most?"

"Redheads," Leo smirked.

"No, Leo! Can you be serious for two seconds?"

"Probably not."

Maddy glared at him.

"I mean, of course, I can," Leo said. "Please, Maddy, enlighten me."

"Boys." Maddy waved her hands. "All the boys in the whole class voted for Belle."

"Not all."

Maddy narrowed her eyes. "I thought you didn't remember."

"Well, I do now, and there was one guy who didn't vote for Belle."

"Who?" Maddy asked.

"This guy." Leo jabbed both thumbs at his chest. "Do you remember who I voted for?"

Maddy hated to admit she *didn't* remember, so she just stared at him.

A smug smile snaked across Leo's lips. "Meg."

"Who?" Maddy stared at him. "There isn't a Disney princess named Meg."

"From *Hercules*." Leo waggled his head in the most irritating way possible. "You know? The Disney movie? *Hercules*?"

Maddy pushed her chair back and stood. "Meg is not a princess."

"Neither is Mulan." Leo rose to his feet too. "And yet, Disney princess she is."

Maddy wished she could argue with that.

Leo continued, "Meg should be everyone's favorite because she's the most real."

"The most real..." Maddy paused to let her words sink in. "...*cartoon* character?"

"Hey." Leo swatted her arm. "You're the one getting all worked up about this. I'm just saying I like Meg because she wasn't perfect. She made mistakes. She was good *and* bad. Just like everyone."

"Everyone is not good *and* bad." Maddy gathered their spoons and napkins, then shoved them into her empty bowl. "People are mostly one or the other."

"And...do you think people can change?"

Maddy groaned inwardly. Despite her best efforts, she was in the middle of a philosophical debate with Leo.

He took the trash from her hands while she rubbed her temples. "Leo, it's simple."

Leo smirked and headed to the garbage can near the front door. He waited for Maddy to catch up before he said, "People aren't simple, Maddy."

She straightened her purse on her shoulder. "Well, I don't think they are that complicated."

Leo bunched up his lips and stood there for a minute longer. "Tell you what. Because it's your birthday, I'm going to let you have this one. Next time, I will argue it until I die. Deal?" He held out his hand.

Maddy slapped her palm into his and shook. "Deal."

TWO

Villainy is often just a form of stupidity

Almost a week later, Maddy was getting ready for school and noticed the necklace Izzy gave her for her birthday sitting on the dresser. She hadn't planned on wearing it that day, but it caught her eye on the way out of her bedroom. Izzy would be excited to see it. Maddy reached for the chain, admiring the amber-colored pendant. Before she quite knew what was happening, it slid through her fingers and disappeared into the gap between the dresser and the wall.

Fiddlesticks.

With a groan, Maddy used her hip to shove the dresser out of the way. Lurking in that mysterious gap was a treasure trove of socks, lint, crumpled papers, and a box she didn't recognize. She rooted through the junk to find her necklace, then picked up the box.

And remembered.

Grams's genealogy test.

"Are you about ready for school?" Maddy's mom poked her head in Maddy's bedroom.

Maddy startled, and the box slipped out of her hand. She fumbled with it long enough for her act to qualify as a comedy routine before setting it firmly on top of her dresser. "Yeah, I'm leaving right now."

Her mom didn't say anything with her mouth; she didn't need to. Her eyes were writing a novel.

"What?" Maddy fastened the necklace around her neck and opened the top drawer for clean socks.

"Is that your DNA test?" Her mom gestured to the box.

Maddy nodded.

"And is it done?"

Maddy shook her head.

"Oh, child." Her mom rubbed her forehead. "It's been days!"

Maddy walked across her room so she could sit while she put on her socks. Talking to her mom, coming up with excuses, and balancing to put a sock on each foot was a recipe for disaster. "I know. I'll get to it."

"And when would that be exactly?"

Maddy shrugged one shoulder. "I don't know. Is it really that important? What if I didn't do it at all?"

"Not do it at all?" Her mom sat on the bed next to Maddy. "Okay, tell me what's going on."

"Nothing's going on."

"Something is going on. There's a reason you haven't done this test yet. What is it?"

Maddy scratched her nose. "Does there have to be a reason?"

Her mom raised one eyebrow so high it disappeared into her bangs, making her face look lop-sided. "You tell me."

"It's just..." Maddy tugged one sock higher so it wouldn't slouch. "There's not, like, a huge reason. I guess I don't get the point. I know who my parents are; I know who my grandparents are. This kind of thing is for people who don't know that stuff or really old people."

"So, you think only adopted and old people care about their family heritage?"

The correct answer was yes, but the look on her mom's face made Maddy rethink her response. "I just don't see the point."

"Mmm hmm," her mom nodded. "Did you know that Grams asks me every night if you've sent in that test yet?"

"No, I didn't know that."

"Well, she does. And every night I tell her you'll do it. Am I lying?"

"No."

Well, maybe.

Maddy slipped her foot into a tennis shoe and pulled the laces way too tight. "Why does it matter so much to her?"

"She's old, Maddy." Her mom placed a hand on Maddy's arm. "All she has left is family. Her history is really important to her, and she wants to share it with us."

Maddy sighed and dropped her foot to the floor. She still didn't really get it, but if it was that important to Grams, she would do it.

Later.

Maddy finished tying her other shoe and stood up. "Did you remember I'm driving to Flagstaff with Savannah and Izzy for the football game tonight?"

"Is that tonight?" Maddy's mom squinted into the distance.

Maddy gathered her hair into a messy bun on top of her head and tried not to sound exasperated. "Yes! Remember? Since the game will be over kind of late, we're spending the night at Izzy's cousin's house."

"I remember all of that," her mom said, waving her hand. "I just didn't remember that it was happening tonight."

Maddy secured her hair with a clip. "We'll be home around ten tomorrow, depending on how late Savannah sleeps in."

"That sounds fun."

"Yeah, Leo says the football team is really good this year. He told me Hayden is the best quarterback we've had in forever."

"So, I bet you're really looking forward to going then, huh?"

Maddy gave her mom a strange look. "Yes."

"Ah," her mom said as she stood up. "I thought we might hit a snag somewhere."

"What snag?"

Maddy's mom folded her arms across her chest. "The snag where you can't go to the football game unless you get that test done."

Maddy froze. "Are you serious?"

Her mom's very un-joking face was the best answer to that question.

"Mom!"

"Maddy! I cannot impress upon your mind enough how very important it is that you do this for your grandma. Aside from common courtesy—which is so very important to you—this means a lot to her. It will take you about two minutes."

Maddy stared at her mom incredulously, then stomped over to the dresser and snatched up the box. She shot a glare over her shoulder as she stomped out the door and down the hall to the bathroom. Anger blurred the words together as Maddy skimmed the instructions. A small, insistent voice inside of her said to tone it down, that this wasn't a big deal. It really would only take two minutes, and it was for Grams.

Maddy squeezed her eyes shut, counted to ten, and tried reading the instructions again.

Grams was right; it was as easy as pie. All Maddy had to do was swab her cheek, put the swab in the sanitized bag, and send it in the prepaid envelope to some fancy lab in California. A quick swab later, she was sealing the bag.

So, maybe it was kind of ridiculous she'd put that off for so long. She kept her scowl in place so her mom couldn't tell what she was really feeling—especially because Mom's satisfied smile reflected in the mirror. They both knew Mom was right, but Maddy didn't have to admit it.

"Happy?" Maddy turned and held out the baggie with her spit-soaked swab.

Her mom took the baggie. "Beyond happy. Joyful, ecstatic, thrilled!"

As hard as she tried to hold it in, Maddy couldn't contain a giggle.

"Thank you, Maddy. I'm so glad I can finally tell Grams you did this."

Maddy picked up her toothbrush to get rid of the weird taste the swab left in her mouth and squeezed on a generous amount of toothpaste. She finished brushing and rinsed out her mouth. "Do you want me to take that to the mailbox?"

Her mom handed her a towel to wipe her mouth. "I'll drop it off at the post office on my way to work. Can I give you a ride?"

"No, I told Leo I'd pick him up." Maddy slipped the towel over the bar and straightened the two edges so to hang evenly. "Plus, I'm driving to Flagstaff, remember?"

"Duh, of course. Silly me." Maddy's mom gave her a ditzy look that made Maddy giggle again. Then she looped her arm across Maddy's shoulders in a side hug and squeezed just the right amount of tight. "I'll see you tomorrow, darling. You girls be careful, please."

Maddy promised they would, kissed her mom good-bye, and started for the front door. A loud bang reverberated down the hall. Neither Maddy nor her mom opened doors like that, so it was either her dad back from his run or Leo being impatient. Maddy hurried into the living room where her overnight bag was already packed and waiting next to the door.

"Hey, punkin." Her dad stood on one leg, stretching his quad. His shirt was soaked to his belly button with sweat.

"Hey, Daddy."

"On your way out?"

Maddy nodded and pulled her backpack over one shoulder and her overnight bag over the other. "See you tomorrow."

"What?" He dropped his leg and spread both arms wide. "You're leaving me for a whole twenty-seven hours with no hug?"

"Ew, no!" She skidded away from him and gripped the doorknob. "Grams can probably smell you all the way in France."

Her dad's arms fell to his side. "Where's the love?"

Maddy blew him a kiss. "There. Love you, sicko."

Her dad caught it and waved with a grin.

On her drive to Leo's house, Maddy reviewed what she needed to get done that day. There was a test in trig, a lab in physics, and the student council wanted to meet at lunch to talk about the senior class gift. Maddy was only the secretary, so her vote didn't matter all that much, but she had to be there to take minutes.

Then there was the drive to Flagstaff and the football game.

It was a full day, sure, but since they were all good things, Maddy was super excited. She pulled her car into the driveway at Leo's house and put it into park. His mom was less than impressed with honking, so Maddy always made it a point to go to the door. She knocked three times and, unlike Leo, waited patiently for someone to answer.

Leo's mom swung it open with a bright smile. "Well, hello there, bimba. What can we do for you?"

Even though the name 'bimba' sounded like it wanted to be derogatory, it was Maddy's favorite word. It meant 'little girl' in Italian, and when Leo's mom said it, it felt like love.

"Good morning, ma'am." Maddy said in a serious voice. "I'm here to pick up your son Leo."

"Mama mia!" Leo's mom put both hands on her hips. "Do we have a Leo? Do I know this Leo? Leo who?"

Maddy cracked up; she never could keep it together through the whole routine. Leo's mom was such a ham; the astonished look on her face never got old.

"Leo, your son?" Maddy swallowed a giggle. "You know, the tall, dark, and annoying one?"

"Boh!" Leo's mom laughed too. "There are many of those here. Which one is this Leo? Are you sure we have a Leo?" She pulled Maddy into the house with a warm hug that smelled like freshly baked bread. Then she kissed both of Maddy's cheeks, one loud smack at a time, and pointed to the stairs. "He's up there, taking forever. Enzo! Tell your brother Madelena is here."

Enzo sighed like he was just asked to donate a kidney, put down his phone, and trudged across the room to the bottom of the stairs. "Leonardo!" he bellowed. "Your bimba is here."

Leo's mom took the towel from her shoulder and swatted him on his way back to the couch. "I could have done that! Rico or Nico, one of you please walk up the stairs and ask your brother nicely and in a normal voice to come downstairs because his ride is here."

The twins bounced up from their game of Uno and thundered up the stairs.

That, in a nutshell, was the difference between a teenager and a child.

"And you, give me that phone. Come load the dishwasher." Leo's mom snatched Enzo's phone and headed for the kitchen. "You come with me, too, bimba. You have a few minutes?"

Whether Maddy did or not depended completely on Leo. She followed his mom into the kitchen with Enzo dragging his Vans on the hardwood floors behind them.

The kitchen was the central hub of the Romanos' entire house. Mostly because all the kids typically congregated there, and because Leo's mom was always cooking up something worth congregating for. Baby Alessandra was in her high chair, sucking on a teething biscuit. Maddy couldn't resist her velvety chubbiness and ran a finger along the baby's cheek as she walked by. Babies were kind of a foreign entity to her, but Maddy adored Alessandra. She was the happiest, sweetest baby in the whole entire world.

"Dishes." Leo's mom pointed to the dishwasher until Enzo reluctantly started rinsing plates. Gianna and Bella worked on homework at the table, and Liliana hopped around the kitchen floor in a frog costume. The only people missing were obviously Leo and the twins, but also his step-dad, David, and David's daughter, Emma, who had this week with her mom.

Leo's mom handed Maddy a wooden spoon and pointed to a pot on the stove. "Stir."

Maddy obeyed but peeked into the pot first. It looked like discolored cottage cheese was bubbling in there. Her stomach rolled over and she leaned away from the pot to avert her eyes before poking the spoon inside.

"No, no, no, no." Leo's mom took the spoon and hunched over the pot, her elbow jutting to the side. "You have to mean it, bimba. Put some muscle into it." She gestured with her head that Maddy should move closer. When she finally took a step, Leo's mom handed the spoon back to Maddy and watched as she tried to mimic the correct way to stir.

Leo's mom grunted but didn't reclaim the stirring. Maddy took that to mean she was satisfied.

The sound of loud feet pounding down the stairs echoed through the house just a few seconds before Leo appeared. "Hey, peasants! Hey, Mami, is the fregola ready?"

"Ask Madelena."

Leo noticed Maddy and stopped walking. His eyes moved to her neckline. "Hey, nice necklace."

Maddy reached for the stone. It was warm when she wrapped her fingers around it. "Thanks, Izzy gave it to me."

"Yeah, I know." Something glinted in his eyes. It was his signature teasing look that was so much a part of Leo, Maddy wouldn't recognize him without it. She just wasn't sure why he was giving her that look at the moment.

"What?" She tucked the necklace into her shirt like that would make Leo forget whatever diabolical thing he was planning.

"Nothing, she just has good taste, that's all."

Maddy narrowed her eyes, but before she could question him further, Leo nudged her out of the way and peered into the pot.

"Oh, whoa, you aren't letting her cook, Mami? We need to be able to eat today."

"Ha-ha." Maddy gave the mash another good stir, making a full circle around the pot. She really had to work those biceps; it was getting so much harder to move the spoon now. The mixture had thickened quite a bit since she started. "Is it supposed to look like this?"

Leo leaned over Maddy's shoulder, his breath tickling her neck. "Yeah, it's good." He turned the heat off and went for a bowl in the cupboard. "You want some?"

Maddy shook her head. "I ate at home."

"Cool." He put one bowl back and loaded the other with the fregola. Maddy watched curiously as he topped it was sauteed apples from the skillet his mom had been working on and sprinkled cinnamon from a steel shaker that looked about a thousand years old. He topped it all with a splash of thick milk from a miniature pitcher. "Gotta go, Mami. See you." He stood still long enough for his mom to wrap him in a hug and kiss him all over his face, then he raised an eyebrow toward Maddy.

The cue to leave.

She waved to all the siblings, submitted to her own round of hugs and kisses, then followed Leo. He shoveled spoonfuls into his mouth while he waited for her next to the half-open door.

"I'm coming." Maddy scooted by him and headed to the driveway. "*What* is that stuff you're eating?"

"Fregola." He slurped and then coughed a couple of times. "You've had it before."

Maddy shook her head as she reached her car and slid into the driver's seat. She reached over to open Leo's side for him since his hands were full.

"You have. You thought it was oatmeal, though." Leo set the bowl on the console between them while he got situated. Maddy peered inside, trying to remember if she liked it or not. It was already almost gone. How did he eat everything so fast? Just thinking about it gave Maddy indigestion.

"Oh, gimme a break." Leo rolled his eyes. "Just try some."

Maddy took his spoon and scooped a tiny bit on the edge. She brought it to her lips, sticking her tongue out like a reptile to taste with just the tip in case it was disgusting.

"Okay, it's not bad. Just a weird texture."

"Like frog eyeballs," Leo said, placing the bowl into his lap.

Maddy's face wrinkled into a grimace as she started the car and looked over her shoulder to check if the driveway was clear before backing out.

"Nice face." Leo burped the words then grinned at her.

Maddy turned the look on him. "Say 'excuse me,' you troglodyte."

"Excuse you," he said in a high falsetto.

"And don't lick the bowl. It's not like you're starving." She turned the corner on Leo's street and headed for the high school.

"How do you know?" Leo asked, but he stopped, the bowl hovering in front of his face, his tongue already half out. With a sigh, he set the unlicked bowl down. "What's with you?"

"Nothing, I'm fine." She said the words automatically and then wondered if they were true. Was she fine? She felt fine two seconds ago when they walked out of Leo's house, but now she felt super-duper cranky. Was that normal? There wasn't a good reason for her emotional one-eighty.

Maddy shook her head and rolled her eyes at herself.

What was she thinking? It was probably just hormones.

She put a smile on her face and aimed it at Leo this time. "So, how was the Magic tournament last night?"

"Crazy! There were a bunch of noobs, so it took forever. I didn't get home until almost midnight."

"Yikes." Maddy shook her head. "That does not seem like it's worth minimum wage."

Leo shrugged. "Maybe not, but it's gotta be better than working fast food. At least at the Cave I get to try out new board games for free and referee epic nerd tournaments instead of dealing with all the Karens and, oh yeah, cleaning fryers. Gross."

Maddy couldn't argue with that logic. And since she didn't have a job at all, she probably wasn't the most qualified to decide what was worth it and what was not. "Are you working this weekend?"

Leo shook his head. "Naw. Mr. Frees gives me the whole weekend off when there's a football game 'cause he's an alumnus."

That's right, Maddy knew that. "I'm really excited about the football game tonight. Is coach going to let you play again?"

Leo puffed out his chest. "If he wants to win, then yeah."

Maddy laughed at his swelling bullfrog impression. "That last game was G.O.A.T., right? Tied until the last ten seconds, then you kicked that field goal and—"

Leo cheered. "The crowd went wild! Maddy"—he placed a hand on her arm and looked at her seriously—"I have to tell you something profound. I'm really, for real, so proud that you understand football now. The fact that you know what a field goal is, it..." He choked and wiped his cheek. "It makes me feel this feeling in my chest..."

"It's probably heartburn. You really need to slow down when you eat."

"No. Stop messing around. It's, like, this is real. This feeling, it makes me..." He paused for so long that Maddy's stomach started to squirm. Then he opened his mouth and let out the world's longest burp. "Never mind, it was gas."

Maddy stopped at a stop sign, the perfect opportunity to give him a stink eye. "There's something wrong with you."

"Probably. That game was *lit,* though." Leo verbally regurgitated the entire game for the rest of the drive to school while Maddy listened, completely determined not to let her thoughts wander.

THREE

Good and bad are not the only options

Maddy, Izzy, and Savannah walked through the entrance to the football field forty-five minutes before the game was supposed to start. They'd made exceptionally good time, even with Maddy driving the exact speed limit and despite Izzy's regularly scheduled quips that it would have been faster to ride snails. The crisp, October air stung Maddy's cheeks, causing her to rethink this whole plan. The sun was still up, albeit low, and she already was freezing her booty off. She always forgot how much colder it was in Flagstaff than it was at home in Phoenix.

The girls paid for their tickets, got their hands stamped, then hurried to the stands on their side of the field. The chances of finding good seats without arriving three hours early were usually dismal, but since it was an away game and unseasonably cold, Maddy had high hopes.

Luck was with them. The front and center row was taken, of course, but they maneuvered around the crowd and found the front right surprisingly uninhabited. They settled there for the night. The last rays of sunshine crept away from their toes, and the sky turned from blue to purple with pinkish streaks. There was nothing in the world like an Arizona sunset. When Maddy pointed it out to her friends, the words came out with wisps of air. Watching the sun go down was suddenly bittersweet.

It was going to be a very long, cold night.

Savannah dropped a thousand-pound backpack on the concrete in front of their bleachers. It wasn't a normal school backpack. Oh no—Savannah had a huge, honking, mammoth thing that people take on a three-week backpacking adventure in Europe. As Maddy and Izzy watched in awe, Savannah began unpacking multiple thermoses, packages of hand and foot warmers, fleece blankets, and a bright yellow snuggy that Izzy called dibs on just seconds before Maddy could get the words out. Savannah spread some of the fleece blankets over the freezing metal benches and then passed around her brother's old sweatshirts.

"The key to surviving in a mountain climate is layers," she said with a college lecture kind of voice. "Then you can shed some as you warm up."

"*If* you warm up," Izzy mumbled as she pawed through Savannah's bag.

Maddy took one of the sweatshirts and unzipped her jacket to pull it over her head. It smelled vaguely of corn chips, but at that point, she didn't care. She would wear a manure-scented jumpsuit if it meant not freezing her booty off.

"Let's save the hand and foot warmers until we get desperate. Stop it, Izzy!" Savannah slapped Izzy's hand as she tried to pull out a plate covered in plastic wrap. "Those are for later."

"But..." Izzy's hand reached for the plate as Savannah tucked it out of sight. "Cookies! They're still warm. I need one! Maddy needs one too. Don't you need one, Maddy?"

Izzy and Savannah looked at her.

Not wanting to offend either one of her friends, Maddy stalled. "How did you keep them warm this whole time?"

Savannah held up a bag. "Insulated lunch bag."

"It does seem like we should eat those while they're gooey..."

Izzy clasped her hands and batted her ridiculously long eyelashes.

"Oh, all right." Savannah pulled the plate back out.

Izzy snatched it and hugged it to her belly. "I could die happy right now." She reached under the plastic for a cookie that left melted chocolate streaks on her fingers as she pulled it apart.

It looked so good and smelled even better. Maddy squirmed. They weren't really supposed to bring outside food to the stadium. That was a rule.

Izzy graciously handed a small cookie to Maddy. As much as she wanted to eat it, Maddy set it on her knee. The warmth soaked through her jeans and wrestled with her moral dilemma. Izzy gave her a look as if she knew exactly what Maddy was thinking and tried to give a cookie to Savannah, who didn't notice. She was too busy organizing her backpack.

"I brought hats. Do you girls need a hat?" Savannah emerged with a fist full of knit beanies.

Maddy took one and jammed it on her head; she instantly felt warmer. Maybe her dad was right when he said people lose 90 percent of their body heat out of the top of their head. She always thought he was parroting an old wives' tale, like the one about sugar water getting rid of hiccups.

"Scarves." Savannah pulled out one, then another, like a magician at a child's birthday party. The scarves just kept coming and coming until there was a multi-colored heap on the ground at their feet. Izzy set the cookies down just long enough to slip into the snuggy and scoop up an armful of scarves. She wrapped them around and around her face until only her eyes and mouth were visible.

"Gloves." Savannah made a pile on the bench next to her backpack.

Maddy grabbed a pair of purple snow gloves and pulled them on, then stared at the cookie on her knee. She was going to have to make a decision sooner or later; it couldn't just sit there all night.

She was just so conflicted. The cookie was in the stadium with her, which was against the rules already. Maddy couldn't decide if that meant eating it would be good or bad. It didn't help that the smell of sugar and butter mocked her with every inhale. She wanted to take a bite super bad.

"And hot cocoa." Savannah set a humongous thermos on the cement with a satisfying thunk.

"Whathaimmatherermoth?"

Maddy and Savannah looked at each other, then at Izzy.

"What?" Maddy asked.

Izzy swallowed a mouthful of cookies and pulled the scarf out of the way. "What's in those other thermoses if that one is hot chocolate?" she asked, pointing to the other smaller thermoses.

"Oh," Savannah said as she pulled on a pair of white ski gloves. "Soup."

The Boy Scouts wished they were as prepared as Savannah.

"Yummy!" Izzy grabbed the blue ombre thermos, shooting Maddy another look. "Eat. It will warm you up, for real."

"So, um," Maddy hesitated, "you know we're not actually supposed to bring outside food and drink into the stadium, right?"

Izzy jutted one hip to the side and stuck her fist onto it. "Did you know you sound like a cafeteria poster?"

That was probably because Maddy read that very phrase on at least half a dozen posters plastered on the chain link fence all the way from her car to the stadium. "It's a school rule."

"No," Izzy said as she twisted the top off the thermos she'd chosen and breathed in the creamy chicken-scented steam. It made Maddy's mouth water instantly. "What it is, is a marketing ploy because if we don't bring our own stuff to eat, we have to buy their totally overpriced and disgusting concessions."

Savannah nodded and reached for a cookie.

"Hey!" Izzy pulled the plate closer to her side.

"What?" Savannah huffed as she tugged Izzy's arm. "I brought them. Technically they are my cookies, Miss Greedy."

"Yeah, but I already gave you one." Izzy relinquished the plate slowly and pouted while Savannah took another cookie. She kept a wary eye on the cookie plate the whole time she sipped her soup.

Maddy turned the cookie around in her hand, stll unsure. "Yeah, I don't think marketing is the reason they have that rule."

Izzy licked her lip before answering. "It's not really a rule, Maddy. It's like a suggestion. A guideline. A recommendation."

Maddy interrupted before Izzy could think of anymore synonyms. "But they asked us not to."

Savannah wrapped her arm across Maddy's shoulders. "You don't have to eat anything if it makes you uncomfortable, but if we asked a teacher, they would say it was fine, I'm pretty sure. They would probably even ask us to share because my mom makes crazy good soup."

Okay, that wasn't a bad idea, actually.

The asking thing.

Maddy stood up and looked around the bleachers. There had to be a responsible adult somewhere. It was completely negligent to leave a bunch of sleep-deprived, caffeine-powered teenagers all alone in the dark.

Their school band director caught Maddy's eye as he shrugged on a huge down jacket.

"What's that teacher's name?" Maddy pointed.

Savannah stood up to look. "You mean Mr. Turner?"

"That's the band director, right?"

Savannah nodded.

"I'm going to go ask him if it's okay to eat outside food."

Izzy blinked at her over the top of the thermos.

"Take the cookies with you." Savannah snatched the plate before Izzy had time to react and handed it to Maddy. "That will convince him."

Maddy held the plate loosely in one hand and her uneaten cookie in the other. Suddenly she felt like she'd been caught with the murder evidence in a game of Mafia.

"No! Come on, give it back!" Izzy scrambled to her feet. "I wasn't done with those!"

Savannah let out a breath and took four cookies from the plate. "These are for you; the rest are bribery. Go on, Maddy. We believe in you."

Izzy fell back onto the bleachers and hunched over her stack of cookies, scowling at Savannah between bites.

Maddy steadied the plate and climbed across the bleachers to the band.

"Mr. Turner?" she said at the exact moment the band kicked up with the school anthem. Maddy didn't have a free hand to tap his shoulder, so she just stood there, waiting for him to turn around. She probably would still be standing there, all frozen into a statue, if he hadn't raised his arms as the music reached a crescendo and almost smacked her in the cheek with his elbow.

A trumpet blew out of sync as Mr. Turner slowly rotated. "Excuse me, young lady," he blustered. "What are you doing?" His piercing blue eyes reminded her of an eagle she'd seen eyeballing the prairie dog habitat at the zoo.

Maddy cleared her throat and held the cookies out as if they would explain themselves to him. That was silly, cookies couldn't talk. Maddy sighed. This was getting awkward. She was going to have to say something. "I, uh, was wondering, um, is it okay that we brought cookies to the game? I mean"—she stumbled as his eyes narrowed—"I know we're not technically supposed to eat outside here, but is it okay?"

Mr. Turner looked down at the plate, back at Maddy's face, then sniffed. "I really couldn't care less." Then he turned and fixed his trumpet problems with a vigorous wave of the arms.

Maddy backed away slowly, her cheeks warming up the rest of her body so that now she was sweating like crazy. It was time to take Savannah's advice and start shedding some layers. On the way back to her friends, she stuffed the hat and gloves in her pockets, then devoured her freezing cookie to make herself feel better. When that didn't work, she ate another one from the plate.

Then two more.

Now her stomach hurt more than her pride, so...mission accomplished.

"What did he say?" Savannah said when Maddy got within asking range. Izzy just yanked the cookie plate out of Maddy's hands and started counting.

"He said he couldn't care less."

Savannah pressed her lips together for a moment, then smiled. "Well, that's good news! Let's party!" She swung a pink thermos into the air, then pressed it into Maddy's hands.

Slowly, Maddy opened the lid and almost cried. The spicy scent of curry swept away the rest of her embarrassment. Bobbing chicken pieces and diced carrots intertwined with thin rice noodles that made her feel like maybe, just maybe, she could go on with life without feeling idiotic every time she walked down the band hall.

Savannah sat on the bench next to Maddy and watched her down the soup with a look of satisfaction. "I'm glad we got that all sorted out. But, seriously, Izzy, those cookies are for sharing. You need to go back to kindergarten."

Izzy took a huge bite and didn't bother swallowing before she answered. "Gimme a break. I'm freezing by bum off and bored out of my mind."

Maddy tipped her head to the side. "Wait, you aren't excited about the game?"

"I hate football." Izzy shivered. "I wouldn't be here at all, except for—Hey, babe!" She stood up and waved her free arm enthusiastically.

Izzy's boyfriend, Ryder, leaned on the chain-link fence that separated the field from the stands. His face lit up when he caught sight of Izzy, then it curled into laughter. "What the heck are you wearing?"

"Don't judge." Izzy dropped the cookies on the bench and stepped down the bleachers towards him. "Maybe you haven't noticed, but this place is a frozen tundra."

"Come here, I'll warm you up."

Maddy and Savannah averted their eyes.

"Seriously?" Maddy lifted one hand to shield her peripheral. "They're in public!"

"Right? Are we glad, or *so* not glad that Leo introduced them? Sometimes I can't decide, but right now I'm for sure not glad." Savannah reached for the cookie plate. "On the other hand, I think I'll finish the cookies while Izzy is *ocupada*." She chewed thoughtfully, "You know, to be completely honest, I wouldn't mind some pregame smooching if it was with the right guy."

"Yeah?" Maddy's teeth chattered, giving the word lots of extra syllables. She put the gloves back on, then shoved the hat on her head. Next, she pulled Savannah's backpack closer and retrieved the hand and foot warmers. She opened four and stuck two in her pockets and two down the shaft of each boot. "Oh, holy cow, that feels so much better. Do it; you won't regret it."

Savannah smiled. "Have we reached desperation already?"

Maddy didn't respond. She just tossed a few warmers into Savannah's lap.

"Okay," Savannah sighed. "You're right. I feel almost cozy now."

Maddy pulled a couple of fleece blankets over their laps. "So, who's this pregame make-out Mr. Right of yours?"

"Guess."

Maddy looked at her.

"What? We might as well do something while we sit here besides think about how cold we are. Come on, see if you can guess."

"Hayden," Maddy said because he happened to be running by with a football tucked under his arm.

Savannah followed him with her eyes until he disappeared into the mass of football players. "No. I mean, he's adorable, but not really my type. Next."

"Um…" Maybe her brain was frozen. Maddy couldn't think of the names of any guys at all, much less guys from their school.

"Don't say Chris." Savannah held out one hand and shook her head emphatically.

Maddy wasn't going to, but now she was curious why she shouldn't. "Why not?"

"He's snarky. So, no, not him. Next."

"Just tell me." Maddy's teeth chattered as a sudden chill took over. She tucked her arms into her armpits to conserve warmth.

"Do you promise you won't laugh?"

"No," Maddy said, sounding suspiciously like Leo. Maybe she should stop spending so much time with him.

Savannah dug her elbow into the ticklish spot on Maddy's ribs.

"Okay, okay, I won't!" Maddy cried. She couldn't even squirm away from Savannah because they were all cocooned in blankets. "Who is it?"

Savannah whispered something just as the band kicked up across the bleachers.

"Who?"

"Kevin." Savannah raised the volume just a teeny tiny bit.

Even then, Maddy wasn't sure she heard right. "Kevin?" she said to clarify.

At the exact moment, the band decided to stop playing.

Maddy's voice rang through the rafters with resonating acoustics. She clamped both hands over her mouth and stared at Savannah wide-eyed.

"Yeah?" Kevin shouted from the tuba section.

Savannah groaned and sunk into the blankets, trying to become one with the fleece.

"Um, did you finish the physics project?" Maddy yelled. It was the first thing that popped into her mind.

"Yes."

"Oh, good. Have a good game playing band-thing."

"Smooth," Savannah said.

Maddy pulled the hood of her jacket up over her beanie and thought happy, not-an-idiot thoughts to herself.

"What about you?"

Maddy hadn't pieced her shredded ego back together yet. That took all her brain power so she had no idea what Savannah was talking about. "What about me?"

"You know, who would you have some pregame warm-up time with?"

"Oh," Maddy stammered. "No one. I don't like anyone like that."

"Come on," Savannah said. "Don't hold out on me. I know you like someone."

"Who would I like?"

Savannah gave Maddy a long suffering look and sighed. "I can't believe you're still not talking. It's so obvious. Why won't you just admit it?"

"I seriously have no idea what you're talking about."

"Leo!"

Maddy looked around, expecting to see him standing somewhere nearby. Why else would Savannah spout his name out like that? He wasn't in sight though. There was no one around them at all.

Wait.

Did Savannah think Maddy liked Leo?

Maddy said the words slowly. "Like, Leo Romano?"

"Do we know any other Leo?" Savannah looked up at the sky.

"Oh, gross, Savannah!" Maddy hissed. "He's like my brother."

"Hmmm." Savannah tossed her head with an irritatingly knowing look.

Maddy took the hand warmers out of her pockets and set them on the bench. It was way too hot in these stands now. She shifted to face Savannah so there would be no misunderstanding her words.

"Listen, I've known Leo since kindergarten. He used to try to spell his name under the table with boogers. By the end of the year, there was a snot-encrusted 'Leonardo Bruno Romano' under the table like braille. He burps in my face, has no trouble passing gas when I'm around, and seriously doesn't understand the concept of personal space. If I made a list of the guys I would consider dating, Leo wouldn't even make the top one billion."

Somewhere in the middle of Maddy's speech, Savannah's eyes left her face to stare into the distance. That should have been a clue, but Maddy didn't notice until she was done talking and Savannah got downright squirmy.

Maddy slowly turned to the side.

Leo stood on the other side of the fence, watching them with no expression on his face.

Yeah, she totally got an F on situational awareness.

"Hey." Leo tapped his knuckle against the leg of his football pants. Knickers? Knickerbockers? What did they call those things? "My mom texted; she said she gave you my house key?"

For a second, Maddy couldn't think what he was talking about; then it came back in a rush. Leo's mom found Maddy right after school when she picked up Enzo. Leo had already left on the bus with the team, so Maddy did have his house key; she had put it in her jeans pocket.

Maddy fumbled with the sausage-like fingers from those stupid purple gloves until she lost all patience and ripped one off with her teeth.

Had Leo heard what she said?

She spit the glove onto the ground and checked her coat pockets, including the pockets of Savannah's brother's sweatshirt, even though it couldn't possibly be in there. Was it in her purse? She pulled the zipper back and searched through all the compartments, including the hidden pocket in the side.

Her eyes wanted to move to Leo, to check his face. He was no good at hiding what he felt, if he'd heard what she said, she could be able to tell by his expression. But she kept pulling her eyes back at the last second. The bigger part of her didn't want to know if he heard, or what he thought about it.

Maddy patted herself down again, and checked her socks and the glove she threw on the ground. Her breath came out faster now, and her cheeks were flaming hot. Leo's gaze was like a laser on the side of her face. Maybe she could find the stupid key if he wouldn't stand there judging her.

Could she have dropped it somewhere between the school and the parking lot back home? Or the parking lot and the bleachers here? Savannah probably had one of those flashlight/pocket knife/survival tools with her. Maddy could use that to retrace her steps.

Or, duh, she could just use her phone.

Apparently, her brain was not functioning.

"You know what?" Leo backed away, his hands in the air like he'd been targeted with a police spotlight. "Don't worry about it. I'll just crawl through a window. No problem."

"No!" Maddy practically shrieked. "It's here somewhere. I'm going to find it."

"It's fine, Maddy. Forget about it."

"It's not fine!"

Seriously, did the band purposely take breaks every time she said something? Now the entire stadium stared at her like she'd lost every single one of her marbles.

Well, except for Izzy and Ryder, who hadn't come up for air yet.

Savannah gave Maddy a wide berth, scrunching into the end of their bleacher. "Did you check your pockets?" she asked gently.

Like that wasn't the first thing Maddy had tried! She wasn't stupid!

Maddy ripped down the zipper of her coat and flung it to the ground.

"Your jean pockets?" Savannah tried again.

"Yes! I've looked everywhere. Stupid key. It's not in my coat, it's not in my jacket, it's not in my purse, it's not—" Maddy shoved her hands in her pants pockets and felt the tell-tale shape of a key against her fingertips.

With a sigh, she pulled it out and looked at it.

"Here it is."

"Yay!" Savannah clapped and scooted a couple of inches closer.

Maddy stepped down the bleachers to the chain link fence and handed Leo his house key. She kept her eyes trained on the ground. Now she wanted to avoid his gaze for a number of reasons. "I found it."

"Thank you." Leo stashed the key somewhere Maddy couldn't see in the dusky light. Did football uniforms even have pockets? It didn't look like there was a spare place to put a breadcrumb, much less a house key.

Leo had his helmet tucked under his arm, making him look as though he was a star in a feel-good family movie, like he could have been any of the guys on *Remember the Titans*. Once the key was safe, he placed the helmet on his head and nodded to Maddy in that cool guy way.

"Thanks, Maddy."

"Leo?"

He was already starting to move away by the time she got the word all the way out.

"Yeah?" He stepped closer and removed his helmet again, probably so he could hear what she said. Those helmets looked very sound-friendly.

"I—"

What?

What did she want to say?

She was sorry she freaked out? Or that she shouldn't have told Savannah about his kindergarten booger art?

No...

"I, um... You have something on your uniform. There." She pointed to his shoulder where a leaf was stuck.

Leo looked at it and then at Maddy without bothering to brush the thing off. "Okay."

"You're just going to leave it there? Seriously?" Maddy grabbed his arm and pulled him closer, keeping a firm grip on him while she wiped whatever it was off his shoulder.

"There, see, that's better." When Maddy looked up, her face was inches away from Leo's nose. The dim light shadowed most of his features, making him seem like a stranger or something more sinister, like his own evil twin. Maddy's breath caught in her throat as Leo's eyes locked in on hers.

He leaned closer.

"What are you doing?" Maddy snapped her head back. She would have fallen on her rear in the mud if she didn't have such a tight, kung-fu grip on Leo's arm.

"What do you mean?" Patches of red dotted his cheeks.

"Were you going to kiss me?"

"No," Leo grimaced. "No way."

"You looked like you were going to kiss me."

"Well, I wasn't."

"Are you sure? It totally looked like it."

"Yes."

"Yes, you were going to kiss me?"

"No!" Leo ran his free hand through his hair. "Yes, I'm sure I wasn't going to kiss you. Maddy, sheesh, I have a game."

Like those two things didn't go together. Like it was impossible to think about kissing when one was about to play football. That was the dumbest thing Maddy had ever heard, especially considering they had a couple of friends still sucking each other's faces off a few feet away.

Leo tried to pull away, but Maddy still clung to his arm. She couldn't let go of him, or the kissing thing, until she knew the truth. It was Savannah's fault for putting the idea in her head. Did Leo like her as more than a friend?

"I think you were about to kiss me, Leo. Just admit it. Just admit you want to kiss me."

A loud laugh sounded from the stands behind them. Maddy glanced over her shoulder, suddenly aware of all the people watching the scene between her and Leo.

On second thought, standing next to a chain link fence with a football game about to start was probably not the best time to declare lifelong love and devotion.

Maddy let go of his arm. "Fine, you can go."

Leo moved toward Maddy so fast that the chain link fence between them rattled and swayed. His face was hard as he cupped her face in his palms and pressed his forehead against hers. "Maddy," he said through gritted teeth, "if I was about to kiss you, you would know."

Then he jammed his helmet back into place and punched Ryder in the shoulder. It knocked him off balance, effectively breaking Ryder's pregame time with Izzy.

"Dude!" Ryder glared at Leo.

Leo picked up Ryder's helmet from the ground and tossed it to him. "Quit messing around; we have a game to win."

"Heck yes!" Ryder gave Izzy one last, slurpy kiss and disappeared into his helmet. Then both guys ran further down the field where the rest of the team waited. Izzy sighed and linked her arm through Maddy's elbow, which was still resting on top of the fence.

"I love football so much."

FOUR

She is one-quarter villain, and he is one-quarter useless

Maddy spent the rest of the weekend trying not to think about Leo.

She almost convinced herself she was successful, except that while she helped Izzy drag Savannah out of bed, ate the breakfast tacos Izzy's cousin made, and drove back down to the Valley, her mind replayed everything that happened in an incessant way that was impossible to ignore.

She noted every word he said. Every flick of his facial features. She knew exactly where he stood on the field at all times and couldn't help but notice the way his eyes searched the crowd for her after Coconino kicked their butts.

The change in temperature and elevation was what did it. By halftime, all the players were huddled together, chests heaving, while they blew on their hands with exaggerated puffs of wispy air. By the end of the game, they dragged themselves around the field like zombies.

First thing Monday morning, Maddy decided there was only one thing she could do about the whole mess.

Pretend it never happened.

She picked Leo up at his house, completely throwing herself into the whole usual routine with his mom. As soon as he came into view, she brought up the game and then kept him talking with well-timed questions from the second they stepped onto his front porch until they reached the front doors of the high school. They walked to their classes together and met up at lunch like everything was A-OK.

Totally normal.

Maddy was a master pretender.

Except for the fact that she couldn't quite bring herself to look Leo in the eyes. When she talked to him, she had to concentrate on his nose, ear, or eyebrow to keep funny things from happening to her stomach. And every time they brushed against each other in the crowded hallway, she leaped away like he was an electric fence to create a sizable gap between them.

So, not actually normal at all.

This hyper-sensitive awareness of everything Leo did went on for a solid three weeks. Then Maddy got busy with peer tutoring and Leo finished football and started working way more hours at the Cave of Wonders. Five weeks after that fateful Friday in Flagstaff, things were back to a semi-normal state. The only weirdness to speak of was once or twice, during a rare moment of silence, Maddy caught Leo watching her with a strange expression on his face.

Not a problem.

Maddy could just pretend that didn't happen too.

Plus, there were other, more pressing things to think about.

"Maddy? Is that you?" Maddy heard her mom as she opened the front door after a particularly long day of state testing.

She dropped her things on the nearest chair and considered collapsing on the couch but was honestly afraid she might not be able to get up again. "Yeah, Mom. I'm home."

Maddy's mom walked into the living room, drying her hand on a towel. When she saw Maddy's face, she tipped her head to the side. "Rough day?"

"I don't even want to talk about it."

"All right." Her mom perched on the edge of a chair. "Well, I have something else we can talk about, if you're up for it."

Maddy closed her eyes. It better be a good something else, like chocolate ice cream, or she was going to blow a gasket. "Yeah?"

"Mmm hmm." Her mom pulled out an envelope and waved it in the air. "Guess what this is?"

Maddy peeked one eye open. "A winning lottery ticket."

"No..."

"Willa Wonka's golden ticket."

"Really?"

"A speeding ticket."

"Oh my goodness, child!"

Maddy couldn't stop now; she was on a roll. "A ticket to ride. Just the ticket. Two tickets to paradise. A raffle ticket—"

"Madelena Agathe Hutton!"

"Yes, Mommy?"

Her mom's stern face melted into laughter. "What am I going to do with you? Would you like to know what is in this envelope?"

Maddy wasn't sure she did want to know, actually, but she nodded anyway.

"This envelope contains your test results from Heritage Hunt."

What the heck was Heritage Hunt?

It took Maddy more than a minute to remember before it all came rushing to the forefront of her brain.

Her birthday, the call with Grams, the cotton swab—all of it felt like a billion years ago. "Oh."

"Oh?" Maddy's mom slumped her shoulders and pooched out her lips. "Is that all you have to say? Come on, daughter, get over here and open this! I've been waiting all afternoon. It's so exciting!"

Maddy reached for the envelope just as someone knocked on the door.

"Are we expecting anyone?" Maddy asked.

Her mom shook her head. "Why don't you grab that, and I'll set up the computer?"

"The computer?"

Her mom laughed again. "Where is your head today? Grams wants to be here when you open your results. Remember?"

Maddy didn't, but whatever. "Isn't it super late there?"

Her mom checked the watch on her wrist. "It's about eleven. That's not too late. She said to call her as soon as you had it. Day or night."

"Okay..." Maddy dragged herself to the living room to open the front door, right in the middle of another round of knocking. "Leo." Her stomach dropped. "What are you doing here?"

He rolled his eyes. "Nice welcome, Maddy."

"Sorry," she said as she opened the door wide enough for him to come in. "Why didn't you just come in? You never knock."

"You're always telling me to knock, and now you complain about it?" He stepped inside and took off his jacket. "Make up your mind, woman."

Frustration welled inside Maddy like a volcano preparing to erupt. Apparently, all the tension between them was catching up to her. "Don't call me 'woman,'"

"Okay," he shrugged. "Make up your mind, girl."

Maddy's shoulder twitched. "Don't call me 'girl,' either."

"Why not?" Leo shifted. "That's what you are, right?"

"Yeah, but when you say it like that, it sounds so derogatory."

"Says you." Leo squinted with one eye. "I meant it in the most respectful way possible. It's not my fault you totally misunderstand me."

"What are you talking about?" Maddy pursed her lips. This sounded like a conversation inside a conversation. Izzy did those all the time, and it made Maddy's head hurt.

"What are *you* talking about?"

"Seriously, Leo. I can't tell if you're mimicking me or asking a real question."

"That's unfortunate."

Both her hands flew up into the air, making Leo take a step back to avoid getting whacked in the nose. Maddy couldn't even with him anymore. "Leo, this is getting ridiculous. There's all this weird space between us, and I'm super sick of it. I know we had that moment at the football game with the kissing thing or whatever. Can we just go back to normal? Let's just be cool, okay? We're best friends."

Leo stared at Maddy for a long time. "You know I just came over here to pick up something for my mom, right?"

Maddy groaned and slumped all the way to the floor, lying on her back with her arms outstretched to the sides. She grabbed a pillow from the couch to cover her face. She needed a way to block the world out. Life was just too awkward.

"Do I hear Leo in there?" Maddy's mom called from the kitchen.

"Hey, Mom," Leo answered.

"Let me finish with this, just a sec, and I'll get those papers for your mom."

"No worries." Leo kicked the bottom of Maddy's shoe. "Get up, bimba. We're cool."

Maddy shook her head even though it gave her nose a rug burn to rub against the pillow that way. Why did her mom have to buy decorative pillows that were as comfortable as rocks instead of the super soft kind people actually wanted to use?

A hand gripped her elbow. "Come on. Do you really want to explain to your mom why you're sprawled on the floor?"

Maddy closed her eyes and became one with the carpet. Her body was getting all heavy with the convenience of gravity, making it impossible for Leo to pull her up.

He let go of her elbow and chuckled. "Okay, no biggie. You lie there like a slug, and when your mom comes in here, I'll take care of everything. I'll start by telling her it was a dark and stormy night, on the brink of the biggest football game of the season. I scored the winning touchdown, and Maddy threw herself at me, begging for a kiss."

"That is not what happened at all. You guys lost that game."

"Ouch." Leo staggered back dramatically. "You really know where to jab, woman. I mean, female personage."

She ignored that last part and used the pillow to wallop Leo in the face. "And I have not, did not, and certainly never will *throw* myself at you, begging for anything."

"That's how I remember it." He held up his arms to ward off the blows.

"Sick, twisted, demented..." Maddy climbed to her feet and smacked him with each word. "Messed up, crazy, freak..."

Leo got a hold of her hands in such a tight grip she couldn't even twist her wrists anymore, much less keep hitting him with the pillow. She stretched her fingers to release some of the pressure, and the pillow dropped to the floor.

"Ha, powerless!" Leo grinned, his voice low and villainous. "I have you in my grasp, peasant. There is no escape for you now."

Maddy pulled her elbows down to see if she could slip out of his grip. When that didn't work, she turned her whole body around, swinging her shoulder and elbows all over the place. What she succeeded in doing was tangling herself even more. Now Leo's arms crisscrossed in front of her torso and the side of her head pressed into his chest. His heart pounded right into her ear.

"Give up?" His breath was hot.

"Never!" Maddy squirmed. "Joke's on you. This is exactly what I planned. Now I can unleash my secret weapon."

The words sounded good, except that she didn't actually have a secret weapon.

"Maddy?" Her mom's voice entered the room just an instant before the rest of her did. It was amazing how quickly Leo and Maddy disentangled themselves and moved into casual stances far away from each other. "Grams just joined FaceTime; she's ready. Here's those papers, Leo." Mom held out an envelope, which Leo took.

"Thanks, Mom," he said.

"Sure, anytime. Do you want to come say hi to Grams?" Mom waved her arm and started back to the kitchen. "You should stick around for Maddy's test results, too. It's so exciting!"

Maddy's mom was trying so hard to conduct the enthusiasm train that Maddy decided to hop on board. "Yeah, stay. We can find out if I'm part troll, like you are."

"Maddy." Leo shook his head with a mournful expression. "You have to let go of these hopeless ambitions. You will never be like me."

She stuck her tongue at him over her shoulder.

"And it's part goblin, not troll."

Whatever. Leo was a solid mix of both.

"Hey, Grams!" Maddy took a seat in front of the computer while Leo slid into the one next to her. "How are you?"

"Lovely, dearie, thank you. How was your day?"

Her day was exhausting, actually, but it felt way better now. Obviously, she wasn't going to go into all that with Grams, so she just said, "Fine."

Maddy's mom handed her the envelope, and she held it up for Grams to see.

Grams clasped her hands together under her chin. "I am on tenterhooks; you cannot open fast enough!"

Leo laughed, and Maddy slipped her finger under the envelope flap. It seemed to take forever to rip it away from the glue, and Maddy had to glance up a few times to make sure Grams was still breathing on the other side of the screen. Grams's face was pale, and her clasped hands were splotchy white. Maddy swallowed the guilt in her throat so that it settled in her belly. If she'd realized how much this whole thing meant to Grams, she would have gotten the test done sooner.

Well, probably.

Maddy pulled out multiple sheets of paper and set the envelope on the table. When she unfolded the papers, the first one she saw was an official cover letter. She moved it aside to reveal a map of the world on page two. Some of the countries were grayed out, while others were highlighted in bright primary colors. There was a legend at the bottom with percentages next to each color and a pie chart to clarify. The third page was a chart of DNA-matched relatives in Maddy's geographical region, as well as related famous people from the last one hundred years. The end sheet of paper was a summary of Maddy's ethnicity results.

"Why don't you read the cover letter out loud," her mom suggested.

"Okay." Maddy cleared her throat. "Dear Madelena, thank you for participating in the Heritage Hunt DNA and Genetics testing. Your Heritage Hunt results include information about your genetic ethnicity. Heritage Hunt utilizes advanced DNA science to revolutionize the way you view your family tree. Our state-of-the-art testing technology surveys your entire genome with a simple saliva sample. This DNA test is the most comprehensive DNA test available, as it covers both the maternal and paternal lines of ancestry. In addition to your test results, our online interface includes tools for you to utilize your results for family history research. It is our hope that these results will be a starting point for a lifetime love of family history research. More information, blah, blah, blah, customer service line, blah, blah, blah, website. I think that's it. Oh, the test results will also be emailed to the address provided on your application." Maddy looked up. "Did I fill out an application?"

"I did it for you, dearie, when I ordered the test."

That made sense.

"Well, come on. Let's find out how trollish you are." Leo jostled her elbow.

Maddy shuffled the papers to the ethnicity results since everything else was pictures and charts. She smoothed out the paper so it was easier to read.

"African, .5 percent. Scandinavian, 2.5 percent. Same with Polish. Russian, 3.25 percent. Italian, 3.25 percent—"

"Represent!" Leo hooted, lifting both fists in the air.

"—Yeah, um, Greek, 5.75 percent. German, 7.75 percent. Irish, 10 percent. British, 15.25 percent. French, 22.5 percent." Maddy paused and brought the paper closer to her face, then busted up laughing.

"What is it? Why are you laughing?" Grams' voice was breathless, like she'd climbed a dozen stairs two at a time.

Maddy had a hard time forming words around her giggles. "This is seriously funny. It has to be a misprint, or maybe it's a joke."

"What?" Maddy's mom raised her eyebrows.

Maddy held up the sheet of paper and pointed so her mom could see. "Look. Right here, it says I'm 25 percent villain!"

"I knew it," Leo whispered.

"Whatever," Maddy said, swatting him with the paper. "You are such a brat!"

"Maddy," her mom warned.

"Well, he is!" she defended herself. "I bet it's a typo. Like, it's supposed to say Vietnamese or, like, Venezuelan-ian, or something. Villain-ness isn't something that shows up in your blood!"

Grams drew a deep breath. "Helen?"

"Yes." Maddy's mom swallowed hard.

"I simply must be there in person."

"I agree."

"We cannot tell her over FaceTime; it just won't do."

Mom pulled out her phone, her fingers working feverishly over the screen.

"Wait." Maddy looked first at Grams's image, then at her mom. "Tell me what?"

Both of them kept doing whatever they were doing as if Maddy hadn't said a word.

"Tell me what?" She appealed to Leo, though the chances of him knowing what was going on were less than her own.

Leo leaned forward, wiggling his fingers in the air. "It's so obvious, Maddy. They're waiting to tell you in person that you were adopted from Transylvania, that you're the only child of Frankenstein the Monster."

The fact that Leo thought the whole thing was still laughable soothed the rolling in Maddy's belly. He was right; this wasn't a big deal. "Dracula lived in Transylvania, doofus. And the villain in that story was Dr. Frankenstein, not his monster."

"Okay, you can be *his* child. I'm flexible."

Maddy tuned back into what her mom and Grams were saying when they started discussing flights.

"Wait, what? Is Grams coming here?"

Her mom waved her hand to get Maddy to hush. "The soonest flight leaves at two in the morning on Sunday, but I don't want you to take that one, Mom. It's so early."

"Oh, I'll be all right. When will it arrive?"

Maddy couldn't help but interrupt. "Are you coming here, Grams?"

"It gets here at ten Monday night. There are three stops. One in Amsterdam, another in Minneapolis, and then Salt Lake City. Each stop is at least two hours long..." Maddy's mom let out a breath of frustration.

"Oh, dearie. That will not do at all. What of the flights with fewer stops?"

Mom was silent while her fingers swiped all over the screen of her phone. "There's a one-stop that leaves... Wait! Mom, a direct flight just opened with one seat! I can't believe this! It will land at Sky Harbor at seven tomorrow night. Can you get to Zurich by midnight your time?"

"That's less than an hour from now!" Maddy said. "And why is Grams coming here? What's the big deal?" Her stomach started clenching again. She looked at Leo, hoping he would crack some more jokes, but he was texting on his phone.

If she was a one-quarter villain, he was one-quarter useless.

"Absolutely, I can." Grams stood up. "You send me all the details. I will see you all tomorrow night." Grams disappeared into nothingness as Maddy stared at the computer screen.

What just happened?

"Close your mouth, Maddy." Leo stretched his arms over his head. "You're catching flies."

FIVE

Even villains need their mommies sometimes

When Maddy picked up Leo the next morning, he hadn't even gotten his seat belt clicked when she started ranting.

"My mom won't tell me anything! She won't even talk about the test results. After she showed them to Dad, she locked them up in the gun safe. She said she'd explain everything when Grams gets here. Can you believe this? I can't believe this." Maddy slammed the brakes at a stop sign, lurching them both forward. "And why is Grams coming here? You can't send an eighty-billion-year-old woman on a flight around the world by herself! I just don't get why she's okay with this! Or why she won't talk about it."

"Did your dad tell you anything?"

"No!" Maddy hit the steering wheel and accidentally slapped the blinker down. "I'm not turning, you dum-dum," she snapped at the car behind them. Obviously, the driver couldn't hear what she said, but she felt better yelling anyway. There were too many feelings bottled inside for Maddy to keep quiet. She pushed the lever back in place to stop the incessant clicking.

"Such language," Leo yawned.

"Don't even start with me." Maddy glared at him out of the corner of her eye.

"Noted," Leo said seriously. "That is weird about your parents, though. Especially your dad. Usually, he is more of an over-sharer than your mom. Remember when he—"

"Stop!" Maddy shuddered. "Don't even say another word. I'm still working on suppressing that memory."

"I thought it was awesome."

"Of course you did." Maddy shook her head. "All Dad will say about this is it's between me, Grams, and Mom. He's staying out of it."

"Maybe it's not a big deal." Leo held out a hand as Maddy opened her mouth to protest. "Hear me out. Maybe Grams has been planning a trip to visit for a long time and they decided to do it now. She hasn't been here in years. It could be a weird coincidence, you know, that makes this look like more of a big deal than it is."

"Meaning, you think I'm overreacting." Maddy chewed her lip. "Okay, that's fair. I had that same thought a couple of times, but I keep coming back to this one thing I can't ignore."

"What's that?"

"It *feels* like a big deal." Maddy kneaded her hands across the top of the steering wheel. "So, I, uh, Googled the villain thing."

"Of course you did," Leo said in a tone so similar to Maddy's, she couldn't stop the corners of her mouth from twitching upward for just a second before they fell back down.

"This has happened to other people before. I mean, there was a whole question-answer thing on Reddit about people who have 'villain' show up in their DNA test."

"What? For reals? That doesn't sound like a typo or a misprint."

Maddy pressed her lips together. "No, it doesn't, does it?"

"It could be a joke, though."

Maddy gave a half-hearted shrug.

"What did people say about it online?"

"I only scanned through the posts; I didn't take the time to read them all. No one said anything that made it seem like a big thing, just that it had shown up on their DNA test. I don't know, Leo. I don't know what to think about this."

"Yeah, maybe that's a sign."

Maddy glanced at him, letting out a huff of breath.

"Hear me out," Leo said. "Maybe you don't know what to think about it because you don't *need* to think about it, you know? It could just be random or whatever. No biggie."

"Maybe." Maddy checked over her shoulder to change lanes. "Maybe not. You know what?"

"No, what?"

Maddy rolled her eyes. Leo couldn't take anything seriously. "I think this is bugging me so much because my mom is acting so weird. If she'd laughed it off, then I could let it go."

"So, it's all your mom's fault?" Leo laughed. "Very cliche."

Okay, maybe a little. It was kind of true, though. Most problems in life were easy to blame on parents or siblings. Parents were responsible for all things unfair while siblings were at fault for everything else. Leo was the one who told her that, so he should understand why she felt this way.

Maddy sighed. "I'm just saying that it's super weird."

"No arguments there." Leo stretched his hands back and thumped the ceiling of the car. "It is definitely super weird."

About a block from the school, Maddy's cell phone rang.

"Who is it?" She glanced at Leo, who was peering into her purse to check the phone screen.

"VDA?"

"I have no idea what you just said. Is that a name?"

"It looks like an acronym or something. It's all capitalized."

"Probably a crank call," Maddy sighed. "Or a telemarketer. Don't answer it."

Leo shrugged and switched the song on the radio. "With the three bazillion tunes on this planet, can you explain to me how the radio manages to play the same three over and over?"

Maddy's phone rang again.

"Uh, that would be the VDA," Leo announced.

"Just turn the ringer off," Maddy said, clipping each word with increased irritation.

Leo chuckled and picked up the phone.

"Leo!" Maddy hissed.

"Hello?" Leo said in a high falsetto. He flapped his hand at Maddy as she sputtered her protests.

What the heck did he think he was he doing?

It was suddenly very hard to concentrate on the road. Maddy glanced over at Leo as often as she dared.

"Yes, I'd like to order a pepperoni pizza with extra cheese and green peppers cut in the shape of dinosaurs. Please deliver to the high school in thirty minutes. The front office will accept the order. Thank you." Leo hung up and giggled like a little girl.

Maddy slapped his arm with the back of her hand. "You are five years old."

"What are you talking about? That was seriously hilarious."

The phone rang for a third time before Leo had a chance to put it back in Maddy's purse.

"Don't answer it," Maddy warned. "Come on, Leo, it's just scammers. You're going to tick them off, and they'll spam me for the rest of my life."

Leo's posture straightened in a robotic way.

"Did you hear me?" Maddy dared a peek at Leo as she turned the corner into the high school parking lot. "What are you staring at? Leo?"

He put the phone up to his ear. "Hello? Yes... Yes... No... She's right here, but she can't talk; she's driving.... Okay, sure. Hold on." He set Maddy's phone on the middle console and hit the speaker button.

Maddy shot him a silent but deadly glare.

"Hello? Yes, am I to be speaking with Madelena Hutton?"

"Yes," Maddy sighed. What were they selling? A knife set that cuts all by itself? An encyclopedia set that you need on your shelf even though all that junk is available online? The most amazing cell phone coverage in the galaxy?

"Hello, Madelena."

"Maddy," she interrupted.

"Me to pardon?"

"Just call me Maddy."

"Yes, Maddy. The name of my is Elle. I to be a Determinator with the VDA—"

Leo seemed to have recovered enough to stifle his snickering with one hand. Maddy couldn't even roll her eyes at him this time; she totally agreed. If scammers wanted to succeed at scamming people, they needed to come up with titles that sounded like something real and not like a preschooler with a stutter.

"It is the importance of most that I speak with you," Elle went on, her voice rising above all the noise Leo was making.

"Why?" Maddy said. "Is the dethroned King of Cloud Cuckoo Land in need of a million dollars to fund his plot to take back his crown? Tragic, really. You must give him my regards, but I can't help him right now. I have a physics test in first period."

"I beg your—"

"Have a nice dayyyyyyyyy! Thanks!" Maddy called in a cheery voice as she pushed the end button and tossed the phone at Leo. "Now, turn that dang ringer off and put my phone away."

He did so with a sheepish look. "That was weird, yeah?"

"Yeah. Why did you answer the phone, anyway? If you don't recognize the person who calls, you don't answer. Common knowledge, right?"

"I know, but I had the pizza thing pop into my head and wanted to try it out. You can't tell me that wasn't funny."

"What about the second time?" Maddy pulled into a parking space, turned off the car, and started gathering her things. When Leo didn't respond, she looked up to see him squirming in the passenger seat. "Leo?" she tried again.

"Yeah, I heard your question." He looked away. "I don't know why I answered, exactly. I just *had* to."

"No, you didn't have to. You're just a booger. Come on." Maddy backed out of the car and waited for Leo to move his booty so she could lock the doors. They walked in silence until they were inside the school, where they parted without ever speaking again. Maddy did lift her hand to wave, but since Leo didn't reciprocate, she figured he didn't see it. With a shrug, she took the stairs to the science hall.

After Maddy finished her physics test, Mr. Thompson gave the class permission to use iPads for educational games while they waited for everyone to finish up. The kids who busted out their headphones were obviously planning on watching YouTube videos instead. Maddy amused herself by imagining what excuse they would come up with to justify their videos as educational.

'But Mr. T., I have to watch Ninja play Fortnight so I can learn how to become a better world-class video game player.'

'Nerd of the Rings was explaining how to reforge a sword. If I'm ever transported to medieval times, I'm going to need to know how to defend myself.'

'Mark Rober has a super educational new video out.'

Actually, that last one was legit. Mr. Thompson already put his stamp of approval on Mark Rober videos.

Maddy opened her email and tried not to gasp.

She had about thirty unopened emails.

This was especially astonishing because she checked her email on her phone while she was eating breakfast, and there were zero unopened. That was less than an hour ago! As Maddy peered closer, she saw that all the emails were from the same place.

The VDA.

What the heck! This VDA thing was worse than the school when parent-teacher conferences were looming. Phone calls, emails...what next?

Maddy clicked all the messages and sent them to the spam folder without reading a single one.

"Maddy?"

She looked up.

Mr. Thompson stood next to her desk, holding a stack of papers. "Would you take these tests to the office for me? I have a TA there who will grade them."

Maddy tucked her phone in her pocket. "Sure, no problem."

"Thanks." He handed them over. "I know you won't peek. You're the only one of these knuckleheads I trust to do this."

"Hey!" a number of her classmates exclaimed.

Mr. Thompson put his fist on his hip. "Don't give me that. You all know Maddy is the most trustworthy person in this room. By a show of hands, who agrees?"

All the hands went up.

"There you have it," Mr. Thompson nodded. "Off you go, then. Thank you."

Maddy left her books and stuff spread out on her desk. There were still about twenty minutes left of class, and it wouldn't take her long to run this errand. Well, unless she ran into Mrs. Thoene and stopped to chat about endangered animal species again. Last time they got so carried away with the plight of the black-footed ferret that Maddy missed half of second period before she realized how late she was.

Maddy hurried through the quiet halls, trying to focus on what she needed to do. The student teachers usually hung out in the teachers' lounge, which was adjacent to the front office. If she took the secret side entrance instead of going through the main doors, she probably wouldn't run into anyone. Sure enough, she sneaked through the door into the teachers' lounge undetected. Well, except for the college-aged guy with a mullet, who sat at one of the tables sipping something steamy.

"Are you the student teacher for Mr. Thompson?" Maddy asked, hugging the papers to her chest.

"Yes, ma'am." He took a sip, fogging up his glasses so his eyes disappeared.

Maddy set the papers on the round table in front of him. "Mr. Thompson asked me to give you these papers to grade."

"Yippee," he said, taking another sip of whatever was in his mug.

Maddy couldn't tell from his tone if he was really happy about the assignment or being sarcastic. She stood there for a minute, trying to figure it out. The TA put his mug down and gathered the papers toward him, the way people do when they win a boatload of poker chips.

So, probably he really was excited to have something to do.

"Okay, then..." Maddy started to say, then stopped when it became obvious that he wasn't paying a bit of attention to anything other than tests that needed some red pencil markings. She left the lounge and headed back to the hall. On her way, Maddy heard her name coming from the front office. For a second, her confused brain thought it was the college guy calling her back with a question or something. Then she realized it was a woman's voice.

"Yes, I understand you. Madelena Hutton." The school secretary was short-tempered on a good day; this conversation made her sound downright cranky. "But you need to understand that you cannot just enter this school and demand information about the students. Seeing as you are not a relation, there is nothing more to be said here. Good day."

Demand information about students?

About...Maddy?

Who in the world was Ms. Harvy talking to?

Maddy pressed herself against the wall to eavesdrop better and try to get a look at who was out there. If she peeked around the corner to observe, the movement would most likely catch their eyes, and her cover would be blown.

"You do not to understand the nature of urgent of this request." The second voice was also female. Softer, but equally insistent. "I must to really speak with the Madelena Hutton."

"Then, speak with her if you must." Ms. Harvey's voice held a note of mocking. "But not right now and not on these school grounds. I'm going to have to ask you to leave before I call security."

Maddy almost snorted and gave herself away. Security? The closest thing the school had to security was a janitor named Gus who was an ex-Marine. Maddy was sure he'd be more than happy to turn his leaf blower or toilet plunger on this pesky visitor. But the odds were not good that it would make any difference.

A huff of air broke the silence briefly, then footsteps faded away. As quickly and as quietly as she could, Maddy took a sharp turn and sneaked into the office, crouching down to follow the curve of the desk so Ms. Harvey wouldn't see her and ask what she was doing. It was her only choice. If she went into the hall now, the person would see her easily, and she wanted to see them first.

She didn't need to bother; Ms. Harvey had left her desk. Maddy stood up so she could walk faster and hurried to the door. There, she paused and peeked both ways before stepping out of the office. She pressed her back into the brick wall, trying to look as flat as possible. No one was in sight, but she didn't want to take the chance. The front of the school was just around the next corner. If she hurried, she'd be able to see the visitor on their way out the doors. Maddy edged along the way until she reached the corner and stopped to peek around. All her neck muscles tensed, ready to pull her head out of sight if needed.

A tall figure pushed the double glass doors open, flinging them to the sides. Maddy knew it was a woman, but she wouldn't have been able to tell that if she hadn't heard the lady talking to Ms. Harvey already. This was because she was wrapped in a long, shapeless, black cloak that dragged along the ground, picking up dust, dirt, and spitballs like some kind of fabric broom.

She looked like an extra from a *Harry Potter* movie.

Had Maddy finally gotten her acceptance letter to Hogwarts?

Maddy watched until the figure swept out of sight. With every step the woman took, especially down the stairs, Maddy expected her to trip over the long hem of her cloak, but she never did. It was almost like she floated instead of walked. When the mystery woman was out of sight, Maddy slowly walked back to her physics class. She had no idea what was going on, but she couldn't blow it off anymore. There was too much circumstantial evidence to ignore. Despite what Leo said in the car, this might be something.

There were five minutes left on the clock when Maddy returned to class, more than enough time to read one of those emails. She went to her spam folder and looked for something from the VDA.

Then she opened it.

Dear Ms. Hutton,

It is with utmost of the urgency that we, the VDA, speak with you. It has come to our attention that you have received the results from your Heritage Hunt DNA and Genetics Test. You want to know of the formed DNA found in your blood that we wish to speak with you about. Please to respond with all the energy of our souls, that we may discuss with you this importance.

We look to forward of your response,

VDA

Maddy stared at the words for a moment. It sounded like it was written by someone who did not speak English as their first language.

Or it could be a big fat joke.

She pulled up a new browser window and typed 'VDA' into Google.

Virginia Dental Academy.

She was willing to bet that wasn't what she was looking for. Same with Virginia Development Academy, the Verband der automobilindustrie—whatever that was—or the VDA Experiential Marketing and Event Design Agency of Boston.

She blew her hair out of her eyes and deleted 'VDA'. To replace the search, she typed, 'words that start with V'.

That was useless. There were, like, a billion of them.

Maddy tapped her thumb against her phone, trying to think of another way to ask the same question.

When Google fails you, who do you ask for help?

Duh.

It was so obvious she almost smacked herself in the forehead with her palm.

Mom.

SIX

Villainy, thy name is high school

After physics, Maddy scooted to the girls' restroom and locked herself in a stall to call her mom. The phone didn't even get through one full ring when Mom picked up, her voice breathless.

"Hello?"

"Hey, Mom?"

"Maddy? I was hoping you were Grams."

Maddy paced the small space to get rid of the pent-up energy in her legs. "Why? Isn't she on a plane or something? Is everything okay?"

Her mom let out a long breath. "Yes, she's on the plane. But sometimes flights are early, or things happen. I'm waiting by the phone, just in case."

Maddy supposed that made sense.

"What do you need?" her mom said in a more even tone. "Aren't you supposed to be in class right now?"

"Yeah. I mean, I'm between classes, but I have a question that can't wait."

"Okay." Now her mom sounded wary like she was sorry she picked up the phone in the first place.

Maddy took a deep breath. Might as well jump right in. "What's the VDA?"

The silence on the line did nothing to soothe Maddy's concerns.

"Mom?"

When her mom finally spoke, the words came out in disjointed croaks. "Where did you hear about that?"

"They've been calling and emailing me all morning." Maddy decided not to mention the cloaked figure at the front desk. That would really freak her mom out, and Maddy wasn't one hundred percent sure that had anything to do with VDA. It could just be an odd coincidence.

"They are fast," her mom breathed. "Really fast. Much faster than they used to be. Oh, I wish my mom were here!"

Which was not the most reassuring thing for a teenage girl to hear her own mom say.

Maddy gripped the phone so hard her fingers blotched red and white. "Mom? Who are these people? What do they want? What should I do?"

"I don't know, I don't know." Her mom gasped. Maddy could picture her pacing the living room, wringing her hands.

"Should I come home, or something?"

"No..." Her mom hesitated, then started again with more momentum. "No, no. They'll expect that. They're probably watching the house already. You just stay where you are, surrounded by people, and you'll be just fine." There was a tapping sound, then she said, "In fact, do you think you can go to Leo's house after school? I'm going to leave for the airport right now, and I don't want you here all alone. You'll be safe at the Romanos'."

Safe?

Was she in danger?

"Maddy?"

"Yeah, I'm here. I'm sure I can totally go over to the Romanos'. But, Mom? What's this all about? I would feel better if you explained."

"I know, honey. Believe me, I wish I could, but this is your grandmother's story to tell. I really can't do it without her. This will all make sense later, I promise. I'm going to let you go now so I can call Adele and double-check that she's okay with you coming over. Unless I text otherwise, go there after school, okay? For now, you stay at school and keep a lot of people around you at all times. Don't go anywhere alone. Not even the bathroom."

Maddy's heart skittered across her chest. She didn't want to imagine a world where it wasn't safe to go to the bathroom alone. "Really, Mom? Are you sure I should stay at school? Maybe you could come get me on the way to the airport."

"No, you'll be just fine. I think." Her mom took a deep breath. "It will be fine. I'm sure. Now get to class and stay with people. I'll pick you up from Leo's house after I get Grams."

"Okay." Maddy didn't bother mentioning she drove her car to school that day and would therefore have it at Leo's house. She didn't think there was room for one more thing in Mom's brain at the moment. "I guess I'll see you then. Love you."

"Oh, I love you too, Maddy. Pay attention to your surroundings, okay? Don't let anything catch you off guard."

Again, not the most reassuring thing to tell your daughter.

Maddy hung up and stared at her phone for a moment before tucking it into her back pocket. It was silent in the bathroom, but she still stuck her head out of the stall to check both ways before leaving, just in case there was a masked ninja waiting to jump her. She scooted along a wall with her back pressed against the pokey bricks for the second time that day, then pushed the door open slowly and surveyed the hallway.

There were a few students meandering to class, but not the usual rush. This was good news because, suddenly, everyone at the school looked like they could be the traitorous villain. After a couple of false starts, Maddy seamlessly inserted herself into a group of girls moving in the same direction as her next class and then jumped from their group to another when the first group turned down a hall opposite the one Maddy needed. If someone had been watching her from above, which at the moment didn't seem all that impossible, Maddy probably looked like a frog jumping lily pads.

The last leg of her journey to her next class was void of any students, so she took a deep breath and sprinted the remaining distance with her backpack thumping against her tailbone. She dashed through the classroom door, dodged milling students, and slid into her seat. When she was settled, she was too busy huffing and puffing and congratulating herself on getting there alive to notice that Leo was staring at her like she was ten apples short of a dozen.

"What?" she breathed, trying to stabilize her heart rate.

"Nothing," Leo said while he shook his head. "I don't want to know. Don't tell me."

Well, she hadn't planned on explaining anything until he said that. Now Maddy realized someone needed to know what was going on in case she was abducted or her brain got sucked out of her ears. Unfortunately, Señora Hernandez had just started class, so she couldn't talk to him anymore, and they weren't allowed to use cell phones, so she couldn't text either.

Maddy waited for Señora to give them their assignment, then she jumped to her feet and hurried to Señora Hernandez's desk. "Can I use the bathroom pass?"

"Sí." She smiled and handed Maddy a maraca.

Maddy took it and hurried to the nearest bathroom, slinking around corners and running serpentine through the halls. Her mom had warned her not to go anywhere alone, but the need to make sure someone else knew what was going on trumped the obedience card. Really, it was the lesser of the two evils.

Maddy bypassed the crowd of girls putting on makeup and tucked herself into a stall in the farthest corner. What she needed to do right now was send Leo a massive text, and since she wasn't sure how to explain everything that was happening, it was probably going to take a while. Maddy tuned out the noise around her and spent almost the entire Spanish class typing out the longest text in history. Then she had to reread what she wrote so it didn't sound too crazy and edit whatever the heck spell-check was thinking.

Seriously, how did it get 'custard flan for dinner' from 'overheard the office lady'?

Once the text made sense all the way through, Maddy read it through a third time for good measure, her thumb hovering over the send arrow. Doubt filled her like a helium balloon. It was strange how all her actions, when viewed through the lens of paranoia, were sketchy. If she sent this text, Leo would know what was going on, but there would also be a paper trail. It suddenly seemed really foolish to have this all written down. Could the VDA use it against her somehow?

On the other hand, if she didn't send it, Leo wouldn't know what was going on, and Maddy needed him to know what was going on. They wouldn't have another good chance to talk this out until the end of the school day.

It could be too late by then.

And actually, a paper trail might work in her favor somehow. Like, evidence. Yeah, evidence. Anyway, talking about it later with Leo might not be safe either. The VDA could have them all bugged.

There was that.

Maddy sent the ridiculously long text, then glanced suspiciously at the light bulbs and ceiling sprinklers. Were any of them cameras in disguise? They could be, but the thought was too disturbing to dwell on. She shook it to the back of her mind, where it was easier to ignore, then made her way through another crowd of girls primping. She ignored their strange looks and stepped into the hall, prepared to sprint with multiple deep breaths. The race through the hallways was hair-raising and had a couple of near misses. Maddy didn't know there were teachers roaming the halls between classes until this moment, and she didn't want to explain to them why she kept looking at the ceiling and running zigzag through the halls.

When she finally made it back to the Spanish classroom, everyone was divided into groups working on dialogue. She scooted through the door and almost ran to Señora Hernandez's desk.

"Here." She set the maraca back into its designated space.

Señora Hernandez adjusted it with one hand and held the other out to Maddy. Her forehead puckered as she spoke. "Tomaste mucho tiempo; estás enferma?"

Maddy's brain was too scrambled to deal with another language. The only word that got through was 'enferma.'

Sick.

"Uh, yeah, my tummy el sicko. Sorry I took so long." Maddy didn't wait for her teacher to respond. She just turned around and headed back to her seat. All she got for her efforts was another alien look from Leo.

Which she ignored.

The bell rang before Maddy had a chance to crack open her book. She stuffed it in her bag and scrambled to her feet. If she didn't leave the classroom with the bulk of students, then she would be all alone and easy to pick out.

Like a wounded gazelle.

Leo watched Maddy whirl around and throw things into her bag. He folded his arms.

"I think you've finally cracked," he said, his expression serious. "No really, I think you are completely, certifiably bonkers."

"Check your texts," Maddy huffed, shoving her jacket into the large front pocket of her bag.

Leo raised his eyebrow as he moved one hand to retrieve his phone. His eyebrows lurched upward when he looked at the screen. "Holy ravioli, Maddy. What the heck is all this?"

"Just read it."

He went silent, which was good. Maddy already couldn't think straight, and it was a billion times worse with him judging her. After a few minutes, it became clear that Leo was a stupendously slow reader. Maddy tapped her foot as she watched people eke into the hall. The classroom was emptying out. Soon they would be left all alone with Señora Hernandez, and, for all Maddy knew, Señora could work for the VDA. Maybe she was a spy posing as a perky Spanish teacher.

"Come on. You read; I'll guide." She took his free elbow and pulled him into the mass of student traffic.

Inside a mob of armpits and cologne was a strange place for Maddy to take a full, deep breath, but that was exactly what she did. It was the first time since she called her mom that she felt calm. There was something strangely comforting about people stomping on her shoes and sticking elbows in places they didn't belong. In this mash of people, there was no way someone could single her out.

She was one in a million here.

"What do you have for third period?" Maddy raised her voice over the noise.

Leo didn't answer. Not only was he super slow at reading, but he also moved his lips along with the words. He paused at the end of every sentence and looked off into space. It was the opposite of skimming, like he was really trying to comprehend the situation. While Maddy appreciated his diligence, she just wanted to see what he thought already. This patience thing was a tough gig.

With no direction from Leo, Maddy decided to head to her own third period. Leo would have to finish reading by then, and he could get to his class from there. Maddy turned them around and headed to the girls' locker room, where she needed to dress for P.E. They were running the mile that day, and Maddy suddenly felt totally and completely drained. All that sprinting through halls and eyeballing passing students suspiciously was exhausting.

Maddy stopped outside the girls' locker room and let go of Leo's arm.

He finally put his phone down and looked at her with an unreadable expression.

"What do you think?" Maddy twisted a ring around her middle finger.

"Seriously?" Leo raised both eyebrows. "If I didn't already know you don't have a sense of humor, I would think you were messing around. Are you for real?"

"Yes," Maddy nodded.

He took a breath. "Okay, if this is for real, it is also completely crazy. Are you sure your mom wants you to stay at school? It seems like it'd be better for you to go home."

"Except she won't be there. Remember? She has to pick up Grams, and Dad's at work. Which reminds me, can I hang out at your house until Mom gets back tonight?"

"Yeah, of course," Leo shrugged. "I'm more worried about the rest of the school day."

"Mom said to stay surrounded by people."

Leo shook his head. "I don't think that's going to work. If these wackos, the VDA or whatever, are going to try something, it will be easier to do it in a hall full of students. No one's going to notice one less."

Maddy's stomach rolled. The small sense of security she'd claimed suddenly fled for the hills.

She hadn't even considered that.

"What do I do?"

Leo tapped his phone against his chin. "You know what? You just go to class; I'll take care of it."

That did not make Maddy feel any better. "What are you going to do, though?"

His eyes narrowed. "Okay, don't freak out. I really think this is our only option."

"What is our only option?"

"I mean, it will get you to all your classes and someone will for sure notice if you disappear, so don't argue with me, Maddy. It's really for your own good."

"Okay, sure. What the heck are you talking about?"

"See!" He lifted his hand in the air and then let it drop back to his side. "You get all worked up without even letting me explain."

"Explain already!" Maddy slugged him in the arm.

"Ouch." Leo rubbed his arm and gave her a wounded look. "Why are you so violent? I'm just trying to help."

Maddy pursed her lips. "Do you realize you haven't actually told me what you're thinking yet?"

"I did too."

Maddy shook her head.

"Girls," Leo said, rolling his eyes to the ceiling. "Okay, listen carefully this time. I'm going to recruit the guys to stand outside your classrooms and make sure you get to the next class safely. I would do it myself, but I can't miss that many classes without someone noticing. If I spread it out among the team, we can all keep an eye on you."

Maddy stared at him, trying to decide whether that was super thoughtful or incredibly offensive. "So, there's going to be a football player outside all of my classes, like a bodyguard? That's your solution?"

"Seriously, Maddy? This is what I'm talking about. Do you realize every girl in this school would trade their phone to have a football bodyguard walk them to all their classes? Why can't you be normal? Just get excited or something."

Maddy crossed her arms and gave him her best evil eye.

"Whatever." Leo dropped his hands to his sides. "You don't have to get excited. You don't even have to like it, but you will have to deal with it because this is the best plan we've got. Just trust me here. I promise it will work great."

This was the same phrase he used when he convinced her to skateboard off the slide at the park the summer before fifth grade and she broke her arm. She missed the river trip because she couldn't get her cast wet.

"Come on." Leo gripped her elbow like she was the president of the United States and he worked for the Secret Service. Maddy half-expected him to put on shades and check his earpiece to make sure the coast was clear from all checkpoints before moving forward. "Let's get you to class."

Maddy shook his arm off her. "I am already at class." She pointed to the girls' locker room. "P.E."

"Oh." He slumped like a deflated balloon. "So, okay, you go in there and do whatever it is girls do, and I'll go find some guys. The biggest, scariest guys on the team. Trolls. Wait out here after class and don't go to your next class without one of them next to you. You promise?"

"I promise," Maddy said because it was a zillion times easier than arguing with Leo.

He gave her his own version of the stink stare and tapped his foot.

Apparently, he didn't appreciate her attitude.

With a sigh, Maddy crossed her heart and raised two fingers in the air. "I solemnly swear that I will wait inside the girls' locker room until I see a big, hairy, scary football player drooling on the carpet outside the hall."

Leo shook his head.

Maddy was sure he was thinking he would let her get away with it this time because that was a zillion times easier than arguing with her when she got like this.

Seven

How do you protect a villain?

The day went by completely uneventfully, considering, or maybe because of, all the fuss Leo made.

Well, except for the part when Ty Goshman picked Maddy up and carried her over his shoulder all the way to trig so no one could touch her. Or when Huxley Thomas cleared the English hall like Andre the Giant in the movie *The Princess Bride* by yelling, "Everybody move!" Yes, he bellowed, and yes, everybody moved. Honestly, that wasn't the weirdest thing that had ever happened in the hallway at school. There were probably people who didn't even think twice about it.

Unfortunately, Maddy was not one of those people.

By the end of the school day, she was one weird look or sarcastic comment away from hiding in a corner with her hood over her head.

Other than those aforementioned gems, it really was a completely uneventful day. No abductions, no brain-melting—other than the kind that usually happened in American government class—and no more VDA sightings. Leo met Maddy at her locker at the end of the school day, flanked by seven guys who each outweighed Maddy by at least a hundred and fifty pounds. They formed a neat circle around her locker while she exchanged books, and they completely ignored the exasperated people trying to get to the lockers they were blocking. When Maddy was ready to go, each one of the guys extended his arms and said the word 'safe' each time they took a step.

Which was a lot.

They said the word a really, really lot.

But that wasn't the worst part. It was trying to coordinate steps in the center of a bunch of football players who were standing shoulder to shoulder and facing outward so they couldn't see when Maddy moved. Because they had no idea when she took a step, their timing was all over the place. It was pretty much a one-act comedy routine. More than once, someone almost face-planted into the carpet. It took over twenty minutes to get to the parking lot.

Then they hit the biggest snag of them all.

Maddy's two-door Toyota Camry.

"There's no way you guys are going to fit in my car," Maddy said. It would be a miracle if two of the behemoths could do it, much less seven. "What's the plan now?"

Leo scrunched his face and stared off into the distance, then he slapped the car hood. "We're going to walk."

"To your house?" Maddy asked to clarify. He had to be joking. It would take them a year and a half to reach his house by walking the way they did through the school.

Leo nodded. "Positions!"

The guys encircled Maddy, stuck their arms straight out in front of them, and chanted in unison. "Safe."

That was Maddy's cue, but she ignored it. "Leo, this really won't work. It's going to take forever."

"Maybe."

"Can we just, like, walk normally?"

Leo looked off into space again, scrunching his face to draw inspiration from thin air. This time Maddy followed his gaze. Maybe there was a big whiteboard in the sky supplying him with ideas.

No, there was nothing but air.

Leo was coming up with this stuff on his own.

Which was super reassuring.

"Okay, I got this. Here's what we're going to do." Leo walked around the group, rearranging guys so that two were in front of Maddy, two behind, and two on the left side and two on the right including Leo.

So, a box now, instead of a circle.

"Leo!" Maddy breathed out all her exasperation. It was not a little bit. She might have caused a hurricane somewhere with all that pent-up air.

"No, this will work. Watch." He cupped his hands around his mouth. "Safe!"

The guys in front took a step, then Maddy and the middle crew, then the back followed. It took them a few tries before they got into a normal pace, and when they did, Maddy actually smiled. Maybe this would work. Leo's house wasn't too far away; it was a beautiful, sunny day; and yes, she was flanked by seven gorgeous guys.

And one village idiot.

They got a lot of strange looks from passing cars, but other than that, everything went smoothly for an entire block. Maddy barely minded when a few of the rubberneckers looped around and came back to take a picture. She couldn't wait to see which Instagram feed they'd end up on with a witty caption that would damage all of their reputations.

And question their sanity.

Maddy was so preoccupied with the passing cars that she didn't notice the limo right away. It wasn't until the hairs on the back of her neck started tingling that she glanced over her shoulder and saw the car slowly following along beside them. For a second, with all the other cars gathering into a line behind it, Maddy thought it was a funeral procession.

That wasn't ominous at all.

And actually, that might have been better than the dawning realization that the limo was keeping perfect time with their group. It took effort for a car to drive as slow as Maddy and company were walking.

That's about the moment Maddy started freaking out.

"Leo?" she said in a shaky voice.

"I see it," he whispered. "I'm watching. Don't worry."

Don't worry.

Such easy words to say, but not so easy to do. In fact, Leo telling her not to worry actually made the worry amp up, and now all she could think about were all the worst-case scenarios. Any moment now, someone was going to jump out of a vehicle and throw her in the trunk. That wasn't horrifying enough, so there was also the scenario where the limo was a distraction for the trained bounty hunter hiding in the bushes up ahead. The boys would all be so busy keeping an eye on the limo that Maddy would be a mere memory by the time everyone realized what happened.

Oh yeah, and there was also the almost real possibility that the black limo could jump the curb and plow down her square of safety. Or someone from inside could shoot her in the butt with a sleeping dart. She would wake up thirty years later in the middle of the desert, where she would be forced to harvest dust until the end of her days.

She never claimed her worries made any sense.

Maddy's attention split in two. With one part of her brain, she kept track of where she put her feet so she didn't trip and upset the whole football brigade. With the other part of her brain, she watched the movements of the limo. Going back and forth like that gave her a headache of epic proportions, but it was all necessary—especially because the car seemed to be getting more aggressive. Now it nosed ahead of them so that the back doors, where the passengers would be, were parallel with their group.

Her worries were looking truer and truer by the second.

"Leo?"

He touched Maddy's wrist. "Don't worry. I got this."

Leo's eyes shifted toward the limo, then, without any warning, he let out a war cry and leaped into the air. Like a jungle cat, he scrambled up the side of the limo and crouched on the top on all fours. As if that wasn't enough, he started banging on the top with his fist.

"Man, I was gonna do that," one of the football players muttered.

Maddy wouldn't have been able to hear what he said except that Leo had to stop yelling to breathe right at that particular moment.

He went one with renewed enthusiasm. "Who are you and what do you want? Leave my friend alone, you psycho. You don't know who you're messing with!" He then followed with a number of other words and phrases that made Maddy's ears itch. She tried to redirect her attention; it would be best for their friendship if she just forgot what he was saying.

In public.

At the top of his lungs.

The limo came to a screeching halt.

And so did their group. The football players watched Leo in silent awe and refused to go a step farther. Leo continued to hang onto the top of the limo like a deranged spider monkey. Some of the football players looked as though they wanted to join Leo in the pounding and shouting; others were checking their cell phones and completely oblivious.

The whole thing seemed quite confuddling for the poor guys. Should they keep walking? Should they join Leo on the limo? Should they search their pockets for gum?

Brent went with the last one and offered a piece to Maddy.

She lifted a hand to stop the gum's progression. "I'm good."

The back door of the limo flung open, startling Brent so much that the gum ended up on the ground. A cloaked figure bolted out of the back seat. Maddy squeaked and shrank to the corner of her disheveled safety square. The air crackled with an electricity that Maddy felt in her bones like she did when a storm was on the way.

The figure straightened into perfect posture and lifted two arms—just two, not six, or twelve, or something otherworldly—which was a huge relief given the circumstances. The arms pulled the hood down, and just like that, the football players turned into drooling piles of goo.

And who could blame them?

The black-cloaked figure was more than just a figure. It was a woman. An insanely beautiful woman with long raven hair that glistened in the sunlight like onyx. Her velvety purple eyes swung from Leo to the slack-jaw football players to Maddy.

There they rested.

"Maddy?" She reached out an ivory hand that might as well have been made from porcelain.

Leo was too involved in vehicle damage to pay any attention to anything else at first. When he heard the woman's voice, that sure caught his attention. It got even worse when he looked up and caught sight of the woman. He stopped pounding the limo and started slobbering on it instead.

Maddy shook her head. Apparently, Leo no longer had this. She tried to shrink even farther into the mass of football players. Leo caught Maddy's eyes and slid off the top of the limo. He pushed the woman out of the way and stood in front of Maddy.

"What do you want? Who are you people?" He was trying to sound tough but kept losing his train of thought. If he glanced back at Maddy, he was fine. As soon as his eyes moved back to the woman, he started talking like his tongue had suddenly expanded to the size of a bounce house. After a moment of confusion, Leo turned his back on the woman so he couldn't see her anymore and raised his voice.

Maddy took a step back so he wasn't spitting on her face while he yelled. "You know you can't just harass people like this? It's against the law. Leave us alone, or we'll call the police. You'll get a restraining order or jail time or something..." He paused as though trying to decide. "...worser."

Nicely done, Leo. Something worser. That totally showed them. No doubt the woman was now rethinking her stalker life choices.

The woman's voice melted into the air like spun sugar. "I mean to not harass. I wish to speak with the words of Maddy for a moment. May I? It is really of important." Her soothing tone lilted with an accent Maddy couldn't identify.

Leo's resolve shuddered. Even though he wasn't looking at the woman, he seemed unable to shake her influence. He blinked slowly, his eyes wide and unfocused.

It was understandable. There's not much a teenage boy can do in the face of such ravishing beauty. Since Maddy appeared to be the only one immune to whatever was going on with the guys, she took a deep breath and stood up.

"I got this now, Leo."

Leo stepped aside but linked his elbow through Maddy's so they would share the same fate, whatever it was.

Maddy stood shoulder to shoulder with Leo and held out her free hand, inviting the woman's attention onto herself instead of whatever she was doing to scramble the guys' brains. "What do you want to talk to me about?"

The woman's face flooded with relief that made her shine like a pearl. All of the football players gasped in unison.

"Seriously, you guys?" Maddy said. "Cut it out. You are super distracting."

They picked their jaws off the ground and had the presence of mind to look sheepish.

Well, some of them did. Others just kept salivating on their shoes.

"I-I do not wish to speak the words of this here in the place of public…" The woman's large eyes darted around the sidewalk with all the boys and all the traffic and all the everything.

"Well, too bad!" Leo raised his fist to intimidate the lemon tree right in front of him. "She's not going anywhere with you!"

The tree might have been cowed; it was tough to tell what a tree was thinking, but since the woman couldn't see Leo's fierce expression, she remained unruffled. "Perhaps there is to be a place of neutrality we could go? Somewhere of where you feel will be safe for you?"

Maddy caught Leo's eyes and raised a brow. They had done something like this before, where they tried to have a conversation without speaking words. It was after they babysat Leo's siblings. Rico and Nico totally read each other's minds. Maddy was pretty sure that was a twin thing, but Leo was convinced they could do it too if they tried hard enough. They'd been practicing for over a year, and sometimes it actually did seem to work.

Sometimes it was a dismal failure.

Like right now.

Leo sighed and widened his eyes, but Maddy still didn't get it. He flicked his gaze to his hand. Specifically, to his phone.

Oh, maybe she did get it.

Maddy pulled her own phone out of her pocket and opened the texts.

> **What are you thinking?**

Maddy glanced at the woman and then back to her phone.

> I don't know. Maybe. If it's somewhere super public. What do you think?

His response was immediate.

> **No way. She's evil.**

What makes you think so?

She's unnatural. I feel weird when I look at her.

Maddy decided not to mention that there were perfectly natural hormones that explained those weird feelings. Because the truth was, something weird was going on. Leo was yelling at a tree, which was definitely not usual for him. And the rest of the guys were building their own swimming pool on the sidewalk. Maddy had serious concerns about mild dehydration if they didn't cut it out. So, despite what she wanted or wished, something was happening. The woman had, like, power over them or something.

Maddy pursed her lips and considered her options. Whenever she had a tough decision to make, it helped to think of the two extremes.

So, she could tell the woman thanks but no thanks, and just leave.

That was probably the safest thing to do.

Or...

She could get in the fancy car with the unnatural woman and have a chat.

Which was probably the stupidest thing she would ever do in her entire life.

What came in the middle of those extremes? Somewhere in there was the right answer; Maddy could feel it.

She could pick a place to go, somewhere super public, and find out what the woman wanted.

Was that completely nuts?

She hated to admit, even to herself, that she was curious. The woman had gone to a whole lot of effort with all those emails and phone calls to track Maddy down today. Maddy couldn't think of a time in her entire life that anyone had tried that hard to talk to her. She looked at Leo, the way his eyebrows furrowed into a long black line above his eyes. He gave a slight shake of his head.

I'm gonna do it.

"What?" Leo said out loud, then looked at Maddy with a horrified expression. His head bowed over his phone again, his thumbs moving feverishly across the screen.

> Are you crazy? What are you thinking?

He followed his text by a billion emojis of explosions, frowny faces, and lightning.

Maddy shook her head.

> I want to hear what she's going to say.

> Bad idea.

Leo glared at her and then went back to his phone.

> BAD IDEA.

> Maybe.

This had the potential to be a really bad idea. But now that the curiosity outweighed the fear, she knew she would lie awake at night for years to come and wonder what would have happened if she'd talked to the woman. She pushed *send* on the text and tucked her phone away.

While Leo growled and grimaced at his phone, Maddy studied the woman with neutral eyes. The beauty and glamor were definitely still there. Movie stars wished they were as poised and flawless as this woman was. She stood so still she could have been a marble statue of a nymph on display in a regency manor. She almost looked fake. Like, if Maddy reached out and touched her hand, would she disappear?

"There's a Wendy's just ahead on the corner," Maddy said. "We can go there and talk."

"Lovely that is to be!" The woman smiled so brightly that Maddy had to blink rapidly for a few moments to get the spots to fade away. "I will to follow you, shall not I?"

Maddy nodded, and Leo groaned as he stuffed his phone into his back pocket.

EIGHT

Villainy shows up in the blood

Maddy tried to send the football players home when they got to Wendy's, but they took their responsibility seriously and refused to leave until she was safe. Well, that and Leo overruled her by talking way louder and using manly grunts. Maddy wasn't fluent in Neanderthal, but she got the impression that Leo promised them all free Frosties if they stuck around for a little while longer.

So, that's why an entourage of football players lounged outside of Wendy's, leaning on the retaining wall and perching on the planters. One or two of them pressed their noses against the window to watch Maddy and Leo walk with the woman to a corner bench and sit down. Maddy waved them away so they wouldn't creep out the other customers, but they didn't see her.

Or pretended they didn't see her.

Either way, they stayed.

It was a good thing they didn't insist on coming inside. Wendy's was so crowded that Maddy bumped into more people than she could count on the way to the only empty table. Leo stuck to her like a super static sock, no matter how hard she tried to reason with him. It wasn't like the woman would vaporize her in the middle of a crowded restaurant. If she wanted to do anything awful, she'd had plenty of chances already. But Leo refused to hear logic and glued himself to Maddy's side as soon as she chose a chair. The woman glided into the seat across from them.

"Who are you, exactly?" Leo blurted as soon as they were all seated. "And why have you been stalking us all day?"

For once, Maddy was glad he didn't have a filter.

The woman opened her mouth, but Leo kept talking right over her.

"And what's this thing you got going on?" Leo waved his hand up and down in front of the woman's nose. "Can you turn it off, or whatever? I can't think straight."

The confusion on her face made it very clear that the woman had no idea what Leo was talking about.

But Maddy knew. "He thinks you're putting a spell on him." She laughed like that was the most ridiculous thing on the planet.

People don't just go walking around putting spells on other people.

"Oh," the woman nodded. "I apologize. This form, in your world, is powerful. Quite. I forget. Please to one moment." She lifted her hood to cover her face, and it was like someone extinguished the spotlight at their table. It took a second for Maddy's eyes to adjust to the dimmer light.

When the woman pulled her hood down again to reveal her face, Maddy had to blink for a different reason.

"Ew—ugh!" Leo pushed his chair back, his face contorted in disgust.

Maddy clasped her hands to the bottom of her chair and wound her feet around the chair legs to keep herself from doing the same thing. Instead of young and stunning, the woman was now old. Not regular, cozy grandma old; like, wicked witch old. Old with a long, crooked nose and a huge wart with an actual hair sticking out of the middle.

The mother of all hairs. Thick and black and wiry.

"How did you do that?" Maddy tried to keep her voice even so they wouldn't attract the attention of everyone in the room. They were already getting stares from people who had seen them walk in and were probably wondering how in the world the beauty queen suddenly morphed into a freakish hag.

"Please." The woman lifted a gnarled hand that was wrinkled with some kind of arthritis. "Please, do let me to explain."

"Yes, absolutely, explain." Maddy's eyes watered. She'd forgotten to blink or maybe was afraid to. What if the next time she looked across the table, the woman was something even worse?

A spider, a vampire, or a clown with a chainsaw?

At this point, she would believe anything was possible.

The woman fixed her rheumy eyes on Maddy's face with such intensity that Maddy had an almost uncontrollable desire to check for boogers and things between her teeth.

"My name is Elle," the woman croaked.

"Hey! You're the chick on the phone?" Leo burst out and Maddy had to elbow him to remind him to lower his voice. "I mean, the lady. You are the lady who called this morning."

"Yes," she nodded. "I called this morning to you. I am Elle, the Head of the Determinator of the VDA."

"What is the VDA?" Maddy asked. There were other questions that wanted their voice heard, but Maddy was barely keeping it together as it was. She didn't want to know too much too fast in case it made her brain decide to actually explode.

"The Villain Detection Agency."

So, that's what VDA stood for. Not that that helped anything. Villain Detection Agency sounded as made up as the word 'determinator.'

"Oh, this is so the much harder than I was to be thinking." Elle tapped her yellow, cracked fingernail on the table. "Let us just say to this: the mission of my job, the agency, and of the Determinator is to be doing the detecting of those who have the villain in their blood. We must to be determined if they will have the villain tendencies, that we might—"

"Hold the flipping phone." Leo held up his palm. "I'm pretty sure everything you just said was gibberish. What the heck are you about?"

"I..." Elle blinked. "I about..." She looked at Maddy in such helpless confusion that Maddy had to intervene, even though she was just as mixed up as Leo was.

"He thinks you're messing with us," Maddy translated. "Are you messing with us?"

It was exceptionally hard to stop there. Maddy had so many other questions building up, like how did Elle change her appearance? And what was Elle's accent, and why did she mix up her words so badly? And why did chicken nuggets sound so incredibly good right then?

The confusion didn't leave Elle's face. "I...I do not... What is messing?"

Maddy tucked her shaking hands into her armpits and looked beyond the wart and the leather skin to the soul of Elle's eyes—which were actually not that different from the eyes of the younger version, now that Maddy looked closer. So, was the hag, like, a cover? Elle said something about her other form being too much. Was Elle trying to make things easier on them by morphing like that?

Maybe Elle was a nice person. Maybe this would be okay. Maybe Maddy hadn't totally lost her marbles all over Wendy's linoleum.

Shapeshifting seemed like a weird way to put people at ease, but if Elle wasn't from around here, it made sense she wouldn't understand what was and wasn't a social norm. That was comforting until Maddy realized that if Elle wasn't from their world, she was from another one. Which meant there *were* other ones. Which meant Maddy's comfort zone was about to be blown to bits.

"Where are you from, Elle?" Maddy asked, squeezing her hands into fists.

Elle's countenance lifted at the change in Maddy's voice. "It is from the land of Skurk that I come to you."

"Is that in Greece?" Leo asked.

"Greece is not of the Skurk." Elle shook her head. "Skurk, my home, it is a world that is different. It is separate." She spread her arms to the sides like that would help us understand what she was saying.

It didn't.

Maddy's brain throbbed. "Okay, so you're from Skurk. Tell me again what you want to talk to me about?"

"Yes, I talk to you of the test, the—it is the test for your heritage. You take this test."

"Umm…"

"When you do this, it shows to you the blood of your ancestors, so you see the blood that comes inside you."

Okay, all the blood talk was disarming, but Maddy nodded to keep the information coming.

"When you to take this test for DNA and in you it finds the villain gene, then the VDA is to be alerted. Our duty we have is to make the contact. We responsibility to find the blood that is dormant or the blood that gives to you the villain tendencies."

"What are you saying, exactly?" Maddy's fists were so sweaty it was hard to keep them clenched tight. Her fingers kept slipping out of formation.

"Madelena—Maddy—you have into you the blood of a villain."

If Elle had stood up and dropped the mic, those words could not have packed a harder punch. Maddy's mind was officially blown. She knew it was happening because her thoughts went completely blank. All gone. This was something that had never actually happened to her before, and she wasn't quite sure how to handle it. She couldn't form words. She couldn't move. She couldn't blink.

Leo didn't seem to have the same problem.

"You are whack, lady!"

"Whack?" Elle rolled the word around like she was trying to figure out the flavor.

"Whack-a-doodle-doo! You're talking crazy! What you're saying isn't even possible. I took biology; there's no villain gene. You can't detect that crap! People choose to be bad guys or not. Even if it were possible, which it isn't, then the government or whoever would round up the bad people before they had a chance to pull a Hitler 2.0."

"Yes," Elle said, looking relieved. "This is what I to do. The rounding."

"Wait, what?" Leo glanced at Maddy. "You round people up? Who gave you the authority to do that? What do you do with them? Where do you take them?"

"I— I do not understand the things what you are meaning." Elle stared at her palms, helplessly. "I am not made for this world."

Leo slapped his palm on the table, causing Maddy to jump in alarm. "Well, who does understand? Who do we talk to so we can get some answers? This is a big deal because you're not taking Maddy anywhere. Especially not because of a nonexistent villain gene."

Elle reached into the folds of her cloak and pulled out a business card. She set it on the table and pushed it across the table so they could read it. "This the site of the web for you to explain. You go there and take the test."

"What test?" Maddy blinked. "I already took the test. I swabbed and everything."

"It for to test the villainous." When Elle turned to Maddy, her image flickered like she was a video game with glitchy graphics. Maddy reached to take the card from Elle's hand and accidentally brushed her skin. Besides feeling freakishly cold, Elle was completely solid despite her hazy image. Maddy turned the card over to see words on the back, printed in thick black strokes against a deep purple background.

Villain Detection Agency
https://www.villaindetectionagency.com/villainoustest
info@villaindetectionagency.com
"There is no Villain without I"

"Maddy?" Leo's voice was tight.

Maddy looked up, and Elle's chair was empty.

"What happened? Where did she go?" Maddy stood so suddenly, she knocked over her chair. The clatter got lost in the noise of the room. Maddy righted the chair, then stood up and twirled a full circle.

She couldn't see Elle anywhere.

Leo's face was an interesting shade of white. "I don't know what happened. I was looking right at her, and she just disappeared. But that's impossible. People don't just disappear. Do they? No, they don't. They don't. They don't."

Yeah, Leo definitely needed some air; Maddy did too for that matter. She grabbed Leo's arm and squeezed around people to get to the front entrance of Wendy's. Elle's black limo wasn't in the parking lot anymore. Maddy pushed the glass door open and yelled at Brent.

"Did you see where that limo went?"

He looked up, shading his eyes from the afternoon sun. "Oh, weird. It's gone."

Maddy tried not to sigh. "You guys can go home now. I don't think I need a square of safety anymore." She cut Brent off when he opened his mouth. "Or a circle of safety. Thanks for your help."

"What about our Frosties?" Ty flexed his arm muscles so they got all bulgy.

Maddy let go of Leo to rub the center of her forehead, where the throbbing was the strongest. "Leo will buy them later."

They grumbled and they growled, but they couldn't do much else besides trudge away from Wendy's in different directions. Maddy watched them go with her hands pressing tightly into her sides. Hopefully, the sun would take care of the goosebumps all over her arms because she had never had so many.

Leo blinked as he stepped into the bright sunshine. "I didn't see what I just saw. I didn't see what I just saw. Maddy?"

"Yeah?"

"Do you think this is a dream? Sometimes I have super realistic dreams. Like the time I was in a blue milk drinking contest on Tatooine, and the alien with the chin that looks like a butt beat me so the whole floor opened into this pit thing, and Jabba the Hut tried to make me jump into it, but I didn't want to because I had to do my history homework."

Maddy just stared at him.

"It was more realistic than it sounds. When I woke up, it took me a minute to remember that it was just a dream and not real. Even when I went downstairs for breakfast, I kept expecting the living room floor to open up into a pit."

Maddy patted Leo's shoulder but didn't respond. She wasn't entirely confident she would be able to say anything without using the word 'mental' to describe Leo or herself, so she kept her thoughts contained.

"What do we do now?" Leo asked.

"Let's go back to the school, get my car, and then go home."

Leo scratched his chin. "Do you still want to come over? I don't think the VDA is going to bug you now that Elle talked to you and gave you that card and stuff."

"I don't think so either, but I'll still come over. Mom's expecting me there." Maddy could easily call her mom and change the plan, but she didn't want to go to her empty house right now. She didn't want to be alone. Leo's house, with all the chaos and noise, sounded fantastic.

They made much better time getting back to the school than they did leaving it, and with a lot less noise. Part of Maddy kind of missed the baritone 'safe' every time she took a step. In a weird way, it did make her feel more secure surrounded by a circle of guys. Without them, she was really exposed.

Maddy and Leo drove to Leo's house without any more out-of-the-ordinary events. It seemed almost unfair that the world could go on like normal when they just saw a young woman change into an old woman and then disappear.

There was something wrong with that.

Entering Leo's house was like walking into the stadium during the half-time show, except that there was a spicy wave of tomato sauce instead of that stale corn chip smell. Rico and Nico zipped by, each carrying a model airplane and making more noise between the two of them than the entire high school band. Enzo jammed out while he swept the floor. She hoped he was enjoying himself because hearing loss was totally in his future. Gianna was on the communal computer in the corner of the living room, typing something in Word, and Bella and Lilianna had their dolls spread out all over the place while Alessandra crawled around trying to eat everything they didn't move in time.

It was beautiful.

Leo tossed his stuff in the walkway and headed to the computer. Before Maddy followed him, she moved his shoes to the rack, hung up his coat, and leaned his backpack against the wall, then did the same with her own things. By the time she finished, Gianna and Leo were in a pretty heated argument over who should have the computer.

"I was here first!" Gianna's eyebrows hung like low clouds over her narrowed eyes. "You can't just come in here and override my computer time."

"This is important, peasant. Now move your babushka."

"No."

"I'm not kidding, Gia. I need the computer. Now!"

"My report is important too!"

"So help me, peasant, if you don't move—"

"You can't make me!"

Leo raised an eyebrow and gripped his sister by the waist. Before Maddy could blink, he picked her up and set her on the floor next to the computer desk.

"I'm telling Mom!" She kicked at him.

Leo took Gia's seat and reached out his hand, palm up. For a second, Maddy didn't know what he wanted, then it dawned on her, and she handed him the VDA business card. He started typing as Gia repeatedly kicked the legs of his chair and screamed creative adjectives. When that got zero reaction, she stuck her tongue out and stomped into the kitchen.

"Is she going to get your mom?" Maddy twisted her fingers together. Leo's mom was scary when she got angry. The last place Maddy wanted to be was next to him when the tornado of Italian words started picking up speed.

"Naw." Leo kept typing and talking, a talent Maddy had yet to master. "She knows Mom will just tell her to work it out. We're good."

Maddy's shoulders unhunched, and she scooted another chair closer to the computer screen. Leo pressed 'Enter' with a flourish and sat back as the website loaded.

"How villainous are you?" Maddy read the words as they appeared on the screen.

Leo let out a scoff. "This is ridiculous."

Maddy totally agreed. The graphics looked like the old Nintendo games her dad showed her, the ones he used to play when he was her age, with the pixels totally pronounced. The word 'villain' blinked red, then green, then purple, then yellow over a cauldron with bubbles that glitched as they tried to float upward. A gawky bat flapped around the outside of the screen.

Leo maneuvered the mouse until it hovered over the 'Click Here' button.

"What do you think? Are we doing this?"

NINE

It's important to understand the heart of a villain, as well as the mind

Maddy shook her head. "No."

"Really?" Leo lifted his index finger away from the mouse clicker. "I mean, really? You aren't even a little curious after what happened at Wendy's?"

"Sure, I'm curious," Maddy admitted. Anybody would be after all the things that had happened in the last hour. "It's just too weird. Let's wait and talk to my mom and Grams before we do anything. Okay?"

Leo shook his head.

"Wait, you want to take the test? Why? I thought you thought it was all ridiculous."

"It is ridiculous," Leo said. "It's completely *pazzesco*."

Crazy.

"But I seriously feel like I'm losing it, Mads. I have to see if maybe something in this test will make everything else make sense."

Yeah, but what if something in the test would make everything else way worse?

"I think we're over our heads, Leo. I want to talk to Grams at least before we go any further. Don't you think this feels like a bigger deal than we know?"

"I don't know." Leo shrugged one shoulder. "So, you're not taking the test?"

"No."

Leo nodded. "Alright, then I'm going to do it." He faced forward, and his index finger pressed hard on the mouse. The screen immediately changed.

Welcome to the Villainous Test.

Please answer all twenty questions to the best of your ability to determine your villainy. The Villain Detection Agency will contact you within twenty-four hours to discuss your test results. Have a nice day.

Maddy waited a billion years for Leo to finish reading before she spoke. "You know this is bananas, right?"

"I love bananas." Leo clicked on the 'Next' button, and a data form appeared to enter his name and email address.

"Don't put that in there!" Maddy pulled on the mouse cord so Leo couldn't orientate the arrow to click. "What if they try to steal your identity?"

Leo rolled his eyes. "Give me a break, Maddy. They aren't going to get much off my first name and email. That stuff is all over the internet. If they ask me for my social security number and my parents' credit card numbers, I promise not to enter them, okay?"

No, it wasn't okay. But she let go of the mouse anyway.

A question replaced the welcome message on the screen. Maddy read it out loud to distract herself from the butterflies flipping out in her stomach. "Question one: are you or have you ever been a hun?"

Leo moved the mouse to the answer box and clicked the word 'yes'.

"Leo! You are not a hun. What are you doing?"

He gave her a look. "My mom calls me 'hon' all the time. That makes me a hun. Now zip it and let me see how villainous I am."

Maddy pressed her lips together, determined to stay out of it, but that didn't stop her from thinking all the thoughts as Leo proceeded to answer the questions.

2. Do you own a pet? If so, what kind(s)?

A dog, a turtle, and a chinchilla.

3. Can you trap a person's voice in a seashell?

Who can't?

4. Are you a step-anything?

I am a step-brother.

5. Have you ever been imprisoned in the body of a beast?

Every day.

6. Can you transform into a snake?

Only on Tuesdays.

7. Have you ever made a house out of candy?

Yes.

8. Does it bother you when other people are happy?

I'm allergic to happy people.

9. Do you like red roses?

Of course I do. I keep some on my dresser where I can admire them first thing when I wake up.

10. Do you ever have the uncontrollable urge to eat children?

Yes.

Okay, Maddy couldn't let that one go. "Leo!" She smacked his arm. "You do not want to eat children! Don't be sick."

"How do you know?" he grinned wickedly.

Maddy rolled her eyes. "That's disgusting! Why are you doing this?"

"It's actually fun. Look at this next one: Can you turn people into frogs or any other unnatural being?"

Maddy smacked him again. "You can't do that! Why did you type 'yes'?"

"See her?" He jerked a thumb at Lilliana, still hopping around in her frog costume. "I got her dressed this morning. One kid turned into a frog. Check."

"That is not what they mean, and you know it!"

"Do I?" He squinted at her. "I am not sure I know anything anymore, so, in the meantime, I'm going to have some fun. Twelve: have you ever blamed the death of the King on his innocent son? Yes."

Maddy clicked her tongue. "When did you do that?"

"In the video game *Castle Serge*. You should play it sometime."

She shook her head.

So not happening.

"Thirteen: Do you want to marry the only child of a crazy inventor? Absolutely."

"Now you're just being ridiculous. Do you even know the only child of a crazy inventor? And what kind of question is that, anyway?"

Leo's mouth quirked to the side. "Really? Do I finally know something you don't know?"

Maddy crossed her leg over her knee and swung it in agitation. "Whatever, just explain already."

"It's in the movie *Beauty and the Beast*, Maddy. Gaston, the *villain*, wanted to marry Belle, right? You of all people should remember that."

She did remember that; she just hadn't connected it. "What does that have to do with how villanous you are?"

Leo's eyebrows drew together for just a moment, then they leap upward. "I think the test is trying to connect you to a villain. That makes sense, yeah?"

"But Gaston wasn't in the original story of Beauty and the Beast. Disney made up that character."

"Yeah, but the Disney version is the version everyone knows. No one reads that old fairy tale stuff anymore. So it makes sense the test would use villains people know."

It did make sense.

It was like Leo was a rational person making logical points and not a tremendous goofball. At least, at this moment. She was pretty sure that made this moment the strangest thing she'd experienced so far that day.

"Does that mean all of these questions are fairy tale-related?" Maddy asked. She made Leo scroll up so she could go back through them.

One, with the huns? Maddy had no idea; maybe it was the legend the movie *Mulan* was based on or something.

Two could be any of them; all the fairy tale people had animal friends.

Three was *The Little Mermaid* movie.

Four could be any of them.

Five was *Beauty and the Beast* again.

Six stumped her.

Seven was *Hansel and Gretel*.

Eight could be any of them.

Nine sounded like *Beauty and the Beast* again, but she also remembered something about roses in *Snow White*.

Ten could be *Hansel and Gretel*, although there was probably more than one fairy tale with witches that had that urge. Maddy just didn't want to think one more minute about that.

So, then, eleven was *The Frog Prince*. Twelve? She had no idea. And thirteen had to be *Beauty and the Beast,* but not the original story. This question was reference to the Disney movie too.

"Huh, that is super intriguing. Go on. I want to see the next question."

"See?" Leo smirked. "It's curious, right? Now you are sucked in like a spit wad."

Maddy wrinkled her nose. "Just get on with it already."

Leo gave her another grin, then typed his answer into thirteen so that fourteen would pop up. "Did you ever put a curse on a baby (or want to)?"

"Don't do it," Maddy warned.

Leo's smirk got even bigger, which was hard to believe considering the size of the original smirk. With exaggerated movements, he hit the 'Y' key, then the 'E' key, then finally the 'S' key, and jabbed the 'Enter' button.

"I don't know why you're always hating on your family," Maddy said, shaking her head. "You know they're amazing, right?"

Leo snorted.

"I know you know you would miss them if they were gone." The words felt vaguely familiar when Maddy said them, like something her mom would say.

"I'd love to test that theory," Leo chuckled.

"No, you wouldn't. Stop it!" She wanted to slap that self-satisfied smile off his face, but she settled for smacking him in the arm for the billionth time. "That question was probably *Sleeping Beauty*. Though, again, the curse thing happens a lot in fairy tales, so it could be any of them. Fifteen: Do you think puppies make good coats?"

"That is sick!" Leo yelled at the computer. "This test is sick!" The keys made angry clicks as he pressed them.

"Then why did you type 'yes'?"

"Because I'm on a roll. But seriously, that's disgusting."

"So, you'd eat children and curse them, but it's sick to make coats out of puppies?" Maddy threw her arms in the air. "I'm seriously concerned about your priorities."

He shot her a don't-mess-with-me look. "Sixteen: Have you ever poisoned a corset, an apple, or a comb? Yes."

"That's *Snow White* for sure," Maddy said before it registered that Leo answered 'yes.' "Wait! How in the world did you do any of those things?"

Leo leaned sideways, a gleam in his eyes. "Don't tell Gia, but I covered her hairbrush with hair-be-gone."

"No, you didn't. Did you really?" Maddy ran her fingers through her hair. "Why would you do that?"

"She's a pest."

Possibly a future bald one. But not if Maddy could help it. "When did you do it?"

"A couple of days ago. Stop freaking out; it didn't work. She obviously has all her hair. I'll have to use more next time."

"Excuse me, did you just say 'next time'?"

"Seventeen." Leo raised his voice above Maddy's screech. "Do you have impeccable fashion taste? Obviously."

"Not," Maddy tugged at the hem of his ratty football jersey. "That sounds like the *Cruella* movie. Is that a fairy tale, though?"

"Dunno," Leo said. "Maybe they don't have to be fairy tales, you know? Maybe they're asking questions from popular stories with villains."

Maddy tapped her chin with her index finger. "Except that all stories have villains; that's what brings the conflict."

"No," Leo shook his head, his smile way too big. "Check your facts, Maddy. All stories have antagonists to bring conflict."

"It's the same thing."

He jabbed his finger in her direction. "No, it's not. I can't believe I got you again. Twice in a row! This is totally my day. Remember in English last year when we read that short story about the guy deserted on the island? He was the only character, but his struggle was with himself. He was the antagonist and protagonist. Good and bad all at once."

Maddy shook her head. "No, that's not how that works. People are good *or* bad. He was the hero; those native people on the island were the villains. They wrecked the canoe he made and stole his food supply. Antagonists are villains."

Leo pressed his lips together and mimicked her head movement, shake for shake. "You're wrong, but that's okay. I know that's hard for you to accept this, so I'll let you think what you want, but know that I know you're wrong and it makes me super happy."

"How nice," Maddy droned. "Question eighteen: Do you believe you are the fairest of them all?"

Leo swished his thick, dark hair out of his eyes. "Is there any doubt?"

"Could your head get any bigger?"

"Probably not. Nineteen: Have you ever tricked peasants into the cave of wonders? Yes." Leo glanced at Maddy. "You're not going to contradict me?"

She shrugged. "Now that I know how your brain works, it's obvious how you justify this one. You work at the Cave of Wonders board game store, and you call everyone peasants."

"Now you're getting it. Last question: Do you believe in happily ever after? That's so cheesy. No way."

Maddy felt a twinge of sadness as he pressed the 'Submit' button. She probably didn't believe in happily ever after either—she wasn't sure—but the thought of not believing in it suddenly seemed supremely sad. It would be nice if happily ever after were a thing. If it were real, Maddy thought she would kind of like one of her own.

"Okay, done. What do you want to do now?"

"Move over." She squished into the chair next to him, bumping him out of the way with her hip.

Leo caught the back of the chair before he landed on the floor and used it to steady himself on his feet. "What are you doing?"

"Taking the test."

"What?" He walked around and sat in the seat she'd vacated. "I thought you thought this was ridiculous."

"I do." The site already redirected them to the homepage, so she clicked the button to start the test over and entered her first name and email. "You made such a mockery of this thing; I feel like I need to show you the right way to do it. Ready to be inspired?" Maddy hit 'Submit' and waited for the questions to appear. "Hun? No. Trapped voice in a seashell? No. Pets? No. Step-something? No. Trapped Beast? No. Snake? No. House of candy? No."

"Hold up," Leo held out a hand. "You've never made a gingerbread house at Christmas?"

"I have, but those are made out of graham crackers, not candy. Candy is just decoration."

Leo clamped his mouth shut and scowled.

"Bothered by other people's happiness? No. Red roses? Yes. Eat children? NO." She shot Leo a look. "Turned someone into a frog? No. Blamed the son for the death of the king? No. Marry the only child of an inventor? No. Curse babies? No. Puppy coats? No. Poisoned stuff? No. Fashion taste? No. Cave of Wonders? No. Happily ever after? Yes. Done and done in waaaaaay less time than you."

"It wasn't a race," Leo grumbled.

Maddy knew he just said that because she was faster. If he had been done sooner than she, he'd be dancing around the living room with multiple 'boo-yah's' already. Maddy clicked 'Submit' and waited for the cheesy fireworks that told her the results would be sent to her email within twenty-four hours. She twirled the computer chair around to face Leo and laced her fingers behind her head. "And that is how it's done, polpetto."

"Do you even know what that means?" Leo asked.

Maddy shook her head, too smug to care. "I know that's what your mom calls you."

Leo narrowed his eyes, a smile playing along the corners of his mouth. "You should find out what something means before you use it. What if you just called me the love of your life?"

Maddy's arms dropped, and the back of her neck tingled with heat. "Did I?"

Now it was Leo's turn to be smug. "I don't know, did you?"

Before Maddy could answer, Leo's mom called them all in for dinner. There was something about homemade ravioli and meatballs with marinara that had the power to drive all other thoughts from Maddy's mind. That's not even to mention the breadsticks fresh from the oven and flourless chocolate cake for dessert. At Leo's house, dinner was an event, not just a meal. It lasted over two hours, and everyone gathered to talk about their day, steal food off each other's plates, and laugh about random things. And in the course of all of that, Maddy discovered that 'polpetto' meant 'meatball,' not 'the love of your life.' A perfect description of Leo.

So, that was good.

Maddy lost all track of her worries from the day until her phone rang and her mom's name popped up. She excused herself from the table and went into the living room to answer.

"Hey, Mom."

"Oh, good. How are you?"

"I'm great. Just finished dinner. Are you close?"

"Almost," her mom said. "Grams is pretty tired from her flight; I want to get her straight home. I was thinking I can send your dad back out to pick you up; I'm waiting to hear back from him."

Maddy picked up a pile of Barbie clothes and dumped them into the plastic bin next to the couch. "I have my car, Mom. I can drive home."

"Oh." Her mom's sigh was too exhausted to stick around long. "That would certainly be easier, but I don't want you to be alone."

In the most condensed way possible, Maddy filled her mom in on what had happened that day, minus the villainous test thing. She'd save that little nugget for later when her mom wasn't so wiped out. "I don't think the VDA is going to bother me anymore."

"Really? Why?"

"I took care of it."

There was a long silence in which Maddy could almost hear her mom's thoughts resonating through the phone. Her mom wanted to know what the heck Maddy meant by that, but was too tired to deal with the answer.

"It's not a big deal," Maddy said to reassure her mom, but also, she meant it. Really, with her belly stuffed to the rafters with delicious Italian food, there wasn't room for troubles and concerns. "I'll get my stuff and meet you at home. When do you think you'll get there?"

"About ten minutes. Oh! Your dad is home now. He just texted Grams."

"Okay, sounds good. Drive safe. I'll see you there in a few." Maddy hung up the phone and went back to the kitchen to thank Leo's parents and let everyone know she was going home now.

"How fun your Grams is here for a visit." Leo's mom kissed both Maddy's cheeks. "You tell her *ciao* for us."

"I will." Maddy waved to the rest of the circus and walked with Leo to the front door.

As she shrugged into her coat, Leo shifted from foot to foot. "This day was something else, huh?"

Maddy couldn't find words to respond to that.

"I—" Leo glanced at her, then down at his feet. "I feel kind of bad I overruled you and did the test and everything."

Maddy froze with her arm halfway inside her coat. "Okay?" It was the only way she could think to answer. Leo never apologized.

"Yeah." He ran his fingers through his hair. "If I was a better friend, I would listen to you more. So, sorry about that."

"It's okay." Maddy pulled her jacket closed and zipped it up. As warm as it was during the day, the desert got nippy after the sun went down. "Really, I get you."

"Okay, thanks." He stooped to grab her backpack and waited until Maddy had her shoes on to hand it to her. "I'm just glad that's all over. If I tried to tell myself about this day before it happened, I would have seriously thought I was losing it."

"Seriously." Maddy slipped her bag over one shoulder and fiddled with her car keys. Since they were in a sharing kind of mood, there was something she wanted to say that she didn't usually say to Leo. Sort of like his apology...

But different.

"Thanks for watching out for me, Leo. You're a really good friend. I actually think you're the best friend ever."

"Yeah?" His features lifted.

"Really."

Leo studied Maddy's face for a minute, his gaze super intense. Then he punched her arm and grinned. "This is getting weird. Go home. I'll see you in the morning."

Maddy stuck her tongue out at him and went through the door he held open for her. When she got to the car, she glanced over her shoulder before unlocking it and saw Leo standing in the doorway watching. He lifted his hand. Maddy waved back, then got in her car. She started it up, backed out of the driveway, and honked a couple of times as she pulled away.

When she glanced in the rear-view mirror before she turned the corner, Leo was still standing in the doorway with his hand in the air.

99

TEN

Not all villains are remembered

Grams was still sleeping the next morning when Maddy had to leave for school. Other than a quick welcome and kiss on the cheek, Maddy hadn't had a chance to say more than a few words to Grams the night before. The poor woman looked so drained; her skin was pale, and she had dark circles hovering under her eyes. Maddy wrote Grams a note while she ate her toast and gave it to her mom before she left so Grams would know how excited Maddy was to have her there and also to finally sit down and talk. Then Maddy left to pick up Leo.

She could hear the chaos raging behind the door before she knocked. No house was large enough for all those huge personalities. After waiting a few minutes with no response, Maddy figured they couldn't hear her and knocked again.

Still, no one answered.

This time, Maddy rang the doorbell, hoping Alessandra wasn't still asleep.

The door creaked open a tiny crack, and Leo's mom peeked out with furrowed eyebrows. "Yes? Can I help you?"

Maddy bobbed on her toes. "It's just the old chauffeur service, here as always."

"We didn't ask for a chauffeur service," Leo's mom said slowly.

Maddy tried to hide a smile. "Oh, you don't need to ask. It's automatic. Every school day like clockwork to pick up that rotten bum Leo."

"Leo? Do we have a Leo?" Leo's mom glanced over her shoulder as Rico, or maybe it was Nico, bumped into the back of her legs.

"Right?" Maddy laughed. "I wouldn't claim him either. Is he ready? I don't want to be late."

Leo's mom shook her head. "I think you have the wrong house. There is no Leo here."

Maddy smiled all the way and nodded, waiting for Leo's mom to open the door wider and usher her inside.

She didn't.

After a moment, Maddy's smile faded. "Is he here? Or did he already leave? I thought he wanted a ride." She searched her memories of the night before to see if she was forgetting something important—that had been known to happen when she ate copious amounts of amazing Italian food at the Romanos' house. Had Leo said anything about leaving early or getting a ride with one of the guys?

She honestly couldn't remember.

"Is he meeting me at school?"

"You are confused. There is no Leo here," Leo's mom said.

So, Maddy got mixed up, then. Whoops.

"Oh, I'm super sorry about that." Maddy waved. "Thanks, I'll see you later."

Leo's mom closed the door without another word. Maddy didn't take it personally. There was a really lot to deal with in that place. Come to think of it, Leo's mom had done this same thing once before a few years ago when one of the kids backed up the toilet trying to flush something super valuable. Just for fun.

Maddy sincerely hoped that wasn't the case today. Maybe she would hit the grocery store on the way home and get Leo's mom some raspberry gelato.

That always seemed to cheer her up.

Maddy sang along to the radio on the way to school, trying not to notice how empty the passenger seat looked without Leo sitting there. When she locked up her car and walked across the parking lot, she felt different.

Oh, right. It was the lack of eye strain.

She hadn't spent the whole drive rolling her eyes all over the place while Leo cracked cheesy jokes. It wasn't that she missed him, exactly. It was just that she didn't realize what a big part of her day he was until he happened to not be in part of it.

That was all.

The same phenomenon happened a few weeks ago when the vending machine in the lunchroom ran out of chocolate milk. The whole afternoon just dragged on after that.

Maddy got her books for her classes, took a sec to straighten her locker, and still had a few minutes before school was supposed to start. She wondered where Leo went so early in the morning and what he was doing right now. He was probably in the weight room. Maddy wasn't about to go looking for him. The last time she did that, it was all dudes crammed in that little room, and the stench got stuck in her nostrils like poignant French cheese. She hadn't been able to smell properly for at least two days.

"Maddy!" Izzy hooked her arm through Maddy's elbow. "Hey, I'm so glad I found you! You will never guess who just asked me out!"

Maddy scrunched her eyebrows. Either that was a trick question or a really lame joke. "Ryder?"

"Ryder?" Izzy wrinkled her nose. "Ew, no! I wouldn't go out with that heathen!"

Maddy sucked her top lip into her mouth and chewed on it. "Really? Because I'm pretty sure you've been dating him for the last two months."

Izzy stopped walking. "What? Are you joking?"

"Are you?" Maddy peered at her friend for signs that she was teasing.

There were zero twitches, flicks, or winks.

That was weird.

"I am so confused," Izzy said. "Are you really talking about Ryder Hanks? I've never been out with him." She gave a half laugh and eyeballed Maddy with a searching look. "Like I would go out with a guy like Ryder, please!"

"Okay, no." Maddy held out her palm. "Two months ago, after the first football game, Leo invited us to Missy's house with some of the guys from the football team, including Ryder. You guys flirted the whole night and dipped french fries in each other's milkshakes." Izzy had to remember that part. It was kind of an epic moment because up until then Izzy always stated very loudly that french fries in ice cream was disgusting.

Somehow Ryder changed all of that.

Izzy unhooked Maddy's elbow and felt her forehead with the back of one hand. "Are you feeling alright?"

"I'm fine." Maddy swatted Izzy's arm away. "You're the one who's having a memory episode. Come on. Two weeks after that, Leo invited us to a scrimmage and that's when Ryder asked you out for the first time."

Izzy's eyebrows drew together. "This isn't a very funny joke, Maddy. I'm actually getting kind of worried about you."

Well, it went both ways. How could Izzy not remember her first date with Ryder? Maybe she got hit in the head during baton practice yesterday. Maddy decided to take it easy on Izzy and use smaller words. "Oh, okay. Not to worry. We can talk later. We better get to class now."

Izzy nodded, but her forehead stayed warped in lines of concern.

Their first-period classes were right across the hall from each other, so they stayed together the whole time they walked. Just, without talking at all. Maddy noticed Izzy shooting glances at her every few seconds, her face all creased with confusion. That bonk on the head must have been a doozy. Maddy wondered if she should call Izzy's mom and explain what was going on. If they didn't take her to the doctor after practice yesterday, she needed to go now. Maddy wasn't sure how concussions worked, but she had a vague idea that memory loss was part of it. That and a super big headache.

"How does your head feel?" she asked Izzy, whispering in case loud noises would make it worse.

Izzy scrunched her lips together. "Fine, why?"

Was denial part of a concussion?

They reached their classrooms and turned to face each other. Maddy was more than ready to say goodbye to her friend; she was tired of the searching looks Izzy kept giving her. Maddy raised one hand and was about to bid Izzy farewell when Izzy laid a hand on her arm.

"Maddy, I really hate to ask...I mean, I don't want to upset you, but I have to know. Something you said is really bothering me."

Maddy nodded patiently, ready to help Izzy out however she could.

"Who's Leo?"

Maddy's mouth dropped open. "What?"

"You kept talking about a guy named Leo like I should know who that is." Izzy twisted her necklace around her finger. "But I don't know who he is."

She didn't know who Leo was?

Obviously Izzy wasn't okay. As soon as first period was over, Maddy was going to force her to go to the nurse. Izzy shouldn't be at school after an injury that scrambled her brain the way this did. She should be at home, resting.

"Oh," Maddy laughed. "That's nothing. Don't you worry about it. We can talk about that later. Have fun in chemistry." She smiled and waved, then worried all the way through physics that Izzy was going to blow up the chem lab because her head wasn't on right. Maddy hoped Izzy had a really competent lab partner.

Right before physics ended, one of the girls at Maddy's table asked for help with the homework. The other two people in their group rushed out as soon as the bell rang, so it was up to Maddy to explain or leave poor Jean totally confused. Maddy was happy to help, of course, but it took so much longer than she thought it would. By the time Jean's understanding dawned, Maddy didn't have time to call Izzy's mom or check on Izzy. Hopefully, Izzy found her second period without too much confusion. Maddy dashed across the school to Spanish.

She slid into her seat just as Señora Hernandez started roll call. Maddy answered when her name was read and organized her stuff, so she was ready for class to begin. Then, she looked around the room. Leo wasn't there yet. No doubt he would breeze in, extra late and extra stinky because he got in some lifting battle with one of the other football players. Maddy wished at that moment that she'd picked a desk a little farther away from his royal smelliness and closer to an open window or an air freshener.

"Carston James."

"Yep."

"Kelsie Monson."

"Here."

"Terrin Travis."

"Yo."

Wait a second.

She didn't call Leo.

Romano should have come before Terrin. Maddy listened closely to see if Señora somehow got confused and out of order. She read through the rest of the names without looking up, then put her tablet down and clapped her hands together.

Maddy shot her arm in the air before Señora had a chance to say anything. "You forgot to call Leo."

Señora Hernandez stared at her. "Quién?"

"Leo," Maddy said slowly, since English was not Señora's first language. "Leo Romano. He sits..." Maddy looked at the chair next to her, which was full of a body that was not Leo's. Well, unless he somehow morphed into a short, red-haired girl.

"Estás bien?" Señora Hernandez began, then stopped as Maddy stood up and swayed.

"I'm...I need...I'm going... Air."

Maddy stumbled out of the classroom to the nearest outside door. She pushed it open and leaned against the stone wall, letting the warmth seep into her skin and the breeze steady her breathing.

Something was seriously wrong here.

Maddy thought back through the morning at rapid speed. Leo's mom, Izzy, Señora Hernandez.

They all didn't remember Leo.

Why didn't they know who Leo was?

It was too random to be random.

They wouldn't all be in on a joke together. And what kind of joke was it to pretend like Leo didn't exist? What was funny about that? Maddy often wished he would take his bodily functions and weird noises and go away, but she didn't actually want it to happen.

Maddy couldn't convince herself it was Leo's mom messing around or Izzy's supposed concussion or Señora's language barrier anymore. Something was seriously wrong here. She pulled her phone out of her pocket, grateful she'd stashed it there instead of in her backpack, which was still sitting next to her desk in the Spanish room. Maddy dialed her mom's number with shaking fingers and held the phone to her ear.

"Hello?" Her mom's voice was so familiar and comforting that tears sprang to Maddy's eyes. It wasn't until that moment that she realized how tense she felt and how thoroughly stressed out she really was.

Maddy tried three times to get the word out. "Mom?"

"Maddy? What's the matter, honey?"

"Do you remember Leo?" She tried to keep her voice steady as she gripped the phone. "Leo Romano, do you remember him?"

"Of course, I remember Leo." Her mom's voice rose in surprise. "What kind of question is that?"

"You do? Really?" Maddy let out the breath she'd been holding. Her shoulders relaxed enough to stop bunching at her earlobes.

"Of course! Maddy, what is going on?"

"I don't know." The words got stuck in Maddy's throat. "No one remembers Leo, Mom. Not Izzy, not even his own mom. He's not at school, and he wasn't at home. It's like he never existed." Her voice lowered to a whisper. "I thought I was losing my mind."

"Okay, okay, okay, okay. Slow down and tell me that again. Start at the very beginning."

Maddy obeyed, explaining her trip to Leo's house to pick him up and ending with what happened a few minutes ago in Spanish class. Maddy remembered to breathe between sentences, which was good, and when she'd finished, some of the burden that had been building since she talked to Izzy lifted. Not only did it feel fantastic to get it all out of her own head, but now she could stand back and let her mom help her figure out what to do.

Maddy was so glad she didn't have to do this alone.

"Where are you right now, Maddy?"

"Outside the school. I needed some air."

"Okay, here's what I want you to do. Right now. Walk to your car and come home. Can you do that?"

"My bag is still—"

"Do you have your keys and license?"

"Yes." She started walking toward the parking lot.

She was leaving school, just like that. Without telling anyone, without asking for permission, without getting the proper excuse, slip, or filling out any paperwork.

Maddy felt dirty.

"Stay on the phone with me, okay? Don't hang up. Let's stay connected until you come home."

She unlocked her car and buckled up. Despite her current truant activities, she couldn't bring herself to drive while talking on a cell phone, so she set the phone on the middle console and pressed the speaker button. "Are you still there?"

"I am."

Maddy started the car and pulled forward. "I'm leaving the school right now."

"Good," her mom breathed out. "Good. You just focus on getting here safely. I'm going to fill Grams in on what's happening."

"Tell her hello for me." Maddy turned right at the red light and pulled into traffic. She felt a million times more collected now that she knew she was on her way home.

Home was good.

Grams responded before Maddy's mom said anything.

Oh yeah, speaker phone.

"Good morning, dearie."

"Morning, Grams." Maddy's smile wavered. She couldn't quite call it 'good,' not just yet. She listened as her mom told Grams everything that had happened. The connection wasn't great and the phone was bouncing around the console, so Maddy missed most of what her mom said and all of what Grams said. It was a tremendous relief to turn onto her street. When she pulled into the driveway at home, she snatched her phone and ran into the house.

"I'm home," Maddy called and felt her knees wobble underneath her.

Her mom caught Maddy up in a big hug and was joined by Grams a few moments later. Her familiar rose-scented perfume made Maddy's eyes prickle again.

"I'm so glad I'm home."

"Me too," her mom said. "I never would have let you leave the house today if I'd known this was going to happen."

"What is happening?" Maddy asked the question that had been squishing her mind to most. "How come no one knows who Leo is anymore? How do I remember him, and you remember him, and no one else does? Not even his mom? That's the craziest part. This doesn't make any sense.

It's a million times worse than Elle disappearing in Wendy's and almost as bad as that stupid test."

"What test?" Maddy's mom looked at her sharply.

Oh yeah, she hadn't actually told her mom about that part yet. The way her mom stood with her fist on her jutted hip made it obvious there was no skirting around this subject, not even if Maddy wanted to. Maddy had been waiting for a better time. Not so sure now was it, but there they were.

"Elle gave us a card for a villain test." She checked her pockets and remembered she was wearing different pants than she was yesterday.

Duh.

Plus, she left the VDA business card next to Leo's computer.

"Did you take the test?" her mom said, her voice rising.

Grams put a hand on her daughter's arm.

"I did. Leo did. We did. We thought it was a joke. It looked like a joke."

"Not a joke." Grams shook her head. "Have you checked your email, dearie?"

Maddy shook her head.

"Would you mind doing so now?"

"Like, right now?" Maddy asked.

Grams nodded.

Since her phone was still in her hand, Maddy pulled up her email immediately. Right at the top was an unopened message from the VDA.

"That was faster than I thought," Maddy murmured.

"I imagine they consider you a priority," Grams said.

Maddy didn't register Grams' words; she was too focused on opening the email. She skimmed it, then read it out loud. "Congratulations, Madelena Hutton. You have passed the Villainous Test as zero percent villainous. Despite your blood composition of one-quarter villain, it is clear that your villain tendencies are dormant. Unless there is a drastic change in your behavior, the VDA clears you to live a normal human life. It was a pleasure working with you. Have a happily ever after. The Villain Detection Agency." Maddy looked up. "Okay, so I'm not a villain—shocker. What does this have to do with Leo?"

Grams placed a hand on Maddy's arm. It was like she'd set a gallon of ice cream there; it was so cold it almost burned. "Come, dearie. I think it's time we had a little talk."

ELEVEN

A villain may be a victim whose story is yet to be told

Maddy's mom went to get her dad from the back office. He was working from home. Maddy wished she'd noticed that sooner. Her dad hated working from home. It would have been a clue that this day was not normal.

Maddy sat numbly at the table, trying to process the world as she now knew it. Maybe she was having some kind of mental breakdown and this was the moment her family chose to tell her about it. That was not the most comforting thought, but it made way more sense than anything else going through Maddy's head. How else could she justify people disappearing right before her eyes and her best friend suddenly not existing? There was a horrified part of Maddy that wondered if Leo had ever been real.

Maybe he was like her imaginary friend or something.

Okay, scratch that.

Even in her tender mental state, that was a stretch. Maddy was positive her brain wouldn't be able to invent a character like Leo. He was a nut, totally one of a kind. And she was not that creative.

Grams bustled around the kitchen in her zippered robe and fluffy slippers, her silvery hair secured in a neat chignon at the base of her neck. She boiled water for tea and made a stack of buttered toast, which she set on the table in front of Maddy before she went to rescue the whistling teapot.

Maddy stared at the toast with her lips curled. Her stomach was so messed up from all the clenching and rolling, there was no way she'd be able to eat any of that. It would be a miracle if even tea made it through the mangled disaster that was her insides.

Maddy's mom and dad returned just as Grams set the kettle and various boxes of tea on the table. They all sat in unison as if they'd planned out how they'd look, each with straight backs and hands on the table, as they faced Maddy.

"Why don't you start?" her mom said to Maddy. "It will be easier for us to assess what's going on if we know what has happened so far."

Maddy knew that made sense, but she was so tired of talking. Not only that, but the thought of reliving the last couple of days made her stomach go from rolling to heaving. Grams's hand moved to rest on Maddy's forearm, and she felt a surge of moxie.

She could do it.

She could tell them everything about everything.

And she did.

Getting started was like an open, itchy wound, but as she went on, she found that talking was soothing, the same as ointment and a Band-Aid. When she finished, she assumed the clasped hands position and peered across the table, ready for some answers.

"Well," Grams sighed. "It's not as bad as I thought."

"Not good either." Maddy's mom's face was grim.

"Wait, who's Leo?" Maddy's dad looked around in confusion. "You're talking about him like I should know him, but I have no memory of anyone named Leo."

Maddy's eyes flew to her mom and then Grams. Neither of them looked surprised at all.

"He doesn't have our DNA, dearie. The VDA's eraser affects your father like everyone else."

"Wait, my mind has been erased?" Maddy's dad looked stricken, then mumbled to himself for a moment. "No, that can't be right. I can still remember the theme song to *The Fresh Prince of Bel-Air*."

"They only erased Leo, hon." Maddy's mom patted his hand. "Leo is Maddy's best friend, and now he's in Skurk. I told you this; you keep forgetting."

"Right." Her dad nodded like that made perfect sense.

"What I want to know," her mom said, facing the rest of them, "is what possessed Leo to treat that test so lightly."

"Leo doesn't take anything seriously." Maddy laughed, then choked on it. Tears sprang to her eyes so suddenly she didn't have time to stop them from rolling down her cheeks. "He thought it was a joke."

Her mom's face softened. "Oh, honey. It's going to be just fine, you'll see. Have you told us everything? You didn't leave anything out? Even the smallest detail might be important."

Maddy shook her head and reached for a napkin to blow her nose.

"Mom?" Maddy's mom looked at Grams, who nodded.

"Now it is my turn, yes." Grams fixed her bright green eyes on Maddy. They were so velvety soft; it was like being wrapped in a fluffy blanket. "What I tell you may be hard for you to understand at first, my Madelena, but I want you to know now that it is all true. So, please keep an open mind and feel free to ask questions as I go. There is much to take in."

Maddy tried to ignore the anxiety rising in her chest and just focused on breathing consistently.

"Our story begins many, many years ago. In history, they call this the middle age of human time. The people of the world were much as they are now, some very good and some very bad. Those who were good produced a type of magic with their selfless deeds."

"Magic?" Maddy didn't interrupt. Grams had stopped to take a breath, and she pounced on the pause. Magic was one of the things that bothered her the most. That was the way her brain had tried to explain what happened with Elle and the VDA. There wasn't a logical explanation otherwise, so it had to be magic.

Except that magic wasn't real.

Was it?

"Yes," Grams smiled. "There are all kinds of magic in the world. You see it every day. The sun on the water is a kind of magic. Budding trees and green things poking out of the ground. All of these are magic."

"But that magic can be explained with science." Maddy wasn't trying to argue; she really wanted to understand.

Grams touched her hand. "This will be easier for you to grasp, dearie, if you let go of everything you think you know."

Maddy took a deep breath and let it out slowly, trying to clear her mind. It was difficult. The thoughts swirled like a tornado, whipping around and around. She took another breath and closed her eyes, picturing her mind as an empty room.

"Are you ready?" Grams whispered.

Maddy fluttered her eyes open. "Why didn't you guys tell me any of this before now?" She had a vague feeling that it would have been a lot easier to swallow a tale of magic if she was younger and less jaded.

"It all depended on your DNA test," her mom said gently. "If the villain bloodline didn't show up, there was no reason to tell you anything. You see?"

Maddy nodded. She understood the reasoning, but she didn't have to like it.

"Shall I go on?" Grams asked with a small smile. "Are you ready now?"

Maddy nodded again and dropped her chin onto her folded arms.

"The people who produced magic from their good deeds created a new world, a perfect, peaceful world that is attached to this one. It grew and expanded, bringing a guardian by the name of Beschermer to watch over and protect it. She called the land Eventyr." Grams paused to make sure Maddy was still with her. The tips of Maddy's fingers itched for her notebook and pen. She had the strangest urge to take notes like she was preparing for a history test.

"When Eventyr's magic stabilized, it created a world that could be inhabited, and Beschermer looked to our world to fill it. She thought it fair that the people whose lives created the magic of Eventyr should inhabit the world itself. But she could not come here—that is the only limit to her magic—so she found people, humans, to help her gather those who deserved an immortal life in Eventyr."

"Why couldn't she come here?" Maddy asked.

Grams pressed her index fingers to her chin. "Her magic is tied to Eventyr. She tried once to leave, but without her, Eventyr is shaken and unstable. She never tried again; it just isn't safe."

That reminded Maddy of something. "Is Elle Beschermer? The longer she was with Leo and I, the more, like, transparent she looked. And she flickered."

"No," Grams pursed her lips. "We will come to Elle, but she is most certainly not Beschermer."

"Who is she then?"

Maddy's mom tapped the table. "Patience, Maddy. We'll get there. Go on, Mom."

"Yes, so, these people Beschermer found to help her were great story collectors. They searched this world for stories of men and women, sometimes children, whose extraordinary choices make them good candidates for Eventyr. They searched, too, for those whose courage in hardships was so great that they earned rest. They compiled the stories and brought them to Beschermer, who read them and chose those who would thereafter live in Eventyr."

"So, not everyone got to go?" Maddy squinted at Grams. "How did she decide who was worthy and who was not?"

"Most of the stories were chosen to go then." Grams said. "Eventyr was new and empty, and it was a simpler time. The lines between good and evil were much more distinct than they are now."

That made sense.

Sort of.

"Those helpers of Beschermer—"

This time Maddy did interrupt. "Who were they?"

"Maddy!" Her mom pointed her finger to accent her words. "Manners."

"Be easy on her; this is much to take in." Grams smiled. "Who was who?"

Maddy looked at Grams instead of the glares her mom sent across the table. "Who were the helpers? Do we know them?"

"We know of them." Grams glanced at Mom. "*You* know of them."

"I do?"

"There were many, but the most well-known are the Brothers Grimm and Mr. Hans Christian Andersen."

"Wait." Maddy held up one hand. "Wait, those are the guys who wrote fairy tales."

"Compiled," Grams corrected.

"Compiled?" Maddy's eyes widened. "So, you're telling me the fairy tales are real? Like, those people in the stories—Cinderella and everyone—they are real people?"

Grams beamed. "Yes! You do understand! The characters we know from fairy tales, they were real people who once lived on this earth just like you and me."

"And now they are…"

"Living on Eventyr, yes." Grams' face was full of sunshine. "They live there forever in peace. They have earned it."

Maddy dropped her head into her hands. So much for keeping an open mind. How was she supposed to believe that fairy tales were real? This was crazy. Fairy godmothers and poison apples and eternal sleep and long, magic hair? Those things were real?

Not possible!

"Maddy?" Grams asked gently.

"Wait," Maddy's head popped up. Her conversation with Leo swirled through her mind. "So, in the story of *Beauty and the Beast*, a man was turned into a beast because he was a jerk, right? That earned him an immortal life in Eventyr?"

"You must remember that the stories as they are told over generations do change. There is a core of fact, but much is elaborated. Especially today with the movies and fairy tale remakes coming from so many writers. Our stories are shifting."

"So, what's the real story? Do you know it?"

"I do." Grams looked at her hands. "I know all the stories."

Something in her voice made Maddy look at her closer. "Are you Beschermer?"

Grams laughed, her countenance lifting. "Oh, dear me, no! The very idea!" She exchanged an amused glance with Maddy's mom.

"Will you tell me the real story of *Beauty and the Beast*?"

"Maddy, that's getting us far off track. Let's focus…" Her mom didn't get to finish.

Grams's hand on her arm made her pause.

"I am happy to share the tale," Grams said. "It will only take a moment. The Beast, whose real name was Adam, lived with his aunt in France. His mother died during his birth, and his father was killed in the great war. His aunt doted on him, too much perhaps, so that he grew to be a selfish and conceited man. His choices turned him into a beast, the worst version of himself. When his aunt tried to help him see who he was becoming and tried to help him change, he did not take it well. He turned her out of the house."

Indignation rose in Maddy's chest. "What? How could he do that? It was her house!"

Grams shook her head. "No. In that time of history, women did not own anything. It was his house when he became a man. She was thrown into the snow at night with nowhere to go."

"She...she died?" What kind of sick story was this? Suddenly the beast went from a dorky, oversized stuffed animal to a vicious, horrible man. Maddy didn't want to hear this anymore. Was it too late to cover her ears and sing "Twinkle, Twinkle Little Star" at the top of her lungs?

"She would have died if she was not found by a neighbor woman who took her in. Her neighbor heard the story, nursed her to health, and offered her a place away from this world of sorrow."

"Eventyr?"

Grams's smile did not reach her eyes. "Adam, when his rage was over, realized what he had done and searched everywhere for his aunt. By then, she was already gone. He thought he had killed her, and he sunk into a deep, dark place within his own mind. It is there that the merchant pilfered his roses, there that Beauty agreed to take her father's place, and there that she learned to love him when he could not love nor forgive himself. When he sacrificed his happiness for her, his repentance was complete. They both earned their place in Eventyr, and there they remain."

No.

No no no no no. That was not how that was supposed to go. How could Broadway and Disney turn *this* story into a movie and make the Beast seem like a good guy when he obviously wasn't? All this time she'd defended him, thought he was misunderstood, and he truly was a beast.

Maddy was very wrong.

Did that mean she was wrong about everything else? Her world was tipping upside down and there was nothing she could do about it

Why had she asked Grams to tell the story? She should have let it be.

Maddy shifted in her chair, unable to sit still. "I don't understand how the Beast ended up in Eventyr. He almost killed his aunt; that should make him a villain."

Grams pulled her glasses from her nose and let them dangle on the chain around her neck. "It is not so simple, my Madelena. People are not so simple. Adam did horrible things, and he did wonderful things. He was so good, and he was so bad. Light and dark. Villain and hero. He was taken to Eventyr when his goodness overshadowed his badness."

Maddy shook her head. "A villain doesn't deserve a place in Eventyr. Is there a villain place? He should have to go there."

Grams rubbed her eyes, her hands traveling to the back of her neck where she gave herself an impromptu neck massage. "There is a place, but we do not need to speak of it now—"

"Why not? I want to know more about this place. Where is it? Is it another world connected to this one, like Eventyr?"

Grams looked at Maddy steadily. "A few bad choices do not make a villain, just as a few good choices do not make a hero. It is when the good overcomes the bad that the hero is made. When the bad consistently overshadows the good, the person becomes a true villain."

Maddy waved all of that away, barely listening to the words. "Is that where the VDA comes from? This opposite of Eventyr place? What do you call it?"

"Skurk," Grams whispered.

Maddy almost laughed, thinking Grams was teasing, except that Grams's face was drawn into serious lines, with absolutely no hint of a smile.

"Skurk?"

It sounded ridiculous, like something a toddler would say when they were hyped up on sugar. But then, Maddy remembered Elle talking about the same place when they were sitting in Wendy's.

So, it was real?

"Yes. Now, Madelena—"

"So, how does this work? Does telling a story activate the world, and then the person gets sucked into Eventyr or Skurk?" Maddy was seized with a determination to get that Beast into the right place. Her sense of justice was going haywire at the thought of him enjoying endless beaches and ice cream with all the people who deserved it when he didn't. "No, that's not right. You just told the story, and it didn't make a difference. Or did it? Can we contact Beschermer and let her know there's been a mistake?"

"There has been no mistake." Gram's eyes drooped at the edges.

"Yes, there has been. The Beast needs to be taken to Skurk. Especially if he's been in Eventyr for all these years. That's not fair. I'll totally do it; just tell me how to get to Eventyr. Or Skurk."

"Maddy." Her mom's voice was tight. "You are absolutely not going to Eventyr or Skurk."

"You do not want to go to Skurk," Grams said.

"Yes, I do. This needs to be sorted out."

Maddy's dad gave her a sorrowful look. "You're missing the point, baby."

Then he and her mom spoke at the same time, their words overlapping.

"You don't understand."

"You aren't listening."

Grams's sigh was so deep that it seemed to shake the table. "You cannot go there, Maddy. You have zero percent of the villain tendancies, as your test states. A way will not open for you to go to Skurk."

"I have one quarter villain blood, though."

"And you choose not to act on it."

Maddy chewed on that for a moment. "Can I go to Eventyr, then?" If she could, then she would have a chat with Bescermer and get the Beast sent to his proper place.

"No."

"Why not?"

Grams placed her palms on the table, as though to steady herself. "Just because you are not a villain does not mean you are automatically a hero. You must prove yourself first. It is not that simple, Madelena."

Again, even with Grams saying it's 'not that simple,' Maddy still didn't think it was all that complicated. "Protagonist, hero. Antagonist, villain. That's how it works, Grams. You're obviously confused."

Maddy's mom's chair screeched across the kitchen as she jumped to her feet. "Madelena Agathe Hutton, you do not talk to your grandmother that way! You need to close your mouth and listen to her words. You have absolutely no idea what you're dealing with here."

Maddy huffed back in her seat with her arms folded across her chest and fumed while Grams and her dad tried to coax her mom back down.

Didn't know what she was talking about—please.

Maddy knew injustice when she saw it. This was obviously a messed-up system. Especially since they erased Leo's memory based on that stupid test alone.

Leo.

Hold on.

This was about what happened to Leo, not the Beast. How could she let herself get so distracted? What seemed so important just a few moments ago, fizzled out like a candle flame seeped in wax.

Maddy took a few deep breaths to steady herself. "Grams, I'm sorry. I'm just trying to understand. Like you said, this is a lot to take in. Mom, Dad, I'm sorry. You're right; I'm not thinking straight. What's most important here is Leo. What happened to him? And how do we fix it?"

Maddy's mom sat heavily in her chair. Grams gave her another hand pat before facing Maddy again.

"I do not know what happened to Leo, but I will wager this guess: If he did not take the test seriously, if he answered as a joke, then his test score would have been the opposite of yours."

Maddy nodded. That made total sense.

"And if his test score is opposite yours, then he would have received a one hundred percent villain mark."

"Okay..."

"And if that was the case, then the VDA would have been alerted."

Maddy's heart skipped a couple of beats. She placed her hand on her chest to keep it from stopping completely.

"And if the VDA was alerted, then our Leo is now"—Grams steeled herself—"in Skurk."

TWELVE

All of us are villains sometimes

"What?" Maddy leaped to her feet so fast she had to grab the table to keep from toppling over. "He can't be in Skurk! Leo is not a villain!"

"Sit down, Maddy," her mom said.

Her dad extended his arm. "You said this Leo friend of yours answered the questions on the test like he is a villain, correct?"

Maddy sputtered. "Yeah, but he was just joking! They can't take him for joking! What kind of organization is this? They should check... They should check their facts before they erase someone!"

Grams picked up her mug of tea and sipped. "The purpose of the Villainous Test *is* to check the facts."

"Maddy, sit down," her mom said louder.

Maddy ignored her mom and started pacing in the small space behind her chair. "But Leo isn't... This is ridiculous! They should know he's just being a goof. Stupid Leo, I told him not to answer like that!"

"Madelena." Grams extended her arm. "Please sit down."

Without thinking, like her body made the decision without her, Maddy plopped into her seat again.

Grams set the mug down with a dull thump. "The VDA is not our enemy, dearie. They are doing what they were designed to do; they are detecting villains."

Maddy refused to go along with that. Someone had to be responsible for what happened, and since Leo had zero sense, he shouldn't be punished forever for one dumb decision. "But Leo—"

Grams raised her hand, and Maddy stopped talking, the words clogging her throat.

"I *know* that Leo is not a villain. I'm worried about him too, Madelena. It is important that you understand the VDA is not the enemy. They are an agency put into place by the power of Beschermer. It is their duty to detect and remove those with villain tendencies to protect the peace of both Eventyr and this world."

"What peace in this world?" Maddy snorted. "Have you *seen* the news?"

"Maddy." Her mom's voice was more akin to a growl than a normal voice. "You watch your tone when speaking to your grandmother."

Grams sighed. "She's worried, love. It is fine."

"It's really not." Maddy's mom narrowed her eyes. "Maddy, we are on the same team here."

"I know that," Maddy grumbled.

"We will find a way to help Leo." Grams touched Maddy's hand. "But first you must understand. If you think the world is without peace now, just imagine what it would be like if the VDA had not already spent centuries removing people with malicious intent."

Maddy took a deep breath, trying to soothe the pounding in her ears. It was like Izzy's brother and his garage band were jamming out in her skull. "Okay, I'm sorry. I'm trying."

Maddy's mom relaxed in the back of her chair but kept a wary eye on Maddy.

Grams went on. "Just as Beschermer watches our world for those whose good deeds have earned them rest, Elle and the VDA watch our world for those who would harm their fellowmen. The good retire to Eventyr. The villainous live in Skurk."

"Forever?" Maddy asked.

"Pardon?"

"Do they have immortality too? That doesn't sound like much of a punishment. You're a bad villain, so, here, you can live forever in a different world."

Grams pressed her lips together. "Skurk is not a reward, Maddy."

"Well, it doesn't sound like a punishment either."

Maddy's dad cleared his throat. "Remember when you dented the car right after you turned sixteen?"

Maddy nodded but couldn't think what that had anything to do with anything.

"How did you feel when you told us about it?"

Maddy recalled the clench in her belly, kind of like she was going to vomit, and her hands began to sweat. "Awful."

"Elaborate, if you please." Her dad's mustache twitched upward at the corners.

Maddy chewed her lip. "I was terrified you would be mad. I was embarrassed I tried to squeeze the car into too small of a space. I was worried how I would pay for the damage..."

Her dad nodded. "Did that feel good?"

"No."

"Then imagine feeling the way you did that day"—her dad paused—"forever."

An eternity of remembering the things you did wrong.

And just like that, Skurk became the most diabolical place Maddy had ever heard of.

"Do they *feel* bad though?" Maddy asked. "They are villains, right? Maybe they enjoy remembering what they did wrong. That would make Skurk like a reward, wouldn't it?"

"Perhaps, for some." Grams patted Maddy's hand. "It is not perfect, but we must trust the VDA."

"Why should we do that, exactly?" Maddy peered at Grams. "You make it sound like you think the VDA is a good thing."

"I do not think they are good, nor do I think they are bad. I simply think they are."

"Grams!" Maddy pulled her hand away to rub her temples. "That doesn't make any sense."

"Perhaps not with what you know at the moment, but I will tell you something that will help you."

Then Grams stopped talking and stared into space.

She didn't seem to notice that Maddy was about to explode.

Maddy's mom interrupted. "I don't know, Mom. This might not be the right time."

"For what?" Maddy couldn't stop fidgeting. "What were you going to say?"

Grams traced the handle of her mug with the tip of her finger. "Madelena, I worked as the Determinator of the VDA for many, many years. Elle replaced me. You see, I was in the position that Elle now holds."

"That's not possible! How is that possible?"

"Let me explain." Grams's face was so kind and full of love that some of Maddy's irritation melted away.

"I was appointed," Grams said. "Beschermer asked me to be the Determinator, and I said I would do it."

"Wouldn't that make you immortal?"

Grams' silvery hair gleamed in the sunlight as she leaned forward. "It would have, yes, if I had not retired. I did not wish to live forever without the chance to have children and grandchildren. I wanted a family more than I wanted immortality."

"Wait." Maddy's mind whirled again. It had spun off the axis so many times today she wondered if it would ever go back to normal. "No, that doesn't make sense. Normal people don't just know Beschermer, do they? How come she asked you to do that? How did she know you?"

"Mom." Maddy's mom's voice held a warning like when she was upset at Maddy.

"She needs to know." Grams's eyes shifted from Maddy's mom and to Maddy. "I lived in Skurk."

"What?" Maddy blinked her eyes, trying to make sense of those words. She needed more imagination to picture her sweet little old Grams living in the world of the villains. "How in the heck did you end up there?"

"More or less the same way that Leo did, the way anyone does," Grams said. "I was measured, and they found more bad than good."

Maddy's opinion of the VDA plummeted once again. If they measured Grams and found her lacking, there was no hope for the rest of humanity. They might as well rename the whole Earth as Skurk.

"No way," Maddy stammered. "No way you lived in Skurk."

"It is true," Grams said.

"But, that would make you a villain, Grams. That's ridiculous! How could anyone think you were a villain? You are the most un-villainous person in the world!" Maddy's words tumbled over each other on their way out of her mouth.

"Thank you, dearie," Grams met Maddy's eyes with a steady gaze. "But, nonetheless, I am one hundred percent villain."

Maddy breathed in sharply.

Grams went on. "When I was a young woman, I made choices that set me on a path. My choices, like all choices, profoundly affected one person in particular and would have been that person's downfall. I was taken to Skurk before the story was finished—"

"That is not fair!" Maddy cried.

"Perhaps not," Grams said. "But it is what happened. I do not have a grudge about my experience. Because I was removed, the person I hurt was able to heal and earn a place in Eventyr. I saw true villainy in Skurk, and I chose not to walk that path."

"Grams, you are not a villain," Maddy said firmly.

"I am by blood, dearie, but I have proved myself to be more good than bad."

"Can you do that in Skurk? Prove yourself?" Maddy was over-whelmed with all the things she didn't understand. Until that moment, she thought of Skurk as some kind of high-security prison where people went in and never came out. "Can Leo do that? Can he show them he's not a villain and come home?"

Maddy's mom and dad looked at each other.

"He cannot," Grams said softly.

"Why not? You did! That's not fair!" Maddy was two seconds from flinging herself out of the chair and pacing again. She would have done it if she hadn't caught her dad's eye and seen the slight shake of his head.

Stay put, he seemed to be telling her with his eyes. *Stick with us a little longer.*

Grams went on. "In my time, one was simply taken to Skurk by nature of a bloodline or heinous actions. To prove that you had changed took years and years and years of hard work and even then it was almost impossible. I was determined not to quit until I earned a place in Eventyr, but I have many friends who gave up. Many who live there still. That is, in part, why we were trying to keep you from Elle. We didn't want you to be taken because of me. Because of your bloodline."

Yeah, Maddy didn't want that either.

"Beschermer and I became good friends. She was overwhelmed with monitoring both worlds and gave me a portion of her magic to watch over Skurk. It made sense; I knew it better than most. I was appointed as Determinator and together, Beschermer and I went to work evaluating the people in Skurk. We thought we had done all that was needed, we thought it was stable, that the worlds had finally reached balance. That is when I asked to leave."

"So you came back here, again?" That had to mean Leo could too.

"Yes, dearie. I was given another chance. I met your grandfather and threw myself into life, determined not to waste a single moment. I lost touch with Beschermer until one day, when your mother was about your age. One of Beschermer's commissioners did some terrible things that disrupted the stability of Eventyr and Skurk. It almost destroyed Beschermer. She called me back and we combined our magic to right the wrongs. We put checks and balances into place so something like that will never happen again. Now, a person with a percentage of villain has another chance to prove themself through the Villainous Test and—"

"But that test was a joke, Grams! It asked about eating children and making coats out of puppies. What does that have to do with anything?"

Grams tried to smile, but it wouldn't stay upright. "It's meant to help determine who a person is becoming. Coupled with bloodlines and actions, it has proven to be a very effective way to measure a person's villanous tendencies. We did the best we could do."

"You wrote that test." Maddy knew the words were true the moment they left her mouth.

"I helped." The lines on Grams face deepened until she looked about a hundred years old. She reached for Maddy's hand. "We had to tighten our hold on Skurk, to keep the people in both worlds safe. Do you understand what I'm saying?"

"Sure." Maddy shrugged as she stared at a spot over Grams shoulder. There was a dent from when Leo parkoured off the kitchen counter and banged into the wall. Everything in this room reminded her of Leo, in fact.

It hurt to think about him, but if Grams had an in with Beschermer, they could totally get Leo back.

It was going to be okay.

"It may not seem like it, but Beschermer does the best she can too." Grams closed her eyes for a moment. When she opened them again, Maddy noticed they were rimmed with red. "And so does Elle. There is simply no way to really measure a person's heart."

"Mom, it's okay." Maddy's mom moved over and wrapped her arm around Grams' shoulder. "You all did the best you could."

Grams nodded. "We did do that, yes. The test is just another step to give those with villain blood the chance to prove they have changed."

Maddy sat up straighter. "So, you think villains can change, then?"

"Just like all of us, they can try." Grams looked very tired. "They have the opportunity to try. Beschermer and Elle have to be very careful they don't let those with villainous tendencies into our world, or into Eventyr. It will damage the magic that sustains them. HC proved that."

Maddy had no idea who or what HC was and she had too many other questions to stop for clarification about that. "So, when people in Skurk prove they're more good than bad, where do they go? Can they come back here?"

"No." Grams was all sympathy. "It is difficult magic to send a person back here. And even more difficult to know that the person has truly reformed. It is a high risk."

Maddy's dad broke in. "Think of how easy it is to squeeze toothpaste out of the tube and how impossible it is to get it back in. That's what your Grams is talking about."

Maddy stared at them. If that was the case, then magic was incredibly weird. "But *you* left Skurk, Grams. You came here."

"Yes, that is true." Grams looked at her hands. "But I had magic of my own. My case is somewhat different from others."

Maddy sat back, her arms flopping to her sides. There was so much whirling around her brain that she was surprised it hadn't helicoptered off her neck and taken flight already.

"Well, I still think it's stupid to call you a villain," Maddy said finally.

"Thank you, dearie. But please remember you know me as a result of the choices I made when I decided I wanted to be a better person. I cannot erase who I was or what I did before that. I am one hundred percent villain in my DNA, Maddy. I simply choose not to act on it."

If Grams was one hundred percent villain, then, Maddy's mom would be half.

And Maddy...

Maddy would be one quarter.

One-quarter villain.

"You are not a villain either, Madelena." Grams's eyes, fixed on Maddy's face, were exceptionally bright. "It is only in your blood. You get to choose who you will be."

Maddy needed a break, a time-out. She really needed to move. The freezer was the first thing to catch her attention when she looked up, so she moved around the kitchen chairs to get a strawberry popsicle. She unwrapped it and had eaten almost half without tasting a single bit of it. The process was far from wasteful, though; the change of scenery and sweet cold soothed her enough to go back to the table calmly.

"Okay, sure. We might be villains. Fine. But Leo is not a villain at all." Maddy tucked the popsicle stick into the wrapper and set it to the side. "He shouldn't be in Skurk just because he didn't take the Villainous Test seriously. We have to get him back. How do we do that?"

Maddy's mom's eyes softened when she looked at her. "We don't."

"We can't, baby," her dad added.

"If he scored high on the test, as we assume, Leo must stay in Skurk," Grams said. "That is what I was trying to tell you, dearie. His villain tendencies, as the VDA deems them, will make him too much of a threat to return to this world. They have already erased him."

"Yeah, why did they erase him?" Maddy's voice rose to a higher pitch. "That seems really abrupt, especially because Leo isn't even a real villain." Maddy's mom opened her mouth, but Maddy kept going. She wanted to get all her thoughts out before someone shut her down. "They don't erase everybody, obviously, I mean, we know the stories of Al Capone and Nero and Mary Tudor... They were not good people. Why didn't the VDA erase *them*?"

Grams rubbed her cheek wearily. "I imagine Beschermer and the VDA left the tales behind to caution others. If I remember correctly, things did not go well for any of those people in the end."

Maddy couldn't really argue with that.

"Regardless, dearie, Leo has been erased and they will not undo it. He cannot come back to this life. He will remain there."

"Forever?"

Grams nodded reluctantly. "Though, if he succeeds in the Reformation Program and proves he is more good than bad, he will have the chance to leave Skurk for Eventyr."

"Wait." Maddy froze as solid as the popsicle she'd just eaten. She'd just made a connection she wanted to unmake. It all came together in the most horrifying way. "Toothpaste, Leo has to go to Eventyr. He can't come back here..." Her voice trailed off.

Maddy had felt all of the feelings in a super short amount of time. Anger, excitement, frustration, entitlement, and many, many others. It wasn't until this moment that she realized all of those other emotions were just a cover for a different one.

This horrible, crushing despair.

It squeezed her chest like someone stuck her in a garlic press.

"There has to be something I can do. We're not just going to give up, are we? We have to get him back. I can reply to the email, or we can track down Elle. This is a mistake, and they have to fix it. You know Beschermer, Grams. Can you call her or whatever you do and explain? She can bring him back. She can, um, unerase him, right?"

When Maddy saw her mom, her dad, and Grams slowly shake their heads in perfect unison, something broke inside her.

She couldn't do life without Leo.

Maddy dropped her head on the table and sobbed.

When Maddy woke up, her whole body ached like she'd been hit by a train. She moved each leg gingerly and rolled over with a groan. Everything hurt, but that wasn't even the worst thing. Her mouth felt like she'd been sucking on a sock. A sock that had spent a full month on a diseased foot. Maddy flicked her tongue around, trying to generate some saliva. She usually kept a water bottle in her room, but when she flung her arm over the side of the bed to look for it, there was nothing there.

Maddy reached for her phone and pushed the button to check the time.

Eleven forty-five.

She dropped her phone on her chest and stared at the ceiling as the memories flooded back. That talk at the table, too much information, crying herself to sleep at eleven in the morning.

So, she slept all day, then.

Tears pricked her eyes at the thought of Leo. She didn't think there were any tears left, and yet, here they were. Two lines slid down the sides of her face and soaked into her pillow. Of all the things she'd had to process, this was the one she couldn't.

Leo was gone.

It couldn't be true, and yet it was.

There had to be something she could do. She couldn't just sit there and go on with her life like everything was fine while Leo was stuck in Skurk.

And that was another thing.

Leo couldn't be stuck in Skurk forever. He had a job and a family and a report due on Friday. Nobody deserved to spend eternity in a place that was one letter away from the word 'skunk'.

Especially not Leo.

He was an idiot and a pain in the rear 80 percent of the time, but he was Maddy's best friend. She couldn't let him disappear. But what *could* she do? There had to be something.

Maddy hugged her fluffiest pillow to her chest.

She knew she wasn't qualified to go to Eventyr or Skurk. She also had no way to contact Beschermer or Elle without Grams' help, and Grams had already decided there was no way to bring Leo home. Maddy wished she hadn't left the VDA card at Leo's house. That was stupid luck. She couldn't barge into his house to retrieve it now. His family would have no idea who she was. And anyway, the VDA probably made the card disappear. If they could completely wipe out the memory of a person, they could easily vanish a business card.

Maddy wished she could remember the name of the website.

Come to think of it, the fact that she couldn't remember was probably another sign of the VDA at work. They might not be able to take her memory of Leo but they would have no trouble making her forget the name of a random website she only briefly saw a few days ago.

Maddy didn't know how Grams could think the VDA wasn't evil. Everything pointed to it. They took people, manipulated memories, and judged people based on one stupid test.

It was beyond unfair.

Grams's words came back to Maddy's mind with such finality, and a knot formed in her chest that not even the fluffy pillow could unwind. 'You cannot go there, Maddy. You are zero percent villain according to your test. A way will not open for you to Skurk.'

A way would not open.

She was zero villain.

A way would not open.

Except.

Maddy sat up and grabbed her phone with fumbling fingers. She opened it up and went to the email app. The message from the VDA was buried amongst a bunch of unopened emails, and for a moment, Maddy thought she had deleted it. When she finally found it, she starred it and then backed it up on the Cloud in case the VDA got any more ideas about vanishing important things. She felt way better after that.

Maddy skimmed the email and came to the place she was looking for.

"Despite your blood composition of one-quarter villain, it is clear that your villain tendencies are dormant. Unless there is a drastic change in your behavior, the VDA clears you to live a normal human life."

Unless there is a drastic change in her behavior.

That was it!

Maddy might not be able to go to Skurk now, but she could if she changed her behavior. Then she would catch the attention of the VDA, and they would have to take her to Skurk. She could bring Leo home! Okay, so, that part was fuzzier. She wasn't sure how that was going to work out, but she was sure the two of them could figure out a way to catch Beschermer's attention and come back home.

It had to work.

But even if it didn't work, she had to try.

What other option did she have?

THIRTEEN
The way of the villain begins with a single step

Once Maddy finished making her plan and went over it three times so she wouldn't forget any important details, she fell back into a deep sleep and didn't wake up again until morning. Birds sang outside her window, and the sun made a buttery pool in the center of the carpet where it peeked through the disheveled curtains. Maddy knew that what she did from this moment on was going to set a tone for the rest of the day. It was crucial to start the day the right way so the rest of her scheme would work.

This was it.

She had to go big or lose Leo forever.

And that wasn't an option.

It was simple. She just needed to do the exact opposite of everything she usually did. Maddy walked to the window, pulled it open, and stuck her head into the cool morning air.

"Shut up, you stupid birds!" she shrieked. "What do you have to sing about? Idiots!"

The silence that followed was eerie and strangely satisfying.

Maddy slammed her window shut and pulled the shades tight so the sun would go away. She couldn't eliminate it completely, but she could block it out enough that the room became cave-like and all the furniture turned into shadows of their former selves. Maddy stumbled through the semi-darkness to her closet and thumbed through her shirts. She wanted a black one with a skull or something on it, but she couldn't seem to find anything even a tiny bit sinister. She didn't even own a black shirt, much less one with something creepy on the front.

Maddy sighed and went back to the start of her shirts. Okay, so, she didn't own any black shirts or skull shirts or shirts with terrifying words on the front. There had to be something else that would work. After another run-through, she found a deep, dark purple tee that almost looked black.

That'll do.

She paired the t-shirt with black leggings and tall black boots that her trendy aunt Danica sent from New York at the beginning of the school year. The result was as dark and brooding as she was going to get without a trip to the mall.

Her hair, however, was a bit of a problem. It was a good shade of dark brown, so she had that going for her, but it was too normal: just below shoulder length and straight. There wasn't even a wave or some layers to give it some sass. She usually just tossed it into a preppy pony, but that was not going to work today.

After experimenting with a couple of possible hairstyles in front of the closet mirror, inspiration struck and Maddy ran to the bathroom. She searched under the cabinet until she found an old bottle of hair gel that belonged to her dad. Maddy squeezed a bunch into her hands and smoothed it through the top of her hair, getting it as close to the scalp as she could. Then she brushed the gel through to the tips of her follicles, creating this greasy, stringy look that made her so proud she almost got teary.

Except that she was pretty sure broody people did not get excited about stringy hair.

When she looked in the mirror to take it all in, she didn't even recognize the person looking back at her. Her big velvety eyes were red rimmed and puffy; her face looked washed out for that same reason, and also because apparently purple was not her color at all. Her dark and now greasy hair hung like Professor Snape from *Harry Potter*. Which was good. He was a villain, right? The only thing that bothered her was the lost look in her eyes. This was not the time to appear weak. Maddy had to be confident and bold. Nobody went villainous while feeling insecure.

Maddy ran back to her bedroom for the necklace Izzy gave her for her birthday. Once it was in place around her neck, courage coursed through her. She could do this. She could totally do this. Maddy threw her shoulders back and went to the closet mirror for one final check before she faced the day.

Her expression needed some work. She narrowed her eyes to hide the puffiness and also because that made her look cynical. Then, she fixed her mouth into a frown, which was just comical, so she tried a straight line instead. The straight line was better; it made her seem unapproachable whereas the frown made her look like an overly sad clown. She didn't want anyone trying to cheer her up; she wanted them to run in fear when they saw her stomping down the hall. She wanted people to clutch their children and hide their faces when she walked by. She wanted them to roll into a ball and suck their thumbs.

It was time.

Maddy clomped down the hallway and grabbed her keys out of her purse. She wasn't taking any books or bags to school with her today. If things went the way she planned, she'd be in Skurk before the bell rang for first period.

The smell of pancakes wafted from the kitchen, but Maddy had already decided to leave without eating breakfast. Both because she didn't want to stick around to explain to her family what she was doing and because she was sure that villains didn't eat square meals. That's why they were so cranky. If they filled their bellies with gluten, butter, and syrup, they would have no more desire to do evil.

It was just a fact.

Her stomach lurched toward the kitchen, but Maddy reined it in with thoughts of Leo. He had already been in Skurk for way too long. She needed to get to school, create some impressive chaos, and rescue him as soon as possible. If going without fluffy, delicious pancakes was part of the sacrifice, then so be it.

No one said it was easy being bad.

"I'm out of here. Later."

Maddy's mom peeked around the corner of the kitchen, her eyes getting wider the longer she took in Maddy's new look. "Maddy, is that you?"

"Yep." Maddy wished she had some gum. Didn't super tough girls always smack their gum when they talked? Unfortunately, her mom used to work for an orthodontist who was convinced that gum chewing was the cause of all major mouth and jaw problems, so there was never any gum in their house.

Maddy's mom stepped closer, wringing a dishrag in her hands. "You look…"

She couldn't seem to find the words. The innocent dishrag wrinkled into a sad state while her mom made noises that tried to be words. Maddy considered that to be her first dastardly deed of the day: ruining the kitchen towel and confuddling Mom.

No, wait! The second dastardly deed. The first was yelling at the birdies.

Maddy was totally killing this villain thing.

"Are you okay?" Her mom peered at her.

"Great," Maddy lied, because lying was rotten. "Never been better. Life is great, nothing to worry about here." She was babbling now; she totally needed to stop talking. "K, gotta go. See ya."

"Wait." Her mom extended a hand. "I think we need to talk some more. I can call the school and excuse you."

"Nope." Maddy pulled the front door open and wished she had a Harley sitting in the driveway instead of an ordinary car.

"Maddy…"

Maddy slammed the door and strolled down the front walk. Her mom was going to be so ticked Maddy did that. It was surprising that her mom hadn't already chased Maddy down, tackled her in the grass, and delivered the first of an epic lecture series on proper manners.

Maddy tossed her nasty hair over her shoulder and turned her stroll into a strut. Strutting wasn't something she'd done before, so it took a minute before she got a good rhythm, but it made her feel pretty awesome, like the whole world wanted to bow at her feet. The wind blew her hair back, and the tops of her fingers tingled with excitement. This moment felt villain-y and super cool.

Maddy followed the traffic laws all the way to school like she was still in driver's training with Mr. Pentegrass in the passenger seat evaluating her every move. While she was indeed forging a new path of rebellion, she didn't want to do it at the expense of causing an accident. That probably lost her some villain points, but that was okay; she would make them up later.

When Maddy reached the parking lot at school, she parked insanely crooked, taking up three spaces instead of one. A few people gave her weird looks. One guy opened his mouth to say something, so Maddy lifted her arms and yelled, "What?"

He closed his mouth and walked away as fast as he could.

Maddy perfected her strut all the way to the entrance of the school. She stood in the doorway, blocking the way so people had to go around her, and surveyed the common area like she was the queen. In reality, she was trying to think what to do next. Now that she was at school and ready to rebel, her brain was annoyingly blank. She needed to find a quiet place where she wouldn't be noticed and think this all through a little better.

Her path of wickedness had reached a momentary dead end.

Someone kicked a sharpie that rolled along the carpet until it hit the side of Maddy's boot. She picked it up and was struck with nefarious inspiration. There were a bunch of student council election posters taped to the walls. Posters with pictures of students with fakey grins. Maddy walked over to one of the pillars that had a bunch of posters and uncapped her marker. She drew mustaches and pirate patches on each one, working her way all around the pillar. When she finished and deemed her work adequate, she noticed a group of kids across from her. They were the kind of kids who didn't pay attention in class, or didn't go in the first place, and didn't seem to care about anything.

This was perfect.

Maddy began making a mental list of all the things they did that she could easily replicate, like rolling their eyes a lot. She could totally do that; she just might need some practice to be able to do it as often as they did without getting a headache.

Also, talking without any emotion at all. Zero voice inflection. Maddy mumbled to herself in a monotone. That wasn't a problem. Easy as pie, as Grams liked to say.

Yeah, Maddy would probably need to get her cotton-candy-sweet Grams out of her head if she was going to pull this villain thing off. Despite what Grams told Maddy about the villain blood, there was nothing evil or malicious about Grams.

Not a single thing.

Maddy noticed the group also didn't make eye contact with anyone. If their eyes weren't rolling, they were staring critically at the floor or ceiling.

This was going to take some practice, but Maddy was confident she could figure it out.

Their appearance caused more of a dilemma than the attitude stuff. Now that Maddy was here instead of in her bedroom, her super evil outfit looked drab, not wicked. She needed better resources to pull off a look that was as convincing as those kids. Like, heavy eyeliner and henna tattoos, jeans with multiple ripped lines, leather jackets, and, yes, the skulls on everything: clothing, bags, fingernails, shoes, belts, and key chains.

Also, there was the guy wearing a spiked collar.

Maddy hoped she got to Skurk before she had to figure out where to get one of those things. She'd never seen a collar like that at the pet store, much less a store that sold things for humans. She didn't even know where to begin looking for one.

When a girl with heavy black lipstick pulled out a silver marker and started drawing frowny faces on her shoes, Maddy jumped out from behind the pillar. It was time to stop thinking and start acting. A trashcan caught the edge of her foot as she walked and clattered to the ground, rolling so that its contents spread across the commons. Maddy ignored it and sashayed toward the group.

A few of the kids watched her with wary eyes.

"Hey," Maddy said in a perfect monotone like she couldn't care less to talk to them and they were lucky she was gracing them with her words.

Not to mention her presence.

The girl with the marker froze and looked somewhere over Maddy's shoulder with zero expression.

Maddy discovered that she sounded way grumpier when she lowered her voice. This also made it easier to do the monotone thing. She pointed to the marker in the girl's hand. "Can you, like, make a skull on my shirt or something? I mean, whatever."

The girl gave a small, one-shouldered shrug, now looking at the ground by Maddy's shoes. "Where do you want it?"

The correct answer was right in the center of her chest where everyone would see it, but Maddy didn't have a different shirt to change into while the girl evilfied her current one, and she knew she wouldn't ever be rebellious enough to walk around school without a shirt on. Maddy puzzled about the problem while pretending to look at the EXIT sign above the entrance doors.

Inspiration struck.

Maddy whirled around and snatched a math book from the hands of a tiny passing freshman, then stuck it under her shirt. It was a good thing the shirt was a spandex mix so that Maddy could stretch it over the book to give the girl a flat surface to work her magic.

"Yeah?" Maddy said, trying not to look too pleased with herself.

"Whatev." The girl shrugged again and went to work.

Maddy tried not to think about all the brain cells she was losing by breathing in those Sharpie fumes. She was pretty sure defiant kids didn't care about their brain cells. Instead, she took this very convenient opportunity to observe the group from the inside. It was strange that all these people milled around each other like they were good buddies, but not a single one spoke to another. Some watched videos on their phones—Maddy was dying to know what they were watching, but she was also slightly afraid. What if, instead of something super dark, they were watching cat videos? That would just wreck her whole image of their heartlessness.

Others touched up their extravagant makeup, making it even more so, or picked at jagged fingernails. A tall guy pulled out a bottle of black nail polish and started painting his super long thumbnail. Maddy's symmetrical brain went bonkers at this. How come he only had one long nail? And why was that the only one he painted black? She had to bite back all her questions and pretend she didn't care.

This was by far the hardest thing she'd had to do so far.

"Hey," Maddy pointed at him with her free hand, the one not supporting the textbook. "Yeah, you. 'Sup? Paint my nails?" Maddy spread her fingers and extended her arm so he knew she was serious.

The guy finished his thumbnail and went to work on Maddy's hand. These people had welcomed her into their group without any resistance. Maddy's mind was officially blown. Who said you had to be bubbly and perky to be friendly?

When the guy finished with Maddy, he drew a wobbly snake on the back of his phone case and then tucked the nail polish bottle away. Maddy almost asked him to do her other hand and then she realized it would be so much more wicked if her hands didn't match.

She was really starting to get the hang of this.

The Sharpie girl let out a breath and stood away from Maddy's shirt to survey it through squinted eyes. Maddy tried to do the same but couldn't get a great view upside down. The girl must have approved because she capped her marker and walked away.

"Thanks!" Maddy called and then cringed.

Villains don't say 'thank you'!

And they totally don't use exclamation marks.

"Or, you know. Whatev," Maddy said louder.

She glared at the people who looked at her until they wilted under her stare, then she left the group.

What could she do next?

What she wanted at the moment was some dark and smokey makeup to give her face that perpetual 'don't care' look. She couldn't ask anyone else for makeup, though, 'cause germs. But maybe she had some mascara in her locker. It could work as an eyeliner substitute at the very least. At the most, she could find something else to do with it too.

Something diabolical.

Maddy swung her arms as she walked down the hall and only then did she realize she still carried the textbook she'd snagged from the freshman earlier.

Wait!

Not snagged, stolen!

Maddy almost shouted in excitement. She totally just stole a book!

Okay, now what should she do with it?

Maddy stewed on this dilemma while she twirled the combination of her locker. The spare mascara was in a case on the top shelf.

Labeled.

She looked at this and everything else in her locker, then sighed heavily. Leo was right; she shouldn't have brought her label maker to school. Her locker looked like it belonged to someone preppy, neat, and motivated. Those were the very qualities she was trying to eradicate at the moment.

Maddy opened the box with the mascara inside and took the tube out. Then, she dumped everything else onto the shelf: lotion, chapstick, hair clips, a small brush, and eye drops. Just for good measure, Maddy shook her hand through the middle of it to mix everything up even more. She wrinkled papers, tore the corner off every one of her notebooks, and uncapped all the markers. She use some to scribble on the labels, making them illegible. The rest she threw on the bottom of the locker to begin the slow and torturous process of drying out.

Once she was satisfied that her locker was a mess—well, as much of a mess as it could be without adding moldy banana peels—Maddy unscrewed the top of the mascara and leaned into the mirror on her locker door. She darkened her lashes and made bold, black lines around the bottom and top of her eyes, the way Cleopatra did in Maddy's history notebook.

Cleopatra was definitely a villain.

Maddy's eyes dropped to the freshman's book. It offended her with its clean cover, crisp pages, tight binding, and new book smell, but Maddy couldn't bring herself to wreck the book. That would be crossing a line she wasn't ready to breach. There had to be something else she could do that would make a point without permanently destroying the book. Maddy opened to the title page, where students were supposed to write their names, and used a deep purple marker to write 'never smiles' in big, bold strokes underneath the name 'Susie Carmichael.'

There. That felt awesome.

It was like she and the book had a little secret. It might look new and perfect, but inside there was proof that it wasn't. Maddy dropped the book on the ground and then kicked it away from her locker. It slid and stopped a few feet away just as the tardy bell rang for first period.

Perfect!

Maddy wasn't just going to be tardy; she was going to be truant. She imagined herself ducking around corners and sliding under bleachers to avoid teachers the whole day, in addition to wreaking havoc whenever the opportunity presented itself.

Knotting shoelaces together.

Switching people's backpacks.

Starting food fights.

Whatever it took.

Maddy was nothing if not flexible.

She went back to the commons, which were now empty, and stood in the center with her hands on her hips. This time, she spun in a slow circle, looking for opportunities. When she made her plan in the middle of the night, she mostly concentrated on what she would be wearing and how bad of an attitude she could cop. Now that she was at school with a skull on her shirt and one hand of black fingernails, she knew she was going to have to do more than look like a villain to catch the VDA's attention.

She needed to do something awful.

With the world so close to Halloween and a school vice principal who used to be a professional cheerleader, the school was draped in cutesy decorations. Jack-o-lantern cut-outs were taped to the front doors and throughout the halls. Real pumpkins that the art students painted sat like fat little sentinels next to every classroom door. Spiderwebs stretched across the display cases with jolly plastic spiders in the center of each one. There were probably fifty of them in the commons alone.

Maddy could work with that.

She walked along the trophy cases, collecting spiders. Their gooey rubber bodies jiggled against her fingers every time Maddy reached for one. She gritted her teeth and tried to ignore the goosebumps on her arms.

It didn't get easier.

With her arms full of spiders, Maddy hurried to the girls' bathroom. There was one person in there, washing her hands, when Maddy walked in. The girl's eyes widened as she took in Maddy's haul, but she didn't say anything. As she tried to pass Maddy to get to the door, Maddy nudged her.

"Hey, gimme some gum!"

The girl stared at Maddy for a minute, then reached into her pocket. She set a stick of cinnamon gum on top of the spiders and then flung open the door and ran without looking back.

Maddy inched her fingers along the sticky bodies, trying to get the gum without dropping spiders on the floor. She was all in on her plan, but she wasn't about to touch anything that hit the bathroom floor. With the gum stick wedged between her middle and ring finger, Maddy dropped all the spiders into a sink and counted them while she unwrapped the gum.

There were actually forty-five.

She stuck the gum in her mouth and chewed without closing her lips, making the most obnoxious lip-smacking sound bounce off the sinks and tile. A slow smile spread across her face. For sure, she knew what she was going to do with the first five spiders.

Maddy gathered them up and dropped one in each of the toilets lined up behind her. Then she took another spider and experimented with wrapping its body around the stall handle so a person wouldn't be able to open the stall without touching the spider. She didn't know what kind of sticky, plastic substance the spiders were made of, but it was perfect for the ick factor.

She couldn't have planned it better.

Once that bathroom was thoroughly creepified, Maddy took the remaining spiders and tied their bodies in knots around the spout of every drinking fountain and door in her vicinity. That took her a while. With seven spiders left, she decided to drop them along the floor at intervals. People would step on something squishy in the crowded hall and then look down to see a nasty black spider staring at them. The freak-out would be epic!

On her way back toward her locker, Maddy took out her flavorless gum and wedged it under the doorknob to the theater. Someone headed to drama next period was going to get a fun surprise.

Now what?

Maddy thought about going back to the bathroom and unrolling all the toilet paper rolls and emptying all the soap dispensers. She could try and clog the sinks like that idiot bandit on *Home Alone*, but then, they lived in a drought state, so that was beyond evil. Oh! She could use the school wi-fi to watch something super edgy.

Like *The Vampire Diaries*.

"Don't you think to move some muscles of yours, Madelena Hutton."

A familiar voice brought a grin that stretched Maddy's mouth to both of her ears. She turned slowly, crossed her arms, and tipped her head to the side. Elle stood in the hallway, wearing her rocking awesome cloak. Two other cloaked figures flanked her sides. They all held their hands out to Maddy like she was a puppy chewing an expensive shoe and they needed to coax her attention somewhere else.

One of the minions spoke next, in a robotic voice that made Maddy wonder if he was in fact a robot. "You have been identified as one entertaining villainous thoughts. With your family background, intervention is necessary to preserve peace in this world. You will come with us for further questioning. You have the right to remain silent. Any magic you use will be counted against you in the assembly of Skurk."

Maddy smirked and placed a hand on her hip. "Took you guys long enough."

FOURTEEN

Villains aren't born; they are created

Something weird happened after the VDA pinned Maddy's hands to-gether with their mind powers and stuffed her in the back seat of their limo between Elle and the silent minion. Maddy blacked out or something because one minute she was in the school parking lot and the next they were driving up a brick road to a dark building with green letters that proclaimed 'The Villain Detection Agency.'

Maddy tried to ask if this was where Leo was, but apparently her mouth was also glued shut.

Well, that was inconvenient.

Elle and company marched Maddy into the building and left her alone in the center of a large, spacious room decorated to look like the inside of a cave. There were even stalactites hanging from the ceiling.

Stalagmites?

Also bats.

There were bats on the ceiling.

Okay, maybe it wasn't just decorated to look like a cave. Maybe it really was one.

Maddy was suddenly grateful her hair stuck to her greasy scalp so none of those nasty things could make a nest in it. That might have seriously driven her over the edge.

"Madelena, this way please." A door opened through the gloom, and Maddy followed the sliver of light to where Elle stood. Maddy almost didn't recognize her voice without the mixing up of words and conjuga-tions. "Come follow me."

Elle led Maddy through a series of tunnels until she was so turned around it would have been impossible for her to escape even if she wanted to. Which she didn't. Inside the bowels of the VDA fortress was exactly where she wanted to be.

Next step: Leo.

Elle opened the door to a circular room with floor-to-ceiling shelves completely covered in books. Even the door was all books, so when Elle shut it, Maddy couldn't tell where the opening was anymore. It slipped seamlessly into the other bookshelves. Someone probably dreamed of being in a room like this, surrounded by books, but it crushed Maddy with the weight of all the things she didn't know.

Maddy wished she was in a room surrounded by chocolate.

Chocolate didn't judge you.

Elle lifted a hand to indicate where Maddy should sit and took the short, stubby chair across from her. As soon as Maddy sank into the seat, it became very clear there was no way in the world she'd be able to get out of it again. Elle settled back with her legs tucked under her, like the two of them were about to talk about crushes and share their skin care routines.

Well, Elle was out of L-U-C-K. Maddy was not talking first.

Though, she actually would love to know what moisturizer Elle used to give her skin that ethereal look.

"Maddy," Elle smiled. Her beauty was back and just as dazzling as it had been that day at Wendy's.

No, that wasn't true; it was more dazzling now. Maddy had to squint when she looked at Elle, and when she blinked, there was a foggy image in the shape of Elle behind Maddy's eyelids. This was probably a part of the magic Grams was talking about. If Elle was unstable in Maddy's world and stronger in her own world, it made sense that in Skurk, she would be achingly beautiful and talk in straight sentences.

All of it made Maddy wonder which Elle was the real one: the hag or the beauty queen? The articulate or the gibberisher.

"There is no reason for the fear or worry, Madelena. I am not your enemy." Elle waved her hand, and a table filled with chocolates appeared in the space between their chairs.

Could Elle read Maddy's mind?

Or did she just think, as most girls did, that chocolate was the first step to fixing everything?

Either way, she wasn't fighting fair.

Somewhere from the depths of Maddy's mind where she'd stuffed all the inactive knowledge she'd gleaned over the years, a memory floated to the forefront. A story. A myth, actually, about a girl who went to the underworld and, because she ate something there—Maddy couldn't remember what—the girl had to go back for six months out of the year.

Forever.

Maddy wasn't about to let that same fate happen to her. She was not going to spend half of her life trapped in Skurk. Not even for beautiful, delectable, yummy, delicious chocolate. She fixed her eyes on a shelf of particularly boring book spines so she wouldn't throw herself face-first at the chocolate. It wasn't easy. The smell that wafted under her nose was rich and sugary, just the way chocolate should smell.

Pure evil!

Maddy avoided looking at Elle and the chocolate with all of her will. She hoped her words would still find a way to jab at Elle without the benefit of eye contact. "You're not my enemy?" Maddy held out her magically bound hands and raised a sassy eyebrow to emphasize her point.

Elle flicked her wrist, and Maddy's hands were free. Where they felt tight before, like someone stuck them together with gorilla glue, they now fell easily and separated in her lap. Maddy stretched her fingers as far as they would extend a couple of times to make sure everything was working the way it was supposed to.

Then she sat on her hands.

Elle went on. "We are both intelligent, seasonable beings..."

Did she mean reasonable?

"...and I know we can figure this about. Let's talk to this."

Maddy shook her head slightly. "Talk to what?"

Forget everything she said about Elle talking straight.

Elle held out her palm like the school crossing guard telling Maddy to stay put until all the cars were gone. "But a moment. It is affecting of the after. The journey to your world words my scrambles. Another moment it will be for me to right myself once upon a time."

Maddy pursed her lips while she waited for that moment to arrive. As she said before, she was so not talking first.

"I to wish for us... No." Elle shook her head, her perfect face lined in frustration. "Moment or two more for to please."

Maddy leaned back and stared at the ceiling, her head mushing into the back of the chair. It was like lying in a pile of Jigglypuffs. If this were her living room and she wasn't on high alert because she was pretty sure an interrogation was coming, she would have fallen asleep in three seconds flat.

"I believe I have recovered," Elle said. "Yes, I seem to be set to rights once more. Now we can have our little chat." She rubbed her hands together with a bright smile.

Maddy lolled her head to the side and twirled a finger in the air. "Yay."

"Now, Maddy," Elle pouted. "Don't be like this. We are great friends, you and I."

This made Maddy sit up straight. Elle's words were a pin poking in her back. "Are we? Funny, I'm usually so good at remembering things like this. Help me out here. Did we get chummy when you were stalking me over the phone and through email? Or was it when your creepy hearse followed me after school? No, wait, I know. It was when you freakified into a hag and then disappeared in the middle of a room full of people at Wendy's. That was when we swore our vows of eternal friendship, yeah?"

"Maddy..."

"No, no, no, no, I got it. It was when you magically handcuffed me and frog-marched me out of my school. That was when we bestied it up? Yes. Oh, I'm so glad I remembered." Maddy scowled at Elle's amused face.

This was so not funny.

Maddy went on. "Listen, I can save us a lot of time here. I'm not a villain; I don't even have tendencies or whatever. I was just trying to get here so I can rescue my friend, Leo. He's not a villain either." It was her turn to hold up a traffic-cop hand to shut Elle up. "I know he scored high on your stupid test, but he's not a villain; he's just an idiot. You wouldn't erase the memory and the life of someone like that, would you? It's practically inhumane, like arresting a child."

When Maddy paused to breathe, Elle snapped her fingers, and a piece of paper appeared in front of Maddy's face. The longer it hovered there, the more the scent of mint filled Maddy's nose.

Maddy took the paper and peered closer at the type.

It was Leo's Villainous Test.

Elle laced her long fingers together and leaned forward. "Never in the history of the VDA have we administered a test with a perfect score."

Maddy tossed it aside. That test was completely irrelevant. "He was messing around, you know? Joking, joshing, being sarcastic."

Elle stared, her face expressionless.

"Don't you guys do that here? Come on, you're villains. You can't tell me villains don't use sarcasm!"

Elle waved her fingers, and the test floated across the room to her hand. "His emotional state when he took this test is irrelevant. We have engineered the test to detect villainous tendencies, and your friend, Leo, has them. I have detained people with much lower scores in the course of my career."

"Detained? Is that what you call abducting, erasing, and imprisoning? 'Cause that's cute."

"Maddy." Elle gave a mournful shake of her head. "What happened to you? I have never seen such a swift transformation. Only a few days ago, you were a sweet girl, and now..." She sighed heavily.

"Now, what?" Maddy leaned forward, her elbows digging into her thighs. She was honestly curious about what Elle thought she had become.

"Now, you are a villain by choice."

"Duh," Maddy tossed her head. "I already told you that. I did that on purpose to come here and rescue Leo. Where is he? We're going home."

Elle's face sank with sorrow. "I am sorry to be right in this case, but I see we made the correct choice to come for you. She will begin her Reformation Program immediately." Elle nodded to the books behind Maddy.

Maddy turned around but didn't see anything new. "Hold on. That's it?"

Urgency rose in her throat. She couldn't save Leo if she was imprisoned here too. The back of her neck tingled like it did when she ate way too much sugar.

Elle paused, "unless, of course, you want to embrace your villainous side entirely. We can arrange induction as the newest resident of Skurk if you prefer."

"No, I don't prefer." Maddy glared at Elle. The lady was totally mocking her, Maddy could tell. Even though she looked all calm and patient, she was full of salty and sass.

Maddy took a deep breath and tried to bring her thoughts out of their spiral. She came for Leo. She came to save him. There had to be a way; there was always a way. Even Grams found a way out of here; she just made that deal with Beschermer.

"Berschermer!" Maddy blurted.

"I beg your pardon?" Elle lifted one eyebrow.

Maddy swallowed. "I want to speak with Beschermer. I want to talk to her about Leo."

Elle laughed softly. "Beschermer does not come to Skurk."

"But you can talk to her, right? Grams told me all about it. Beschermer's power created this place. She gave you whatever power you have. I want to talk to her. I demand to talk to her!"

"You are not in a position to make demands, Madelena. Skurk is not the same as your world; the rules you know do not apply here. You do not get a last phone call, you do not have a fast pass, and you are not entitled to anything."

"But—"

Elle's voice rose, but her mannerisms and expression were perfectly composed. "I am the Determinator now. I am the Guardian of Skurk. Beschermer has entrusted me to take care of things here, and I do. I answer to no one."

Her words settled in Maddy's ears like dying embers.

So, that was it?

That couldn't be it!

Maddy's anger ignited as suddenly as flambe. An electrical current flew down her arm and tingled at the end of her fingertips like it was looking for a way out. Without thinking, Maddy lifted her twitching finger and pointed at Elle. "You can't keep Leo; I won't let you!"

As she spat out the last word, something happened. Something completely impossible.

Jagged purple lines moved from Maddy's fingertips toward Elle's chest. With a jerk of Maddy's arm, the lines bypassed Elle, skimming her shoulder enough to make her flinch, then exploded against the bookshelf behind her. Hundreds of books flew into the air but moved around the room in slow motion. Maddy watched them hover for a breath before falling to the ground with a unanimous crash that shook the room.

Did she just shoot lightning out of her fingers?

Was she, like, a Jedi?

Maddy stared at the mess of books for a long time, afraid to look at Elle. When she finally got the courage, Elle's face was as expressionless as ever. If Maddy didn't have a horrible ache in her shoulder and Jell-O-y arm muscles, she would think she imagined the whole thing.

"There has to be something I can do," Maddy said as she slumped back into her chair, suddenly exhausted. "Leo's innocent. He doesn't deserve to be here. I just want to bring him home."

Elle tapped one of her long fingers against her knee as she surveyed Maddy. The cushions of Elle's chair did not enfold her the way Maddy's chair did.

It seemed that everything followed Elle's will.

"Leo cannot come home—"

"But..." Maddy interrupted without knowing what she was going to say.

There had to be a way through this, but coming up with a plan when her life and the life of her best friend were at stake was not a fertile garden of helpful ideas. Maddy's eyes scanned the room, looking for inspiration from something, anything. She just wanted to save Leo. Stupid Leo and his stupid sense of humor. If he'd just listened to her and not been sooooooo clever, none of this would have happened. He would have scored normally on the villain scale, and they would be eating ice cream after one of their legendary movie marathons.

Wait.

Wait!

"Elle!" Maddy sat up, pulling her arms out of the chair with a squelching noise that was incredibly disturbing. "I scored zero percent villain."

"I am aware."

Maddy paused for dramatic effect. "How many people do *that*?"

Elle's mouth pursed into a perfect circle. She glanced over Maddy's head, squinted, then nodded. "You, it appears, are the first. It is that pet question that gets people; we must change it to animal familiar. I believe the word 'pet' is not specific enough."

"I am zero percent villain," Maddy said again.

Elle nodded. "According to the test, yes; however, your actions today proved otherwise."

"I was just trying to save Leo!" Maddy flung her hands in the air. "You erased my best friend! It was the only thing I could think of, but what I did today doesn't change who I am! I'm still the same Maddy I was before."

"Your actions prove otherwise," Elle said again, her eyebrows drawing a thin line across her eyes.

"I didn't do anything awful, not really. Other than the lying and the stealing, it was silly pranks. I was just trying to get your attention. Listen, I'm not a villain. Leo's not a villain. What can we work out here?"

"The VDA does not make deals. A villain is as a villain does. You know this to be true. You said yourself that you would take the Beast from Eventyr and put him in Skurk, though he has reformed. We are not so different, you and I."

"So, you *can* read minds, then?"

Elle laughed like this was the funniest thing she ever heard. "No, I simply have access to your life while you are under surveillance. Eighteen months from the date of your villainous test. You said these words to Agathe. You did not think them."

That was true; she did do that.

Maddy let out a long breath. "My perfect score has to be worth something. What if I could reform Leo?" The words popped out without Maddy thinking about them and as soon as they sunk in, her heart sped up. "Can I go to where he is? Can I prove to you that he's changed?"

"Leo cannot leave Skurk unless he passes the Reformation Program. He has begun the process and is reforming as we speak."

What was this program? How exactly did the VDA go about reforming a villain? Maddy hoped it wasn't like shock therapy. Or that they didn't have him all chained up in an orange jumper working in the coal mine.

Maddy shook her head to clear the plethora of super unhelpful thoughts. She had to stay focused. Elle hadn't said no, so the answer could be yes. "How long will that program thing take?"

"Not long. If he proves he is reformed, he will leave for Eventyr. That is, if he achieves the requirements to prove he has reformed."

Maddy didn't like the sound of Elle's voice. There was a glitch in it that made Maddy think the Reformation Program might not be all it was cracked up to be. "How often does that happen? You know, how often does someone get to go leave Skurk?"

Elle reached forward, chose a chocolate from the table, and nibbled the corner without looking at Maddy. "It has never happened."

Maddy knew it!

She knew that sounded like hooey! She was not going to accept it though. If there was a teeny tiny way, an itsy bitsy gap to get Leo out of there, Maddy was going to find it.

"You have to let me try. I can show you he's harmless. I know Leo better than anyone." Maddy extended her hand. "Please, Elle. You have to let me try." She was so close. All Elle had to do was say yes and then, once Maddy got Leo out of Skurk, she was going to pull some strings with Beschermer to get him unerased and back home. There had to be a way to do it. These people had magic and magic was supposed to make everything possible.

Everybody knew that.

Elle clasped her hands in her lap. The chocolate she'd been holding hovered in the air by her ear.

Maddy stared at Elle steadily, afraid that if she looked away, Elle wouldn't agree. And Elle had to agree. This had to work because Maddy didn't have a backup plan.

"As you wish," Elle said, her voice as soothing as wind chimes. "You may try."

FIFTEEN

Villains, too, come in all shapes and sizes

Maddy sat up, gripping the arms of the chair with her fingernails. The fluff oozed against her skin like silly putty. "Really?" Maddy was sure she heard Elle say she could try, but she was having a hard time trusting her own ears.

Did Elle mean it?

Was she really going to let Maddy help Leo?

"I will." Elle stood up and snapped her fingers.

The book-encrusted room faded and blurred around the edges of Maddy's eyesight. When everything came back into focus, Maddy and Elle stood on a grassy glen in full sunshine. The contrast was brutal. Maddy couldn't open her eyes all the way for a few moments while her eyes adjusted, and then everything stayed blurry until she could blink enough to clear all the welled-up water.

When Maddy could finally see normally again, she took in everything as quickly as she could, not sure if it would blink out and become somewhere new again. She stood outside another building. Unlike the VDA, this one was made of brick that was tinted lime green and had big purple flowers painted on the side. It looked cheerful, sort of like Maddy's preschool back in the day. There wasn't a sign to specify what the building was, but Maddy didn't need one. Ten to one this was the reformation place.

"Is Leo in there?" Maddy asked Elle, who appeared beside her.

Elle nodded and held up a lanyard that dangled from the ends of her long fingers. Maddy took it and examined the card attached to the end. It reminded her of those door keys at hotels, but it was totally blank instead of embossed with a logo.

"I grant you clearance to enter the building, clearance to find Leo, and clearance to leave this world should Leo reform adequately."

At the end of each phrase, Elle paused until a small, green circle appeared on the edge of the blank card; she stopped when there were three.

No, not circles. Apples. Maddy could just make out the little stem and leaf.

"When you accomplish each task, the apple will change from green to red. When you have three red apples, you and Leo can go home."

That didn't sound too hard.

"What does 'reform adequately' mean exactly?" For the first time in her life, Maddy was glad her dad was a lawyer. Now, instead of enduring everybody's super funny corrupt lawyer jokes, she could put years' worth of advice to use, starting with never make a deal unless you are one hundred percent clear on the expectations. Maddy turned the card over and examined both sides carefully. There were no other distinguishing features to speak of. Just a blank white card with three green apples on one side. "I mean, does he have to save a cat from a tree or, like, slay a dragon? Or can he just say he was messing around, and we're good to go?"

"To leave Skurk, one must achieve a higher percentage of good than bad. You will see each person with a Neckticator like yours." Elle indicated to the lanyard she'd given Maddy. "Except, instead of apples, there is a percentage that measures their degree of villain. To prove I am not your enemy, I will consider your task complete when Leo's percentage lowers to 49 percent."

"I bet I could get him to 5 percent," Maddy mumbled, slipping the lanyard over her head.

"You can certainly try, but you should know that humans are always at least 10 percent villain. They cannot help it; it is their nature." Elle glanced over Maddy's head. "Go now; they are between classes. This is your best chance to locate your friend."

Maddy stared at the building, her mind running with tasks. Walk to the building, go inside, find out where Leo is, get him, and run for it. "Thank you—" Maddy turned to Elle, but she was gone. There was nothing to prove that Elle had ever been there at all.

Maddy rolled her eyes and hurried to the tall, black door of the building. With her heart beating in her ears, she pushed the door open and stepped inside.

Unlike the dark, dank, and dreary office of the VDA, this place was bright with high ceilings and tall windows. Maddy looked around for someone to ask for help and almost jumped to the moon when something appeared at her elbow.

At the height of her elbow to be exact.

And that would be someone, not something.

It appeared to be a little, goblin-like creature with long ears and eyes bigger than dinner plates. Its long, crooked nose threatened to disappear into its mouth when it spoke. "Clearance, you?"

A clipboard appeared in its hands. A black, cracked fingernail went down the list as it muttered to itself. "Stringy, dark eyes, scowl. It looks like a villain, yes it does, but it is not on the list."

"How do you know I'm not on the list?" Maddy finally recovered enough to toss her head. "You don't know who I am. You don't know my name."

"Oh, I knows it, Madelena Hutton, called Maddy, it is. But it is not on my list. What is it doing here?"

Maddy gaped, too startled to respond right away.

How did that weird little thing know her name?

"I know everything that happens inside this school. I knows it." The goblin held the clipboard in the air, where it remained visible for approximately three seconds before the creature let go and the clipboard vanished. Then the creature folded its long, hairy arms over its chest. "But the outsides, theys don't always tell me what's I don't know. And I's don't know what it is doing here. What, I asks of it. What?"

"It's..." Maddy swallowed. "I mean, I'm here because...Elle, she..." Maddy sighed because...words. She held up her lanyard card. "I have clearance, see?"

The goblin snapped its thin fingers, and a small pair of square pincher glasses appeared in the middle of its nose. The thing leaned forward and examined Maddy's card without touching it. After a moment, it flicked its tongue, and the glasses disappeared. "Cleared it is. Go it may."

"Thank you." Maddy wrapped her hand around the card. "Um, where can I find Leo?"

"It wants to know where Leo is, does it?" The goblin smiled, revealing mossy green teeth. "It must find him. That is its task."

Oh yeah. That was what Elle said.

"Thanks, anyways." Maddy tried not to glare at the thing. It wasn't its fault it looked like an unhelpful booger and Elle was mean. With a sigh, Maddy turned a full circle and then started walking toward the brightest hall. She'd had her fill of small, dark, and cave-like places for the day. The little thing cackled behind her. The sound followed her all the way to the end of the hall before it faded away.

A dead-end hall.

Of course it was.

Maddy turned and went back the way she'd come only to find that the foyer where she'd entered wasn't there anymore.

Of course it wasn't.

So, then, where was she?

It was just a long, empty hall. No classrooms, no windows, and no doors. Even as she watched, the walls shifted colors and shapes, making corridors that didn't exist moments before.

Fabulous.

Hallways that moved and rooms that changed. It was like Hog-flipping-warts without pumpkin pasties or a House Cup. Maddy turned around again and found a big, round room behind her instead of the bright hall.

"This is bonkers!" she yelled to no one in particular. "How am I supposed to find anything when everything keeps moving?"

And where the heck were the students? This was a school, wasn't it?

Maddy chose the hall directly across from where she stood and started down it with the same results. Another room, a square one this time, replaced where she'd come with a statue of an octopus right in the middle.

Ridiculous!

Maddy stalked over to the statue and stared at it for a minute. The whole thing smelled like the underside of a lake boat that had been sitting in the water for way too long. Maddy pinched her nose and peered at the octopus statue. It had a human face that scowled right back at her. Each of the eight arms was curved in such a way that they could spew water into the basin underneath if they wanted to. Obviously, they didn't want to, though, because the whole thing was bone dry and crumbling like it had never seen water in its existence.

This whole thing was ridiculous!

So, Maddy kicked the statue.

'Cause that made sense.

It also hurt super bad. Maddy grabbed her toe and rubbed it until the sharp pain dulled to bearable.

"That was rude," the face said, water spilling out of the mouth with the words.

Maddy screamed and jumped back, tripping over her own feet in the process so she now sat on her rump, staring at the human octopus thing.

"When one does something rude, one should apologize. It does not do to kick things that have done one no harm." More water spewed. The octopus's arms came to life, flicking in and out of the tiny pool gathering beneath it.

"I'm...sorry?"

"Are you? One should not apologize until one is sure one is really sorry for the thing which one has done that needs apologizing."

Maddy blinked, and a dull headache started pounding behind her eyes.

"Are you sorry for what you have done?"

The sincerity of the question made her pause to consider. So, okay. It wasn't the statue's fault this place was kooky dukes. She shouldn't have kicked it. There were better ways to deal with frustration than kicking an innocent thing.

Apparently, statues had feelings too.

Maddy clasped her hands in front of her stomach, hoping that it would make her look more sincere. "I am sorry. I apologize for kicking you. I shouldn't have done that."

"Thank you!" The octopus man opened his mouth and laughed, water gushing to the basin. "But I am not sorry! Not at all. You bring with you the breath of life. I have not seen nor spoken to a soul in thousands of years."

Maddy's heart plummeted all the way down to her shoes. "Are you telling me you haven't seen anyone at all in over a thousand years?"

He shook his head. "Speech brings water, and water is life."

"Yeah, but how have you not seen or spoken to anyone in that long? There should be people all over the place. This is a school, isn't it? Or a Reformation Program thing? Whatever it is, there should be people, right?"

The octopus man splashed his tentacles in the water and flung droplets in the air, which he tried to catch with his tongue. "Water, water, everywhere, and all the drops to drink."

The more he talked, the more water there was to play in, which meant the more he ignored Maddy.

"Hey!" Maddy shouted, waving her hands in front of his face. "Where are all the people?"

"Water! Water! Water!"

Okay, this was pointless.

Maddy shot him a filthy look and turned toward one of the many halls branching from the square room. She wasn't going to stay here and talk in circles anymore. Leo was waiting at the end of one of these random halls, and Maddy was determined to find him. She took only a small step before something wrapped around her waist and lifted her in the air.

It was a great stone tentacle.

Ew!

"Hey!" Maddy tried to push the tentacle away, but the wet, sticky surface felt like chewed-up gum against her skin and gave her the heebie-jeebies. It was way worse than the sticky spiders. She raised her arms in the air to avoid touching the grossness as she looked around for the octopus's face. It wasn't easy to find with the way the tentacle waved her through the air and looped her under other tentacles. Finally, she caught sight of a great big eye and pointed straight at it. "Put me down, you thug!"

The eye blinked. "I cannot let you go. One is not resigned to one's fate when one has a way to change it."

Maddy twisted her head so she could see the face after the tentacle moved her again. "What are you going to do? Keep me here forever? You know I'm human, right? I have to do things like eat and sleep and go to the... The point is you have to let me go eventually. Can't you just talk to yourself and get your precious water that way?"

"One does not have much to say to oneself, one has found." The tentacle turned so that Maddy hung upside down in front of the octopus man's face. This was not going to end well. Maddy and being upside down had never gotten along very well—not since the third-grade monkey bars incident. And she didn't even want to think about that ride at the makeshift fair in the mall parking lot the year before.

"You want to turn me back around, or your water's going to get polluted," Maddy gulped.

"One does not understand."

"Just trust me, buddy."

The tentacle whirled again, and Maddy found herself the right way again. The blood drained away from her face, relieving the rushing in her ears so that she could breathe again without feeling like she was going to explode.

"Thanks. Now let me go."

"One cannot."

Maddy looked around in frustration. There was nothing within reach to smack the thing with until it let her go. She'd been hoping for a baseball bat but would settle for a pool noodle. Now that she thought more about it, that probably wouldn't work. Stone statues most likely didn't feel much pain.

Then again, Maddy didn't think stone could be slimy and sticky either.

Maddy rocked from side to side, trying to wiggle her way out of the tentacle grip. Occasionally, the octopus thing would zip her up into the air, almost like a twitch, and then bring her back down again. This was not super conducive to producing good ideas. So, she had zero. Not a single, solitary, realistic one.

She could do nothing.

The frustration burned slowly this time. The more she thought about how stupid and hopeless this situation was, the more it built. The breaking point came when the octopus man started singing a stupid song about water that didn't even rhyme.

Plus, the thing was totally tone-deaf.

It was excruciating.

Maddy's fingertips tingled with rage. She shook them out in case they were falling asleep from lack of blood flow because of the tentacle squeezing her waist, even though that didn't make a lot of sense. Wouldn't it be her legs tingling if that were the case? The shaking only made the tingle get worse. Maddy was about to stop when jagged, purple lines went flying in all directions.

And they were coming from Maddy's fingertips.

One hit the octopus man's tentacle, making it writhe.

So, apparently, the stone could feel pain. At least, it could feel the jagged purple lines coming from Maddy's fingertips. She didn't know if those were painful or not, actually. She didn't feel anything other than that weird tingle.

"One did not like that." The octopus man stared at her mournfully and stuck his wounded tentacle in his mouth like a giant thumb.

"Yeah?" Maddy flung more sparks. "Well, this one doesn't like to be trapped forever by a nasty, stinky, sticky tentacle."

The other tentacles wiggled in agitation as they tried to avoid the purple sparks. Maddy aimed her fingers at the octopus man's face and held them steady, squinting one eye like she was about to shoot a rifle.

"Let me go by the count of three, or I'm shooting this lightning stuff at your eyeballs."

The octopus man pulled his tentacle out of his mouth with a disgusting squelching noise. "One does not—"

"One," Maddy interrupted.

"It is most—"

"Two."

"Quite unlike—"

"Two and a half." Maddy flicked her fingers, and a sparkler flung out, fizzling before it hit the man's face.

"One will let you go!" Two tentacles covered his eyes, and the one that had her trapped dropped to the ground. "One will let you go with your purple stings and beautiful conversation. One will dry up and crumble to the dust." The octopus man's head hung on his chest in the perfect picture of despair.

The tentacle unfurled and lay still like a giant, disgusting snake.

"Thank you." Maddy wiped at her shirt. There was no way that goop was coming out; it had already seeped across the Sharpie skull like a blindfold. "Goodbye." Maddy started to walk away, and then the guilt got to her.

"Fine." Maddy stomped back to the statue. "Here, I'm going to tell you a story so you can talk to yourself and keep the water flowing or whatever, okay?"

One of the tentacles lifted and then flopped back into the water.

"I don't have to help you out, you know," Maddy said in an irritated tone. "I could just leave you here to dry up like crusty old bread. Doesn't matter to me."

"Wait." The octopus man lifted his head. "Wait! One does not want to dry up. One wants to learn this story to stay the water so that it might not flow away and leave us in the depths of dusty despair."

And that's how Maddy ended up cross-legged on a stone floor telling the story of Goldilocks and the Three Bears to a huge octopus statue with a human man's face. She had to repeat the story three times until he could retell it without leaving out important plot points because he kept trying to make Goldilocks a good guy. She was just misunderstood with a hankering for porridge, apparently. Maddy gave up after way too many minutes of sideways arguing. If it made him happy and let her go, then he could tell the dang story however he wanted to tell it.

Yeah, Leo was never going to believe this.

SIXTEEN

The way of the villain is rarely smooth

In retrospect, Maddy should have asked the octopus man for directions.

After wandering the ever-changing halls for what felt like a million years, the only living things she came across were a tank of electric eels and a garden of multi-colored poppies the size of poodles having a bubble-gum-blowing contest.

Maddy sighed and stopped walking. One bare wall ran parallel to the other in both directions until the end of time. Her feet were killing her, and the rumblings of her empty stomach made it hard to think about anything else.

"Where is Leo? How am I supposed to find him in this mess?" Maddy said aloud.

She'd been saying the same thing in her head for such a long time that the next natural step was for the words to blurt out of her mouth.

An arrow appeared in the hallway in front of Maddy's face.

It was a very large arrow, sunshiny yellow in color with ripples of silver that ran along each edge. The arrow pointed straight ahead, which, honestly, wasn't all that helpful since that was the direction Maddy was going anyway. What caught her attention was the wobbly way the arrow hung in the empty space. It reminded Maddy of those times when she held a device for someone else to watch a funny video or see a silly picture. Because Maddy laughed along, the screen shook and distorted the image.

The arrow shook like an invisible dancing gorilla held it up in the air.

"Is someone there?" Maddy slowly reached a hand forward and swiped the air to the left of the arrow. Her hand came in contact with a giant fur ball. For just a moment, a striped tail appeared. It was gone by the time Maddy blinked.

"Hey!" Maddy jumped backward. She was learning caution in this new world. Caution enough to want to put space between herself and whatever creature was attached to that tail until she knew if it was going to mock her, imprison her, or eat her.

All three sounded equally inconvenient.

The arrow wobbled even more, so Maddy took a chance and swiped at the air to the right side this time. Her fingers flowed along the smooth profile of what felt like a stuffed animal. A pointed ear and half a face appeared, then disappeared. It happened so quickly again that Maddy wasn't sure if she'd actually seen anything or was hallucinating from lack of food. It was a partial relief to hear a low chuckle fill the air.

Nice to know she wasn't imagining things.

Not nice to know that whatever it was already thought she was hilarious.

Probably not in a good way.

"Uh, uh, uh," a voice cackled. "Mustn't touch."

"Who are you?" Maddy almost asked 'what' instead of 'who' but changed it at the last minute. "And why are you invisible?"

More giggles, more wobbling arrow. "That is not the right question."

"Which question? I asked two." Maddy squinted, wondering if that would help her see the figure around the arrow better. Maybe it was like those brain teaser pictures; once you knew that the picture was an old lady and a young woman, then it was easier to spot either one. "Are you talking about the 'who are you' question or the 'why are you invisible' question?"

"Either, or neither. One or both." The voice hiccupped.

Maddy's patience was the last bit of jam in the bottom of a jar. She didn't have much left for this business.

"Okay, let's try this question. Am I supposed to follow the arrow? Is that how I get out of this mess?"

"Is it?"

Maddy let out a loud breath. "I don't know, is it? I'm asking you if you know."

"No?"

"No!" Maddy looked down at her feet, trying to steady herself. She didn't know what it meant about her mental state that she was arguing with an invisible voice holding an arrow, but she knew it wasn't anything good. "Look, I just want to find my friend Leo. Is he in the direction of this arrow you're holding?"

"Is he?"

"Is he?"

"He is."

"Wait, he is?" Maddy squelched the hope that bubbled up her throat.

"He is?"

Maddy knew it was too good to be true. "You're just messing with me again, aren't you?"

"Messing, messing. Are you, you are." The voice laughed heartily for a few moments. "Words are fun. Fun are words. Front they go and backward too. Is he, he is. Fun, fun, fun."

Maddy totally and completely disagreed. There was nothing about this conversation that was fun. In fact, whatever the exact opposite of fun was, she felt it from the tips of her head to the crown of her toes.

Wait, what?

That's not what she meant.

The crown of her ears to the tips of her nose.

No, no, no, no! That wasn't it either.

Maddy shook her head as the laughter grew louder.

Suddenly she wished for the silent hallways of endless nothingness. Why did she ever think that was frustrating? Compared to conversing with an invisible, mocking fur ball, that was amazing! Oh, how she longed for those bygone minutes walking and walking with no one laughing at her or wobbling stupid arrows in front of her face.

One just doesn't know how good one has it until it gets worse.

She must really be losing it now that she was drawing wisdom in the language of an octopus statue come to life.

"Okay." Maddy held up her palm in what she hoped was the creature's face. "You have fun with that. I'm going to go find Leo."

Maddy glared at the arrow and tossed her hair over her shoulder. Maybe she was naive in thinking the creature and its confounded arrow would stay where they were while she walked as quickly as she could to the part of this loopy building that was the farthest away from the creature. If she was in her world, it would have been obvious from her social cues that following her would result in a meltdown or a blowup. Everybody knows that you let a person go if they give you an evil glare and stomp away.

Apparently, normal social rules and common courtesy didn't apply in Skurk.

The arrow bobbed in the air next to Maddy's left shoulder. When she sped up, it stayed in the same position.

"Where is Leo?" the voice asked.

Maddy gritted her teeth but stayed silent. There were so many things she could say, and none of them was nice or polite, so she settled with muttering, "I don't know."

"You don't know?"

"No."

"How do you find that which you do not know?"

A flick of electricity wound down Maddy's arm and settled in her fingertips. Now she recognized that as more than a random twitch. It was the precursor to purple lightning that stung whatever it touched. Maddy resisted the urge to blast the creature and its obnoxious arrow out of the air. That would for sure teach it to mess with her, but it would also be really mean.

"I don't know how I find what I don't know. If you're just going to talk circles, I wish you would go away."

"We don't talk circles; we talk words."

"Apparently not," Maddy grumbled.

"Apparently what?"

"What?" Maddy jiggled the tension out of her shoulders. "You know what? No, I'm not playing anymore. You can dork around in the space around me, but as of now, I'm pretending you don't exist. If you're not going to help me, you can leave."

"I'm going to help you."

"Wait." Maddy stopped walking. "Really?"

"That's why I'm here, to help."

"Is that what you've been doing?" Maddy snorted. "You have got to be kidding me."

"Kidding me, kid in knee, kid anemone," the voice sang.

Maddy stared into the shapeless void for a second longer, then started walking again, picking up the pace. Why she even bothered trying to have a real conversation was the real question here. It was clearly incapable of being capable.

"That wasn't the right question," the voice said on her right side.

Maddy shook her head and increased her pace even more.

"To find what you don't know when you want to know it, you must ask the proper question, or you will find what you know you didn't want to know."

"What?" When Maddy blew the word out, a bunch of sparks exploded from her hand.

The voice giggled. "Temper, temper. Temper your temper."

Maddy stopped so abruptly that the arrow stuttered to a stop and swung around to face her. "Either leave or be helpful, all right?"

"All right." The arrow floated upside down, then right side up, but didn't do anything else.

"It is so flipping annoying to talk to something you can't see!" Maddy exploded. "Just show yourself!"

The faded outline of a large, plump shape appeared around the arrow as if someone else, just as invisible, traced the curves with a black pencil. The shape filled in slowly with shadowy stripes and wispy lines of fur. A few moments later, a super furry gray cat with stripes that were so dark gray they looked purple suddenly appeared in the air near Maddy's right elbow. The cat's eyes were yellow, and its mouth stretched to the very edges of its face as if the corners wanted to leap off and go farther.

Maddy sighed.

It was just her luck to run into the Cheshire Cat.

Of all the creatures she could have met up with in Skurk, it had to be the most annoying thing in creation. Maddy had never liked the Cheshire Cat, not even when she was a kid. In fact, she refused to watch *Alice in Wonderland* after that first time because the cat ticked her off with all its meandering and twirling. She donated her copy of the book to the nearest lending library with a silent apology to the poor schmuck who picked it up. There was nothing to like about a creature that twisted everything into confusing knots.

Have an opinion.

Take a side.

Do something other than float there and grin like an ape.

Stupid grin.

"Here, you see. I am me."

"I see." Maddy folded her arms and shifted her weight to one hip. "Now, are you going to tell me what the deal is with the arrow?"

"Does the arrow have a deal?"

Maddy spoke very slowly, pronouncing each word carefully so it would not be misunderstood by accident. It could still be misunderstood on purpose and probably would be, but she realized she had no control over that. "Am I supposed to go in the direction of the arrow?"

"Are you?"

Oh boy.

Maddy took a couple of deep breaths to stop the lightning from shooting out of her fingers and singeing the Cheshire Cat into one of those creepy hairless breeds. She just had to be more direct and simplify the questions. That was the key, right?

She hoped right.

"I want to find Leo. Does the arrow point to Leo?"

"Point to Leo."

"So, it does?"

"It does."

Maddy couldn't tell if the Cheshire Cat was answering her question or parroting all the last words she said like an immature first grader. Whatever. She blew out a long breath. It didn't matter. Her only options were to try and work with the kooky thing or wander these halls until the end of time.

So, obviously, she was going to work with it.

What was the most direct way to find out where Leo was?

Maddy pasted a smile on her face and tried, "Where is Leo?"

The Cheshire Cat went rigid, pointing the arrow straight down the hall in front of them. Maddy started walking, her steps lighter than cotton candy. She couldn't believe something finally worked, but she was so glad it did. This was a much better solution than flambé cat.

She could do this, with small words and short sentences.

After only a few minutes of walking, the hall opened into a four-way intersection. When Maddy stepped into the center of it, the way she came disappeared into a straight wall, making the intersection a T.

"Where is Leo?" Maddy asked the Cheshire Cat.

Again, it went rigid, like someone controlled it with puppet strings, the arrow rotated to the right.

Maddy turned and headed in that direction. This hall was as clear blue as the ocean on a sunny day. The air even felt crisp and salty, like this was a relaxing day at the beach instead of a rescue mission in the hands of the Cheshire Cat. At first, the walls were smooth and flat, but as Maddy walked, she noticed texture pop up. When she ran her hands along the wall, she felt bumps and ridges like a grainy piece of wood. Soon after, the doors appeared.

They were not identical doors like a person would expect to see in a school or doctor's office. Each was a different color; some were twice as tall as Maddy, and others were three times as wide. One looked like it wouldn't have fit a starving mouse, and another must have been made for a moose, complete with antler-shaped wings on either side. After passing over a dozen of these doors, Maddy began to worry.

What if Leo was behind one of the doors?

What if she passed him?

Maddy stopped walking and glanced at the Cheshire Cat, who hovered beside her. Why not? That was what he was there for, wasn't it? "Where is Leo?" she asked.

The arrow continued to point forward.

So Maddy continued walking down the hall. The next step she took, something bothered her, like when she knew she was forgetting something but couldn't remember what it was or what it had to do with. Maddy stopped walking again and looked around to see what had changed. Something was different.

It took a moment, then she heard it, more distinct this time.

Voices.

They were distant, yes, but definitely voices.

Maddy could have kissed the stupid Cheshire Cat. Instead, she picked up her pace, almost running now. The muted, buzzing conversations got louder, like the noise of a classroom before the teacher called everyone to order. There weren't any words clear enough to decipher, but it was beyond encouraging to hear the sounds of people.

"Where is Leo?" she asked the Cheshire Cat again, just in case. She was so close now she didn't want to miss him if the sounds were coming from a door, or if the halls had shifted and she needed to turn around, or if something else entirely unimaginable happened in this impossible place.

The arrow pointed forward.

Maddy passed her first window, and her feet faltered. When she'd arrived at Skurk, all magically bound and ready for a fight, she hadn't noticed the actual world. She stopped now to peer out the window, overcome with curiosity. The sun shone through clouds that moved very quickly like they were jostling for position, each wanting the chance to cover the sun. Because of this, the rays were stilted and jagged, unable to get through all the way.

There was a thicket of trees just beyond the window. It was full of tall, tangly trees with branches that looked like crooked arms and gnarly fingers. Maddy couldn't see beyond the first row of trees because the shadows were so thick they seemed to suck the light out of everything. A crow cawed and erupted from the trees in a flurry along with a bunch of other crows, making what Maddy believed was called a murder.

She shivered.

Rain began to fall, and a streak of lightning lit the darkness, lighting the area enough for her to see a pair of yellow eyes watching from the trees.

So, yeah, not a super chipper place.

Maddy turned around and was relieved that the Cheshire Cat waited patiently, still holding his sign and hovering behind her. It didn't occur to her until this moment that, like everything else in this place, the Cheshire Cat could abandon her before she got to Leo. That wasn't worth window-gazing at a creepy forest and a murder of crows. From now until the moment she stared into Leo's face, she wasn't going to take her eyes off the Cheshire Cat again.

She stepped away from the window and paused as a thought struck her. Why had the Cheshire Cat stayed with her? She hadn't been particularly nice to it. If her mom were here, she would have gone hoarse from yelling, "Maddy, manners!"

"Why are you still here?" Maddy asked, blinking at the Cheshire Cat. It was actually kind of cute, in a weird way. The smile was too big and the ears a little too pointy, but all in all it looked like Izzy's cat Tigger, except gray instead of orange.

The Cheshire Cat blinked its enormous yellow eyes. "You need help."

Yeah, that was obvious. "Yes, but why are you helping me?"

"I am the Cheshire Cat."

That didn't answer Maddy's question, exactly, but she thought she was starting to understand. "So, you help people? Is that your job?"

"I help. I guide."

Maddy scratched her chin as she thought about that. "Do you have to guide people?"

"I choose to guide."

"Why?"

"I like to help."

Maddy wrinkled her nose. "You weren't all that helpful at first."

"Helpful, not helpful. To each his own."

"Do you mean to say that what is helpful to me might not be helpful to someone else and vice versa?"

"As you like it."

That actually made a lot of sense. "So, when I asked if I was supposed to go in the direction of the sign..."

"I am not your oracle; I am your guide."

Okay, yeah, the cat couldn't answer vague questions. So, that meant that a person needed to know what they wanted before the Cheshire Cat could help them.

Fascinating.

"Where is Leo?"

The Cheshire Cat went rigid and pointed down the hall. She looked at its bright, banana eyes and smiled.

"Thank you."

SEVENTEEN
Villains cannot be reformed

The Cheshire Cat led Maddy through the halls just a little farther until they reached a large room bustling with people.

Maddy had to pause and catch her breath for a moment. It felt like she'd been alone in the world for longer than forever, and now there was so much noise! So much going on! It gave her a headache trying to process all the sounds and movements.

She'd sort of forgotten what it was like to be around a lot of people.

It was almost overwhelming.

The Cheshire Cat bobbed ahead of Maddy, weaving through the people until it came to a table. There it stopped and tipped the sign facing downward. That could only mean one thing. Leo was there.

"Excuse me, Madam?"

Maddy didn't want to pull her eyes away from Leo. What if he disappeared like a mirage or something? Whoever was talking to her had already repeated the question and stepped closer. She could sense their presence to her right.

Turning just enough to see the person without losing sight of Leo in her peripheral, Maddy said, "What?"

A stooped man in a black cloak took another step closer. He obviously had no concept of personal space.

Or hygiene.

A rotten smell moved through the air with him. Maddy tried to breathe through her mouth, but then she tasted it too. There was no escape.

He smiled, revealing a handful of graying teeth. "Allow me to introduce myself. My name is Zephyr. I am an Andersen." He paused, as though expecting something. His shoulders straightened slightly as he puffed out his chest.

Maddy had no idea what she was supposed to say to that. Was it some kind of villain custom? Like how people were supposed to kiss the King's ring or something? What did that even mean, that he was an Andersen? She glanced over at Leo. Whew, he was still there. "Okay, um, nice to meet you. I'm trying to get to—"

"Forgive me." He fell into a bow that was so low that Maddy wondered if his nose grazed the floor. "I could not help but notice the draw of your magic."

"I don't have any magic." Impatience made her voice sharp and her memory fuzzy. "I'm just here to...whatever. It was nice to meet you and all, but I have to go." Without giving him a second more of her time, Maddy plunged into the crowd. She wasn't going to take her eyes off Leo's head again until she was right next to him.

"Excuse me. Sorry. Pardon me. Oops!" That last was because she stepped on someone's toes. Or hoof. It was a hoof, actually. So, then, she didn't really need to apologize. The person, or creature, or whatever, probably didn't feel a thing.

Maddy ignored all the weird looks as she elbowed her way through the crowd to the Cheshire Cat.

And Leo.

She could reach out her fingers and touch his shoulder. He was right there.

Maddy's breath caught in her throat as she looked at his tousled brown hair, which still needed a haircut super bad. If he turned around, she'd be able to see his bright blue eyes.

Maddy wanted to throw her arms around him and never let go.

Wait, what?

She tucked her arms into her sides so she didn't do *that* and smiled at the Cheshire Cat. "Thank you. You have been super helpful, but your services are no longer needed."

The Cheshire Cat tipped its head to Maddy, then disappeared. First, the arrow got hazy, then the body faded, then the tail, and last of all, his smile.

Leo looked up at the sound of Maddy's voice. "Maddy!" He stood up so fast that his chair screeched across the floor and flipped onto its back. He threw his arms around her, his words muffled into her hair. "Maddy! What are you doing here?"

Maddy's heart pounded a drum solo in her ears. Could Leo feel it? She pulled away and gripped his forearms, trying not to think about how flushed her face was. "Rescuing you, polpetto. Let's get out of here." She jerked her head toward the entrance she'd just come through.

Thank goodness it was still there.

Maddy didn't know if all the rooms changed the way the hallways had, but she wasn't taking anything for granted. The sooner they got out of this place, the better.

Leo's eyes flickered around the table, then back to Maddy. "I can't just leave. They won't let me. I have to finish the Reformation Program."

"No, you don't." Maddy held out her lanyard so he would see the card. The first apple that marked her task to get into the building was already red. Maddy hadn't noticed that before. The second, to find Leo morphed from lime green to a deep red right before their eyes. "I made a deal. You can come with me right now. Well, as soon as you say you're not a villain."

There was a gasp, followed by low murmuring that swung in an arc around the table. Maddy took her attention from Leo long enough to assess the people around them. There was a girl wearing black-leather everything with short, white hair; a red-headed guy in a tunic; a dark-haired guy with a wicked scar under his eye; a gorgeous blonde girl with a serious pout; and another blond guy wearing a straw hat.

Maddy was sure they were lovely people, but she and Leo had to get out of there. She didn't trust Elle even a tiny little bit—especially after having navigated the halls of this fun house. If they didn't leave now, Maddy had an aching feeling that they might be stuck there forever.

And ever.

After.

"Come on, Leo." Maddy urged him with her eyes. "Let's go."

"I don't know; this seems too easy." Leo looked around the table again, chewing on his lips. "What do you think, guys?"

Maddy blinked. Why was he asking their opinion? She narrowed her eyes and folded her arms tightly against her stomach.

The leather girl sat back with her fingers linked behind her head. "She has a Covenant Card. That's legit, dude."

"A what?" Maddy tore her eyes away from the hoop in the girl's nose to ask Leo.

"A Covenant Card." Leo reached under his shirt and pulled out a lanyard like Maddy's, except his had a 65 percent in large, purple numbers. "But yours looks different. What are those apples and why are they two colors?"

Maddy shrugged, heat creeping up her neck from the stares of the other people at Leo's table. "Elle just told me to enter the building, find you, and prove you aren't a villain. Then we can leave. I found you, so the second apple turned red."

Leo stared at the card. "I don't get it," he mumbled to himself.

"Yeah, how did she get in here, anyway?"

Maddy's eyes swiveled to the straw hat guy. "Through the front door."

Leo sighed. "You better sit down, Maddy. This is going to take a little while to sort through."

Sit down?

Maddy shook her head, causing her hair to brush against her shoulders like a feather duster. "Are you crazy? We have to get out of here, like, now!"

Leo yelled to the nearest table and asked for a chair. No one responded. They didn't even look over.

"Dude." The scar guy flipped his hair off his forehead. "Those are Andersens. They're not gonna talk to you. They're all still butt hurt. Don't bother."

Leo rolled his eyes and gestured towards another table to ask the same question. A guy with ridiculously long hair slid a chair towards them. Leo caught the rails on the back and pushed the chair closer to Maddy. "Sit down."

She really didn't want to. Maddy's skin prickled as she sat primly on the edge of the chair. She wasn't going to be there long enough to get comfortable.

The scar guy smirked.

Maddy looked at him. "What does that mean, when you said that thing about Andersens?"

He tipped his chin down. "What do you mean, what does that mean? They're Andersens. That's it."

"Yeah, but what does that mean?" Maddy spoke slower, emphasizing each word. This guy was clearly not getting it.

Leo held out a hand between them, like tension was something he could karate chop away. "The people at that table are Andersen villains, Maddy." He waved his hand towards the nearest table that hadn't responded when he asked for a chair. "Hans Christian Andersen. From his tales. Everyone else around here hangs out with other people; they don't care if they're from a story or not. But not the Andersen tales. Hunter's right; Andersens stick together. I don't know why I keep trying."

"You're an optimist." The dewy-eyed blonde smiled at Leo in a way that made Maddy want to throw ketchup at her face. "And you never know. Years have passed since that horrid display with their Fairy Teller. Some of them may have a change of heart. In fact, the Snow Queen almost smiled at me yesterday." She moved a glistening lock of hair off her shoulder. "We want to be here for them when they're ready."

Maddy glanced over her shoulder. She didn't want to be there for anybody. She wanted to leave. Right now. With Leo.

The blonde girl switched her dazzling smile from Leo to Maddy and leaned her elbows on the table. "Maddy? Is that right? Such a pretty name! Leo told us a lot about you. I feel like we're already friends. I know this is confusing, and you've obviously been through a lot. Let's go around the table and tell her our names, everyone. I think that will help her feel more comfortable." She placed a graceful hand on her chest. "I'm Gwen."

The leather girl rolled her eyes and cracked a loud bubble. "Saylor."

"Hunter," said the guy with the scar.

The straw hat guy dipped his head. "Tim."

"Camden." The redhead gave a goofy grin.

Gwen clapped her hands. "Oh, good job everyone. Now, Maddy, please tell us how you got here. Leo said you scored very low on the Villainous Test. I thought it was impossible for someone to come to Skurk without a single villainous percentage. I would love to know how you came to be here."

"How do you know about my score?" Maddy looked at Leo.

He shrugged in an oh-so-familiar way that made Maddy wish they were back home watching a random reality TV show and sharing a carton of Rocky Road. A wave of exhaustion washed over Maddy, and her stomach growled.

"Oh, you poor thing! You need some food. Stay right there." Gwen rushed away and actually glided to a series of tables. She was back in a moment with a tray of mashed potatoes, gravy, roast, green beans, and a dinner roll.

Maddy was starving but still worried about that six-months-in-the-underworld story. "Is it safe to eat the food?"

"Course it is." Camden handed Maddy a utensil set wrapped in plastic. "I've been eating it for a hundred years."

"That's reassuring," Saylor smirked.

That's exactly what Maddy was thinking. Was he serious about the hundred years thing? Maddy knew people said stuff like that all the time: this drive is taking forever; I've done this a billion times; I'm starving. Gross exaggerations. Was this one of those cases, or had Camden really been there for a hundred years?

If so, it was totally not reassuring.

"The food is safe," Leo said. "You can eat it."

That was good enough for Maddy.

She unwrapped the utensil set, spread the napkin in her lap, and picked up the fork to dig in. The food was so good and the perfect amount of comforting. Mashed potatoes filled in that hollow place she'd had in her stomach since she realized Leo was missing, and gravy poured over everything else, warming away the chill. Maddy was about halfway done with the tray of food when she realized everyone was sitting there, just watching her eat.

Yeah, that wasn't awkward at all.

Maddy dabbed her face with her napkin and tried to be more conscious about not eating like a pig at a trough. When she was finished and laid the fork on the tray, Gwen clapped again, as if Maddy had done something worth celebrating. She then asked Maddy the same question she had earlier, almost word for word.

Feeling like a ridiculous puppet of déjà vu, Maddy turned to Leo and asked, "How do you know my score?"

"Elle told me when they picked me up. She wanted to know how we could be such good friends when my score was one hundred percent and yours was zero."

"What did you tell her?"

Leo looked at Maddy in a way she didn't recognize. He was Leo; she knew he was. He had all the same mannerisms and the same stupid gorgeous hair, but something was different. Something was off. Maddy couldn't quite put her finger on what it was, and it bothered her a lot.

"I told her opposites attract." The side of his mouth quirked up in a familiar way, settling her mind.

This was just Leo. It was fine. He'd been through stuff, and she'd been through stuff. They'd both practically lived a lifetime since they last saw each other. Maybe more. Maddy didn't actually know how time worked in Skurk.

"Yeah, so, to answer your question," Maddy turned to Gwen, "I made myself look like a villain and broke some rules. I wanted the VDA to pick me up."

Leo snorted. "You broke some rules?" The smile that toyed along his lips was so familiar that it lifted her spirits enough to smile back.

"You wanted to come to Skurk?" Hunter's look was not a compliment.

"Well, yeah. I wanted to save Leo, and this is where he is, so, yeah."

"I love that so much!" Gwen clasped her hands under her chin. "Maybe let us start at the beginning. Is that okay, Maddy? Would you tell us everything that has happened in your world since Leo left? That would be so helpful!"

Maddy nodded. She wasn't quite sure what to think about Gwen. The girl was like the human combination of a puppy and a cheerleader, except that she was so beautiful it hurt Maddy's eyes to look at her straight on. Sort of the way Elle looked, except more solid. Maddy glanced at Leo to see if he was as captivated by Gwen's beauty as he had been by Elle, but he wasn't looking at Gwen.

He was looking at Maddy.

His eyes had this icy intensity that made her cheeks flush.

Not familiar.

To distract herself from Leo, Maddy told the group what had happened from the morning Leo disappeared when she tried to pick Leo up to go to school, to the moment the VDA caught up to her. She left out the stuff Grams had told her, planning on filling Leo in later. She didn't think that was a topic for group sharing. Especially this group.

They were all villains, after all.

"So, that's it." Maddy pressed her palms onto the top of the table and glanced at the entrance to this room. She let out a relieved breath that it looked the same as when she arrived. Nothing had changed yet.

"Yeah," Leo said. "That's not it. I want to hear more about this breaking the rules thing. What did you do? Jaywalk?"

Maddy glared at him and then briefly explained what she'd done.

Leo shook his head while his friends chuckled.

Except for Saylor, who rolled her eyes. "That's, none of that, is all that villainous. You really shouldn't be here. There's something going on."

"You always think there's something going on." Tim nudged her. "Paranoid, much?"

"Oh, Maddy, I'm just so glad you didn't do anything too awful to get here!" Gwen fluttered her luscious eyelashes. "We wouldn't want you to become a real villain!"

"Gasp." Saylor fanned her fingers over her cheeks.

Tim punched her arm this time. "Aw, cut it out, Saylor. Don't tease Gwen."

Gwen just giggled. "Oh, Saylor, you're so silly. Now, Maddy, I'm just confused about one, tiny, baby thing. You said that everyone at school, your friend—uh, Izzy, was it?"

Maddy nodded stiffly.

"You said they all forgot Leo, but you didn't. I don't understand that part. The VDA's Villain Eraser is so thorough. Do you have any ideas why you didn't forget Leo?"

Maddy narrowed her eyes. Did Gwen know Maddy had villain blood? The innocent way she tipped her head and caused her flaxen hair to flow like liquid gold down the side of her arm was almost too much. Maddy was 98 percent certain Gwen was putting on a show, and if that was the case, what for? Was she trying to get Maddy to own it? Was she sizing Maddy up like competition?

Maddy had no idea, but she did know there was no way she could answer Gwen's question. She didn't trust any of them—except Leo of course—enough to tell them that her villain blood made it so the VDA couldn't completely manipulate her memory. Information like that was volatile. They might set Maddy on a throne to idolize her or burn her to a crisp.

Really.

It could go either way.

"I think," Maddy said, slowly, "it's because Leo and I have known each other since we were in kindergarten..."

Half of them gave Maddy blank stares. Only Tim and Camden seemed to understand what she meant.

"Since we were little kids," Maddy clarified. "He's so much a part of my life that they would have to erase all of my memories to get Leo out of them, and if they did that, they might as well erase me too, you know?"

Maddy tensed her shoulders and waited for someone to call bull crap. It was a weak explanation at best. Especially considering she just told everyone that Leo's own mother completely forgot about him. Much to Maddy's surprise, no one questioned her. At least, not out loud. Leo did stare at her for more than a few moments in that dark and brooding way.

Unfamiliar.

"So, about the building." Hunter leaned forward. "You explained how you got to Skurk, but how did you get inside the Reformation building?"

"I told you that already," Maddy said. "I just walked in the front door."

Leo shook his head. "There is no front door, Maddy."

"Okay, then maybe it was a side door. Whatever, it doesn't matter. I came through the door."

"No, no, no, Maddy," Gwen shook her beautiful head. "You don't understand. There are no doors to the building at all."

"What?" Maddy's eyes flicked from each nodding person to the next. "That doesn't make any sense. I definitely came through a door—two of them actually. Big, old, fat doors that were super heavy."

All six heads now shook at different rhythms. They should have coordinated better; the random movement made Maddy's head start pounding again.

"What do you mean, no?" Maddy said sharply. "There has to be a door, at least one. Otherwise, how did you all get in here?"

"We were placed here," Camden explained. "All the villains are placed here after they are taken from their time. It just happens. No one really remembers it exactly."

"That's right," Tim nodded. "I was walking through the forest, then blinked, and I was walking through the halls of this place."

"I went to sleep last night and woke up in the lobby," Leo said.

Maddy remembered that she thought she'd blacked out in the car from school to Skurk. "Did someone explain to you what was happening when you got here? Or were you just left alone to figure it out?"

"Oh, don't you worry," Saylor smirked. "The good guardians of Skurk are more than happy to harp on all the reasons and all the things, over and over. We are all very, very clear on why we're here."

Hunter reached for Maddy's plastic knife and ran it under his fingernails. "This building ain't normal. No one comes in, and no one goes out."

No one goes out?

Maddy's heart rate picked up so fast she thought her heart might actually burst out of her throat. "Elle told me we could leave once Leo proves he's not a villain."

"We can," Leo said. "Hunter was being dramatic. Lots of people leave the building. There are whole colonies of people living out there in Skurk. Normal lives like we do at home. They have kids, they work, they go to school."

"Those are just the saps who give up," Hunter grunted. "Everyone else stays here, trying to get to Eventyr. Trying to change their status until the end of time."

Leo glared at Hunter, who clamped his mouth shut. "Elle doesn't lie. If she told you we can leave, she meant it."

Saylor snorted.

Was Leo just being naive? Were they stuck here forever? Hunter and Saylor certainly didn't seem to agree with him, and even Ms. Perky Gwen had doubt lines marring her perfect features. Maddy rubbed her temples, trying to figure out what to do next. She thought she was being all savvy, asking questions like her dad would have done, but now she realized she had left a bunch of vital information untapped. She was so antsy to save Leo, she'd jumped in too fast.

Too hasty.

Maddy couldn't let herself think about failure. The situation was what it was, and the only way to change it was to complete the tasks and hope Elle wasn't a big fat liar. This had to work because the alternative—spending the rest of forever trapped in a place called Skurk with the memory of her old life erased—was totally unacceptable.

EIGHTEEN

Some villains don't know they are villains

"So," Maddy spoke to her hands. She didn't want to see any discouraging expressions on anyone's face. It was hard enough trying to keep her own inner gremlins from grumbling without doubtful eyebrows confirming her fears. "How would a person go about proving they aren't a villain around here?"

Saylor blew an enormous bubble and cracked it against her teeth, then sucked it back in noisily. "You can't."

Maddy twisted her ring around her finger, still not looking up. Just because Saylor said that didn't mean it was true. She could be wrong, right? Maddy concentrated on butterflies, springtime, and Savannah's chocolate chip cookies.

"Oh, dear, you are discouraging her." Gwen shook her head, her sympathetic voice ringing like wind chimes. "Never fear, Madelena. There's surely a way to prove Leo's not a villain. It's just that no one knows how to do it because no one has ever done it before. But that doesn't mean you can't figure it out!"

Maddy stared at Gwen. She honestly couldn't tell if Gwen was trying to be encouraging or patronizing. Maddy shifted her eyes to Leo. "That sounds like there's no way."

"No, there is a way," Leo said.

"Yeah." Saylor sucked another big bubble back into her mouth. "You just gotta bypass all the crap they tell you when you get here and believe in yourself because you're special, and you deserve this."

"Listen here," Camden smiled. "What they mean to say is it ain't easy. It used to be, before the Andersen takeover—"

"What is that?" Maddy interrupted, her head pounding ferociously. "What is this Andersen thing you guys keep talking about?" Since they kept bringing it up, it had to be important. Maddy didn't like that everyone seemed to know something she didn't. It was giving her serious FOMO.

They all exchanged shifty eye glances. Finally, Gwen spoke. "We don't know the details. It was hushed up. But lots of years back, one of the Fairy Tellers—"

"What's a Fairy Teller?" Maddy rubbed her temples.

"Oh," Gwen giggled, "I'm so sorry. A Fairy Teller is a human who is commissioned from Beschermer—"

"For Ursula's sake, just call her Bea. It makes my ears hurt to hear her full name," Saylor scowled.

Gwen gave Saylor an indulgent smile. "*Bea* gives a commission to certain humans so they can watch over the tales they've written or collected. It's, like, a responsibility and a portion of Bea's magic to help them do their job—at least, that's what I've heard. I also heard that Eventyr is separated into tales, Grimm and Andersen mostly, the way Skurk is separated into villains who reform and villans who accept their status." She waved her hand delicately. "As for the Andersen takeover, the Andersen Fairy Teller, I think his name was HC, manipulated the magic from his commission and took villains from Skurk."

HC? What kind of a name was that?

"How did he do that, exactly? Where did he take them?" Leo leaned forward. So, he hadn't heard this before either? The look on his face was so intense it made Maddy want to pay closer attention to what was going on.

Gwen shrugged. "I don't know any details. I'm sorry. Zephyr might know. I've heard people say he was there."

"I don't want to talk to Zephyr." Leo sat back with a disgusted look on his face.

Maddy knew exactly how that felt. That guy was creepy upon creepy.

"Those Andersens had a hard time coming back, that's for dang sure. Elle don't trust none of them; she only gived them a chance to reform because Bea made her do it, but most of them didn't take it," Camden said. "They stick together in Skurk, and those guys still here, trying to reform..."

He jabbed a thumb at the corner table. "They don't want nothing to do with none of us. It's hard to reform, Maddy, but I gotta believe it can be done. If anyone can do it, Leo can, for sure. He ain't a real villain, and now he's got you here to help him."

Maddy closed her eyes for a long time, overwhelmed with all the things she didn't understand.

Leo nudged her side with his elbow. "Hey, buck up, little soldier. We can figure this out. Let's break it down." He didn't say anything else until Maddy opened her eyes and looked at him. "The VDA designed this place to reform the people they think are villains, right?"

"Sure," Maddy shrugged.

"But some people have been here a really long time, so that means they don't have a lot of confidence that villains can reform enough to leave Skurk."

"Okay?" This was starting to take a downward turn. Maddy didn't need any more reasons why it wasn't going to work. She needed hope that they wouldn't be stuck here forever.

"But we have these trials—they call them classes—we have to complete to prove our humanity."

"Like what?" Maddy leaned forward. "What do you have to do?"

Leo looked at the card on his lanyard. "I went down 5 percent when I picked up a library book that was on the floor."

"They really love their books," Tim nodded.

"That's it?" Maddy straightened. If all they had to do to get his percentage down was pick up books, they could do that right now. Four more books, and Leo would be under 50 percent.

"Hold up." Leo held out a hand. "The same thing never works twice, Maddy. I tried that. The VDA throws challenges at us all day long to measure our strength of character. We never know what counts and what doesn't. But I did discover that we get bonus points if we do something of our own accord, outside of a challenge. I gave someone the last dessert at lunch, just out of common courtesy, you know? Anyway, my percentage went down 10 percent then."

"They also go up," Hunter said, and he launched into a big story about how he tripped someone or something. Maddy wasn't really listening. She was too busy plotting. If a small act of service involving dessert would knock ten points off, how far would Leo go down if he did something really nice and unexpected?

Maddy was willing to bet the VDA would send them home instantly. And she knew just the thing they could do.

"Leo!" Maddy blurted.

Everyone looked at her in surprise. Except for Hunter; his mouth was half open and his eyebrows furrowed, meaning he was probably in the middle of his story and Maddy had interrupted. She was only half sorry. This was super important.

"I know how we can get out of here. When I was wandering the halls looking for you—"

"You wandered the halls?" Leo interrupted. "Wait, you entered the building through a door and wandered the halls? How did you do that?"

Maddy waved her hand impatiently. "You're missing the point. I met a statue of an octopus man who dries up if he doesn't talk. I taught him a story so he could talk to himself and keep the water flowing, but it's going to get old really fast."

Leo shook his head. "You told stories to an octopus statue? Maddy…"

"Stick with me, here. Could we take him some library books? If he could read aloud to himself, he wouldn't get bored of the same old stories as quickly. That would be a huge service that would prove you aren't a villain. And we could go home."

They all stared at Maddy.

"I don't think your friend is who you think she is," Saylor said, sounding so much like the Cheshire Cat that Maddy actually looked over her shoulder to see if it was hovering there.

"That is a most extraordinary story!" Gwen's eyebrows furrowed together, giving her gorgeous wrinkles. "We aren't allowed in the halls without guides. It is a labyrinth, you see, meant to keep us here. People have vanished forever trying to escape through the halls."

Leo's face furrowed. "I don't get how you went through the halls and found me. It's practically impossible that you're here."

"The Cheshire Cat helped me," Maddy said.

Hunter snorted. "The Cheshire Cat doesn't help. The Cheshire Cat is a menace."

"He helped *me*," Maddy said in a small voice.

"Listen." Saylor cracked her gum. "We take classes on how to be model citizens that never actually tell us what to do. Then, we are given trials completely out of the blue. The halls swallow people, and there are creatures that would test the patience of a saint. The point I'm trying to make here is that this Reformation Program is a total bunk. It's impossible. No one reforms. They either give up, accept Villainous Status, and become citizens of Skurk forever, or they stay here hoping to find a way through eventually because they are stupid and optimistic, like Gwen."

"Hurtful," Gwen pouted.

"How long have you been here?" Maddy asked the group in general but looked at Gwen.

"I bin here a hundred years, like I said." Camden tipped his hat. "But Gwen's been here for thousands of years."

Maddy gaped. "What?"

Gwen didn't look a day over seventeen.

But then, Camden didn't look one hundred either.

That was probably the immortal thing at work. It must start the instant a person comes into Skurk.

"Right-o," Camden went on. "She's Guinevere, you know? From the King Arthur tale?"

Maddy's eyes narrowed. Guinevere? That wasn't possible. Maybe this was how villains kept themselves entertained, by messing with people.

Camden smiled. "You know that story? I growed up hearing that story at bedtime. It was a right honor to meet Gwen until I realized they put her here before they had that there Villainous Test. There ain't a way in Twiddly Dumb that Gwen would have ended up here if they had given her a fighting chance. She's the nicest person I ever knowed."

Gwen blushed prettily and ducked her head. But Maddy wasn't so sure. No one was that nice or that perfect, and now that Maddy knew who Gwen really was and what she did, well, no wonder she was stuck in Skurk. Guinevere was the downfall of everything Arthur created. All the peace, prosperity, and unity crumbled because of Guinevere.

And Lancelot.

So, it was good she was here and couldn't leave. Maddy couldn't imagine what horrible things Gwen could and would do to the world if she were free.

"Dear Camden," Gwen said after she had recovered herself. Tears glistened like jewels in the corners of her eyes. "Thank you. You are a true and valiant friend. I must clarify, however; Camden is almost correct. I have lived here not quite two thousand years."

Maddy didn't care if she was two thousand or two million years old. She didn't want to listen to any more of this. She just wanted to get out of there right now.

"And I also must clarify," Gwen continued, "that I did earn my place in this world. I did not live without fault. At the time, I felt I had good reasons for the choices I made, and I know I learned from my mistakes. So, I stay here, and I continue to hope for a way out so that I might prove to myself and others that people can change."

Such pretty words, but Maddy had had enough.

"Leo, let's go."

He looked at her incredulously. "I can't leave, Maddy."

"Yes, you can. We just call the Cheshire Cat to show us the way to the library and then give the octopus statue some books to prove you're not a villain anymore, and then we leave."

"No," he shook his head. "That's not what I mean. I can't just leave my friends. They don't deserve to be here either."

His friends?

His friends!

He'd been in this place with his 'friends' for less than twenty-four hours. He'd known Maddy most of his life. So, what did that make her?

Heat burned up and down Maddy's arms, making the tiny hairs tingle.

"Tim and Camden are just like me," Leo continued. "They thought the test was a joke and answered the questions that way. They don't have any villain DNA at all. The VDA brought them here just because of their test scores."

"Now, don't you get your knickers in a twist," Camden said. "I right think we deserved this fate for not taking the test seriously."

"That's just one of their many tricks." Hunter flicked guck from his nails to the floor. "They want you to think that so you give up."

Leo waved away Hunter's words like they were noxious fumes. "The point is, I can't just leave them behind, Maddy. They aren't villains."

"What about the rest of them?" Maddy asked, sarcasm tinting the edges of her words as she pointed around the crowded room. "Are they all innocent too?"

Leo clamped his mouth shut and stared at Maddy with an unreadable expression.

"Not everyone deserves to be here." Gwen shook her beautiful head. "Hunter's fate is like unto mine."

By that, did she mean Hunter was wrongly accused? Because that sounded like denial to Maddy.

"And who are you supposed to be?" Maddy folded her arms.

Hunter shook his head. "I'm not going there."

He acted like a modern tough guy, like someone Maddy might see at school coloring his shoes with a Sharpie or driving too fast through the parking lot. He'd strut down the halls with his super coolness, looking down on everyone around him.

Saylor covered the side of her mouth and leaned forward. "He's the Huntsman from Snow White."

Hunter chucked the plastic knife at Saylor, which she dodged with a grin. The percentage on Hunter's card went up 5 percent.

"But he's not a villain either. He let Snow White go," Leo insisted.

Hunter glowered at them all. "You're just thinking about one part of one little story, smart guy. Do you want to hear the other stories? I have many from my years and years of serving the Evil Queen, and you can bet your baby blues they aren't heroic."

Maddy had always wondered about that. The Huntsman's part in the story was small, but in that short piece, he saved Snow White's life. He seemed villainous but acted with kindness; although, it never said what happened after he went back to the Queen. Whatever kindness made him let Snow White go obviously wasn't enough to cancel out the other evil things he did.

Maddy scooted away from him as discreetly as she could; he didn't notice. Hunter got all broody and stared into the dramatic mid-distance as though the rest of the people at the table no longer existed.

He probably let Snow White go because she paid him.

Leo caught Maddy's eye. His face was wrinkled into a thousand lines. Unfamiliar lines.

He opened his mouth to say something, but Maddy interrupted.

She didn't want to hear whatever was on his mind.

"I suppose you're misunderstood too?" Maddy said to Saylor, who was still gloating at Hunter. "Wrongfully accused? Don't deserve to be here?"

Saylor snorted. "Heck no. I deserve to be here. I'm 60 percent villain, most of it pure Sea Witch DNA, thank you, thank you. And that's not even talking about my actions. Try to withhold your jealousy."

"The Sea Witch?" Maddy's lips curled. "Like, Ursula?"

"No, not like Ursula," Saylor said in a mocking tone. "Ursula is a Disney brainchild. My great-whatever grammsie-poo was the actual Sea Witch. She stole the mermaid's voice and gave her legs so she could try and get that brainless male mortal to notice her. But Grammy-kins tricked the little idiot, and she would have turned to dust except Bea rescued her at the last minute so she could go to Eventyr." Saylor said the word like she was spitting out a mouthful of dog doo. "Happily freaking ever after."

"But"—Maddy's forehead wrinkled as she considered this new information—"I was told all the tales have a basis in truth. See, the Beast was actually just a really beastly human being. There's no such thing as mermaids and sea witches, so that story can't be real."

"How do you know?" Saylor raised an eyebrow. "Just because you don't see those things doesn't mean they aren't there."

Maddy shook her head; she refused to talk about it anymore. It was time for her and Leo to leave this place. She tugged on his sleeve and, when he looked at her, she gestured toward the doorway out of the noisy room with a toss of her head.

Maddy stood up and pushed her chair away from the table. "Well, thanks for lunch. It was nice to meet you all and all, but we have to be going."

"Maddy." Leo looked up at her with drawn eyebrows. "Were you listening to anything I said?"

"Yes," she said defensively.

"Are you sure? Because if you were listening, you would have heard the part where I said I'm not leaving without these guys. It's not fair that I get out while they are stuck here forever. I'd feel like garbage if I just ditched them."

Maddy nodded in her most understanding way. "Can I talk to you privately?"

Maybe if she could get him away from the others, he would be more reasonable.

Leo stood up very, very slowly. "We'll be right back," he said.

"Byeeeee." Maddy waved with her fingers and grabbed Leo's arm to pull him through the crowd. He didn't move out of her grip, but his arm felt like an oversized noodle, all limp and useless. Maddy maneuvered around tables and groups of people, accidently bumping that Zephyr guy with her elbow on their way to the hallway just outside the room.

Maddy dropped Leo's arm, and it flopped back down to his side. "Look, this hallway didn't change. It's exactly the same as it was when I came here. We'll just call the Cheshire Cat and get this show on the road."

"Maddy," Leo said.

She flipped her hand in the air. "Cheshire Cat, where is the library?"

While she waited for the Cheshire Cat to appear, Maddy tried to ignore Leo. He kept staring at her in that weird way. And Maddy suddenly wondered if he was measuring all the ways she had changed the way she was measuring him.

That was not a comfortable thought.

And it was also ridiculous. Maddy hadn't changed. She was the same person as always, except with super greasy hair. Maddy ran her fingers through it and cringed. Yeah, the first thing she was going to do when they got home was take a shower. It was really starting to get to her.

"Cheshire Cat!"

Leo sighed heavily.

"What?" Maddy glared at him.

"Maddy, I'm not sure how to make you hear these words."

"I heard everything you said," she snapped.

"Okay," he rubbed his eyes. "And yet, here we are. Even if that cat shows up, I'm not going anywhere. It wouldn't be right."

"Whatever." Maddy turned to call the Cheshire Cat again. Even with her back turned, she could feel Leo's disappointment seeping through the back of her head.

"Why do you keep looking at me like that?" Maddy said evenly, trying not to sound as frustrated as she felt.

"Like what?"

Maddy faced him. "Like you don't know me."

"Is that what I'm doing?" Leo's eyes were guarded.

"Where is that stupid Cat? It said it liked to guide, and here we are in need of a guide. Idiot!"

"There," Leo said.

Maddy looked over her shoulder. "What? Where? I don't see the cat."

"That's not what I meant," Leo said. "I've been trying to figure out what's different about you, and that's it. What you did just now."

"What? Look over my shoulder? That's what's different about me?"

No." Leo shook his head.

Maddy had seen the same look on his face when he challenged himself to eat a dozen glazed donuts then had to throw them all up ten minutes later. "That snarkiness and sarcasm you've got going on. That is not the Maddy I know."

"I'm the same, Leo. You're the one who's different."

He grabbed Maddy's hand. "Look at me."

She shook him off and stared down the hall. Where was that blasted Cheshire Cat?

"Maddy?" He gripped her hand again and pulled her gently. Maddy finally turned to face him, but she lolled her head to the side in a lazy way.

"What happened to you?" His voice was small.

"I told you everything I did until I found you," Maddy said, trying to shake him off again. "I don't get you right now."

"That's not what I meant." Leo kept a firm grip on her hand. "There's something else. Like, your skin; it's hot to the touch."

Maddy yanked her hand away, leaving sparks in the air between them.

Leo yelped and drew his hand back, shaking it. "Galloping ravioli, Maddy! You just shot sparks out of your fingers!"

"I did not." If Maddy pretended it didn't happen, she was pretty sure that would make it true. "Cheshire Cat! Library!" She couldn't think of how to be more direct than that.

Leo stepped in front of Maddy, so she turned around. But he was fast and turned with her.

"Stop messing around, Leo. I need to find that cat so we can get out of here."

"Maddy." The change in his voice made her stop and look at him.

"What?"

"Why did you come to Skurk?"

She'd already told him that. How many times did she have to repeat the same things over and over before he got it?

"Do you remember?" he asked, watching her carefully.

That was a stupid question. Clearly, she'd come to Skurk to…

To…

Maddy looked at Leo again, trying to read his face.

"Who am I?" Leo asked in a small voice.

"You're Leo, you nerd bomber. Did you forget your name?"

Some of the heaviness lifted from his features. "And why are you here?"

"To get you home, duh. Why do you keep asking me weird questions?"

Leo took both of Maddy's hands in his, and she suddenly found it extremely hard to breathe. "And why did you want me to come home?"

Maddy blinked. That was another stupid question. He was her best friend. Didn't he know that?

He lifted their hands close to her face and stroked her cheek with his finger. "Did you miss me?"

"It's only been, like, a day." Maddy's words came out in halting bursts.

Leo leaned forward so their noses were almost touching. "Why did you come here for me, Maddy?"

Her breath turned ragged as she tried to think. Leo was standing so close. Every time he exhaled, Maddy breathed in the smell that was just so Leo. Something sweet and tangy, like the marinara sauce his mom made. His eyes were as deep as the ocean, and Maddy felt herself falling into them while her thoughts flew around like the crows that she'd seen from the window earlier.

The window.

Maddy gasped and pulled away from Leo, looking all around the hall.

There was no window.

Maddy walked to the wall across from them and ran her hand over the space where the window should have been.

So, they weren't in the same place. This wasn't the same hall she'd taken to get to the cafeteria.

Maddy whipped around and placed her hands on her hips. She's had quite enough of this garbage. "Forget that stupid cat. We're going to find the way out of here by ourselves."

Leo's shoulders sagged. "And how are we going to do that? You can't get through the halls without a guide."

"Don't tell me what I can't do." Maddy narrowed her eyes. Pent-up energy scored through her body like adrenaline. She flexed her hand and watched the purple sparks gather like a tornado in her palm.

"Maddy, I'm going back in there." Leo jabbed his thumb toward the cafeteria. "I meant it when I said I don't want to leave without my friends. We've been talking about options, and I think we've almost got a plan that will work. Come with me?"

Maddy shook her head. The whole point of this whole stupid thing was for him to come with her. "Elle and I made a deal."

"Yeah, but it doesn't include everyone."

"So?" Maddy narrowed her eyes. "You'd rather stay here with people you barely know than come home with me. Is that what you're saying?"

Leo's mouth drooped. "I'm not so sure I know you very well at the moment."

Maddy flung her hand, and sparks sizzled into the wall. "I can't believe you're choosing them over me. Those people are villains, Leo. Do you realize that?"

Leo stared at the wall for a moment, even though the sparks hadn't left any kind of mark. "Not everyone here is a villain."

"Yes, they are." A breeze whipped around Maddy's shoulders, lifting her hair. She looked around for the source, an open door or window, and was astonished to discover the wind was coming from her hands. Maddy lifted them to her face and watched another tornado form in her empty palm. Maddy closed her hands tightly to contain the energy until she was ready to use it. "That's why they are here."

"Am I a villain?"

Maddy rolled her eyes. "No, you're an idiot. You had to go and be all clever, and look where it got us. Super fun, huh?"

Leo stared at Maddy. "Thank you for coming for me. I'm going to go back to my friends."

"*I'm* your friend."

"Are you?"

"Yes." Maddy reached for his hand, her palms tingling. She wasn't sure how this was going to work, but she knew it would. Leo met her halfway, his palm sliding into place against hers.

Maddy closed her eyes and unleashed all the energy she held back. It erupted like a hurricane, blowing their hair and clothes around. Leo opened his mouth and yelled something she couldn't hear over the rush and pounding. Maddy gripped Leo as hard as she could and concentrated on home.

Hey, it worked for Dorothy.

She pictured her white house with the gray stone halfway up the siding. The front yard with xeriscaping because Arizona didn't have enough water for both plants and people. She focused her memories on the glistening swimming pool in the backyard. When the picture was formed in her mind, when it was so clear she could have reached out to touch it, Maddy opened her eyes and shouted.

"Home!"

Then the roaring got louder and all that surrounded them was black.

NINETEEN
You say villain like it's a bad thing

I t worked.

Whatever it was and whatever Maddy did, it totally worked.

She knew before she opened her eyes that they were home. She could smell that distinct home smell. Her dad's sweaty running shoes, her mom's fruity perfume, laundry soap, and cinnamon air freshener. Never again would she take those things for granted.

Maddy was so happy to be home that she almost kissed the carpet.

Leo groaned, and Maddy opened her eyes to make sure he was okay. He lay on his back with one arm thrown over his eyes.

"Are you hurt? Did you land funny?" She stretched her leg to prod him with her shoe.

He scooted away from Maddy, just out of reach, and groaned again. "I feel like I've been hit by a truck."

Maddy wiggled her fingers and toes, checking for stiffness or injury. She felt totally fine. "Can you move?"

"No."

Yeah, Maddy was pretty sure he was faking it. "Well, you better buck up, buttercup. Who knows what will happen if my parents or Grams come in here and find you groaning on the floor."

"What do you mean?" Leo peeked an eye open and shot into a sitting position. "Fat olives! We're at your house! How did we get here?"

Maddy flexed her tingling fingers. There was so much built-up energy that she still felt it surging up and down her arm, but in a faint way, almost like an afterthought. "I think I brought us here."

"How?" Leo looked at Maddy for the first time since they left Skurk. "Why did you do that?"

"What do you mean, why? You didn't really want to stay there?"

He drew his legs to his chest and wrapped his arms around them. "No, but—"

"Leo!" Maddy jumped to her feet and patted her clothes for her phone. "We have to call your mom to see if she remembers you. Do you have a cell phone? I think mine is still with all my stuff at school. Never mind, I'll get the landline." Maddy's parents still kept one for emergencies, but she'd never used it before. Maddy ran down the hall, peeking through doors as she went to see if anyone was around.

The house seemed so empty.

Maddy snatched the cordless phone from the base and raced back to the living room. She slid into the space next to Leo and dropped the phone on his shoes. "Call your mom."

Leo moved slowly but didn't argue. He pushed talk, punched in seven numbers, and held the phone up to his ear.

"Hello?" He glanced at Maddy. "Hey, Mom? How's it going?"

She could hear the chatter of talking on the other line, though she couldn't make out any distinct words.

"No, it's Leo." His voice was strained.

More chatter.

"Your son?"

Wait, what? That wasn't supposed to happen. Maddy brought Leo back; now everyone should know him again.

"You know what? I think I have the wrong number. Sorry to bother you." Leo turned the phone off and let it drop to the floor. "She doesn't know who I am. Maddy, I knew this wasn't going to work. You should have let me stay there and finish the reforming thing. It was our best option."

"No, it wasn't," Maddy snapped. "I don't trust Elle or the VDA. I don't think they would have let you go. The halls were different, and the Cheshire Cat wasn't coming. I had to do something—"

"How did you do that?"

"—to bring you home, and I did, so why do you care?"

Leo pushed his hair out of his eyes. "That's a very nice 'why' answer. Now tell me *how*."

Obviously, he wasn't going to let the subject go. His face was firm, the same way it was a few months ago when Maddy ended up sitting on the freezing bleachers at a hockey game with him, eating super-hot Takis.

Her taste buds were messed up for a week after that.

"Does it matter how we got home? Isn't it enough that we're here?"

Leo shook his head. "What's the point of being here? My mom doesn't know who I am, Maddy. I don't exist in this world anymore."

Maddy refused to let that be true. "I bet she was just distracted. I'm sure she remembers who you are."

"Uh, no. There's distracted and there's what-the-heck-are-you-talking-about? She said she didn't have a son named Leo. It was definitely the second one."

Maddy looked down at her hands and saw purple sparks swirling in her palm.

That was new.

Not that she'd spent a ton of time analyzing it—she'd been sort of occupied with the whole rescuing Leo thing—but she thought the power was some kind of weird byproduct of being in Skurk, like it activated the villain in her blood and gave her a little something extra. But what did it mean that she still had power in her world? Could she make things happen here? Could she override that VDA and make Leo exist again?

Maddy sat up straight and flung her fist into the air. "Restore the memory of Leo Romano to this world." She opened her palm to unleash the beast. Sparks grew into jagged lines like purple lightning that shot to the ceiling. The house shook for a moment, then settled and was still.

"What the heck was that?" Leo's hands were pressed flat into the floor like he was trying to anchor himself somewhere. "What did you do? Who *are* you?"

Maddy ignored his questions and pushed the phone back to him with the toe of my shoe. "Call your mom now."

"I'm not doing that again." He watched Maddy warily. "It was bad enough the first time."

"Fine." Maddy picked up the phone. "I'll do it." She punched the numbers in and waited.

"Hello?" Leo's mom answered quickly, like she'd been waiting for this phone call.

"Hey, Adele! It's Maddy. Can I talk to Leo?"

"Maddy! Bimba! I thought he was at your house already."

Maddy almost giggled, and then stopped herself just in time. Out of context, spontaneous giggling might sound a little crazy. "Oh, he is, but he wanted to talk to you. He couldn't dial because his hands were messy, so hold on."

The lies came so easy it was almost scary. Maddy held the phone out to Leo, who took it like it was a creepy bug.

"Hello? Yeah, I was going to ask you if you remember me. I mean, if you remember that I'm eating dinner at the Huttons' house. Yeah. Okay, sounds good. See you, then. Love you." Leo handed Maddy the phone. "Good news. My mom says I can stay for dinner." His face did not look like he thought this was actually good news.

"Congratulations." Maddy hung up the phone. "You exist. You're welcome!"

Leo stared at the phone for a minute, then looked at Maddy. "What is going on with you, Maddy?"

"What do you mean?"

He raised an eyebrow. "You know how long I've known you?"

"Duh, forever."

"Then that was a stupid question. You know what I mean."

Maddy leaned against the couch and spread her legs out straight in front of her. It looked like they were doing this, so she might as well get comfortable. "So, funny story. I think going to Skurk gave me superpowers. Also, my Grams is one hundred percent villain by blood, so that quarter villain in me wasn't a typo. I guess it, like, woke up when I went to Skurk 'cause now I can do this." Maddy shot her hand in the air and turned the lights on and off and on and off and on.

Just because she could.

"Maddy..."

Maddy's hand dropped to her side. "What's your problem? Lighten up. This is super cool." Maddy flicked her finger, and Leo spun in a circle on his bottom.

He scrambled to his feet. "Don't do that again!"

Maddy looked up at him lazily. "Why not?"

Leo didn't answer; he just jammed his hands into his armpits and hugged his arms close.

"Come on, Leo," Maddy said in a wheedling tone as she laced her fingers behind her head. "Think about it this way: no one can mess with us anymore. If the VDA came back and stalked us in their stupid car, I'd just..." She swung her arm and made the couch across the room move against the wall. "Did you see that? That's awesome! Right?"

He still didn't answer. Instead, he stared at his feet.

"Leo?" A surge of anger flicked down Maddy's arm. She clenched her fist to keep it contained. "What is your problem? Why are you all doomsday? We can have so much fun with this!"

He slowly raised his head and looked at her. His face was drawn into jagged lines that made him look like an old, wrinkly man. "I don't even know who you are anymore, Maddy."

Another surge ran down Maddy's other arm. She clenched both fists and kept them rigid at her sides while she stood to face him. "Yeah? Well, I'm not the only one who is different around here. The Leo I know would think this is the greatest. He would already be planning the pranks we can pull and the people we can annoy with my Jedi mind powers."

His face fell, his eyes drooping. "If you think that, then you don't really know me either."

"Whatever!" Maddy pressed her fists into her legs. "Remember the Villainous Test? You were the one who was all, 'this is such a joke. I put curses on babies'! Where's that Leo?"

His eyebrows drew a thick line above his eyes. "You're right. I should have taken that test more seriously. I realize that now. Even if I thought it was all a joke, I shouldn't have made light of it the way I did. And maybe that means I've changed, or at least, I've learned. But it doesn't mean I'm a different person than I was before I took that test. Just, hopefully, a wiser one."

He was fooling himself if he really thought that. He had changed. Not only was he less fun and super lame, but he kept looking at Maddy with that judgy face. And she thought she might know why.

"You like Gwen, don't you?"

"What?" Leo blinked. "What are you talking about?"

"You like Gwen. That's what this is all about. That's why you didn't want to leave without them, and that's why you're acting this way about being home. You want to be back there with her and the rest of those villains." Maddy's arms trembled from the effort of holding the lightning contained in her palms. "Which is pretty ungrateful, don't you think?"

"They aren't villains!" Leo snapped, then took a deep breath. "I'm sorry, I shouldn't have yelled. But you're missing the point, Maddy. Those guys in the reform school are just people. They aren't villains. They are normal, flawed, imperfect people who did stupid or thoughtless things. Sometimes on purpose and sometimes by accident. Just like you and me."

"I am not like that!" Maddy hissed.

"No?" Leo's lips turned up into a smile. "You never, ever make mistakes or do anything wrong?"

Maddy tossed her head. "Well, yeah, I do. I have good reasons for what I do."

"And you don't think they do? Don't you think everyone else in the world has good reasons for what they do? I bet they could give you a novel justifying their actions. Anybody could." Leo sighed. "You're my friend, Maddy. They are my friends. What you did for me, that's what I was doing for them. I think they deserve a chance, is all. A chance to prove they don't belong in Skurk. I care about all of them and want them to be free. Do you get that?"

Maddy wasn't going to be drawn into a circular tangent. Leo was the master of those. "Do you know what I went through to rescue you? Do you have any idea how hard that was? It would have been a billion times easier to leave you there and forget about you like everyone else did. But I didn't do that, did I?"

"No, you didn't forget me, but you never saw me either." Leo's voice was so heavy that it pulled his shoulders forward.

"What are you talking about? I see you all the time. I see you right now. That doesn't make any sense, Leo."

"You're wearing your birthday necklace," Leo said softly.

The change in subject threw Maddy off for a moment. She reached up and gripped the pendant. "Yeah, so?"

"I gave you that necklace, Maddy."

"No, you didn.'t. It was from Izzy."

Leo shook his head. "I gave it to Izzy to give to you for your birthday. I chickened out. I wanted you to have it but didn't want to give it to you."

Talking to him right now was like deciphering a complicated riddle. "What?"

"Maddy." He extended his hand, then seemed to think again and lowered it to his side. "I've been in love with you since the third grade."

She scoffed before his words had a chance to fade. "No, you haven't."

Leo shoved his hands in his pockets. "That's exactly what I mean. You don't see it."

"That's because it's ridiculous. You don't feel that way about me! We're like brother and sister."

"To you."

"To you too, idiot!" Maddy folded her shaking arms into her chest. "What do you call all those pranks and teasing me all the time and acting like a moron?"

Leo tipped his head to the side. "Flirting."

No.

Maddy refused to believe that what Leo did was flirting.

It couldn't be.

In the movies, flirting was cute and fun. The guy adored the girl and showed it in cute little ways that had all the girls in the audience melting into puddles of goo and all the guys vomiting into their popcorn cups. Leo was never like that. He never looked at Maddy like she hung the moon or whatever.

Well, except for maybe at the football game...

Maddy shook herself. She couldn't get distracted. Whatever happened at the football game was not the issue. Right now, the issue was that her *supposed* best friend was a complete alien.

"Maddy," Leo said, letting out a long breath, "I don't want to fight with you. I do appreciate what you did for me, but you gotta see that this is way bigger, right? The way people are held in the Reformation Program, the fact that you walked right in and have powers now—the whole stupid thing is so much bigger than us. Instead of fighting, let's figure this out together, okay? We have at least one whole brain between the two of us." His wavering smile almost worked. It was almost like none of this other stuff had ever happened when he looked at Maddy that way.

Almost.

But it was too late to forget all that other stuff now.

He took a step forward, his eyes pleading. "Let's find Grams, maybe bring Elle here, and talk with all of them. There's a lot going on that needs to be sorted out."

"I'm not bringing Elle here." Maddy pressed her lips into a straight line. "That woman is pure evil."

Leo stopped moving. "Elle's a villain now? My friends are villains. Is everyone a villain to you?"

Maybe.

Maybe they all were.

"Maddy," Leo shuffled backward, his face a mask. "Have you thought that maybe *you* are the villain?"

"I am not!" Maddy shrieked. "How dare you say that to me? I rescued you from Skurk I am the exact opposite of a villain, the least villainous of all the villains. If you knew me at all, you would know that. Maybe you aren't my friend!"

Leo's eyes flashed. "Maybe I'm not. My best friend is Maddy Hutton, the girl who woke up at three in the morning to paint Mrs. Erbe's house as a surprise. I'm friends with the Maddy who loves people and is friends with everyone. The Maddy I love is not the version I'm looking at right now. I want that Maddy back. When you find her, you come see me." He turned and stalked to the door.

"Don't you turn your back on me, Leo!" Maddy shot her arms toward him and opened her palms. She forgot about all the pent-up energy she had been holding on to until it whooshed out of her hands and hit Leo in the small of the back, knocking him onto his knees. A deep purple shadow encompassed his whole body so that Maddy couldn't even see his outline in the mist.

Maddy shook her hands out; they felt so much better now that all that pressure was gone. She walked to where Leo knelt and waited for the purple haze to clear so she could tell him she forgave him for being a jerk. They would be able to talk much more rationally now that all that power was out of her body.

Except that when the fog finally cleared, Leo was gone.

"Leo?" Maddy waved her hands in the air where his body should have been. "Leo? Where are you? This isn't funny. Come out." A movement caught her eye, and she jerked her head toward the wall where a lizard ran along the baseboards.

Maddy crawled over to the wall and cupped her hand around the thing. It squirmed against her skin, its four blue legs flailing.

It wasn't a lizard; its head was the wrong shape.

It was a newt.

A newt with skin the color of Leo's eyes and black spots that looked like scoops of ice cream.

Maddy shut her eyes and squeezed them. She already knew it was pointless. The newt was still there, writhing inside her hands. She could feel the tiny poke of its fingers looking for a way out.

It was real.

Maddy opened her eyes and tried to smile. "Hi, Leo."

She had just turned her best friend into a newt.

We need villains so we have someone to blame when things go wrong

Maddy's heart bubbled into her throat as she stared at Leo, who was squirming around in her hand.

She couldn't believe it.

She had actually shot lightning out of her fingertips and changed Leo into a newt.

Not that she was happy about the newt part—obviously that was a mistake—but she couldn't deny it felt pretty awesome to know she had the power to change people. If she could change people, she could change things. And with that kind of power, she could do anything! Rearrange the house into a castle. Modify Phoenix until it became Hawaii.

Wait...

Could she stop time? How powerful was she exactly?

Maddy's mind whirled with the possibilities.

"Quit freaking out," she said to Leo. The way his slimy limbs rubbed against her fingers was kind of giving her the heebie-jeebies. "I'll change you back, just give me a minute." Maddy focused her attention inward to the core of her body where the energy had converged before it shot to her fingertips. There weren't any of the mysterious tingles anymore, just surges of excitement as she contemplated all the things she could do.

The power didn't feel accessible like it had a few minutes ago. Did she have to be angry for it to work?

Maddy carried Leo into the kitchen and searched the cupboards for something Leo could chill in while she figured out what to do next. He almost escaped a few times because he was so slippery, and she only held him with one hand while she opened the cupboards with the other. To keep him from splatting on the tile, Maddy had to grip him tight enough that his eyeballs bulged.

It wasn't a big deal. He could still breathe. He was fine.

Maddy finally found something in the back of the cupboard where Mom put steel bowls and glass baking dishes: a tall bowl with a convenient little stand that looked like it was used for fancy desserts. The sides were high enough that Leo wouldn't be able to slip over them, and the glass made it easy for Maddy to keep an eye on him. Maddy carried the bowl with one hand and Leo with the other.

"Don't squirm," she scolded him.

Maddy set the bowl in the sink, then she put a splash of water into the bowl. She gently lowered Leo into the bowl. "How's that? Not too cold?"

Leo eyed the puddle for a minute, then dipped his toe in. The rest of his body followed, leaving Maddy to conclude that the water was good. She filled his bowl a little more with enough water to cover the bottom, but not cover him all the way. She had a vague memory from, like, middle school biology or something that amphibians needed to stay wet but didn't have to be submerged all the time. Maddy hoped she remembered that right, for Leo's sake.

With him splashing around in his temporary home, Maddy was free to concentrate on how she was going to turn him back into a human.

The phone rang in the other room, interrupting her thoughts.

"Stay where you are." Maddy pointed a finger at Leo, then went into the living room to retrieve the phone. "Hello?"

"Maddy?" Her mom's voice came through the line. "Why aren't you answering your phone?"

"Oh, um…" Maddy was caught off guard. Her mom's voice was completely normal as if nothing had happened. Like, for example, Maddy leaving the house dressed like a vampire movie extra and disappearing for hours to Skurk. Didn't her mom remember any of that? She couldn't, or she wouldn't be shooting the breeze about Maddy's phone. Instead, she'd be telling Maddy off for going after Leo.

"I left it at school," Maddy said finally.

"Maddy, Maddy," her mom laughed. "What am I going to do with you?"

That was a question Maddy didn't know how to answer.

"Anyway, Dad has to work late tonight, so Grams and I are bringing home pizza. Does Leo want to stay for dinner?"

Did newts eat pizza?

"How did you know Leo was here?"

Mom laughed again, a high, tinkling sound. "Leo's always there. But, also, you told me he was coming over to do homework this afternoon."

"Right." Maddy was one hundred percent sure she hadn't said anything close to that. Apparently, when one plays with memories, one opens a can of worms. "Yeah, Leo will probably want dinner. Thanks."

"We'll be home in about twenty." Her mom called goodbye cheerily and hung up the phone.

Maddy pressed the button to end the call and set the phone on the counter. "All right, bucko. Turn back into a boy," she commanded, pointing her finger at Leo.

It didn't work.

She didn't really expect it to work, but it was still a letdown when it didn't.

"How do people undo curses in movies?" Maddy asked Leo. "I can't remember, and you can't talk. Oh, wait!" Maddy ran to the other room and took a huge volume of all the fairy tales off the shelf. It was an ancient book with hand-tipped drawings that Maddy wasn't usually allowed to touch. She figured this was an emergency and so normal rules didn't apply.

Maddy carried the book to the kitchen and plopped it in front of Leo's bowl. "Let's see what the fairy tales have to say about curses." She opened a page at random and skimmed the story. "Kissing: true love's kiss will undo a curse." Maddy looked at Leo's squished, slimy face with his wet mouth and eyes that were way too far apart. Yeah, that was so not happening. There had to be another solution. Maddy went back to the book and skimmed through a half dozen more stories.

"Oh, hey! In *The Frog Prince*, she actually throws him against the wall to break the curse."

Leo looked, shrinking as far away from Maddy as he could get.

"Relax, you big baby. I'm not going to do that." Maddy shook her head and turned the page, but part of her wondered if it would work.

After skimming for a few more minutes without finding anything, Maddy closed the book with a huffy breath. "Kissing or throwing you against the wall; those are our options? Pathetic!" Maddy pulled a bar stool to the counter and relaxed into it. "Looks like we're going to have to wait for Grams. Grams will know what to do."

That is, assuming Grams remembered that she told Maddy about the villain blood thing. Maddy wasn't sure how far her magic blow-up went into the past or how much it messed with everyone's minds.

Maddy watched Leo roll around in the water as though he didn't have a care in the world. Leaving him as a newt wasn't an option, but he looked so happy that the thought crossed her mind more than once. Life wouldn't be so bad as someone's pet. You just did what you liked, and someone fed you, cleaned up after you, and took total care of you.

That sounded like a pretty good deal to Maddy.

Leo noticed Maddy watching him and clumsily walked to the edge of the bowl closest to her ginormous face. He placed a hand or paw, or whatever it was called, on the glass in front of Maddy's eye and left a slimy streak down the side.

Gross.

Okay, it was probably better for Leo to be a human than a newt.

The door opened, and happy chatter seeped into the room. Grams entered first, carrying a grocery bag that totally better have ice cream inside, and her mom followed with the pizza. The tangy smell of tomatoes and cheese was like flipping a switch on Maddy's hunger cues. Her mouth started salivating, her stomach growled, and her fingers itched to snatch the whole box out of her mom's hand and devour the entire thing.

"Hello, my Madelena!" Grams smiled all the way to her eyes.

Maddy glanced at Leo, saw that he was fine, and went to Grams for a hug. The scent of mint filled the air.

"Where's Leo?" Mom set the box on the table and looked around the room.

Maddy braced herself for the moment her mom saw the newt that was Leo. It was a good thing too, because her mom shrieked and backed into a chair, knocking it to the ground with a bang. She lifted a shaking finger and pointed at the bowl. "What the heck is that thing doing in my bowl?"

What would happen if Maddy pretended not to see anything? A smile tickled the corner of her mouth as she contemplated the chaos.

"Maddy?" Her mom's voice snapped Maddy out of her revelry. "Explanation."

"Um..." Maddy glanced at Grams, wondering again what they remembered about the last few days. "Would you believe that's Leo?"

Maddy's mom's mouth dropped into a perfect O shape.

Grams peered at Maddy. "Oh, dear. Perhaps we should sit down." She pulled a chair out for Maddy's mom and gestured for Maddy to join them. "Bring Leo here, please."

Maddy's mom's eyes widened, and she leaned toward Grams. In her agitation, she didn't keep her voice low enough to keep Maddy from hearing every word. "You don't really think that thing is Leo, do you? It can't be."

Grams didn't answer. Maddy double-checked to make sure Grams wasn't mouthing a response or using sign language or something behind her back. Then, she carefully picked up Leo's bowl and hugged it to her chest. She took short, shuffling steps to keep the water from sloshing out, then set Leo in the center of the table.

"How did this happen, Madelena?" Grams's mouth pressed into a straight line without even the slightest hint of a smile. This made Grams look super severe; Maddy had never seen her without that twinkle in her eyes.

The phone rang before Maddy had a chance to open her mouth. They all looked at each other for a moment, then Maddy realized Grams didn't have a cell phone and hers was still somewhere at school. Her mom realized this at the same time and left the table to retrieve her phone from her purse.

"Hello? Oh, hey, hon. Yep, just a sec." She covered the phone with her hand. "It's Dad. I need to talk to him. You two go ahead. You can fill me in later."

Grams nodded and Maddy gave a thumbs up. Her mom went back to the phone, talking as she left the room.

When Grams fixed her eyes on Maddy, they looked velvety purple instead of dark blue. Maddy squirmed in her seat. The force of that gaze made Maddy feel like Grams was downloading all the thoughts, mistakes, and embarrassing moments directly from her brain.

"Please, tell me what has happened, dearie," Grams said.

Maddy bit her lip. "What do you remember about the last few days?"

"What an interesting question." Grams crossed her arms on the table. "It sounds like what I remember and what has happened might not align."

"Yeah," Maddy twirled a piece of hair around her finger. "So, maybe that might be true. I need to know what you remember, so I know what to tell you."

Grams tapped a finger against the tabletop. "Assume I know everything."

"Okay," Maddy nodded. If she assumed Grams knew everything, then she didn't have to admit to anything. It seemed like a good deal to her. "So, Leo got erased, right, 'cause he didn't take the Villainous Test seriously. Then I went to save him, and I brought him back. The end." Maddy raised her eyebrows, wondering if Grams would let her get away with that.

Grams's eyebrows arched to the top of her forehead.

Yeah, Maddy didn't think Grams would be satisfied with that. But she didn't want to incriminate herself more than she had to, so she pasted a complacent look on her face and stared at Grams without blinking.

Blinking was sus.

After a long time of fidgeting silence on Maddy's part, Grams said, "You brought Leo back from Skurk?"

"Yes."

"How ever did you manage that?"

Maddy looked at the ceiling to escape Grams's eyes. They were piercing and uncomfortable. "Um, with my mind powers."

"Pardon?"

Maddy sighed. "I don't know how I did it. We were arguing in the hall at Skurk, then we were lying on the floor in the living room."

"That is all?"

No, that wasn't all. Maddy traced a circle on the table. "Um, so, I felt all this energy build up, and I exploded it into getting us home."

Grams leaned back in her chair. "Has anything like this ever happened to you before?"

Maddy shook her head, then realized that wasn't exactly true. The energy thing happened in Elle's office and in Skurk, she'd just been so focused on finding Leo she hadn't stopped to figure out when it was or what it meant. Grams's eyes never left Maddy's face while she waited for an answer. Maddy could tell Grams knew she wasn't sharing everything, but still, she didn't elaborate.

Grams sighed. "When did you first feel this power, or energy, start to build?"

Maddy felt like she was in a police interrogation room with a spotlight over her head, like she'd done something wrong. Irritation sizzled from her shoulder to her elbow. "I guess I first noticed it when I was looking for Leo." Maddy paused as another memory replaced that one. "No, actually, I was talking to Elle in the library room, and I felt the tingle in my fingertips. Also, I might have shot some sparks into the air."

"So, then, Elle knows." Grams sat back.

If Elle didn't know before, she for sure did now. Maddy couldn't imagine that her big tornado in Skurk went undetected. "Probably."

"I see." Grams's face fell into exaggerated lines, making her look so much older.

"Did I do something naughty?" Maddy quirked a smile.

Grams looked at Maddy sharply. "I know you had the best intentions, but I wish you had talked to me and your parents before you took matters into your own hands."

Maddy shrugged. If she asked the grown-ups for help, they would have told her to wait while they talked it through for a billion years. What a waste of time. It was better that Maddy did what she did.

Well, except for the newt thing.

"Can you fix Leo, Grams?"

"That remains to be seen." Grams's eyes shifted to the bowl where Leo sat perfectly still, watching them. "Tell me how Leo came to be this way."

Maddy let out a breath of air. "He was mad that I rescued him, and we got in a fight."

"Why was he mad?"

"Because he had a plan or something with his stupid villain friends." A flicker ignited in Maddy's belly. "A plan that wasn't going to work. And when I, his real friend, actually did rescue him, he was all offended." The flicker turned into a flame that swirled around and around, picking up momentum as Maddy thought about Leo's stupid, stubborn plan. "He didn't even say thank you."

"Maddy..."

Maddy took a deep breath, and the swirling settled into a breeze, the type that ruffled leaves along the sidewalk. "Anyways, I got mad and turned him into a newt."

Grams' eyes flew open. "You did this?"

"Not on purpose!" Maddy defended herself. "And anyway, he was being such a jerk. If you could have heard him, you would totally agree. I bet you would have done the same thing if you had powers. He was a cretin about the whole thing."

"Your power did this?" Grams gestured to Leo in his bowl.

The side of Maddy's mouth twitched into a smile. She pressed her lips together tight to hide it when she noticed Grams watching her. "Yeah, I mean, I guess. Anyway, can you change him back?"

"You want me to change him back?" Grams said, annunciating each word. "How do you suggest I do that?"

Maddy faltered. "I thought you could talk to Elle or Bea or someone with powers, and they could help us out. I tried to do it, but I think I can only use my powers when I'm angry."

Leo stood on his back two legs, his front hands pressed against the glass. His head swiveled from Grams to Maddy, which made her wonder how much he understood. Did he know they were talking about him?

Grams removed her glasses and rubbed her eyes. "If you were angry enough to turn Leo into a newt, I wonder why you want to turn him back."

"I'm not angry anymore," Maddy said impatiently. "And, yes, he's a twit, but he's Leo. I mean, he's my best friend. I can't just leave him like this."

"Can you not?"

Maddy wrinkled her nose and tipped her head to the side. "Do you think we should keep Leo a newt?"

"No, I do not think that."

"Then why do you keep asking me all these weird questions?"

Grams looked at Maddy, her eyes sagging in the corners. "I am trying to determine where your heart is, dearie. I hear that you were angry enough to turn him into a newt, but you love him enough to want him to come back. Which is more? The anger or the love?"

Maddy balked at the word 'love'; it seared her ears like a blow horn and made the hairs on her arms stand straight up. "I don't know." Maddy rubbed her arms until the hairs quit tingling.

Grams laid her hands one on top of the other and rested her chin on the back of her hand. "You do not know?"

"No, okay?" Maddy snapped. "I don't know. Leo makes me crazy, but he's my friend. So maybe I want him back to normal and maybe I don't."

"You feel both?"

Grams's question startled Maddy enough to push her back in the chair.

She wanted both.

Yes and no.

It wasn't so long ago that Maddy shouted to Leo that it couldn't be both. It had to be one or the other.

Had she...changed, then?

Maddy's stomach flipped over at the thought, draining all the confidence she felt previously until there was only an inkling left. Was she wrong?

Was she the villain?

Grams sat across the table with an irritating knowing look, like she knew exactly what was going on inside Maddy's head. Each flick of her eyes made Maddy feel smaller and smaller until she was afraid she would disappear.

Maddy sat up straighter, looking for that power or energy or lightning or whatever to draw upon to bring back some of her self-assurance. She hated this feeling of nothingness.

"Maddy?" Grams said gently.

Maddy met Grams's eyes and felt that flick in her belly. Grams shouldn't be sitting there all judgy, making Maddy feel worthless. It was her job to help Maddy figure things out. It was just stupid that they were talking about Maddy's powers when Leo was still a newt. Grams completely missed the point.

"I want him back to normal," Maddy said in a low voice.

Grams waved her hand over Leo's bowl. "Then *you* must change him back."

Maddy made a noise somewhere between a scoff and a snort. "Are you serious?"

"Yes."

Maddy sat up straighter. "Didn't you hear me say that I tried? It didn't work. What do you expect me to do?"

"Nothing," Grams said.

"Nothing?" Maddy blinked. "Do you mean that I can't change Leo back or that this newt thing will wear off eventually and I don't need to do anything?"

It had to be the second one. Maddy was pretty sure she could do anything with her power—she felt how strong it was. She just didn't know how to use it. Why wasn't Grams explaining that?

"Maddy," Grams reached out a hand. "Take a look at your heart. It has grown so cold."

What was she talking about? There was nothing wrong with Maddy's heart. Just because she got a little angry and turned her best friend into a newt didn't mean her heart was hard. People got mad all the time; everybody did. Leo threw a ginormous baby fit that time his video game glitched on the boss level. He threw a controller at the wall and left a dent. Getting mad and doing stupid things was what humans did. So, why were

Grams and Leo so convinced there was something wrong with Maddy? There wasn't. She was the same person she'd always been.

They were so frustrating.

A few purple sparks shot out of Maddy's palm. She closed her hand around them, but not fast enough to hide them from Grams.

"Maddy?"

"What?"

"You are not yourself. Surely, you must see this."

Maddy placed her hand under the table and opened her fingers halfway to release some of the energy. It was a lot stronger than it had been before, and it almost burned her palm the more she tried to contain it. The table rattled, swishing the water in Leo's bowl up the side.

"There's nothing different about me." Maddy narrowed her eyes. "You're the one who keeps accusing me of whatever. All I want you to do is change Leo back into a human. Is that so much to ask?"

Grams tried to touch Maddy's arm, but Maddy jerked it out of reach.

"Even if I had the power," Grams said, looking at her hands, "I would not use it to help you. This is a mistake you must fix, or you will truly be lost forever."

What the heck did that mean?

"So, you're refusing to help Leo?" Maddy's voice was low and icy enough to produce goosebumps on her arms.

No." Grams shook her head. "I refuse to help you."

Maddy slapped her hand on the table, causing it to quake. Grams grabbed Leo's bowl before it toppled over. Maddy always suspected that Grams cared more about Leo than she did about her own granddaughter.

There was proof.

Maddy lurched to her feet. "This is so unfair! You should help me! I thought you loved me!"

Grams looked up with sorrow in her eyes. "I do love you, Madelena. It is because I love you that I cannot fix this for you."

"What kind of crap is that?" Maddy's vision swam so that three Grams sat at the table, each clutching a trifle bowl with a newt quivering inside. "You have to help me."

"I do not."

"You have to." Maddy's words came in a visible gust that fogged the side of Leo's bowl.

Grams did not flinch. "I will not."

"Yes, you will!" Maddy pushed her hands toward Grams.

The energy flew at Grams, who sat calmly, looking at Maddy instead of the cloud of purple lightning headed her way. It should have smacked her right in the torso, but when it made contact, the energy bounced off Grams, creating a ring of light that was so bright Maddy lifted both arms to shield her face. The cloud of energy flew back toward Maddy, hitting her square in the chest, where it vibrated.

Maddy's body shook like she was stuck inside a salad spinner. She tried to gather the energy so she could push it back out, but it swirled so fast she couldn't grasp it. Somehow, when it backed off from Grams, it went rogue. Maddy couldn't do anything to stop it.

Was it possible for people to spontaneously combust?

That was the last thought she had before she completely blacked out.

TWENTY

There is a little bit of beast inside each of us

When Maddy opened her eyes, the kitchen was gone. No table, no chairs, no counters, sink, or refrigerator. No Leo in his glass bowl. The sun shown in her eyes with relentless focus, stinging her eyes enough to produce tears. Maddy lifted her arms to cover her face and screamed.

These were not her arms.

Instead, they were big, hairy logs of muscle with hands that ended in claws.

And that was not her voice.

Her lovely soprano was replaced by a deep baritone that rattled her eardrums. It was like strep throat times a billion.

Her stomach, her legs, her feet!

Not hers.

Not hers.

Not hers!

Maddy closed her eyes and squeezed them as tightly as she could, hoping that that simple action would clear away whatever this nonsense was.

"You are not dreaming." A musical voice reached Maddy like tires squealing. It was so beautiful, it rankled enough to make her teeth grind.

"What is going on?" Maddy growled.

She cleared her throat and tried again. "What happened?"

That didn't make any difference at all. She still heard that nasty growl, a deep, guttural, animistic sound that was apparently coming out of her mouth.

"Open your eyes," the voice instructed.

Maddy didn't want to. Opening her eyes was so final. She couldn't pretend everything was fine if she was forced to see the opposite for herself.

221

The more she tried to resist the urge to open her eyes, the stronger the urge became. She didn't seem to have a choice anymore as her eyelashes fluttered open, and she was stuck staring at bright nothingness. It took a few minutes for her vision to adjust so that she could make out recognizable shapes in her surroundings. A tree here, a flower there. A big thing of water.

Water, that was weird.

There was no concrete, palm trees, or rush hour traffic.

Okay, she was obviously not in Phoenix anymore.

Maddy lay in a grassy glen next to a dark, shimmering lake. Surrounding her on all sides was a forest of tall, creepy trees like those she saw through the window of the Reformation Building. The branches reached out like gnarly fingers that couldn't wait to get a piece of her. Maddy used her crooked, hairy legs to push herself away from the trees, and she landed on something wet and sticky.

It was mud.

Of course.

"It will take you a moment to adjust to your new body." The voice spoke again, drawing Maddy's eyes away from the alien scenery to a woman. She was tall and lithe and wore a glittering white gown that fell to the ground but didn't pick up a speck of dirt. Her blonde, wavy hair flowed around her like a cape, moving even though there was no breeze. Around her neck was the necklace Izzy—no, Leo—gave her for her birthday, except it looked different. Maddy squinted, but she couldn't make out more than an amber colored blob.

Apparently, her new creature body was near-sighted.

Lovely.

"What the heck happened to me?" Maddy grumbled. "Did you do this?" She pointed a finger at the woman, then got distracted from what she was saying. Her hands were exactly the same as the paws of Leo's dog. Maddy held them close to her pathetic eyes and poked the pad of each one. The inside skin was leathery and tough while the outside was covered in thick, dark fur. The claws protruding from each 'finger' were long and sharp, curling around the pads of Maddy's hands and almost touching the leathery skin.

"I did not."

Maddy looked up because she seriously forgot the woman was there. And also, what they were talking about. "You didn't what?"

The woman smiled, setting off a chorus of birds in the nearby branches. "I did not do this to you."

Oh yeah, that's what they were talking about.

"Then who did?" Maddy demanded.

"You did."

That was so ridiculous. Maddy tried to scoff, but it came out as a growling, snorting sound that was loud enough to make an entire flock of chirping birds find a new roosting place. "Whatever, I did not! What kind of moron would turn themselves into a—" Maddy looked at her hulking body. "What would you call this, exactly?"

The woman's face was so horribly beautiful it made Maddy's eyes water. "A beast."

"I am not a beast!" Maddy spat, drool hanging from the corner of her mouth in a string long enough to touch the ground. "That's ridiculous."

The woman extended her arm to the lake. "See for yourself."

Maddy rolled her eyes and sat still, her back straight. She wanted to go look in the lake but not because the woman told her to. After a moment, Maddy sniffed. "I'm thirsty."

"Of course you are," the woman said. "Drink all you like. This water will never run dry."

Maddy gave her a suspicious look, then flopped onto her belly and army-crawled to the lake. She wasn't sure she could walk on those crooked legs, and she wasn't about to try it out for the first time with the woman looking all perfect and judgy. It was hard enough to get her unwieldy new limbs to work together enough to crawl. When she reached the bank of the lake, she was totally out of breath and sweating in places she didn't want to think about.

Maddy stuck her face over the water and waited for the ripples from tiny, darting fish to clear so she could see.

Okay, maybe she was a beast.

It was hard to live in denial with the evidence staring right at her.

Where her cute human face used to be was a hairy mass of dark brown fur that extinguished her pixie features. All that she could make out from the matted mess were beady black eyes and a large wet nose. Oh, yeah, and the two twisted horns that stuck to each side of her head. Those were kind of hard to ignore. Maddy touched them gingerly, running her fingers to the very tips. It seemed from the look of them that the horns would be rough and gritty, but they were as smooth as the inside of a seashell.

She had horns.

When Maddy was younger, she thought being a unicorn would be the coolest.

This was a tremendous letdown.

Maddy flopped onto her bottom in the mud and hunched over so far that her nose almost touched the water. It was quite easy to hunch. This beast's body seemed to be made for it with its hulking, heavy shoulders and massive, fat head. Maddy would probably never learn to walk correctly; her top part was so much bigger than her bottom part that she would always be fighting against her center mass to keep her balance.

It suddenly made a ton of sense why most animals walk on all fours.

"Madelena."

Maddy didn't answer. She was too busy cradling her huge face in her weird hands and trying not to cry.

Beasts didn't cry.

"Madelena, look at me."

Just like when she tried to keep her eyes closed, Maddy didn't seem to have the option to continue staring at the ground. Her neck muscles contracted to raise her head before the words left the woman's mouth. Totally against her will. Totally unfair.

Maddy shielded her eyes with a paw because the woman's brightness made Maddy slightly nauseous.

"I'm a beast," Maddy sniffed.

"In a way." The woman sat in the mud next to Maddy without a bit of it sullying her white silkiness. She seemed to hover in the air millimeters from the guck and grime. "You have become one."

In a way.

It sure looked like more than 'in a way' to Maddy. From pointy top to furry bottom was beast and more beast. Maddy had a great imagination, but there was no way she could pretend she was something different like a butterfly or, perhaps, human again.

"How did this happen?" Maddy asked. She knew the woman already said Maddy did this to herself, but she didn't want to believe that was true. "How did I turn into a beast?"

"How does one ever become a beast?" the woman said, bringing to Maddy's mind the same obnoxious clarity that the statue of the octopus man used. Or in other words, no clarity.

Answering questions with questions was her new pet peeve.

"One small choice at a time," the woman went on. "Your outside only reflects what you have become on the inside."

Hold the phone.

Was the woman saying she was a beast on the inside too?

What the heck?

If that were true, she wouldn't have tried to save Leo; she wouldn't have cared.

Also, she wouldn't have tried to fix the whole newt thing.

She wasn't a beast.

She wasn't!

"Even if that were true," Maddy said, silently adding 'which it's not,' "that I have been a beast on the inside, why did I just now become one on the outside?"

"I imagine," the woman said gently, "that your body could no longer maintain your outward appearance when your choices were creating something so opposite."

Ah-ha! Maddy knew this was rubbish! If what the woman said was true, then dudes like Napoleon and Ghengis Khan would have looked like big, ugly hyena creatures because of the choices they made. That wasn't how it worked. Bad people still looked human.

The woman seemed to know what Maddy was thinking. She put a soft hand on Maddy's furry forearm. "Not everyone has the chance to see what they are becoming before it is too late for them to change. You are lucky."

Lucky?

Lucky, her big, hairy butt.

Maddy scowled and moved her arm away from the woman's touch. "You didn't really answer my question."

"What were you doing before you woke up as a beast?" The woman folded her hands in her lap. "What do you last remember?"

That was easy.

Maddy was trying to get Grams to stop talking in riddles and help her turn Leo into a human again. In fact, now that she thought about it, this conversation with the woman mirrored her conversation with Grams. Lots of questions, lots of randomness. No action and no answers. Maddy plucked a long piece of grass and flicked it into the water. "I was arguing with my Grams."

"And then?"

And then, well, then Maddy shot Grams with purple lightning.

That's what happened.

Something that felt a lot like shame crept up Maddy's curved back and burned the base of her neck. She didn't want to tell the woman about that. Though, she had a sinking feeling the woman already knew.

"Then, I, uh, shot purple sparks at her."

The woman nodded, the sun glinting off her hair like streams of gold. "You used your power to attack someone you love, in anger."

It sounded so bad when she said it that way.

"That is why you are a beast. You used your power against its nature."

Power had a nature now?

"All power in this world is born from light and goodness, especially the magic that sustains Eventyr and Skurk," the woman explained. "It cannot abide evil intentions."

Maddy grunted. "Villains have power."

"Some do."

"And they do not use their powers for light and selflessness."

"Some don't."

"So, then what you said about all power isn't true."

"Villains do not use their power for good," the woman said sadly. "The moment one uses the power gifted to them in anger or malice, it leaves a mark on their soul." The woman waved a hand over Maddy's big, hairy, smelly self. "People may not always be able to see it on the outside, but power used this way has great cost."

"Fabulous." Maddy spit out a bristly strand of hair. Even without a breeze, all that thick fur kept finding its way into her mouth. Any second now she'd be hunched over, hawking up a hairball on the woman's dress like Savannah's cat, Tootsie Roll. "So, my power turned me into a beast. That's what you're saying?" Maddy waited for the woman to nod, then spun a sausage finger in the air. "Yippee."

"This beast form is merely the personification of your choices. It reflects the process you became when you began caring more for yourself than for others."

Maddy let her finger drop to the ground, where it sank entirely into the mud before she had a chance to blink. "Yeah, you keep poking at that. Was I really so bad? I ate my vegetables and loved my family and rescued Leo. How does that make me a beast?"

The woman didn't answer; she looked out over the lake. When Maddy followed her gaze, she saw scenes from the past few days floating on the water like a movie screen.

The high school vice principal climbed a ladder that was held steady by two janitors to hang webs over the trophy cases. Then she arranged the gross, gooey spiders. It took her forever to do it; she kept moving the spiders and then squinting at them critically. Like it mattered. The scene didn't speed up, so for almost an hour, Maddy watched the vice principal climb up and down the ladder, spread the cotton web, and move spiders around.

Then, the scene flipped to Maddy, with greasy hair and a sharpie skull on her shirt, throwing soda cans at the spiders to knock them to the ground. One of the soda cans got stuck in the web when the spider fell, and Maddy cheered. Then she gathered all the spiders and stuck them in the toilets, around door handles, and on the spouts of drinking fountains.

The scene flipped again, and Maddy watched girls run screaming out of the bathroom, and a janitor spent way longer than was comfortable trying to unravel one of the drinking fountain spiders without cutting off the legs with his knife. She saw the vice principal standing under the ripped webs, soda cans at her feet, staring sorrowfully at the gaping holes.

The scenes flipped quicker now: a small freshman explaining to a stern teacher what happened to her math book; a girl laughing with her friends until she put her hand on the spider-covered doorknob to the theater; a frustrated student council member ripping down all the posters Maddy defaced; another janitor picking up the trash that people had strewn down the halls from the garbage can Maddy knocked over.

She tried to ignore each and every one of the twinges she felt as she watched people deal with the consequences of her actions. "Okay, so, what I did wasn't exactly nice, but it's not the worst thing ever either. No one really got hurt. For sure no one died."

The woman pressed her lips together in an expression that reminded Maddy of someone, though she couldn't quite put her finger on it.

Probably because she didn't have fingers anymore.

"The road to villainy must start somewhere," the woman said simply.

Maddy turned back to the lake and saw Leo sitting at the table in Skurk with Hunter, Gwen, Saylor, Tim, and Camden. They all leaned forward, talking with their hands, their mouths moving quickly. Maddy watched Gwen put her hand on Leo's arm, and instead of feeling that raging jealousy that fueled their flight back home, she noticed something else: Gwen's eyes were as wide and innocent as a Disney princess trapped in a tower.

All traces of comparison and competition melted away like a tub of ice cream left on the counter all night. Maddy recognized that look on Gwen's face because she'd felt the same expression on her own face. Gwen's eyes were full of longing. She wanted to believe whatever it was that Leo said; she wanted it to be possible. That was not the face of a dastardly villain that couldn't wait to break out and wreak more havoc. That was the face of a girl who knew she made mistakes and wanted to believe she could rise above them.

Maddy's heart ached inside her nasty, beastly body.

She hadn't given Gwen a chance to be a different person than she'd been in the past. She hadn't heard any of Leo's friends out. She'd never asked Leo what his plan was to free them all from Skurk. She'd been so focused on getting the two of them out of there that she hadn't listened to a thing he said.

Maddy watched the rest of the scene play out with Leo trying to get Maddy to listen: Maddy's eyes shifting to the exit more than they shifted to any of the people at the table; Leo following her reluctantly to the hall; the dark swirl of magic; the landing in the living room; their fight and Leo shrinking, shrinking, shrinking into a newt.

The next scene started with Grams in the kitchen, but Maddy couldn't see it anymore. Water—okay fine, they were tears—blurred her vision so that Grams and herself disappeared into wavering lines of color. Maddy's shame climbed higher and grew hotter as she watched Grams trying to reason with her, Leo cowering in his bowl, the table shaking, and Mom on the phone in the other room stopping to listen. By then it was too late. Maddy struck her beloved Grams, and the scene disappeared. In its place were water and lily pads, thin aquatic vines, and small fish that moved in sporadic patterns through the reeds.

Maddy watched it all without seeing. Her attention drew inward and focused on her heart.

Now she understood what Grams meant. In place of a beating, fleshy organ, Maddy saw a heart chipped from granite. It weighed so heavily in her chest. She lifted one hand to clutch it. Though she felt the beats against her palm, she saw with her mind's eye the hardened, cold lump.

The woman was right about her. Actually, the woman was right about all of it.

Maddy had done this to herself because all she cared about was herself.

Okay, so...maybe she was a little bit of a beast.

Dang it.

TWENTY-ONE

Sometimes a villain is a princess who hasn't been rescued yet

The anger Maddy had felt for way longer than she was ready to admit finally dissolved, leaving behind a nasty, stagnant pool of regret. "So that's it, then. I'm, like, a nasty beast for eternity?"

The woman tutted gently. "That is not how the story goes."

"Wait, what?" Maddy looked up, hope lifting her shoulders at least two inches. "Do you mean I can fix this? What do I have to do to fix this?"

"You know this tale," the woman smiled. "You tell me."

The only tale Maddy could think of with a person that was turned into a beast was, well, duh, *Beauty and the Beast*. So, if this tale was like *Beauty and the Beast*, Maddy was in luck. Not only had she just seen the Broadway play with Leo—so it was super fresh in her mind—but she also happened to know this tale from the inside out and upside down. "So, I need to, like, find someone to prove they love me even though I look like this? Is that right? So, true love's kiss?"

The woman smiled her serene smile and intertwined her hands inside the bell sleeves of her gown so that they were now invisible. Her head bobbed forward once, though she didn't say a word.

Maddy took that as a yes.

"Great," Maddy pursed her lips together. Which, incidentally, made her fangs protrude in a quite ferocious way. "Perfect. That's fantastic." She looked around the deserted glen. Now that the birds had fled, it was eerily silent. Her eyes settled on the woman, who watched the clouds with a half-smile. "So, uh, how do you feel about beasts?"

The woman's eyes flicked from the sky to Maddy's face. "I do have a bit of a soft spot for creatures such as yourself."

Maddy nodded. That didn't sound like the kind of love that would break her curse. A soft spot didn't sound the same as love at all, more like interest or curiosity.

The woman confirmed Maddy's thoughts. "I cannot break this curse for you."

"Yeah," Maddy nodded. "I know. So, I just need to find someone to love me like that. Right?"

The woman smiled.

"Perfect." Maddy set her mouth into a thin line. "I'm going to be a beast for eternity."

"You do not have much faith in finding true love?" the woman asked.

That wasn't true. Maddy absolutely believed in love. She even believed in true love. And she definitely knew it existed. Her parents were proof of that if nothing else. They were the opposite of each other in every way, and they loved each other fiercely. Maddy believed it was out there; she just hadn't ever experienced it for herself, so she didn't have much faith in true love finding *her*.

Her cheeks warmed up as she remembered Leo's words right after they got back from Skurk. 'I've loved you since the third grade.' Had he meant that? It was Leo, after all. He could have been messing around.

Maddy shook her huge, hairy head.

No.

Leo was a goof, a total goof. It drove her crazy most of the time, but it also made it really easy to determine when he was joking and when he was serious. There was nothing in the memory of his stiff shoulders and tight face that was farcical. She knew Leo meant what he said.

So, maybe Leo loved her with *that* kind of love, but Leo was now a newt.

Plus, she was the one who turned him into one, so there was that.

She didn't know the exact percentages, but she was confident the chances of him overlooking what she had done and still loving her enough to kiss her weren't looking good.

Regret tugged her stomach towards her toes. What would have happened if she'd let everything else go in that moment and focused on Leo? What if she'd given herself a chance to process his words and consider what she felt in return? She'd never done that. When he told her how he felt, she completely blew him off. And now she would probably never know the answers to her questions.

"How's Leo?" Maddy ran her finger through the mud, making deep gouges with her claw that traced the shape of the letter L. "Do you know? I mean, can you check on him? I didn't really get a chance to turn him into a human again before I went kablooey all over the kitchen."

The woman's tinkling laugh made the hair on the back of Maddy's neck stand up. It was clear this body didn't appreciate the woman's pure goodness. The body of the beast was repelled by anything lovely, but Maddy's spirits were soothed, which gave her hope that she wasn't rotten all the way to the core.

"Leo is well."

"Is he...still a newt?"

"He is."

Wait, so, how was he well?

Maybe what she meant was that he was alive, which was better than destroyed. So Maddy supposed that would qualify as well.

In a weird way.

Wait a second!

"How am I supposed make this right with Leo when I'm here, like this, I mean?" Maddy did a quick scan of her insides to look for the ball of energy, but she couldn't find it. Her powers were gone, or dormant, or something.

It made sense, really. It wouldn't be fair if this beast's body also came with the powers to change back into a human. That would sort of defeat the purpose. "And how is he supposed to change me into a human again if he's a newt?"

You know, assuming he was willing to.

"Oh, Madelena. You will find a way."

Maddy peered at the woman, searching her features for something recognizable. "Do I know you?"

"You do not recognize me?" Her words disappeared into a laugh like wind chimes.

Maddy looked closer, trying to find something around the mouth or the eyes that wasrecognizable. For a moment, Maddy thought the woman's nose was familiar, or maybe her left ear lobe, a little bit.

Maddy shrugged. "I have no idea who you are. Who are you?"

"My name is Agathe." She spread her arms wide.

Maddy nodded. "That's the same name as my Grams. Are you a relative or something?"

That didn't seem likely. That wasn't the type of detail most people kept hidden, like the crazy uncle who sold antiquated toys on eBay or the eccentric aunt with five hundred ceramic cats. A fairy queen would be something to brag about.

"You don't look anything like my Grams, though." Maddy's throat ran raw from the effort it took to talk. She wished there was a Handels nearby with a soothing strawberry milkshake.

"By now, I would think you have learned that the outside does not determine the inside, just as the inside does not determine the outside. There is more to someone than what you see and more than you know."

The woman was as bad as the Cheshire Cat.

Maddy sighed, suddenly exhausted. "Can you just tell me what you're trying to say without all the randomness?"

Agathe clicked her tongue and shook her head, her hair glittering like fireworks as it fell across her shoulders. "This will not do, Madelena. Look closer."

Maddy took a deep breath like she was asked to remove one of her muscled limbs, and turned her ginormous body to face Agathe. Maddy squinted into her beauteous face and tried to see what wasn't there.

'Cause that wasn't impossible or anything.

As she looked, Agathe's face slowly drew wrinkles around the mouth and forehead. Her features grew, especially her nose and ears. Her long, wavy hair was cropped into a gray bob.

Maddy almost fell into the lake.

"Grams?" she whispered. "Is that you?"

"Now, you see." Grams smiled, a dimple appearing on her left cheek as her face morphed back into the beautiful Agathe.

Maddy waved a hand in front of Grams's face, wondering if it would change between old and young. Grams stayed young and breathtaking no matter which direction Maddy's hand went. After several minutes, Grams took Maddy's hand to get her to stop.

That was fair.

The smell every time Maddy lifted her arms was worse than a freshly road-killed skunk. She had heard that a skunk couldn't smell its own scent, but she was beginning to think that was a made-up thing, like the boogeyman. It was just an old wives' tale or urban legend to keep life interesting, and Maddy knew it because she was keenly aware that the smells wafting from her body were killing the grass where she sat.

"I will explain." Grams ran her hands over the top of Maddy's hand like she was petting a purse dog. "Remember when I told you about my villainous past?"

"Do *you* remember that day?" Maddy still wasn't sure if or how much she had changed the course of time with her little Skurk trick.

"Of course, I do. Magic knows magic, Maddy. I can sense and see what you do, just as you can sense and see what I do. When things change, magic leaves a mark, a wisp of what was real, of what could be. I can see the difference, as can you."

"No, I can't." Maddy had no idea what she was talking about. Wisps and marks sounded like insects, not magic.

Grams patted Maddy's hand. "You can. You have yet to learn how."

"Okay," Maddy was willing to take her word for it. "So, what about that day?"

"I did not tell you all." Grams paused, her perfect forehead wrinkling into very humanly worrying lines. "I did not tell you why I went to Skurk. I did not tell you who I am."

Maddy felt a shiver run through her body. "Who are you?"

"I am..." She seemed unable to get the words out. "I am the aunt of the Beast from your favorite tale, *Beauty and the Beast*."

The words sunk in but didn't make any sense. "How can that be? That story has to be a billion years old, and you're my Grams."

"Yes," she smiled. "I am your Grams, but I am also the Beast's aunt. His name is Adam. You see, I lived my life long ago, as I told you. I spoiled Adam; I did not teach him how to be a good man. When he threw me from the house, I was found by Gabrielle-Suzanne de Villeneuve. She lived in the manor house nearest to Adam and me. When I told her my tale, she recorded it in an old book. She cared for me until I was strong, and then she explained. She was a searcher of stories, one commissioned by Berschermer to build the magic of Eventyr. Because my story was tied to Adam's and his story was not complete, I lived with her while we watched it unfold. We saw how the Beast he had become changed with the love of Belle, and I watched as Beschermer called them to Eventyr to live forever in peace. It was the happy ending I wanted for Adam. He was no longer a beast. But what to do with me? I was not a villain, not really, but neither was I a hero. Because of my indulgence, Adam became a beast."

Maddy took the pause to ask a question. "What happened?"

Grams stared over the lake. "Magic in Eventyr is created from goodness; Beschermer herself was born from it. At the time of my story and Adam's, there was so much contention between the heroes and the villains, or the protagonists and antagonists of the stories, that it was compromising the stability of Eventyr. Beschermer needed a place for the villains to go, where they could live in peace, separate from the heroes. She felt they deserved that, that their part in the story was important. Without the conflict they created, there would have been no goodness to rise above it, and no magic. The villains, too, deserved immortality. Beschermer created Skurk with her own limited power, and those who did not qualify for Eventyr were taken there."

"So, that's where they took you? To Skurk?"

Grams nodded. "As I told you, I proved my worth. I earned a place as Determinator and worked hard to make sure the people in Skurk were treated fairly and could live after a manner of peace."

Usually, when Maddy thought hard about something, she liked to chew her bottom lip. That was impossible in this form; she might actually draw blood. Maddy resisted the urge by running her fingers through the mud to create deep chasms that quickly filled with water. It was strangely therapeutic.

"What is on your mind, Madelena? You can speak freely to me. I wish you would."

Maddy created a crater by swirling her claw around and around. Grams's request didn't give her the magical urge to speak as some of her other commands had. It was Maddy's choice to share her thoughts and, given the freedom, she found that she really did want to talk it out with Grams. "There's something I don't understand."

"Please." Grams extended both hands.

"You told me that fairy tales are true." Maddy watched the crater saturate. "You told me the people were real."

"I did, and they are."

"But," Maddy looked up, "magic doesn't exist in our world—"

Grams lifted her hand to interrupt. "Rather, magic doesn't thrive in our world. Every day magic is created, but it doesn't grow or stay or attach to anyone."

"Why?"

"I don't know," Grams said simply. "I am not a student of magic. I just know how to wield that which has been given to me."

Wait a second.

"Magic was given to you?" Maddy thought Grams said she didn't have power.

Or maybe she said she wouldn't use it.

It was all a little fuzzy now.

Just like Maddy's toes.

"When I became the Determinator of Skurk, I was gifted a seed of magic from Beschermer to act in that position. Magic given this way never leaves you. It grows with you and becomes part of your DNA. This is how you have magic, my Madelena. It passed to you, through me."

"But that means Mom has magic?" Maddy couldn't really picture that.

"She may; she is one half villain, after all. Thus far, it has not awakened. Perhaps yours would have remained dormant if you hadn't gone to Skurk to rescue Leo. That seems to have been enough to wake it up. You will always have magic now, Maddy, just as I do. I do not always choose to use it. You will have to decide what you choose."

Maddy didn't want to think about that. The implications of a choice that big were too much to handle for her tiny beast brain. She'd think about that later. For now, she wanted to know everything about Grams's story. There had to be something in it that would help her change. If Adam could become more than a beast, maybe Maddy could too.

"Grams, how did you enchant Adam and turn him into a beast if you weren't born with magic?"

"I did not enchant him," Grams smiled. "I know it is difficult but try to understand. When a storyteller creates a story, they do not record it as it happened, exactly. That would make them a news reporter, sticking to the facts. A storyteller embellishes what they are given to make a better story. The same is true for *Beauty and the Beast*. I did not have the power to turn Adam into a beast, but I did not stop Adam from becoming the heartless human he was. His choices turned him into a beast, yes; however I had the influence to change him, and I didn't do it. When my story was recorded by Madame de Villeneuve, she embellished my influence into magical power and me into an enchantress. In the tale, I physically transformed Adam as he internally transformed himself in reality. Do you see? Therefore, I am the villain in Adam's story."

Maddy did see. It was painful the way her mind bent and expanded to accommodate this new idea, but she did understand.

That didn't mean she had to agree, though.

"You might have been the antagonist, Grams, but you were not a villain. Loving someone so much that you spoil them is maybe foolish, but not inherently evil."

"Perhaps," she patted Maddy's hand. "It is hard to say. If brought up differently, would Attila the Hun have been a different man? Or King Henry the Eighth? I made mistakes, dearie. I am not without fault in my story."

Oh, that reminded Maddy of another thing that was bothering her. "Grams, the story of *Beauty and the Beast* has been around forever. How are you still alive?"

"I was given immortality, Maddy."

"Even in our world?"

"When I was taken to Skurk, immortality settled upon me while I lived there."

"But you left Skurk; you don't live there anymore."

"Yes," Grams agreed. "You may not believe it, but immortality loses its appeal as time passes. I wished for a real life, a second chance, if you will. I wanted to prove to myself that I had learned from my experience with

Adam and could have a different kind of family. It was risky; no one had done that before. Beschermer warned me that I might step into your world and disappear like dust, but it was worth the risk for me."

Tears trickled out of the corners of Maddy's eyes, getting lost in the voluminous fur surrounding her face. "That's really cool, Grams."

"It was so worth it. I came to your world and did not turn to dust, thank goodness. My magic clung to me, preserving my youth until I learned to direct it. Over time, I began to age naturally."

"Wait, so, like, your power preserved you? Is that what will happen to me? Will I be immortal?"

"That remains to be seen."

If Maddy didn't convince someone to love her, she might never return to her world or get her power back, and then it wouldn't matter if she was immortal or not. But she was so curious to know what Grams thought, she couldn't stop herself from asking. "Based on what?"

"Your choices, dearie. I chose a mortal life with your grandfather and our family. Inside I am young, as you see me now, but outside, my body is old as you know me in your world. Eventually, my body will wear out, and I will die as all mortals do."

"Why would you choose that?" Maddy exclaimed, her voice coming as a grunt that echoed in the clearing. "Why would you want to die?"

Grams' dimple appeared on the left side. "The question is, why would I want to live without those I love? When I met your grandfather and we fell in love, I knew I did not want to live forever if it was without him. That feeling was magnified with each child we had. I have never regretted my choice. I would not trade any part of this life I have lived."

The ideas were so new that Maddy had trouble keeping up. "You wouldn't even trade the awful parts?"

Grams looked at Maddy in surprise. "There have been no awful parts."

"Sure there are." Maddy waved her free hand. "Sickness, sorrow, death, war. Awful parts."

"Those are just parts, Madelena; just parts of life. I would take the sickness and sorrow to know the health and joy. I could take death and war to really live. All of it is precious to me, the good and the bad."

More tears welled underneath Maddy's eyes so that her vision blurred into grays, greens, browns, and blues. Leo said the same thing: good and bad, not one or the other. Both. Maddy's heart ached as she thought about her family and Leo, her friends and school.

Her life.

She wanted another chance too.

"There, my dear Madelena. You let those tears all come." Grams kissed the back of Maddy's paw and pulled her close. "You let them come and wash away what you have been. You have time to change, my Maddy. There is always time for a change."

TWENTY-TWO
Villainy feels like loneliness sometimes

Grams and Maddy stayed snuggled in the glen for a while. Maddy wasn't sure how long, exactly. Everything felt slower somehow. It was impossible for her to figure out the time without a watch or phone under normal circumstances, and these circumstances were as far from normal as a person could get.

After some quite peaceful moments of listening to Grams breathe in and out, watching the sun wink off the surface of the lake, and feeling the wind rustle her fur back and forth, Maddy was startled when Grams moved away.

"I must go now," she said, rising to her feet as if gravity lifted her instead of her legs.

Maddy looked up, shielding her eyes from the sun. "What do you mean, you have to go?"

Grams extended her hands to the side. "I must go back to our world."

"This isn't our world?" Maddy had a vague idea that they were somewhere in the backwoods of Montana where there were still empty spaces in the world.

"No, dearie," Grams laughed. "You have arrived in Skurk."

"This is Skurk?" Maddy looked around with new eyes.

The glen and lake were so serene that it was hard to picture them in a place for villains. There should have been crows and lightning and dark, murky waters with something sinister lurking beneath.

Okay, that was actually kind of freaky.

Maddy shivered and scooted away from the lake. She wished she could see the bottom. It gave her the willies.

"Yes, this is Skurk." Grams lifted one hand and pointed slightly to the right. "A small part of it. If you follow the path through there, you will come upon a village. I believe you may find some help."

Yeah, Maddy still wasn't one hundred percent clear on that part.

"Find help to do what?"

"Dear Maddy, you must find help to break this curse, of course."

"Wait, I have to do that here?"

Alone?

Beastified?

"Without you?"

Grams smiled, her eyes disappearing into the creases her cheeks created. "I cannot stay here, Madelena. I was granted this time from Beschermer to help you see, and now that you do, you must find your own way."

"But—" Maddy stopped to swallow. "But I thought I was going home to break the curse."

With family and Leo. That made the most sense. They mostly already sort of loved her, so she wouldn't have to start from scratch. Maddy's neck was starting to ache from looking at Grams. She still wasn't sure she could stand on these beastly legs, so she stayed put, enjoying a nice crick in the neck along with whatever it was that squeezed her heart until she thought it might explode.

"You cannot go home, dearie." Grams was all sympathy.

"Why not?"

Grams brought her hands together on her stomach like a belt. "The VDA cannot allow. You have proven that your bad outweighs your good."

Okay, that was fair.

But, so not.

Maddy sighed, hunching over so that her chin almost touched the mud. "Do I have to stay here forever?"

"You have so little faith in your ability?"

"No, it's not that." Maddy ran her claws through the mud. "Well, it kind of is, but mostly it's that you told me people can't go back to our world once they're taken. Remember the toothpaste tube?"

Grams patted her head, careful of the horns. "Look at me, dearie."

Maddy did, but it was hard. Her head felt as dense as yeastless wheat bread.

"This is a *test*, Madelena. A chance just for you. You will find a way to return to us. I have great faith in you." Then she kissed Maddy's wide, hairy forehead and disappeared with the wafting smell of mint.

Maddy stared at the place where Grams stood long after she disappeared. A small part of Maddy wanted to throw an almighty fit for her leaving. It was tempting; her muscles twitched with the effort it took to stop herself from flinging clumps of mud in the air and roaring until she was hoarse. But she didn't give in this time. She knew she deserved everything she was going through.

This was her lesson to learn.

Her beast to conquer.

But not right this second. Maddy wasn't sure she had it in her to move just yet. She sat in the mud until her bottom got cold and Grams's scent faded.

Now she was truly alone.

Maddy took a long drink from the lake, unsure when she would find water again, and finally took a stab at this walking-on-two-feet thing. It seemed easier to start from a kneeling position than on her rear, so she groaned onto her knees. From there, she placed one gargantuan foot in the mud and squashed it down good so it would stay put. She pressed her palms into the thigh of that same leg to leverage herself onto the other foot. In an awkward, semi-squat position, Maddy stopped to catch her breath. She was probably moving around a thousand pounds worth of fur. That's what it felt like, anway.

Slowly, she straightened and took one, wobbly step forward.

Then fell face-first into the mud.

It did not taste delicious.

And the smell...

Ugh!

Maddy rolled onto her back and spit the mud out of her mouth. Which, you know, would have been a great idea if Skurk didn't have gravity. But it did, and the mud came right back down. This time splatting into her eyes.

"This is awesome," Maddy grumbled, rolling back onto her stomach and crawling to the edge of the lake. When her front paws felt the cool water, she moved forward a little bit more and stuck her whole face in.

It actually felt amazing.

Rejuvenating.

Maddy immediately climbed back onto her knees. She wasn't sure how, but she knew it was going to work this time. She anchored one foot, leaned onto that leg, raised the other, and straightened. One wobbly step, then another, then another, and holy Toledo! She was walking.

It was a legit miracle.

Maddy shrieked for joy and twirled in a circle. That might have been a bit ambitious for her new legs, but she caught herself just before she landed back on her bottom, and she stopped to regain her balance.

Now she was all turned around.

Where did Grams say to go?

She could still see the imprint of her body in the mud where she was sitting when Grams was there. If she pointed straight from that spot, that might be the right direction. It was worth a try. She was for sure not getting anywhere standing there doing nothing.

Maddy headed towards the woods, her body adjusting quickly to the beastish gait so that by the time she reached the edge of the trees, she almost felt like she was walking normally. Or at least not weirdly anymore. The woods, however, presented a different problem.

The sun had already dimmed as she left the edge of the lake. Now the forest was shadowed and beyond creepy. She didn't want to go in.

That's when she realized—oh yeah—she was a beast. Maddy was probably the scariest thing she was going to see in that place.

She found the faint outline of a path and headed toward it. Maddy was careful to stay in the very center of the path. It felt more secure, or something. One foot in front of the other, she wove through the trees, gaining confidence with every step. She could do this. She was bomb at following a path.

The darkness of the forest didn't seem so awful as it had before. Without the comparison of light, the dim enclosure of bushes and trees started to look brighter. Or maybe this beast's body gave her night vision.

Okay, that was awesome!

It for sure gave her tremendous hearing. Maddy could hear the sound of bugs scuttling in burrows under the ground and leaves whispering to each other in actual words. It was creepy cool and kept her entertained throughout the long walk to the village.

And it was a long walk.

Maddy suddenly had sympathy for Hansel and Gretel. If she came upon a house entirely made of candy, she could have devoured it too—partly out of relief to not be alone in the world and partly to have something to do. This walk was the opposite of entertaining.

Not that she wanted to meet a witch and end up in a cage. That wasn't the type of entertainment she was looking for. Just some variation in the trees would be nice, and maybe some different birds. A person could only hear the same song over and over for so long before it became an obnoxious brain worm.

Was it Maddy's imagination, or were the trees beginning to thin out?

And was that the scent of baking bread?

Maddy sped up, fueled by the thought of houses and people and bread. She reached the line of trees and paused in their shadow to survey the village spread out in front of her. There were several tight rows of squatty houses. A well in the center. No, two wells. One surrounded by animals, and one probably for the people. On the backside of every house was a large field with a different crop. At least, Maddy assumed they were a variety of crops. She didn't know a ton about farming, but the plants were different sizes and shapes.

Though, not green. She thought crops were supposed to be green. Maybe the food was different in Skurk. A world with princesses and beasts and giant beanstalks probably had weird plants too.

A young woman in a simple homespun dress packed bundles wrapped in brown paper into the back of a cart. Little children wove between the houses, giggling and squealing like piglets. Men walked from the fields with tools over their shoulders. Maddy watched it all for a moment, wondering if Skurk was five hundred years behind the now or if this village just chose to live without modern conveniences, kind of like the Amish.

It didn't really matter if they were a little behind the times or not; the young woman looked about Maddy's age and was pink-cheeked and cheerful, singing a haunting song as she worked. If anyone would help her in this place, Maddy was sure it was this girl.

Maddy rambled out of the darkness and started towards the village. Her big, clomping feet made enormous marks in the dusty path and the same amount of noise as a rampaging bull elephant. The young woman looked up. She stopped working, her eyes widening as she opened her mouth and...

Screamed.

Not a scream of excitement, like finding a pair of Tevas on sale for 80 percent off. And not a scream of happiness, like when you run into a friend you haven't seen since middle school. No way; this was a scream of terror, a million times worse than any Maddy had heard in real life or movies.

"Beast!" The young woman screamed, running to the front of the cart and snatching a small child from the seat. "Beast!"

Was she protecting the baby from Maddy?

Did she seriously think Maddy was going to eat the kid? Unlike Leo, joking or not, Maddy had *never* had the urge to eat a child. She sort of wished she had a copy of the Villainous Test with her so she could show the girl her answer to that question. Though, come to think of it, the girl probably wouldn't let Maddy get close enough to point it out.

The town bustle stopped abruptly. A silence more still than mere quiet followed, and then gasps, screams, crying, and shouts.

Torches and pitchforks.

Yes, pitchforks.

Seriously, could they be a little more cliché?

Maddy stopped walking and stood stupidly in the middle of the path, watching the mob of villagers form a tight line along the entrance to the village. They stood ready with their pitchforks aimed at Maddy's head.

"Back, Beast," one man called.

Maddy lifted her hand, making the line gasp in unison and fall back a step. She lifted her voice so they would be sure to hear her over the constant pounding of their terror. "I'm not going to hurt anyone. I just need some help."

More exclamations. "The Beast wishes to ravage our village."

"It will carry our children away in the night."

"And plunder our stores for the winter."

"The village will starve."

"Hey!" Maddy put her hand on her hip. "That is not what I said!"

"Listen to it roar! We must strike, swift and sure, to preserve the lives of our people."

"Are you guys kidding me right now? I just need some help!" Maddy cupped her hands over her mouth to help her voice carry.

The men shuddered down the line like they were practicing the wave for a football game. "It calls for its foul allies. Courage, men! On three."

At that moment, it occurred to Maddy that maybe they couldn't understand what she was saying. She assumed they would be able to, since Gram understood her just fine. But maybe the villagers weren't fluent in Beast.

By the count of two, with the line of men swinging their pitchforks into the air, Maddy decided to let this village alone. Whatever they were planning with those tools turned into weapons was obviously not going to end well. She turned and loped off the path, skirting the village but not going back into the trees. Grams had pointed her this way, so this is where she wanted to be. Just not here, here. Maybe there was another village close by, one that liked animals and didn't jump to conclusions.

Something hard hit Maddy's shoulder, almost knocking her to the ground.

"Beast!" a childish voice cried.

A group of children, old and young, stood in a cluster behind one of the cottages, their arms filled with rocks.

"Back into the abyss with you!" one cried, letting another rock fly.

Maddy sidestepped the rock and stuck her tongue at the kids.

One pointed a shaking finger. "It has put the evil tongue on you, Phillip. You are doomed."

More children wailed, and the one who must have been Phillip went as white as paper and sank to the ground. "I had so much to live for." He lay in the dirt and covered his face with a handkerchief one small girl flung at him through her tears.

Up ahead there were more groups of women and children armed with sticks and stones that weren't as painful as the words they shouted: beast, miscreant, baddie, brute, fiend, monster, ogre, savage.

Just hurtful, really. They didn't even know Maddy.

It seemed her only choice was to run back into the trees and out of sight. She veered to the left and disappeared behind a particularly large tree with a trunk wide enough to shelter her from sight. Maddy waited for the people to wander back to their lives before moving so she wouldn't catch anyone's eye. The line of trees followed the length of the village to a path that breached in three directions. Maddy stayed in the shelter of the trees until the path was in sight, then cautiously stepped into the open.

"BEAST!" A barrage of stones, sticks, mud, and stuff that looked like mud but for sure didn't smell like it showered over Maddy's head so rapidly that she lost her sense of direction. Each way she turned was brown and unfriendly.

Where had these people even come from? The coast was totally clear just a few moments ago.

Maddy covered her head and ran in the direction she hoped was the forest and not the center of the village. She didn't want to imagine what would happen if she ended up there. The words 'stake' and 'bonfire' kept coming to mind, along with a whole lot of images that were going to give her nightmares later on. Maddy swiped her eyes and blinked around the goo until she could make out the faint line of trees.

Oh, thank goodness.

She dove into the cover of their lofty branches and wondered how she ever thought the forest was unfriendly. It was the nicest thing she'd come across since she left the glen. What was wrong with these people anyway? Why didn't they give her a chance to explain who she was and what was going on? Just because she was a billion feet tall with feet the size of plows and covered in matted, muddy fur didn't mean she was bad. They could have at least tried to understand her.

Oh, yeah.

Like, the way she'd tried to understand Leo's villain friends.

Dang it.

Maddy leaned her back against the trunk of a tree and used the fur on the back of her hands to clean her face. It wasn't perfect, since her hands were not exactly clean, but it was the best she could do. She blinked a few times and tipped her chin up to look at the swaying branches overhead.

Why did karma have such a savage sense of humor?

She wished she could redo her whole first visit to Skurk. She would try to be more understanding, try to help Leo's friends, and, at the very least, listen to their stories and give them a chance. Maddy would do a lot of things differently.

She sighed, ruffling the fur around her face. Honestly, Maddy couldn't even blame the villagers. She would have done the exact same thing in their shoes. But it was a little ironic that a world full of villains treated her like an outcast. It seemed logical that they would all band together, but maybe it was human nature to form classes and ranks, making some people above others, even in a world where everyone was considered the bad guy. It was just bad luck that beastliness seemed to be ranked at the very bottom.

Maddy's shoulder, where the first stone had hit with impressive accuracy, ached like a mo, and there was blood drying on her leg. She couldn't find the motivation to check where the wound was and take care of it. It would take forever to find it through the thick, matted fur and drying mud. Maybe when the sun went down and all the people went to sleep, Maddy could explore the area and find a place to take a bath. For now, there wasn't anything to do but sleep.

TWENTY-THREE
Villains can change their spots

When Maddy opened her eyes, she had to close them and open them a second time, then a third. Opening her eyes was the same as having them closed. Even with her supposed super-enhanced beast vision, the darkness was so profound that she became one with it, another dark thing in the sea of dark things.

Or maybe she wasn't quite awake yet?

She shifted and groaned. No, she was definitely awake. The mossy rock that had looked almost comfy when she leaned against it was now jabbing mercilessly into her back. Maddy sat up and rubbed both hands up and down her fur to relieve some of the aches. Her eyes were still clouded and dim, but the larger outlines of trees were visible when she squinted. The more she looked around, the more she realized it wasn't a vision problem at all; she was surrounded by a thick, black fog. It wasn't like any other fog she'd seen with wispy gray tendrils. This one encompassed Maddy and everything else around her.

It wasn't natural.

As she moved, the fog expanded to stay with her. Someone had put it there, and though it didn't feel dangerous, it was mysterious enough to make Maddy shiver.

Maddy moved her leg to stand up and stopped when she bumped into something that sloshed against her leg.

That's when she noticed the smell.

Food.

Holy cow, Maddy was starving.

She didn't know how time worked in Skurk, but she was pretty sure she hadn't eaten anything in a million years. The way her stomach rolled and clenched, making noises Maddy's mom would not approve of, was starting to freak Maddy out. Her arms shook from holding her body back because what she really wanted to do was launch herself face first into the steaming bowl of whatever it was.

Maddy eyed the food and wondered if it was a trick. It for sure wasn't a mirage like what people experience when they are trapped in the desert for way too long. The steam wafting into Maddy's face and the small, round loaf of bread barely visible through the fog was very real. But it could be poisoned. Maddy reached for the bread to inspect it closer and noticed a white bandage wrapped around her leg.

Okay, that really didn't make any sense. Maddy couldn't fathom someone from the village searching the woods for her so that they could doctor her boo-boo and leave poisoned food for her to eat. That seemed a little inconsistent. That had to mean the food was fine to eat. Yes, she might have been thinking with her stomach, but suddenly the decision became would she rather die of starvation or die of poison? Supposed poison. The poison thing might not be real, but starvation certainly was.

She was totally going to risk it.

Her beast metabolism must have been insane. She was suddenly so hungry she would have eaten the mud off her fur if she thought it would fill the ache in her belly. Maddy scooted closer to the rock and leaned over so she could see better. A face full of yummy scents was all it took for the animal side of her to kick in and attack the food like a ravenous—that's right—beast.

When her stomach was appeased, she waited about five minutes to see if she was going to die a horrible death. When she didn't feel any different, Maddy began to think about other details. That bandage on her leg, for one. The food, for another. The crocheted tablecloth under the dishes of food, most of all.

Grams tried to teach Maddy to crochet when she was eleven. After about two hours of instruction, the only thing Maddy could do was chain ten. It was awkward trying to loop the yarn around a slippery crochet hook with normal human fingers, Maddy couldn't imagine how that would work with her new beast hands.

The tablecloth was made with thin white string that shimmered in the fog, and the stitches were perfectly even all the way through. It probably took forever to make, and someone used it to cover a dirty old rock for Maddy's food.

There had to be a person nearby, someone who did all of this for her.

"Hello?" she said in a gruff voice.

It was going to be super hard to make friends with a voice like that. Maddy tried to lighten it with a cheery English accent, but that only made her sound like she was about to sneeze. With a sigh, she gave up the voice thing and went back to the low growl. "Look, I know I sound like I want to eat you and pillage your village, but I don't. I just want to say thank you for giving me food and bandaging my wounds. This tablecloth is really pretty. You did a good job with it. So, yeah. I don't know if I'm talking to myself and sounding like a loony bird, but I wanted to tell you thank you."

There was only silence for a moment.

Then,

"You're welcome."

The sound startled Maddy so much, even though she was squinting through the fog, hoping for an answer. She shrieked and scrambled backward until her back jammed into the trunk of a tree. "Where are you?"

"I'm here."

The fog lifted, and a stooped, old woman walked forward, leaning heavily on a thick, carved stick. Stringy gray hair hung off each shoulder and looked greasy like Maddy's did when she went all villain with the hair gel. The old woman's eyes glowed yellow in the dark, drawing Maddy's eyes to her face. Shadows blended all her features, except a large, crooked nose that hung so low she would easily win the touch-your-tongue-to-your-nose game. Her knobby legs shook as she stood, and her claw-like hands clutched the moth-eaten shawl at her chest.

All the gratitude vanished as Maddy took in the wizened creature. She tried not to show how disgusted she felt. This was a good time to be a beast, actually. Maddy didn't have to worry about her feelings showing up on her face. As a beast she only had one expression: equal parts terrifying and ferocious.

Maddy took a deep breath and pushed aside thoughts of how grotesque the old woman was. Instead, she tried to concentrate on the things the old woman had done for her. Kindness to a stranger, especially one that looked the way Maddy did, was nothing to sneeze at.

And really, the old woman was probably equally disgusted by Maddy's appearance.

Yet, she'd given food and care.

For all the old woman knew, Maddy was a real-life beast that would eat her up. Not only was the old woman kind, but she was courageous. And Maddy could really use a friend right about now.

As Maddy's thoughts shifted from seeing the old woman's outward appearance to seeing the heart behind her actions, the old woman became the most beautiful creature in the world.

"Can you understand me? Don't be scared." Maddy extended a hand—or claw, really. "I'm not a beast; I'm a human girl. I turned myself into a beast because...actually, never mind. You don't care. The point is, I'm here and I need to figure out a way to break the curse, and you're the first person that's shown me any kindness, so I love you forever. Also, I'm super rambling, so sorry about that."

The old woman's shoulders relaxed. "I cannot quite see a human girl while looking at you. But I know you are telling the truth." She leaned hard on her staff.

Maddy stared at it. "Hey! I have one of those! My Grams made it for me. Do you know my Grams? Agathe?"

"Agathe." The old woman's face softened. "I have not heard that name for many years. Yes, I know her."

"How?" Maddy realized her enthusiasm might be a bit overpowering and tried to tone it down. "I mean, how do you know my Grams? Did you work together?" Maddy had a vague idea that their matching staffs might mean they were in the same department of the VDA, kind of the way people who work at fast food chains usually wear visors.

"Oh no." The old woman's face cracked into a toothless smile. "No, no, no. We took a whittling class together."

That was a weird answer that just led to a bunch more questions. Was that really how Grams and the woman met? Why did they take a class together and why whittling? Did Skurk offer other classes? Maddy could just picture a bunch of old women learning archery or underwater basket weaving together.

Why not? It wasn't the strangest thing in the world.

Maddy decided to let the questions go. People usually had good reasons for not telling others every detail about themselves. She scrambled to her feet and picked up the tablecloth, folding it into a neat square before she handed it to the old woman. "Anyway, thank you so much for the food and stuff. You really didn't have to do that."

"I did." The old woman took the bundle and tucked it under her arm. "It was the right thing to do."

Something in the way her wistful gaze went right through the trees tugged at Maddy's heart. "Would you like to sit down?" Maddy waved her hand at the dirt and instantly felt stupid. How hospitable of her, offering the old woman some pine needle-strewn ground to rest upon.

Oh, Maddy.

"I would like that very much," the old woman said, unfazed. She hobbled closer and eased to the ground with her many cloaks poofing all around her. "My name is Hepzibah."

"I'm Maddy." Maddy sat across from her as crisscross applesauce as the beast's legs would go.

Hepzibah said Maddy's name a few times, as though trying out how the sound felt on her tongue. "That is a foreign name to me."

"My full name is Madelena," Maddy offered.

Maybe that would be more comfortable for her to say.

When Hepzibah tried this time, she nodded. "Yes, that is much more palatable."

Maddy studied Hepzibah's face now that she was no longer in the shadows. Other than the nose thing, her face looked like one that was quite lovely once upon a time and had fallen into lines of care and concern. "Will you tell me your story?" Maddy blurted, then groaned to herself. She was really rocking this social interaction thing. "I mean, I'd like to know more about you. How did you end up in Skurk?"

Was that an appropriate thing to ask?

Maddy really didn't know the customs of Skurk. Maybe asking someone to tell you their story was the equivalent of asking someone back home how much they weighed. It was too late for Maddy to take the words back now, so she just waited to see if Hepzibah would answer or slap Maddy in the face.

Hepzibah simply said, "Oh, I am of no importance," and shrugged her shawl tighter across her shoulders.

Maddy shook her head. "I refuse to believe that. You just saved my life." Which might have been an exaggeration and might have been a perfect truth, depending on the perspective. "What I mean is, you are very important to *me.*"

"Oh, I didn't do much."

Maddy swung her arm towards the village. "Know what happened when I showed my face in that village?" Maddy then waved her hand across the bandages on her legs. "This is what happened. Trust me, what you did wasn't nothing. It was some...thing. At least, way more something than anyone else did."

Not that Maddy was bitter or anything.

Okay, maybe she was, a little.

"Perhaps." Hepzibah leaned forward, resting her elbows on her knees. "Perhaps not. Be careful when casting judgment. Everyone has reasons for the things they do. The village you see there has fallen on hard times."

Maddy didn't see how hard times justified throwing rocks at an innocent beast just passing through.

Hepzibah went on. "It has not rained these thirteen months. When there is no food to feed the children, people do desperate things."

Maddy could relate to that, actually. Leo tried intermittent fasting a few months ago, and it did not go well. Speaking of beasts, the dude put the 'angry' in 'hangry.'

Times a zillion.

Maddy really missed that guy.

She shook her head to keep her wandering thoughts on track. She imagined it would be pretty awful to have to watch your children go to bed hungry at night and listen to them cry.

A wave of compassion swept over Maddy. "Is there anything I can do to help them?"

"Can you make it rain?" Hepzibah smiled sadly.

"No," Maddy hesitated, trying to think. There had to be something she could do. She came from Arizona, for heaven's sake, the very epitome of no water. Her pioneer ancestors were the ones who learned to farm the desert and turn it into the thriving metropolis it was today. But that meant some form of ingenuity had to be in her DNA somewhere, didn't it? Maddy wrinkled her forehead, searching her memories all the way back to the fourth-grade Arizona unit. She had an idea, like an itch that she couldn't reach, that farmers used to do something—maybe they still did it—to bring water to the farms.

Oh,

Irritation!

No, that wasn't right.

Irrigation. Yes, that was it.

Holy cannoli. That could totally work!

"Is there water nearby?" Maddy said, her excitement making her voice way louder. Poor Hepzibah startled and almost fell over in the dirt. "I mean, is there a river somewhere close?"

Hepzibah shook her head. "I'm afraid not anymore."

Maddy refused to be deterred. There had to be something nearby because this irrigation thing would totally work. It would revive all those dry and shriveled crops she saw and make the villagers so happy they wouldn't be mean to people passing through.

Or maybe they still would; it was Skurk. A villain village, after all.

It didn't matter. Whether they would be mean or kind in the future wasn't Maddy's business. She knew a way to help them grow their crops and feed their children. That meant it was her responsibility to figure out how to make it happen.

There was water in her memory. Her tiny animal mind had a harder time thinking, but Maddy wasn't going to give up until she remembered what she knew she knew. There was water in there somewhere, and she was going to find it.

That's right!

"There's water in the glen, Hepzibah! A lake. Grams told me it never runs dry, and she is always right. If I made a, a—" Maddy couldn't think of the word, but she could picture it. Like those tracks she made in the mud with her claws that then filled with water. "Like, a river—no, canal! That's it, canal. I can dig a canal from the lake to the village, and the people will have the water they need, forever."

Hepzibah studied Maddy. "I thought you did not like these villagers."

"I don't." Maddy scraped her claw against a rock accidentally and got the shivers. It was like nails down a chalkboard. "I mean, I didn't. They weren't very nice to me. But they do need help, and I know how to help them."

Well, she knew what to do to help them, at least. How she was going to do it was another problem. She couldn't waltz into the village looking the way she did and tell them her plan. They didn't understand her words. And now that they knew she was out here, they'd be on high alert. Maddy would be mincemeat before she could even open her mouth.

Maddy studied Hepzibah. The old woman understood her, maybe she would translate for the villagers?

No.

Hepzibah lived alone in the woods instead of in the village with the others. That probably meant they weren't on the best of terms either. So, talking to the villagers was out.

But maybe Maddy could do the canal anyway.

Like a surprise.

Maddy perked up as the ideas started flooding in. She could elves-and-shoemaker this whole thing by building a canal while they slept. It would be all ready and amazing when they woke up. Best surprise ever!

Now for the nitty gritty. What was the hour now? It was dark, but that could mean a lot of things. Did she have time to do it tonight, or would she have to wait? She wanted to get this done as soon as possible so she could move on to the next village to find whatever help Grams said was waiting for her there. How fast could Maddy work as a beast, exactly? Did she have super strength and super digging speed along with her night vision? That would be super handy right now.

"I'm going to help them." Maddy nodded, placing her hands on her hips.

Hepzibah shone in a way that Grams had earlier. It was like Maddy could see the young version and the old version flickering back and forth. "That is very kind of you."

"I'm not sure exactly how this whole thing will work." Maddy looked over her shoulder. "But I'm going to get started right now. I want to try and finish it tonight before the sun comes up."

"Very wise." Hepzibah stood, resting her cane under one hand. "I must tend to my garden."

Maddy wasn't sure what to do next. She didn't know where Hepzibah lived, and it seemed a little inappropriate to ask. So, was this it? Her heart sank a little at the thought. Hepzibah was her one friend in this place. Maddy didn't want to lose her so soon.

Hepzibah patted Maddy's arm. "I will find you when you are finished."

Just like Grams. They both seemed to know what Maddy was thinking.

Maddy wanted to hug her or something before she left, but she was afraid that would freak the poor old woman out. "Thank you again, Hepzibah. I think there is a happily ever after waiting for you somewhere. Don't give up hope."

"Thank you, child." Hepzibah turned to go, her voice hazy. "I won't."

TWENTY-FOUR

Sometimes, the only difference between a hero and a villain is one simple act

It was crazy cool how fast Maddy could run on all fours. She wished there was a cheetah nearby that she could challenge to race because she was pretty positive that she would leave it in the dust. Except, she was on her way to save the village from drought and destruction. She didn't have time to get distracted, even if it would be an interesting experiment.

Maddy loped through the forest, careful to stay on the path so she could get right back to the glen. It was tricky because she was moving so fast, but she discovered that it helped to stare at the ground instead of the scenery. The dirt on the path was packed down and a light brown color, but after a time, the dirt became darker, and Maddy could feel more moisture when her paws hit the ground. Maddy dared to look up when patches of light flecked the path. The trees were beginning to thin out again. A couple more strides, and there was the lake. Beautiful and bottomless.

Maddy stopped at the edge and looked into the depths at her wavering reflection.

It was okay for her to use this water, right?

She didn't know who to ask for permission, but since it was for a good cause, it should be fine. Just in case, she lifted her head and bellowed, "I'm going to make a canal from the lake to the village so they can grow crops and stop hating on things that are ugly. Is that okay?"

Maddy waited a minute or two with no response except for the twittering of birds and tried again. "I'm digging now. Say something if this is a sacred pool; otherwise, I'm going for it."

Another minute or two with nothing meant it was fine, Maddy was pretty sure. She slowly dug her claws into the soft dirt and started digging. It was like her body was made for this moment. As soon as that initial hesitation was over, Maddy moved like a canal-digging machine. Mud flew in all directions, sometimes onto her back and up her nose, but that didn't stop her for a second. She kept moving, imagining the excitement on the villagers' faces when they realized they weren't going to starve.

Crouch, scoop, fling. Crouch, scoop, fling.

Maddy was making so much noise that it took her a sec to hear the giggling. She stopped, her chest heaving, and looked around. "Is someone there?"

More giggling.

"I hear you...I think." Maddy wasn't sure. It could have been her imagination. Sometimes when she was doing homework in her room, she thought she heard her mom calling her name. And the sounds of laughter had been so tiny, like the tinkling of dishes getting put away in the cupboard. Yeah, it was probably nothing. She felt incredibly stupid but went ahead and asked again. "Is someone there? Or am I just enjoying the sultry sound of my voice?"

"It's funny." More giggles.

"Funny beasties."

"I like fun beasties."

Okay, so, not her imagination. The voices swirled around Maddy's head like a confused breeze. She couldn't see whatever was making the sounds, but those voices were for sure not in her head. Her imagination liked her too much to create such squeaky, high-pitched little voices. Especially with these dog-like ears. The sound of their talking was pretty much excruciating.

"Where are you?" Maddy asked. "I can't see you; I can just hear you."

The voices went on as if Maddy hadn't asked a question at all.

"We be helping beasties?"

"Beasties helping be fun!"

Maddy thought so too, but she wasn't about to interject her opinion just in case it would change the outcome of the decision-making process.

"We's always be helping beasties."

"Help the beasties. Yes!"

Almost like someone snapped their fingers in front of her nose, two little pixies appeared. They hovered in the air on translucent wings that reflected the water back onto themselves. A black and purple rainbow flowed from their tiny bodies to the lake.

One pixie covered her mouth with her hands and giggled. "Hello, beasties."

"Hello," Maddy said.

The other laughed like bells. "You fun beasties."

"Fun beasties, you."

"Uh, thanks." Maddy ran a hand along her cheek to scratch an itch just seconds before she remembered she was covered in mud. The pixies shrieked with laughter and flickered in and out of sight until they finished cracking up.

Maddy just waited. There was no point in trying to clean herself up with all this fur. It picked up everything way worse than microfiber towels.

One of the pixies hovered near Maddy's nose, her wings tickling the end until Maddy knew she was going to sneeze or explode. She didn't want to do either. A sneeze from her ginormous nose would blow those poor pixies to Wonderland. Both of them together would have been able to make a house in her left nostril alone. Exploding, on the other hand, was super bad.

Maddy squeezed her eyes shut and thought about eggplants until the sensation faded.

"We know secret," a pixie with wild blue hair whispered near Maddy's ear, then fluttered back to the other. "Secret we know, beasties. Water secret."

"Secret water."

Maddy's head spun as she tried to keep up with their darting movements and silly words. This bunch of nonsense sounded like it might be actual sense, though. "What do you know about the water?"

"Asks us nice."

Maddy took a deep breath. "Will you, most honored and renowned pixies, please grace me with the knowledge of the water that I lack?"

That might have been laying it on a little thick, Maddy realized, but it was totally worth it if they quit giggling and gave her useful information.

The pixies flew into each other from the force of their giggles this time. They wrapped their tiny arms around each other's shoulders and laughed themselves silly.

Finally, the red pixie moved forward. "Water doesn't need beastie to move."

"Water moves without beastie," the blue pixie echoed, moving beside the red.

Meaning what?

"I don't understand," Maddy said.

"Water moves without beastie."

"Water moves when beastie asks."

Maddy scrunched her face. Did they mean Maddy didn't need to dig a canal? She could just ask the water to move and it would? But how? Maddy had never seen water without something to contain it. Riverbanks, beaches, swimming pools, glass cups. She had no context for what the pixies were saying.

"Beastie funny when it thinks."

"Funny thinky face."

Maddy ignored the pixies and surveyed her work. It was a good thing she did. There was absolutely no water in her canal, even though she removed the lip of the lake's bank to let the water flow out more easily. The canal was muddy and deep, and excellent workmanship, but there was no water in it.

That was strange.

The red giggled. "Beastie! Ask water to move."

"Water moves when ask, beastie," the blue added.

Maddy sat back on her haunches and shrugged. It was worth a shot. Asking the water to move was a billion times easier than digging a trench all the way through the forest to the village. What did she have to lose? "Hey, water, nice to see you. You're looking lovely today. Love the sparkles, by the way. They really go with your shimmers. Um, will you fill this canal thing I made?"

The pixies swirled around Maddy's head so fast she was positive she couldn't follow them unless she wanted a migraine. Even if she was willing to risk it, her eyeballs probably wouldn't be able to keep up. They moved so fast that red and blue blurred into purple. Their combined forces made streaks through the air. Maddy turned her attention to the water.

A wave broke above the smooth surface like the head of a spoon. It lifted in front of Maddy's eyes, growing taller and wider until it hovered over her like the ridge of a cliff. Maddy cricked her neck to watch it. The water just hovered there for a minute and tipped over Maddy like it was scanning her soul. It must have deemed her more than the scum of the earth because it sloshed into the canal she'd carved out of the dirt.

Just like that.

"See, beastie?"

"Beastie, see?"

The pixies fell over each other giggling. This beast body apparently couldn't giggle. When Maddy tried, it sounded like she needed to hawk something up, so she giggled on the inside and watched the pixies celebrate.

"Thank you," Maddy said. "This will be so much easier. Thank you so much for telling me about the water. That was really nice of you."

"It was not nice. We are not nice, beasties."

"We's just having fun."

"Well, thank you all the same. I wouldn't have figured that out without you."

The pixies gushed about what a nice beastie Maddy was, then brushed their dark, moth-like wings against her face, tickling her cheeks.

Fairy kisses.

No, pixie kisses.

Grams told Maddy about fairy kisses when she was just a little girl and still believed in fairies. Maddy saw the whole thing like it was yesterday instead of years ago. They were building a fairy garden next to the swing set so fairies would come to play with her. Grams said fairy kisses were supposed to be tremendous luck. Maddy hoped with all her soul that pixie kisses worked the same way. She could use all the luck she could get right about now.

Maddy smiled her creepy, beastie smile and thanked the pixies again and again until they got sick of the whole business and disappeared. Then Maddy backed a few steps away from the water and stared at it. "All right water, that was awesome. Let's see if you can follow me all the way to the village." Maddy wasn't quite sure how this part was going to work. Without a canal, would the water just spill everywhere and disappear into the ground, or would it be able to follow her?

The head like a spoon appeared out of the water again, looked at Maddy—it totally did—then surged forward to lap at her toes. It stayed in a line as if there were borders of mud and dirt to contain it, just invisible.

Maddy could work with that.

She waved her hand to invite the water along and marched into the woods. Every once in a while, she checked over her shoulder to make sure the water was still there. A few times, she asked it to keep coming. It never stopped following her, but just in case it got any funny ideas about what it was supposed to do, she wanted to be totally clear.

The water continued behind Maddy like a Fourth of July parade, following the path through the woods to the edge of the village. When Maddy stopped, the water tickled her heels, flicking up to her knees and back down again. Maddy surveyed the area, trying to decide the best way to get the water to the people. The village probably needed water in the well in the center of the village, but Maddy wasn't sure how to make that happen without anyone noticing. There was sure to be an insomniac or stargazer or new mother up with a baby watching out a window. They would raise the alarm, and Maddy would become a beast kabob before they even noticed there was water with her.

It was a much better idea to get the water to the fields. All of the crops came out from the back sides of the cottages, where there were fewer windows, if any. And the villagers could probably think of a way to move the water to the well. If nothing else, they could carry it by the bucket. That would be no problem now that the water was never-ending.

Maddy directed the water to the fields, walking in front of it and trying to hunch down so she wasn't so unsightly. She hoped she was doing this right. Maddy wished she knew more about agriculture. Why didn't they teach that in school? It would at least be as useful as P.E.

Except that most of the food she ate came from chain grocery stores and packages. Phoenix wasn't really an agricultural hot spot.

Maddy sighed.

The water pooled around her ankles, seeping into the cracked ground. It was like the poor dirt couldn't get enough. It lapped and gulped and glugged. Maddy could hear it. Her heart filled with resolution. She was going to figure this out; the dirt needed water, and the crops needed water. The people needed the crops.

A memory bubbled to the surface of Maddy's mind.

She and her dad were planting a little garden in the fall when it finally cooled down enough to go outside without jumping straight into the pool. They didn't have a huge backyard, but her dad loved to see things grow, so he always carved out a small area near the house to grow zucchini, green beans, tomatoes, and corn. This particular time, her dad used his trowel to dig trenches through each row they planted, then he set the hose in one corner, and the water went all around the garden and through each trench, so all the roots got wet.

Maddy could do that here!

It would totally work.

"Let's go, lake!" Maddy swung her arm and dug her clawed feet into the dirt, then shuffled forward. Her feet were large enough to create a nice holding place for the water to follow behind her. She shuffled up to the sun-bleached rows of corn and carefully maneuvered down the line to the wilted peas. Maddy was going to call this move the Garden Shuffle and make millions on YouTube one day.

She could cover so much area in such a short amount of time with her monstrous feet that it took no time at all to transverse every row of the crop fields. The most satisfying moment of her life came when she turned around and watched the lake water seep into the trenches, wetting the soil into a dark brown instead of a dusty gray. Some of the plants perked up immediately, the leaves reaching for the sky now instead of wilting on the ground. Maddy smiled as she amused herself by imagining their roots clapping for joy.

Okay, that was weird.

But seriously, Maddy felt amazing.

A rooster crowed, bringing Maddy to the moment with a jerk. That was her cue to hoof it out of there. Maddy raced behind a huge stack of hay to hide. It would be safer for her in the forest, but she couldn't resist the chance to see the faces of the villagers when they saw her handiwork.

In the meantime, watching the town come to life was fascinating enough to keep Maddy from hopping out of her skin with anticipation. Bleary-eyed children spilled out of back doors to collect eggs and feed pigs. Men followed with axes and hoes slung over their shoulders. Women called from windows and flapped towels in the breeze.

Maddy held her breath as the men moved closer and closer to the fields.

"Wha—" A farmer in blue overalls dropped to his knees, scooping the wet soil in his hands.

Some followed his example while others stood as still as trees, their eyes tracing the lines of the water.

"'Tis a miracle, 'tis!" One flung his hands in the hair, spraying muddy water all over the guy next to him. Neither of them seemed to care. Tears poured down their faces as they shouted thanks to the sky.

"What's happened?" A child tugged on the plaid shirt of one farmer, who squatted to speak at eye level.

"Rouse the village. Bring them all to see the miracle before us."

The child scooted away on tiny legs that really moved. In a short time, their whole village had gathered to stare at the water.

"The water comes from the forest there," a woman pointed. "It comes just for us!"

Another woman clasped her hands under her chin. "It was Hepzibah, I warrant."

"The witch?" A man looked around in alarm.

"Oh, posh." The woman with clasped hands gave him a solid stink eye. "Your own great-grand-mama was the Evil Queen, Orem. Speak not ill of witches."

He scuffed his toe in the mud.

"We must find her. Hepzibah has saved us. Who knows where she be?" The villagers spoke over each other, their voices blending into the happiest chaos Maddy had ever heard.

It didn't bother Maddy one tiny little bit that Hepzibah was getting the credit for her hard work. If that meant the villagers would find a place for the woman, where she didn't have to live alone as an outcast, then Maddy was thrilled. It was not the outcome she anticipated when she planned to help the village, but it was flipping awesome. It was like the old saying about killing two birds with one stone—which was actually a horrible saying that meant she just solved two life-altering dilemmas with one good deed.

Epic.

Maddy hugged herself and thanked her beastly body and the silly pixies for getting them to this place. It felt pretty ding, dong, dang amazing!

A shadow moved in the corner of Maddy's eyes, snapping her out of her love-fest and into an awkward automatic ninja pose that made her lose her balance. She landed face first in the hay, then jumped to her feet in case the shadow wasn't friendly and she really did need to defend herself.

Maddy rose to her full height and came face to face with the most beautiful woman she had ever seen. Even more so than Grams, or Elle, though that seemed impossible until this moment. The woman looked human in form, but so not. There wasn't a word in Maddy's language to describe her. She was more than beautiful, so much more. Maddy's eyes watered trying to stare at her. If Leo thought Elle was something else, he would turn into a drooling puddle of goo at this lady.

Her wide, silvery eyes watched Maddy as she extended one perfect hand. "Come with me, Maddy. You no longer belong here."

TWENTY-FIVE
A little bit light and a little bit dark

Maddy took the lady's hand with complete disregard for stranger danger, mostly because the woman was the antithesis of evil or alarming. She was like a big bowl of popcorn, snuggly blankets, and favorite movies. Although, Maddy would rather stay a beast forever than say that analogy out loud.

The lady pulled Maddy gently so that she had to take a step. Instead of squishing her feet in the dirt, Maddy stepped into a large, circular room with windows along one side and floor-to-ceiling bookshelves on the other. The books in this place had silvery covers that seemed to dance in front of Maddy's eyes. They shifted around the shelves every few minutes as if to prove that nothing could hold them. It was wondrous and magical, but all Maddy would think about was the poor librarians. It brought to mind the interrogation dungeon where she sat with Elle, but this room was so different. It felt different. Light and airy and...and good. Maddy wondered if this room was supposed to be opposite the room at Skurk, to, like, give a perspective or something.

Light and dark.

Good and bad.

Moldy and...not.

Both things.

The lady led Maddy along a plush carpet that looked like it was woven with threads of real gold. It may have been. Maddy didn't want to let go of the lady's hand to get on her hands and knees for a close-up inspection. That would be awkward.

Maddy's beastly feet sunk into the carpet, except where the gold threads crossed. They stood out against the pads of her feet, snagging on the ragged nails of her toes. Straight above, the ceiling was painted a bright, eggshell blue with white crown molding.

At least, Maddy thought it was painted blue until she saw a wisp of clouds float by, and then she began to think the ceiling was the actual sky, even though she couldn't figure out how it fit within the confines of the crown molding.

The lady let go of Maddy's hand when they reached the window. She swung one arm as though inviting Maddy closer.

"Eventyr." That was all she said.

Maddy walked forward until her nose brushed the cool glass. There were so many sights and colors that she had a hard time processing them all at once. Her eyes darted around more than they did when she was trying to keep track of the pixies.

Eventyr was beautiful.

Glittering castles, crystal clear waters with rainbow-scaled fish that jumped in delight, ivy and honeysuckle, maple trees and aspens, thick green grass, and twinkling stars that Maddy could see perfectly clearly even with the sun shining. More striking than the sights of beauty that surrounded the tower was the feeling. This was more peaceful than an empty beach on a sunny day with a good book and nowhere to be.

Maddy couldn't imagine a more perfect place to spend your immortality.

The view shifted every so often; Maddy wondered if the tower they were in rotated to view all of Eventyr at once. Even then, Maddy didn't know how it was possible to see a whole world from a small window. But then, Maddy had spent her whole life not knowing that she was surrounded by magic. She totally forgot that, somehow, magic made everything that was so impossible possible.

When Maddy had seen all she could handle, she leaned her forehead against the glass and squeezed her eyes shut. Tears leaked from the corners of her eyes almost without Maddy realizing what was happening. Eventyr was perfect, so very different from Skurk, and it hurt her heart in a way she didn't quite understand.

It felt wrong.

It was wrong that people were judged by something in their blood and an online test, then sent to spend forever in a place they couldn't escape. It was wrong that the Reformation Program kept people shut away without any hope of actually reforming. It was wrong that Eventyr was available to some, but not to all.

It was all very, very wrong.

"Are you Beschermer?" Maddy asked without turning around.

"I am." Her voice was more soothing than a bubble bath, but Maddy refused to be soothed. She wanted to feel hurt for all the people in Skurk that didn't really deserve to be there. It was wrong to forget that.

The hairs on Maddy's arm ruffled, and she glanced over to see Bechermer take the space beside her.

"Why did you bring me here?" Maddy asked.

"You are not a villain." Beschermer smiled, lighting up the room. "You have proven it to be so."

Maddy stared straight again, still unable to look at Beschermer for very long at a time. "I did a lot of bad things."

"Yes," Beschermer nodded. "But the good you have done now outweighs the bad. You were not sent to Skurk to stay, Madelena. You were sent there to choose."

Maddy pictured herself standing with her arms out to the side. In each hand was a big weight attached to a heavy ball. One with the word 'good', the other with the word 'bad.' She tipped to the side as if the good ball was heavier now, but what would happen if she tipped to the bad side again? Maddy knew she was going to mess up at one point or another. She was human. When it happened, would they bring her straight back to Skurk? At what point would she be left alone to live her life without the VDA or Beschermer yanking her back and forth?

"Your system is super messed up," Maddy said, the words flying out before she had the chance to stop them. They were like an itch that kept moving around so that it could not be scratched. The only relief came from getting those words out.

She wouldn't have stopped them, even if she thought about it ahead of time. But she realized she could have said that in a nicer way.

"Sorry, I didn't mean to sound critical or whatever. I just...I've been all over this place in a short amount of time and it's...it's not working."

"Oh?"

Maddy went on. "I don't think you can determine who a person is or where they belong based on a few things that they have done or answers on a test. I mean, those things are better than taking people just because they have villain ancestors, but still, people are not a math problem. You have to look at their heart, way down inside, to determine if a person is really more good than bad."

Maddy thought for a moment. "Or more bad than good."

"There are many people in the world," Beschermer said after a lengthy pause. "So many people to watch over." The way her voice drifted to a stop filled Maddy with a sense of hopelessness.

Was that what Beschermer felt?

Maddy nodded. "That's true. But don't you think there's a better way to judge people than their Villainous Test score or their bloodline? You have access to magic. There has to be a better way. Can't you use magic to see a person's heart? Not the sum total of their actions, but who they really are on the inside?"

Beschermer's hand lifted to her porcelain cheek. "A way to determine the inside..."

Maddy hoped her pause was to think of a way to make that happen. Grams's Villainous Test was a super good start. The Reformation Program was a good idea too, if they would actually let it reform people. But Maddy wanted there to be a way for Gwen and Hepzibah and all the others to earn a happily ever after based on who they were now.

Not what they had done in the past.

"I also think"—Maddy hesitated, hoping she wasn't pushing it—"that you should change the Reformation Program so it gives people a real chance to show that they've changed. Maybe evaluate once a month or...something." She thought for a moment. "And Eventyr needs to be evaluated too. People change, you know? You want to make sure the people in Eventyr still deserve to be there just like you want to be sure that the people in Skurk still deserve to be there."

"Madelena." Beschermer's eyes glowed like candles. "I now know what to do."

"Did you know the system was broken?" Maddy's eyes slid over to Beschermer. "Were you ignoring it?"

"No," Beschermer said quietly. "I am very aware. It has weighed upon my mind for longer than you know." She clapped her hands together and faced Maddy. "It seems I need to bring my problems to the family of Agathe for solutions."

Beschermer closed her eyes and muttered words Maddy did not understand. A strong citrus scent came with a breeze, like lemon but foreign and flowery. It filled the air around them, rippling the hem of Beschermer's white gown. It swirled around her knees and up her body to the palm of her hand, which she extended. The breeze swirled into a tornado in Beschermer's hand, and when it cleared, a silver-gilded mirror rested in its place.

Beschermer lifted the mirror to her face and whispered the word, "Miro," in musical tones.

"My lady," a voice sounded seconds before a bodiless face appeared in the glass. It tipped slightly forward in a bow. "I am at thy service."

Beschermer returned the gesture and flipped the mirror around, holding the handle with one hand, her fingers falling over the top, but ending where the glass began. "Miro, tell me about this girl. What do you see?"

The mirror breathed in a long breath of air as if he was trying to draw all of Maddy's secrets to him. Part of Maddy wanted to lean into the mirror, but her strongest urge was to resist. It was beyond uncomfortable to let something see into those parts that no one else ever saw. Maddy closed her eyes and tried to cooperate so that Miro could gather whatever he needed to determine who she was on the inside. She would let him and try to bear it gracefully.

No toddler temper tantrums this time.

Miro began to speak. "Madelena Agathe Hutton. One-quarter villain, on her mother's side. Sensitive and kind, with a streak of stubbornness. Strong sense of right and wrong. Often blunt. Sees not the outward appearance, but the heart."

Maddy blinked rapidly to keep the tears from coming. She knew they were coming because her eyes were beginning to sting like she was enormously tired. She placed a paw on her cheek and hoped Beschermer and Miro didn't notice her emotion. It's just that what Miro described was what she wanted to be.

Could it be true?

Was she that person? *Could* she be?

"The mirror never lies," Berschermer said with a slight smile.

Maybe Maddy already had all the qualities she wanted, deep inside; she just needed to build on them to truly become the best version of herself.

"Conclusion," Miro went on." Madelena Agathe Hutton is one-quarter villain by birth, but hero by choice." His face swirled into the mist and was gone.

The smooth glass of the mirror reflected Maddy's beastly face.

Holy cannoli, she looked way worse than she thought.

Beschermer bowed her head, as though confirming a blessing, and lowered the mirror so that it disappeared into the folds of her gown.

"Thank you," Maddy said.

"No." Beschermer took her hand. "Thank you. I believe Miro will suit our purposes well."

"He's perfect." Maddy wished she wasn't still a freak so she could hug Beschermer without making a mess of her. "That will make such a huge difference for so many people."

Beschermer ran her hand along the fur surrounding Maddy's face. "Miro will travel through any reflective surface. In this way, he will watch over Eventyr and Skurk in a way I cannot. He will determine the hearts of the people."

"And..." Maddy swallowed. "And if they don't belong in the place they are?"

"I will place them where their heart lies." Beschermer folded her long fingers across her middle. "I do not wish to hold people unfairly."

"I know." Maddy nodded. "Your power is limited. I get it. I know you do the best you can."

Beschermer looked at Maddy for a moment longer than was comfortable. "You are an extraordinary human, Madelena. And now, dear child, we must see about getting you home."

Home.

Now Maddy understood how Dorothy felt when she finally made it to the Wizard. The mere thought of going home sent Maddy's head spinning and her stomach whirling. Home was where her mom, dad, and Grams were. Home was Leo and Izzy and all her other friends. Home was berry cheesecake air freshener that made everyone hungry when they walked through the door. Her dad's sweaty socks. The freezer that always had a full shelf devoted to ice cream. Thick carpet and smooth tile. Comfortable couches with uncomfortable pillows.

Suddenly, Maddy couldn't stand the thought of not being there anymore.

"I'm ready," she said. "I'm ready to go home."

TWENTY-SIX

Who says villains can't have a happily ever after?

Maddy was expecting some big hoopla.

She didn't know why. Maybe because going home was such an epic thing. But Beschermer simply smiled at her, wished her well, and leaned forward to kiss her forehead. When she next blinked her eyes, Maddy stood in her kitchen.

Home.

Maddy let out a cheer and threw her arms around one of the table chairs since it was the closest thing to where she was standing. She ran into the living room and made a snow angel on the carpet, then opened and closed the front door a few times, just because she could.

"I'm home!" she shrieked.

Footsteps hurried down the hall from the bedrooms. If Maddy was expecting a super bouncy group hug with tears and exclamations of how glad everyone was to see her face, she was way off. Her dad skidded to a stop, his eyes the size of a full moon as he looked around until he found an umbrella. He pushed Maddy's mom and Grams behind him and pointed the umbrella at Maddy's chest.

"Stay back," he said.

Mom clung to his arm. "What is that thing?"

For reals? Like they didn't know their own daughter?

Wait a second.

Maddy moved over to the fireplace where a mirror hung above the mantle. Her movement startled her dad so much that he dropped the umbrella. His face was bright red as he stooped to snatch it off the ground. The tip shook while he tried to get it back between them and Maddy.

"Call animal control and the FBI," he hissed to Grams.

Maddy usually had to stand on tip-toe to see the mirror, so when she walked up to it and the top was even with her horns, Maddy realized things weren't going to be exactly the way she pictured them when she thought about coming home.

"I'm still a beast? Seriously?"

This was probably one of those moments Maddy should just be grateful for what she had, but coming home as a beast wasn't even on her radar. She thought she'd be normal. Did that mean she was still a beast inside? Or that she still needed to do something to break that curse?

It was all so confusing. Part of her just wanted to give up and be a beast forever.

Except that when she tried to imagine herself going to prom or college or the grocery store like this, she hit a snag.

Looking like a beast didn't play nicely with her life plans.

Grams stepped forward, placing a hand on the umbrella to get Maddy's dad to lower it. His arms were so jiggly from the adrenaline that he dropped the umbrella again. "Welcome home, Maddy."

"Maddy!" Her mom stood up straight. "Maddy?"

"What?" Her dad shook his head, like that might help turn Maddy from a beast back into a teenage girl.

Grams opened her arms and enveloped Maddy in a hug. "It is so good to have you home." Her head barely reached Maddy's waist. Maddy didn't want to break her Grams, so she settled for patting Grams's head a few times. "We must call Leo; he's been worried." Grams nodded to Maddy's mom, who immediately pulled out her phone.

"When you said Maddy was a beast, I..." Maddy's dad's eyes widened. "I had no idea."

"Why am I still a beast?" Maddy looked down at Grams, who had to take a few steps back so she could see Maddy's face without breaking her neck. "Beschermer said I wasn't a villain anymore," Maddy went on. "I proved myself. Why do I still look like this?"

"What is she saying?" her dad whispered. "It sounds like my stomach after a marathon."

Grams waved her hand behind her to hush him up. "What does the story tell you?"

Maddy twirled a lock of fur near her ear around her finger. "The Beast proved his heart was changed when he rescued the girl and when he told her she could leave. He was sacrificing himself for her, right? So, do I need to do that still?"

Grams shook her head. "You did your good deed, dearie. Go a little further."

"Okay, so then, the girl came back to the castle, and became friends with the Beast, and eventually..."

Grams nodded. "Now you see."

Maddy did, but she didn't.

She may have done some good deeds to help other people, but part of the reason she became a beast in the first place was because she got so angry at Leo that she turned him into a newt. She hadn't done anything to right that wrong. So, maybe that was the next step? It made sense she needed to make things right with Leo before her curse could be over.

"Wait, did you call Leo?" Maddy pointed at her mom, who was just tucking her phone away.

Her mom nodded. "Yes, he's on his way."

"You can understand it...her?" Her dad's face opened to a startled expression. "Am I the only one who can't?"

Maddy's mom waved her hands to shush him.

"So, does that mean he's not a newt anymore?" Maddy looked at Grams. "Did you fix him?"

"I did not. You did."

But Maddy didn't. When she left for Skurk, he was still all slimy in the trifle bowl.

"You did something in Skurk, Madelena. You created magic that transformed Leo."

"I didn't do any magic. I can't do magic as a beast." Maddy held her hands out to the side so Grams could see there were no sparks.

Grams's smile was lovely. "Magic comes from what? What did I tell you?"

Maddy scratched her head, trying to remember. Thank goodness human brains were more evolved. It was so much work trying to remember even the simplest things.

Grams told her Eventyr was created from the magic that came from...

"Good deeds?"

"Yes!" Grams bopped her finger against Maddy's nose.

Then, did that mean Leo was changed when Maddy helped the village? So, it was like a three-for-one. Maddy's head spun. It was crazy how that one little decision affected so many things.

And so many people.

"I'm glad," Maddy breathed in deeply. "I'm glad Leo's okay."

Then, Maddy walked to the couch and sat heavily. So, Leo was a human again. And when he arrived, Maddy had to face him as a beast. That was not a super pleasant thought. Would he even want to talk to her, much less be her friend again? Maddy wasn't so sure she would want to be best buds with a person who yelled at her and called her names and wouldn't help her friends and, oh yeah, turned her into a newt.

What if he hated Maddy now?

Maybe he was coming over just to tell her that.

Maddy wished there was a closet or space that was big enough for her to hide in. She didn't want to see Leo.

Well, she did, but she didn't.

Maddy definitely wanted to tell him she was sorry for everything she did, and for the person she became for a while. But she really didn't want him to see her this way.

Maddy groaned and dropped her head into her lap.

Her mom sat gingerly next to Maddy, her legs tensed like she was ready to run if Maddy decided she looked tasty. Her mom lifted her hand to touch Maddy's fur. "Oh! She's really soft. Hon, come feel Maddy's fur; it's like those minky blankets."

Her dad sat on Maddy's other side. "Whoa, you're right! It looks like it would be all stiff and course, but it's really cozy." He leaned his cheek against Maddy's side and ran both hands down her back.

Parents were so weird.

The front door burst open without any knocking just as Maddy's mom and dad were putting Maddy to sleep with all that petting. Leo stood in the doorway, his chest rising and falling like he'd run the whole way there. He looked so good in his worn jeans and the school T-shirt Maddy had given him for his birthday last year. His eyes went straight for her. "Maddy?" He took a tentative step forward.

Maddy's mom and dad leaned away so Maddy could stand, but she didn't move. She shrugged one shoulder and tried to hide her face in her armpit.

"This is, indeed, our Madelena." Grams extended her arm toward Maddy. "It is her, Leo."

Leo dashed across the space between them and threw his arms around Maddy's ribcage. He couldn't get his arms all the way around, but what he could reach, he squeezed so tightly Maddy couldn't breathe.

"Holy meatballs, Maddy. What the heck! I've been crazy worried about you. Next time you want to go all villainous, would you give a guy some warning?"

Maddy tapped his elbows to get him to ease up so she could get enough air to talk. "Leo, I am so sorry. About everything."

"I don't even care. I'm just glad you're back."

Wait.

He answered right away. He didn't need Grams to translate for him.

"You can understand me? I mean, I'm not growling or grunting?"

His chin dug into Maddy's chest when he lifted his head to look at her face without removing his python death grip. "You sound normal."

How was that possible? Her own father couldn't understand her. Grams and her mom probably could because they had that villain DNA. What did it mean that Leo understood her? Maddy looked over Leo's head to Grams, who just shrugged with a smile.

Maddy decided to roll with that. It really didn't matter why; it was just so great that he could. It made her feel less alone.

"Listen, Leo." Maddy took his hands and pulled them away from her sides so Leo could step back, and she could see him better. As much fun as it was to talk to the top of his head, Maddy wanted to see his eyes. "I really messed up. I was an idiot, and I feel terrible about everything. I mean, I was so mean to your friends... Oh! Guess what? Beschermer is going to take care of them. She made a mirror to determine people's hearts. Now your friends in the Reformation School can come out. They'll go where they deserve to go. So, they'll be free."

"Are you kidding me?" Leo's face lit up, and Maddy wondered if he was thinking about Gwen. "That's lit, Maddy, really!"

Maddy took a deep breath. "Yeah, so, I'm also really sorry about the, um, the newt thing."

"Are you sure you're sorry about that? I think you've wanted to turn me into a newt since first grade."

"Kindergarten," Maddy laughed. It sounded terrifying. "No, really. I'm sorry. Will you... Do you, uh, forgive me?"

"For what?" Maddy was honestly surprised. What could he possibly be sorry for? He didn't do anything to her even remotely close to what she did to him.

His grin faded as he took a step back. "I've teased you and bugged you and mocked you for, like, your whole life. I kind of drove you over the edge with that villain thing. I kept pushing it. I mean, I didn't help you through it."

Maddy tried to protest, but Leo held up his hand.

"And I haven't been totally honest with you about something. I didn't tell you. When you disappeared and Grams explained what was going on, I didn't understand much because that newt brain was not cool. I get it now, though. I see where I was wrong for a lot of years."

"What are you even talking about?" Maddy broke in, the words bursting to come out. "You really have nothing to apologize for. We didn't know what was happening. It was way confusing. But if it makes you feel better, I will forgive you if you forgive me. Let's just go back to normal, okay? Friends forever?" Maddy held out her paw for him to shake.

Leo looked at her hand but didn't take it. "No."

Maddy's hand dropped to her side. But that was nothing compared to the drop she felt in her heart. So, that was it? The fear she felt the moment she got back home and realized she was still a beast came back immediately. It was the fear that her family, that Leo wouldn't be able to accept her. She couldn't blame him really. She was super hideous. If he couldn't deal with it, she would try to understand even though her heart was squished and broken on the floor.

"It's okay, Leo. I get it."

"No," he shook his head. "You don't get it. I can see you don't get it. You are the smartest, dumbest person in this whole, weird world, Maddy. I swear!"

She lifted her chin just a little. "What do you mean? I do get it. This beast form is horrible, and you can't be my friend when I'm like this. I'm not really sure how to change back, so it's okay if we—"

"Stop talking." Leo shook his head. "Seriously, stop talking. You are running so far in the opposite direction that I'm not going to be able to see you in a couple of minutes."

"What?" Maddy pushed her fur away from her massive forehead. "I don't understand."

Leo grabbed her hand. "No, you don't. So, listen really carefully before you talk again, okay? Stick with me. I can't go back to normal, Maddy, because it's killing me trying to be your friend."

Maddy hoped she wouldn't burst into big, hairy tears. She heard him, and she understood perfectly, despite what Leo said. She had never made things easy for him, and it was probably really difficult to overlook her faults. It was too much for him, and that was understandable; she'd put him through a lot. She took a deep breath. She could do this. She could handle whatever he said and try to be understanding, even if it broke her beastly heart.

"Maddy, look at me." Leo tugged Maddy's hand until she lifted her chin. "I can't read your face when you're a beast—you just look like you want to eat forest creatures—so I'm just going to say it and use small words, okay? I love you."

Maddy blinked, unsure if she really just heard what she thought she just heard.

"And I have for a really long time. I can't do the friends thing anymore. What would you think if we tried something more than friends?"

Maddy blinked rapidly.

"Maddy?" Leo pursed his lips. "Are you still in there?"

Maddy nodded, a grin bursting forth. "I would like that a lot. A really, really lot. A super ton of a lot!"

Leo let out a breath. "Really? Oh crap. I thought you were going to give me to the count of three to get out of here. You're pretty intimidating as a beast, you know?"

Maddy laughed as she brushed a lock of hair out of Leo's eyes, careful not to nick him with her claws. "I love you too, Leo. So much!"

Maddy's dad cleared his throat.

Maddy jumped back, heat creeping up the back of her neck. She legitimately forgot there were other people in the room. It was hard to take her eyes off Leo. Kind of like when you're a little kid and you get a bike for Christmas, the perfect bike you always wanted, and you think if you move your eyes away it will disappear.

Did he really still love her?

She could hardly believe it, though she wanted to, so much.

It would be the perfect ending.

And for the first time ever, Maddy wanted a happy ending for the villain.

So, even if it was too good to be true, Maddy was going to believe it with all of her heart. Leo was exactly what she wanted. If she didn't have arms that were the size of Leo's whole body and ended in vicious claws, she would hug him so dang hard.

And maybe never let go.

Instead, she looked at Grams. "Is there something else we have to do to change me into a human? I mean, Leo and I made it right. Do we have to link arms and skip or twirl in a circle, or..."

Leo snorted and bent in half. "Are you for reals?"

"Hey!" Maddy smacked his arm. "You never know! We've seen weirder things."

"That's true," Leo nodded. "That is very, very true."

Grams smiled. "Have patience, my Madelena. Sometimes magic takes time."

Maddy took a deep breath and relaxed her shoulders. Leo took her hand and pet it adoringly. It was such a good thing he was so obsessed with his dog; that was really working in Maddy's favor.

Then Leo sneezed.

Twice.

Okay, three times.

Make that four.

"Bless you." Maddy pulled her hand away. "Are you okay?"

"I think—" Leo sneezed again, wiping his nose on his sleeve. "I think I might be allergic to you."

"But you have pets."

"True." Leo rubbed his eyes. "But they are short-haired and hypoallergenic. I don't think you are."

Maddy stepped back, but Leo grabbed her hand and pulled her closer.

"You really shouldn't be this close to me if you're allergic to my beast hair." Maddy tried to dislodge her hand, but Leo wouldn't let go.

He sneezed again, an explosive one that sprayed spit all over the inside of his elbow. "Sobethigs are worth gedding allergies."

And that's when the magic happened.

Gold sparkles erupted before Maddy's eyes, then surrounded her whole body. Leo's grip tightened on her paw, but he stood back to give the magic space. Maddy's limbs tingled like they'd all fallen asleep. The sound of rushing waves filled Maddy's head so thoroughly, she couldn't keep her eyes open. The swirl of magic in the dark reminded Maddy of the few times Leo bullied her into riding a roller coaster. There were tugs and pulls and then suddenly everything stopped.

When Maddy opened her eyes again, her body felt weird.

Lighter.

Way less hairy.

The first thing she saw was her hands. Beautiful, smooth skin with cute little nubby fingernails at the tips.

Totally perfect.

Maddy looked up at Leo and grinned.

"I'm back!" Maddy threw her arms around him, laughing. "We did it; I'm back!"

"Right on!" Leo yelled.

They twirled around the living room in a spastic but joyous jig until they were both so dizzy they had to lean into each other to stay upright. Leo pulled away enough to look at Maddy's face. He stared into her eyes with such hardcore intensity that her fingers and toes started tingling again.

"Leo?" Maddy whispered.

"Yeah?"

"You're totally going to kiss me."

He grinned as he moved closer. "You're right."

TWENTY-SEVEN
The perfect ending

A few hours later, after all the hubbub died down, Leo and Maddy snuggled on a beanbag chair, watching a movie with Maddy's parents and Grams. Right in the middle of an intense sword fight scene, Leo bolted upright.

"Crap!"

Maddy sat up too. If there was a spider or something crawling on the beanbag, she was prepared to freak out. "What?"

"I just realized something." Leo's head whipped around to face her; his eyes wide. "You were a beast; I broke your curse."

"Yeah?" Maddy nodded. "Okay?"

Leo dropped his head into one hand. "Crap, Maddy. I think that makes me Belle."

Acknowledgements

This book began with one of those random conversations I have with my kiddos. What would happen if your DNA test said you were a villain? Then it morphed into a five-book series of Fairy Tale mashing. One-Quarter Villain is a stand-alone, but stay tuned for more of Maddy and Leo. They will be back!

As always, there are SO many people who need props here. My publishing team- LOVE your guts y'all! Staci Olsen- for OH EM GOSHing my book pitch. Holli Andersen- for loving me enough to assign Bridget as my editor. Bridget- for being the BEST editor in this world (and all the other worlds too, I'm pretty sure). It is a thing of joy and beauty forever to work with all of you guys.

This book is as much the brainchild of my kids as it is mine. If they tell you they came up with the funniest parts, they are totally right. You guys are my world! Thanks for doing and being all the things. You are amazing humans.

And to you, dear Reader, I hope you have as much fun with Maddy and Leo as I did. (I kind of fell in love with these weirdos.) Thanks for reading, you're the bestest.

No, really.

About the Author

By day, Cori Cooper is the mild-mannered (sort of) Wife to her high school love, the Mother of four punny, movie-quoting, awesome-sauce kiddos who are adults and teens now, (yeah, that happened fast), and the Writer of stories that (hopefully) leave readers with a warm and slightly squishy feeling. (That's not weird at all). And by night... Cori Cooper is sleeping because that's her fifth favorite thing to do.

Writing and publishing books is a long-time dream come true. Sometimes she has to pinch herself (also not at all weird) that she's actually doing the thing she imagined hen she was six years old. It's surreal, and yet, stinking amazing.

So when she's not hanging out with her fabulous family, or writing stories, Cori loves reading or listening to books that make her want to be a better person. She has a fetish for watching cheesy Hallmark movies with her girls - the cheesier the better. She's passionate about baking anything that has copious amounts of butter, and quite frequently, she can be found rearranging furniture, organizing closets, and changing the color of paint on interior walls.

Connect with Cori